THE SECRETS OF TERCAST

SOURCE'S EDGE BOOK ONE

Cover art and illustrations by Tiziana Federica Ruiu
Edited by Crystal Shelley
Layout by Ryan Sivek

The Secrets of Tercast (Source's Edge Book One)
First Edition (Revision 1, Oct 2022)

ISBN: 979-8-9863686-0-3
Library of Congress Control Number: 2022910696

Published By Ryan Sivek
Cary, North Carolina
www.ryansivek.com

In loving memory of Aaron Randall Hill

Acknowledgments

It is impossible for me to recognize everyone who has influenced this novel, but I'll try to cover those who perhaps had the most significant and specific impacts, in no particular order.

First, I want to express my gratitude to Aaron Hill, to whom this book is dedicated. A few of those ideas we bounced around between rocking out in a garage and playing *Halo* eventually found their way into this story. I think you would have liked it. No magical penguins though, sorry. At least . . . not yet?

I am immensely grateful to those family members and friends who read through the very rough second draft of this novel: Janet Sivek, Ethan Sivek, Adam Smith, Katrina Smith, and Ashley Reigada. Your feedback, honest reactions, and enthusiasm gave me hope that this effort might one day be worthy of publication.

To my wonderful beta readers and critique partners—Dr. Kristen Fread, Eli Malone-Shkukin, Preethi Ashwin, Adam Smith, Matthew Guan, Callie C, and Lacey K—I likewise express tremendous gratitude for the time you invested in the story, and for your fantastic feedback and suggestions.

I sought out feedback from the blind community on the portrayal of blindness in my story, and am so very glad that I did. I am profoundly thankful to you, Rachel Ng, Ellie Wallwork, and

Layne Johnson, for your essential thoughts, perspectives, and suggestions regarding this significant aspect of the story.

Two content creators in particular helped me get through that critical first draft. Thank you Merphy Napier. Your enthusiastic discussions on books and reading gave me confidence that my narrative was heading in the right direction, and dared give me hope that readers might find the story enjoyable. And thank you, Molly Burke, for your open and thoughtful observations regarding your experiences as a blind woman. While many sources were helpful, I felt that your content in particular expanded my understanding to the level I needed for that first draft.

My thanks also go out to Audiomachine, Really Slow Motion, Two Steps from Hell, Epic North, Tommee Profit, and Ruelle. Your music has fed inspiration to many key moments in this story.

To my wonderful editor, Crystal Shelley, I wish to express the utmost appreciation. Your impressive eye for detail, and absolutely phenomenal edits have significantly enhanced the narrative beyond my own abilities. Your praiseworthy dedication to thoughtful, inclusive, and respectful language has been a marvelous boon to the story as well.

I also want to express gratitude to my incredible artist, Tiziana Federica Ruiu. Your passion, expertise, and creativity are awe inspiring. You gave visual life to concepts that have bounced around in my head for years, and I find the results astounding.

The abilities of my audiobook narrator, Lisa Angelini, have likewise impressed me. Thank you so much, Lisa, for giving the story and its many characters such brilliant presence in that important medium.

Last, but absolutely not least, I am immeasurably grateful for the love and support of my wife, Alyson. Your tolerance for my mental excursions to these fantastical worlds is exceptional. I can't thank you enough for the time you have spent helping me refine this passion project throughout all the stages of its development. I love you.

Contents

Chapter 1   Lasagna   1
Chapter 2   The Facility   13
Chapter 3   Orientation   25
Chapter 4   The Library   35
Chapter 5   Perspective   40
Chapter 6   Alvior   51
Chapter 7   Resolve   57
Chapter 8   Probability   64
Chapter 9   Oblivion   75
Chapter 10 Decisions   80
Chapter 11 Tercast   86
Chapter 12 Rwenmar   96
Chapter 13 Amy   110
Chapter 14 Breakfast   117
Chapter 15 Vitalization   125
Chapter 16 Chipper and Sunset   137
Chapter 17 Potions   146
Chapter 18 Belze   154
Chapter 19 Two Steps Closer   166

Chapter 20 Elemorb 176

Chapter 21 Connections 189

Chapter 22 Just a Scratch 198

Chapter 23 To See or Not to See 205

Chapter 24 Fire 212

Chapter 25 Into Focus 221

Chapter 26 Tools 230

Chapter 27 The Quick and Thwarted 236

Chapter 28 Ilkuth 246

Chapter 29 Science 255

Chapter 30 Books 263

Chapter 31 Special Designation 266

Chapter 32 Enchantments 273

Chapter 33 Gilmar Company 280

Chapter 34 Ya'ir 286

Chapter 35 Preparations 296

Chapter 36 Healer 301

Chapter 37 Action 308

Chapter 38 Discovery 310

Chapter 39 The Mission 322

Chapter 40 Land 329

Chapter 41 Air 342

Chapter 42 An Odd Conversation 350

Chapter 43 Water 353

Chapter 44 Cyborgs and Sorcerers 365

Chapter 45 Choosing a Side 371

Chapter 46 Lightning 374

Chapter 47 Deceived 385

Chapter 48 Convergence 387

Chapter 49 The Deia 392

Chapter 50 Reconciliation 397

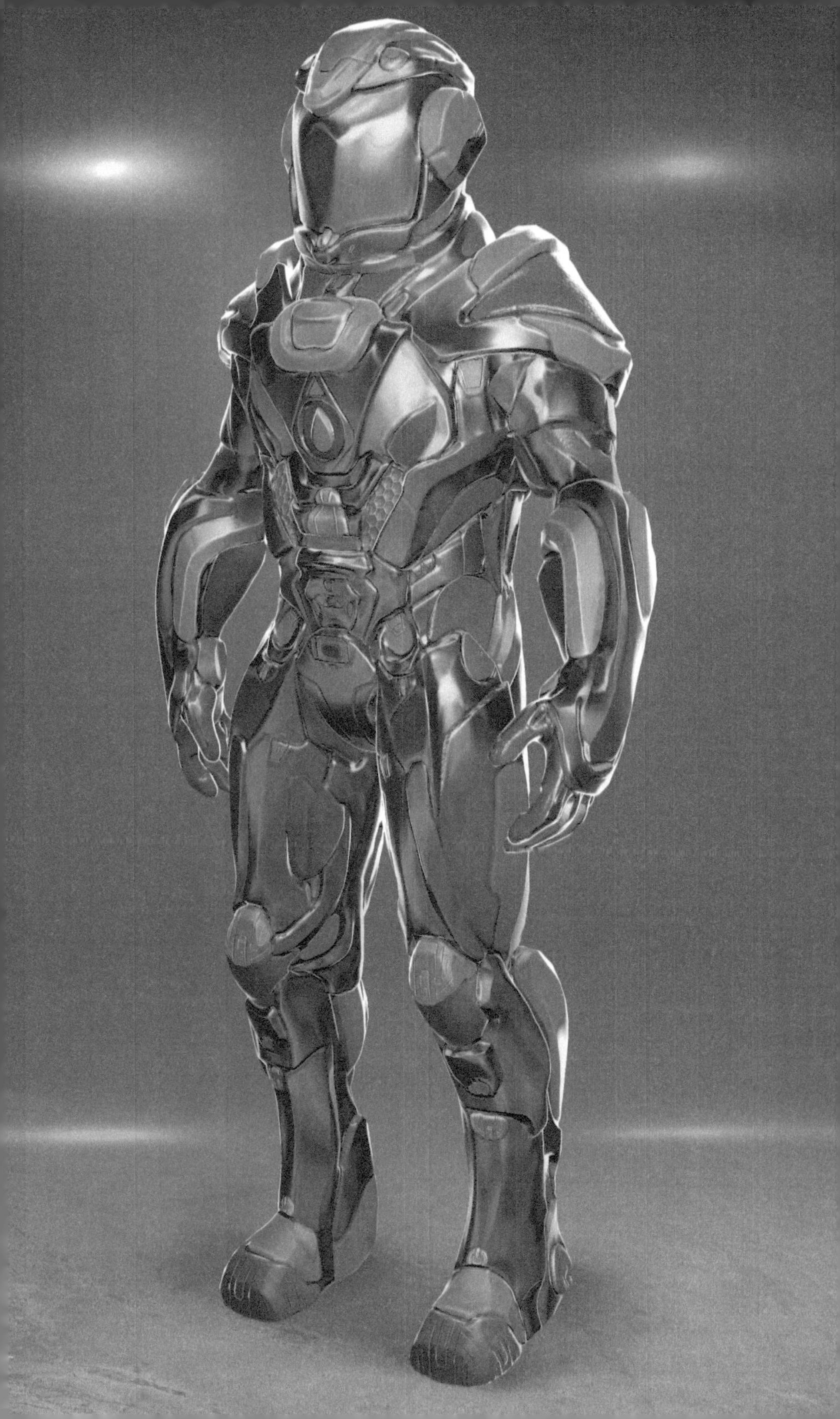

Chapter 1

Lasagna

Breathe.

Focus.

Kara Jones bowed to her opponent across the mat, attempting to isolate the sound of his breathing from the rest of the noise. Years of instruction saturated her thoughts: *Focus on your opponent's impressions on the world around them.* The mat rustled. She could feel it pull ever so slightly at her feet. He was likely entering a combat stance. The scent of body odor permeated the room, but she suppressed her sensation of it—smell wasn't useful at the moment. Filtering the other sounds in the room from her perception, she crouched into a wide stance.

"Go!"

Kara launched herself forward. Her opponent's steps shifted to her right, and she leapt toward his new position with her arms out for a grapple. Air rushed past her as the expected collision never came. She rolled forward, hoping her opponent didn't press his advantage. After righting herself and pivoting, she strained her ears for sounds of movement.

Steps slapped against the mat toward her position.

Kara lurched toward them, arms outstretched. She connected with his abdomen and locked her arms around his torso. Her opponent stumbled but remained upright. He seized the opportunity, pinning her head in a choke hold. She brought a hand inward to grab his arm and relieve the pressure against her neck.

As she remained trapped under the muscular arm, body odor and musky deodorant broke through her sensory filter. Adrenaline pulsed through her. *I need to do something quickly, or this is over.*

Kara wrapped her right arm across her opponent's shoulder, letting all her weight fall against it. He stood firm. He was too strong, too well grounded, and she was too lightweight. His legs deftly evaded her attempts to grab them. She twisted her feet around him, trying desperately to loosen his footing. But his stance was solid.

Time to try something new.

She pulled her arm down and wrapped it around his waist once more. She crouched and sprung upward, using the momentum to bend her back into an extreme angle. Her feet landed perfectly on her opponent's shoulders; she brought them together, applying pressure to his neck.

Gasps erupted from the surrounding crowd.

The arm around her neck loosed. She swung her head around and landed on her back with a thud, knocking the wind out of her. As expected, her opponent pounced on her as soon as she hit the floor. Kara wrapped her legs around his torso as he fell.

A hand slapped the mat near her left ear, causing it to ring.

She smirked.

Kara crunched upward, looping her right arm around the thick arm to her left. Muscles tightened as she pulled against the inside of his elbow while pushing against his hand. The hand slipped out from under him, forcing him to use his other arm for support.

Deftly planting her left foot on her opponent's side, she wiggled her hip and right shoulder to maneuver out from underneath him. As soon as she had a good angle, she reengaged the leg lock around his waist.

He strained to slip away, but her lock was firm. She pressed his right arm upward, causing him to inhale sharply as the shoulder moved too far in the wrong direction.

He struggled for a few more seconds before several taps against the mat told her that her opponent had finally given in.

Samuel Williams watched in awe as the contestants disentangled from their pretzel of an interlock and shook hands. Kara beamed, her gaze shooting into the distance, and Sam couldn't help but grin with her. The instructor approached Kara and said something indecipherable over the noise of the academy. She tucked a strand of light brown hair behind her ear, which had fallen loose from her ponytail, and said something inaudible back to him. The instructor shook his head with a smile and moved to address Kara's opponent, a large, muscular young man Sam didn't know. He was around their age—perhaps nineteen—and easily stood a foot or so taller than Kara.

Jeanette, who stood next to Sam, moved to intercept her sister, and Sam followed. The women hugged, both of them glowing.

"That was amazing!" Jeanette said, towering over her.

Kara laughed. "You know it!"

"I had no idea you could bend like that," Sam said as he approached. "Do you even have a spine?"

She shrugged, her bright blue eyes subtly dancing about. "Figured he wouldn't expect it."

"I'll say," Liam said, chuckling in his rapid-fire way as he stepped in beside Sam. "I thought he had you with that headlock." He adjusted his thick glasses. "It *was* a headlock, right?"

As they continued their discussion of Kara's incredible skills, Sam found himself distracted by the way the sweat dripped down her round face and onto her chest. Her white uniform, while somewhat loose, still outlined her attractive features. She was easily the shortest among them.

Liam cut into the discussion. "Can we head out? I think I've smelled enough ninja sweat for one day."

Jeanette laughed and gave Kara her arm. The group emerged into the parking lot, lit orange by the evening sky. Sam stared at Kara's ponytail as it swung with her gait and shimmered in the sunlight. He was glad they had decided to accompany her to class at the academy. She seemed to relish the attention, and he thoroughly enjoyed watching her crush the others during free roll. Her fierce determination and skill were incredibly inspiring.

Liam elbowed Sam's arm. "I think you should give it a shot."

Anxiety flared in Sam's chest and rippled across his skin. He glanced briefly at his friend's long, pale face beneath ever-messy blond hair and glasses. As usual, Liam's tall frame was drowned in a large graphic T-shirt and baggy pants.

"Give what a shot?" Sam asked, turning his gaze forward.

"Oh, stop pretending," Liam said. "You're over there grinning at her like a puppy. We all see it—except her, of course. Never know until you ask, right?"

That was precisely the point. Sam *didn't* want to know. The most likely outcome was certainly not in his favor. It was the one secret of the universe he was happy to leave undiscovered.

"Things are best left the way they are," Sam finally said.

Liam shrugged and, thankfully, dropped the subject.

Jeanette and Kara discussed celebrity gossip and fashion trends as they took their seats at the front of the sedan. Liam and Sam settled into the back.

Sam turned to the window, finding his semitransparent reflection looking back at him as the vehicle pulled out of the parking lot. Curly black hair sprung up above his monolid eyes, which exhibited his partial Eastern heritage. A prominent, round chin graced his deep-brown face. His figure was a little chubbier than he would have liked.

He stared out the window, thoughts turning to the future.

His future.

He'd recently accepted entry into the physics program of a prestigious university, one of several offers. He didn't really have a strong preference, though. All he really wanted was to dive into the mysteries of the universe—to explore its limits, its origin, the building blocks of existence—and get out of his parents' house as soon as possible.

The sun dropped low beyond the passing office buildings outside his window, casting the sky in vibrant pinks and purples above waves of orange-lit clouds. Several green elms lined the street, with the occasional pedestrian walking under them along the sidewalk. The brilliant colors of the evening scene reminded him of one of his favorite lectures. It had been given in his senior-year physics class, which had ended with his graduation a few weeks ago.

"Consider color," Mr. Nowell had suggested. "We tend to think of it as an inherent property of an object. When the setting sun reflects off of the ocean, we still think of the ocean as blue. In reality, however, the water is a different color at sunset than it is at midday. The colors we perceive inherently depend on the light that bounces off the materials we're looking at. That is the physical truth. Even though our minds compensate for changes in ambient light to preserve continuity, that does not change what is real. Perception is not reality."

Mr. Nowell had paused in a futile attempt at dramatic effect. Most of the class had been whispering together or asleep by that point.

"It can be valuable to think of all scientific knowledge this way," he'd continued. "Strictly speaking, science doesn't give us answers. Science gives us results. Answers are interpretations of the results by people with imperfect perceptions of reality. Progressive experimentation has often completely revised the scientific 'answers' of history. Accurately recorded results will always be relevant, but the interpretations of those results may change drastically with additional research."

"True scientists are skeptics," he'd said. "They question every-thing—including their own perceptions of reality."

Sam had always found Mr. Nowell's philosophical digressions to be interesting and, occasionally, entertaining. This one had resonated with him in particular. He now considered himself an empiricist. A true agnostic.

His parents and religious leaders had always emphasized the importance of faith, but faith was problematic. It caused people to assume truth based on purely subjective experiences. Without an external observer, one could never be sure of *anything*. Faith had caused some of the most horrendous acts in history.

"Hey, Sam?" Jeanette's voice cut into Sam's musing.

"Yeah?" he replied.

"You want to come to our place for dinner tonight?"

This was a fairly frequent—and welcome—invitation. Ever since he'd informed his parents of his decision to leave their religion several months ago, he'd come to despise family dinners at his own home. His father, in particular, could not seem to accept his son as a nonbeliever.

Besides, dinner at the Jones household was always an opportunity to spend more time with Kara.

"That would be great," he replied. "Thanks!"

"What about you, Liam?" Jeanette asked, glancing through the rearview mirror.

"Hmm?" Liam said. Glasses in his left hand, he refused to divert his gaze from the phone he held two inches from his face.

Kara sighed. "Dinner? Our place?" she asked.

"Oh, nah. We're getting the Goon Squad together for a raid tonight."

Uh-oh, Sam thought.

"You're going to ditch us for that stupid game *again*?" Kara exclaimed.

Liam's eyes remained glued to his device. "Don't be bitter just because you can't enjoy the awesomeness."

Kara snorted. "I've played the game. It sucks."

"Pfft, that doesn't count. You can't really experience it without being able to see what you're doing."

"You can only *barely* see what you're doing."

"It's enough!" Liam said, finally looking up and placing the thick circular glasses back on his face. "Like I said, you just can't appreciate the awesomeness."

"Oh *no*," Kara said. "I can't appreciate the riveting experience of a bunch of people screaming over colors on a computer screen. I must miss sooo much by living in reality."

Liam chuckled, turned back to his device, and pulled his glasses off once again. "Glad we understand each other."

Kara released an exasperated sigh. Sam considered pushing Liam to accept their offer but ultimately decided the effort would be useless. Instead, he returned his gaze to the scene of deep oranges and purples whizzing by.

The setting sun slowly gave way to darkness as they pulled up the driveway to Liam's home. He gave them a quick "see you later" and strode into the house with his nose still buried in his phone.

The minutes passed with light conversation, and they soon drove down the sparsely populated road to the Joneses' home.

"That's weird," Jeanette said as they approached the house from the long driveway.

"What's weird?" Kara asked.

"The lights are all off. I didn't think Mom and Dad were going anywhere tonight."

"Maybe they went on a spur-of-the moment date night?"

Jeanette turned toward her sister with a look of concern. "I don't think so. Mom told me earlier that she was making lasagna."

Kara shrugged.

Jeanette switched the car engine off. The three of them stepped out of the vehicle in unison, with Kara taking an extra moment to extend her cane. A gust of wind picked up, fluttering Jeanette's top and Kara's uniform.

Light taps of the cane accompanied their walk to the front of the white two-story home. The colonial-style architecture sat amid pristine landscaping within their wooded lot, which spanned several acres. Smooth river stones lined the walkway, and a middle-aged red oak sprung out of the middle of the lush front lawn, surrounded by multicolored stones at its base.

Jeanette unlocked and opened the door to reveal an eerily dark interior. Sam could barely make out the banister at the foot of the stairs. They stepped inside as Jeanette flipped a switch, causing light to illuminate the entryway. Dark hardwood floors sat in planks parallel to the front door, butting up to the staircase straight ahead. To the left was an open foyer, beyond which Sam could see the kitchen island through the archway on the other side. Paintings and other decorations added a modest touch of color. The distinct smell of baking lasagna aroused Sam's senses.

"Mom? Dad?" Jeanette called out.

The room remained silent.

"Well, clearly they must be around somewhere. Lasagna is in the oven," Kara concluded, pointing at the kitchen. "And I need to pee." She turned on her heel and headed around the other side of the stairway toward the small bathroom, not bothering to use her cane.

"I'm going to go upstairs. I'll be back down in a minute," Jeanette said.

"Sure, no problem," Sam replied.

The staircase creaked above him as Sam made his way into the foyer.

Something definitely felt off. He couldn't come up with any rational explanation for the situation. Cooking dinner without any lights on didn't make sense at all.

"Mr. and Mrs. Jones?" he called out tentatively.

Sam entered the kitchen, flicked on the lights, and peeked at the oven. Sure enough, the timer had been set, counting down from a little over seven minutes. He pressed the button for the oven light and observed the lasagna bubbling in its stoneware baker. The pleasant aroma of cheesy herbs and spices made his mouth water.

He turned his attention past the kitchen to the dining room, where a handsome dark wood table sat on a neutral patterned rug. Sam reached around the small wall separating the oven from the dining room and flipped the switch he knew was there. Light spiraled and waved across the steel backdrop of the light fixture hovering over the table.

A shadow moved outside the sliding glass door.

Sam fixed his gaze on the glass between the dining and living rooms. His heart burst into action, and possibilities assaulted his mind. A burglar? Some kind of animal? He approached the glass door, not taking his eyes off the location of prior movement. The lock snapped free easily. His breathing quickened as he slid the door open. Even without the glare of the window, it was too dark to see clearly. He hit the switch next to the glass door, illuminating the back porch.

Sam jumped.

A branch of the large backyard tree waved in the breeze.

He clutched his chest, willing his heart to slow. *Stupid tree nearly gave me a heart attack. They really need to trim that thing.*

Something shimmered in his peripheral vision. Before he had time to react, a large metallic figure dropped out of the sky, landing a few feet in front of him with a loud *thump* against the concrete patio. Sam stumbled backward and crashed painfully against the hardwood floor.

The metal object ran with incredible speed toward the base of the tree. It looked like some kind of humanoid robot. Along its limbs and back was a series of sleek dark metal plates, giving an armor-like impression.

Sam sat propped against his arms, transfixed at the scene before him. The armored robot reached the base of the tree, past the limits of the porch lights. A thunderous *clang* accompanied a flash of light, which illuminated its metal body and the well-kept backyard landscaping.

Another flash revealed the silhouette of a cloaked figure. It was wielding a sword.

The flashes of light coincided with the sound of the sword striking the robot's metallic armor.

More bangs and flashes of light erupted in quick succession, and the two figures moved into the porch light. Sam squinted as he tried to follow their movements. What he'd thought was a cloak was more like a coat, and its wearer stood with its back toward the house, the robot now facing toward Sam. Between its two large shoulder guards sat a round metallic head bearing a dark glass face shield. It looked like a helmet.

Sam's eyes widened in realization. It wasn't a robot. It was some kind of *suit*.

Instinct pushed him to run, but shock, terror, and fascination froze him in place.

The two danced in a fierce, impossibly fast clash of sword against steel. As the blade struck out again, the suit grabbed it and yanked the cloaked figure from its feet. A crackle of sparks erupted from the blade, causing the suit to release its grip. As the cloaked figure landed, it stretched a pale hand forward.

BOOM.

The shockwave echoed through the house, shaking its contents. The suit flew backward and smashed into the base of the massive tree. Bark and splinters exploded across the yard.

The cloaked figure turned toward the house. Fear spiked in Sam's chest as the faint porch light revealed only a darkly bearded chin under the hood. The man wore a traditional vest with a dark red sash, and a leather belt was wrapped around his torso. He still held the sword in his right hand.

A scream rang out from the stairway.

Long coat billowing behind him, the man bolted in through the open sliding door, stepping—almost floating—silently through the house and up the stairs, completely ignoring Sam.

Jeanette. Jeanette is upstairs! Sam thought with a jolt.

He rose, sprinting back through the kitchen and foyer. Rounding the stair banister, he nearly collided with Kara, who screamed and assumed a defensive stance.

"Kara!"

"Sam?" Her stance softened. "What's happening?"

Jeanette. Sam pushed past Kara. He didn't think he could even begin to describe the situation.

"I have no idea," he replied through heavy breaths as he sprinted up the steps. "Stay there!"

Another piercing scream rang through the house.

Sam turned the corner at the top of the staircase, feeling light-headed. *What am I going to do? Fight?* He shoved those thoughts to the side—he had to do *something*. Another scream came from Jeanette's bedroom at the end of the hall. The door was open, light pouring from it into the dark hallway.

In the distance, he could partially make out Jeanette struggling to free herself from the hooded man.

"Let me go!" she cried.

Sam raced down the hallway as she went limp in the man's arms. Her assailant pulled her further into the bedroom, beyond view.

Just as Sam entered the doorway, the suit crashed through the room's window and part of the exterior wall, scattering shards of glass, wood, and drywall across the room. Sam instinctively brought his arms up to cover his head, then peeked through with wide eyes. The white dresser on the wall near the cloaked man abruptly lurched forward—opposite the direction of flying debris. It smashed into the suit with a loud *crack*, exploding in a whirlwind of splinters and clothing. The suit fell with the debris outside the giant hole in the wall.

Arms lowering, Sam watched wide-eyed as the cloaked figure slung Jeanette's limp body over his shoulder. He glanced briefly at Sam, then flew out the gaping hole and into the night.

Sam stepped into the destroyed bedroom, ears ringing. Slowly, the sounds of crickets chirping became discernible outside the giant hole. The scent of lasagna mixed oddly with drywall dust and debris. He stepped past the rubble, peeking out over the edge of the destroyed exterior. The mysterious flying man was nowhere to be seen. Down below, the remains of the dresser and Jeanette's clothes lay in disarray on the back lawn. The suit wasn't there either.

Sam's pulse slowed, though his breathing was still heavy from the physical exertion and surge of adrenaline.

"Sam?" Kara's quivering voice came from behind him.

He turned and quickly made his way to her through the rubble.

"I'm here," he replied. He tried to catch his breath and silently cursed his level of physical fitness.

She nodded, eyes watering. "Wh—Where is Jeanette? What happened?"

"She was . . . kidnapped."

Tears streamed down Kara's face as she squeezed her eyes shut and placed a hand to her mouth.

Not knowing what else to do, Sam put his arms around her, holding her close. They stood together in silence that was broken only by Kara's occasional sniffling.

Sam felt numb. Stupefied. He was glad she didn't ask for any more details, because he was sure he couldn't give them. The things he had seen were impossible. A suit of power armor *breaking through a wall*? An ominous, cloak-wearing, sword-wielding . . . *wizard* who could apparently fly? It was bizarre. Beyond bizarre. Sam considered himself an empiricist, but he had a hard time accepting this sensory experience as reality.

A knock at the door interrupted their long embrace, causing them both to jump.

"It's probably the police," Kara said through her tears. "I called them."

"Good thinking," Sam said.

As they pivoted to enter the upstairs hallway, movement from the destroyed wall almost caused Sam to stumble in alarm. He whirled around to see that the suited figure had returned. It stood just inside the hole. He prepared to run with Kara in tow, but a gauntleted hand pulled the helmet off, revealing the face of a middle-aged, brown-skinned woman with short black hair.

"Wait!" the woman said, stretching her free hand out in a stopping motion. "Please don't be afraid. My name is Elysia."

She had an accent that Sam couldn't place, but it seemed to be Eastern European.

"Are you with the police?" Kara asked through her sobs.

"We have someone talking to them," the woman said. "I'm very sorry, but you two must come with me. You may be in great danger."

A distant *ding* rang from the hallway, announcing that lasagna was ready.

Chapter 2

The Facility

Sam looked over the woman's intimidating exosuit and wondered what kind of secret government organization could have built it.

"What happened to my parents?" Kara asked.

A pang of guilt gnawed at Sam's insides. He'd completely forgotten about her parents in the turmoil.

Elysia's gaze fell to the floor, and Sam's stomach dropped.

"I'm afraid that the assailant murdered them in the bedroom down the hall," Elysia said. "That is why I am here."

An uneasy silence ensued. Crickets chirped and wind rustled through the trees outside the giant hole in the wall. Though Sam had not known them well, Kara's parents were kind people. Memories of Mrs. Jones's delicious meals and his science discussions with Mr. Jones over dinner played in his mind.

Now they were gone. And their murderer had kidnapped Jeanette.

Kara was alone.

She wept quietly, and a lump formed in Sam's throat. He couldn't fathom what she must be feeling. Unable to look at her face, he squeezed her hand to comfort her.

She tore herself away, with tears streaming down her face.

The weight of her grief slammed into Sam. Tears of his own fell from his eyes. He wanted to tell her that he was here for her, but his lips wouldn't move.

Kara turned and left, nearly tripping over a piece of drywall. Elysia stretched an arm out but seemed to stop herself from responding. Sam hesitantly followed Kara out of the room but paused at the doorway. She strode down the dimly lit hall, fingers lightly brushing the wall, until she reached her parent's bedroom.

Only a faint outline of the bodies were visible to Sam. Kara crumpled next to them. Her sobs echoed across the hall. Sam stood motionless, feeling numb as he wiped the tears from his face with a sleeve. Soft mechanical noises echoed off the walls behind him as Elysia approached.

"I am very sorry, but we must leave quickly. The attacker may return."

Sam nodded, more out of reflex than true acknowledgment. He walked down the dark hallway and slowly approached Kara.

He had failed Jeanette, but he could still do his part to help keep Kara safe.

Making a concerted effort not to look at the bodies, he put soft hands on Kara's shoulders and lifted upward. She followed his motion without protest. He kept one arm on her shoulder as they returned to the bedroom with Elysia.

"It will be faster if we fly," Elysia said. "May I carry you both?"

The idea of flying gave Sam a tiny pinch of excitement through the grief. "You can carry both of us?"

"Yes, though it will not be comfortable."

Sam looked at Kara. She was gone—a shell of her normal self. The sight was agonizing.

"Okay," he replied on their behalf.

"Good," Elysia said.

A sharp sense of panic rose in Sam at seeing the suit advance toward him. Kara flinched at the sound. He convinced himself that if Elysia really meant them harm, there wouldn't be anything they could do about it.

The woman placed the helmet back on, wedged herself between them, and wrapped her cold, stiff arms under their shoulders. They rose upward smoothly and sped out of the large hole, forcing Sam to close his eyes briefly as his stomach lurched. There was no audible means of propulsion. How could it move so quietly? How did they power such a thing?

Queries faded from his mind as the exhilaration of flying above barely visible trees took over. Cool wind howled in his ears. The small pond behind the Joneses' house shimmered in the moonlight below. Curiously, Elysia took them over the nature preserve behind the property.

The suit slowed and deftly put them down on the wild forest floor in front of a large egg-shaped device. A side of the metal egg slid inward and upward of its own accord, revealing gray seats inside. Sam's jaw dropped. *Some kind of vehicle!* He glanced at Kara to find her staring blankly at the ground—lost, distant.

"Please, take a seat inside," Elysia said.

Admiring the sleek aesthetic, Sam entered the strange vehicle and sat down in the second seat to his left, leading Kara by the hand to sit in the seat next to him by the open door. The interior was tiny—only four spots with barely enough room for four pairs of adult legs to squeeze into the center. Other than the seats and a soft light overhead, the interior was empty.

Once Elysia walked in, the door slid back downward and locked into place.

"Please engage your harnesses," she instructed as she removed her helmet. She attached it to a point near her waist before sitting down.

Sam noticed the buckles on either side of his head. He helped Kara click her belts into place and then attended to his own. They pulled down across his chest and attached magnetically to the register between his legs. The seat was remarkably comfortable.

As soon as they strapped in, a nearly inaudible force rumbled under their feet. Kara felt around for Sam's hand and gripped his fingers, causing his insides to flutter in reaction. The vehicle felt like an elevator with seats—and without the noise. As it picked up speed, loud winds beat against the outer hull.

Where were they going?

Sam glanced at Elysia, who maintained a distant gaze toward the door. He wanted to ask the strange woman questions, but he doubted he'd be able to with the wind noise.

As the minutes went by, he expected a change in direction, but it never came. They seemed to accelerate upward indefinitely, though there were a few moments where his sense of balance tipped a bit.

Sam felt a slight pull to the side as his sensation of gravity weakened, then disappeared. His stomach lurched. The wind continued to roar outside. *We must be descending now.*

Gradually, the winds subsided, and a steady sense of gravity returned. Elysia unbuckled herself. Kara's sweaty hand released Sam's, and the two of them freed their own harnesses.

The sliding door opened again, revealing an enormous steel room. Through the opening, Sam could make out a few more egg-shaped vehicles outside.

Elysia motioned for them to follow.

Kara took Sam's arm, and he led them out onto a large landing pad of sorts. Steel plates lined the floor and walls, and the flat ceiling in the distance overhead had a single small hole in the center, presumably for the egg-like craft to descend through. Besides the other vehicles, the enormous room was empty.

They followed Elysia toward a semicircular door at the side of the landing pad. Were they in a space station? If so, where was gravity coming from?

"Where are we?" Sam asked.

"I am not permitted to explain much at the moment," Elysia said over the taps of her enormous boots on the steel floor, "but your questions will be answered soon."

"Are we in space?"

"Oh no, no," she replied, chuckling slightly. "We are in an underground facility beneath Europe. That much I can say."

Europe! Sam nearly tripped over himself with surprise. They had traveled from the United States to Europe in a matter of minutes?

Elysia continued, "I know that you both must have many questions. I promise you will receive answers."

They reached a circular white door on one side of the massive wall, which whisked apart into the walls as they approached. Inside stood a bearded man wearing a strange silver-and-blue uniform. A large, well-lit, domed hallway surrounded him, plunging far into the distance.

"Elysia," he said, nodding to the armored woman.

She nodded back. "Kerlo. Has he been located?"

Kerlo's reply was dense with frustration. "Unfortunately, no." He waved in a large, almost comical motion for them to follow as he turned. "No trace of him yet."

The bright hallway caused Sam to squint as they entered. The man named Kerlo had a strange accent of his own, resembling an unusual mixture of Australian and Southern drawl, with occasional consonants missing. He stood tall—taller than Sam— and strode with purpose, falling into step beside Elysia.

"Oblivion copycat, ya think, wearing that cloak?"

Elysia shook her head. "No. The attack was targeted."

Kerlo gave her a skeptical glance. "Fought with some kinda sword, eh?"

"Yes, and with superhuman speed. The sword was no ordinary weapon. It did not pierce the armor, of course, but it did cause strange electrical discharges. Strikes of the weapon momentarily disabled a few of the suit's functions."

"Advanced tech, then?" he asked.

"Probably. I've seen things like it before, though never as a sword."

They continued to an impression in the right wall, which encompassed another circular door. It spread open as they approached. Sam allowed himself a smidgen of fascination with the technology, despite the tragic situation.

Inside was what appeared to be a break room, in the shape of a half circle. Plush blue chairs stood around four circular marble tables. Odd white pedestals with screens lined the straight wall. They looked almost like touch screen soda fountains, though sleeker and with larger openings. There were no other occupants.

Kerlo spun on his heel. "Make yourself comfortable," he said, before turning to Kara. "I'll look into this a bit more and see if I can find out why the man targeted your family. Be back soon."

Kara gave no reply or acknowledgment, her empty gaze fading into the floor. Her abnormal behavior was agonizing to watch.

Kerlo glanced at Elysia. "Will you stay with them?"

"I can spare some time, but then I must return to my patrol," she replied.

"Very well. I'll try to be quick."

He turned, striding briskly from the room; the circular door shut with a whisper behind him.

Elysia led them to the white soda-fountain-looking pedestals, which apparently provided food. Some familiar meals on display included burgers and fries, pasta dishes, and salads. Others were unrecognizable. For all he knew, they could be normal meals from other countries.

The emotional turbulence in Sam's stomach left little room for hunger, despite having missed dinner. However, out of numb reaction or some automatic desire to be agreeable, he accepted the offer of food on their behalf.

Kara ignored his attempts to engage her, and he decided to just choose a meal for her. He selected chicken and broccoli Alfredo, knowing it was a dish she would normally enjoy. Somehow, Elysia selected it without touching or saying anything. Sam watched in awe as the machine came to life and spat a saucer out into the opening. Sizzling sounds accompanied mechanical noises behind the wall. In less than thirty seconds, stringy fettuccine plopped out from the hole above into the saucer, followed by thin-cut slices of grilled chicken, creamy Alfredo sauce, and broccoli. Steam rose from the ensemble. A section of the area in front of the saucer flipped around, revealing a simple metal fork.

Delightful cheesy scents rose from the dish, causing Sam's hunger to peek through the knot in his stomach. He removed

Kara's meal from the machine and got the same for himself, wondering how Elysia could communicate with the device without physical interaction.

Though still quite unlike her usual self, Kara accepted her meal. They ate together in silence for several minutes. Elysia sat across the table, looking distant. The meal tasted as delicious as it smelled; it even seemed to improve Kara's mood.

"Kerlo has found something," Elysia said, speaking to Kara. "A relative of your mother's may have some answers. He is coming this way to explain."

Kara's eyebrows scrunched up in confusion. "We don't have any other family," she said toward the table. "My parents were both only children, and my grandparents died before I was born."

"Kerlo will explain," Elysia replied.

How was Kerlo communicating with her? She didn't seem to have any visible communication device. Were these people telepathic or something? Sam considered asking but decided against it and turned back to his meal. She said the answers would come later, and he was starving.

The circular door whisked open to reveal Kerlo striding toward them. Kara placed her fork down and Sam followed suit, anticipation rippling through him.

"I just spoke with your mother's cousin," Kerlo said as he approached. "She's devastated to hear about your parents, but wants to meet you. She's kindly offered to let the two of you stay at her home for a while."

Sam struggled to follow the man's meaning with his thick, odd accent. He glanced at Kara, trying to gauge her reaction. Her brow furrowed.

"Where does she live?" Kara asked.

Kerlo seemed startled by the simple question. "Well . . ." He glanced at Elysia. "You'll need to go through orientation first before I can answer that."

"*Orientation?*" Kara and Sam said in unison.

"Into this secret organization of yours?" Sam asked.

Kerlo waved the question aside. "Sam, you are of age, so you're welcome to join Kara if you choose. However, if you decide to continue, returning to your parents' home will have certain . . . requirements."

Definitely some kind of secret organization.

Though why put them through orientation just to send them off to a family member? That didn't add up. Unless perhaps Mrs. Jones's cousin was *a member* of this organization.

Sam glanced at Kara, who turned toward him with a concerned look—her stunning blue eyes darted about as usual. He couldn't leave her. She needed him.

This is also a chance to leave home, Sam realized.

He had been anxious to leave home, but this was extremely abrupt. He thought of his parents and decided he could leave his father pretty easily, given the man's constant condescending attitude. His mother was also frequently disapproving, but he would miss her. Most of all, he would miss his younger sister, Lillian. Compared to his parents, she seemed to be more understanding of his new worldview.

His closest friends were Kara, Liam, and Jeanette, so the only one he'd really be leaving behind was Liam. Sam felt remorseful at that prospect, particularly since Kara and Jeanette would be gone as well. Liam had other friend groups, though. Besides, staying for Liam's sake would mean having Kara go it alone, and she needed him far more right now.

"I won't leave Kara," Sam said. "I'm going with her. May I call my family, though? We haven't seen eye to eye recently, but I still wouldn't want to disappear without telling them anything."

"Absolutely," Kerlo said without hesitation. "You'll need to use one of our devices, though; your phone wont operate in here."

He motioned for them to follow him in that emphatic way of his, and they rose from their seats.

"I must return to my duties," Elysia said, rising with them. "I'm deeply sorry that I was unable to stop this tragedy." She made her way to Kara. "We will do everything we can to find your sister. I promise."

"Thank you," Kara replied.

Elysia held her hand out toward the small woman she towered over. After a moment, she realized her error and placed her hand gently on Kara's shoulder, looking embarrassed. Kara jumped at the touch.

Walking over to Sam, Elysia extended her hand toward him, and he shook it tentatively. Despite the obvious power inherent to the suit, she controlled it with exceptional precision, gripping his hand firmly but without too much pressure.

"I wish you both well," she said. "Please take care."

Elysia turned on her heel and left. Sam guided Kara by his arm around the tables and chairs toward Kerlo, who led them back down the hall to a small office. Inside, three chairs accompanied three plain white desks. Atop each was a monitor with corresponding keyboard and mouse, along with an old-looking office telephone. A large white poster hung from the far wall, decorated with the flags of countries around the world. Several clocks hung on the other walls, displaying the time in different time zones. Clearly, the room had seen little use, if any.

"I recommend you avoid sharing details about the things ya experienced this evening," Kerlo said. "It's unlikely to cause any harm, but it may create more difficulties." He motioned toward the phone on the nearest desk. "Best to keep it to yourself for now if you can."

The idea of hiding the truth made Sam uneasy, but the alternative meant admitting that he had been in serious danger. If his parents knew that, they'd be much less likely to support his decision to leave.

"Okay," Sam said.

Kerlo nodded, backing out through the doorway. "I'll be outside."

Kara moved to leave as well.

"Please stay," Sam asked. "I'd like you to stay with me. Please."

She turned to him with a look of utter torment. "I . . . I can't, Sam. I'm sorry." She turned and left, leaving Sam with anguish twisting in his chest.

Sam sat and picked up the telephone while attempting to

smother his sorrow. He realized he'd likely have to make an international call, since they were apparently in Europe. The poster with various flags on it also happened to have instructions for international calls and a calling code next to each flag.

Sam followed the listed instructions to dial his mother's number. Soon enough, the line started ringing, so it appeared to be working.

"Hello?" His mother's voice came from the speaker. It struck Sam that he had absolutely no idea what to say. How would someone tell their mother that they were leaving home unexpectedly?

"Hello?" she said again.

Better say something soon or she's going to hang up.

"Hi, Mom."

"Sam? What number are you calling from? Did you lose your phone?"

"No, I just . . . don't have service here."

This was going to be harder than he thought.

"I . . ." He trailed off, unable to find the right words.

"Are you okay? What's happened?" she asked, her concern clearly flaring up.

"I'm fine," he said. "I'm just having a hard time knowing what to say."

Thankfully, she remained quiet for a moment, allowing Sam to collect his thoughts. He decided it was best to be honest, without sharing specific details.

"Kara has to leave, and I have decided to go with her," he said. "I can't say where I'll be going. I don't even know where it is. But I won't be coming home for a while, and I'm not sure when I'll be able to call again."

There. He'd said the hardest part. He waited anxiously for his mother to say something, but the line was silent for several seconds. "But . . . the university. . . your friends . . . so sudden . . ."

"I love you, but I need to do this."

"I love you too," she replied. "I know you've been anxious to leave home, Sam, but this is so sudden! Why don't you come home and we can talk before you rush into something?"

Sam ran his hand through his hair, feeling inadequate. "I would, but . . . I won't get another shot at this. If I don't take this opportunity now, it will be gone. Forever." He leaned back in the chair. "Please . . . I know this is sudden, but please accept my decision. I will be okay. I promise." He wasn't certain he could keep that promise, since he was venturing into the unknown, but his confident words would help her feel more comfortable about the situation.

Narrowly avoiding her probing questions about the "opportunity," Sam continued consoling his mother and reiterating his determination to continue. Though she never completely conceded to his decision, she seemed to become more at ease as they spoke. Soon, she handed the phone to his sister.

"What's this?" Lillian said. "You're dropping off the face of the earth to hunt dragons with Kara or something?"

Sam chuckled. "Something like that."

"So I get all your stuff, then?"

"I'll miss you too, Lil."

Nothing but soft static occupied the line for several seconds.

"You really are leaving," she said finally.

"Yes."

Silence again.

"Well . . ." she said. "I love you. Don't do anything stupid."

He smiled. "Oh, I will, don't worry. And I love you too."

"Give Kara a hug for me, all right?"

"Sure."

"Just don't make it weird," Lil said. "She doesn't like you like that."

The ache in Sam's chest resurfaced as Lil handed the phone back to their mother, who continued to weep and stall for time. Eventually, Sam couldn't take it anymore.

"I have to go now. I love you, Mom. And I'll communicate when I can. Promise."

"Okay, okay!" she said. "But please call your father."

He hung up the line without responding, knowing it would never end if he did. He leaned back, sighing.

His father.

His mother knew that Sam's relationship with the man was a rocky one. Recently, they'd spent more time shouting at each other than having any kind of civil conversation. But Sam couldn't just leave without speaking to him. He was still family, after all.

"All right. I guess I will," Sam muttered to himself.

He pulled up the number on his phone and followed the procedure of making the call. The line rang—and continued to ring. Sam's muscles tensed. Soon enough, the system default voicemail message played through the speaker. Panic flooded his mind. What was he supposed to say in a voicemail? "Bye, Dad, I may never see you again"? He wasn't ready for this.

Beep.

"Um . . . Hi, Dad. It's Sam. I . . . uh . . . have an opportunity to do something unique with Kara, but to take advantage of it, I have to go tonight. Sorry, I can't say much more about it. I already spoke to Mom and Lil. I won't be able to communicate for a while, and I'm not sure when I'll be back." He took a deep breath. "I just wanted to say . . . I'm sorry we haven't been getting along much recently. I'm not leaving because of you. Promise. This is just . . . something I can't pass up." He paused. What else was there to say? "Um . . . bye."

The phone clicked as he placed it back in the receiver.

After giving his nerves a moment to settle, he emerged from the room. Kerlo sat on a small chair outside, staring into the distance. Sam's arrival seemed to snap him out of his trance. Kara sat across the hall with a pensive look.

"Done?" Kerlo asked.

Sam nodded. "Yes."

"Excellent. Please follow me to orientation." Kerlo motioned for them to follow him in his exaggerated way.

Here goes nothing.

Chapter 3

Orientation

Sam, leading Kara by the arm, followed Kerlo down a section of the bright hallway, which opened into the orientation section of the strange facility. The large room contained many smaller rooms, almost like an office arranged with cubicles, except that each one was fully enclosed. Long bright lights lined the plain ceiling overhead, and a faint scent resembling chemical disinfectant lingered in the air. The enclosed spaces to the right had glass on one side, through which Sam could see a comfortable-looking armchair that faced the opposite wall. The other walls were solid black—their interiors a mystery.

Kerlo turned to Kara, scratching his short brown beard. "You'll each need to undergo orientation separately. Given your condition, you should use one of the seated rooms." He then turned to Sam. "You can use a seated room too if you'd like, but the holo rooms"—he motioned to one of the black rooms—"are more visually engaging. Alice'll answer all your questions."

Fatigue made the plush armchair a tempting choice, but Sam couldn't ignore his curiosity surrounding those "holo" rooms. As

Kerlo led Kara to her room, Sam let himself into one of the black ones, finding himself surrounded by darkness.

Half of the room in front of him came alive a moment after he entered, revealing a middle-aged woman in a modest blue dress standing poised with her hands together. Golden blond hair fell across her attractive face and down to her shoulders. She stood in the half of the room that had become a small office. Skyscrapers lit up the night through the window behind her. The only other visible item in the simulated area was a model of the solar system off to the side.

"Hello," she said with a warm smile.

"Hi," Sam replied, walking toward her along the too-black floor.

"Is English your primary language?" she asked. Unlike Kerlo and Elysia, the woman's accent was clearly British.

"Yes."

Continuing his casual stride forward, Sam looked around, amazed at how the room and the perspective of the exterior followed his movements as if he were actually walking into it. He held out a hand as he approached the seam, expecting to run into the wall, but the collision never came. He stepped tentatively from the solid black onto what appeared to be a wood floor.

"Excellent," she said. "My name is Alice. I am a synthetic personality. You might call me an artificial intelligence, or AI."

Sam squinted at her face, his interest piqued. Dark eye shadow surrounded deep-green eyes, which posed a stunning contrast to the artificial woman's pale skin. He'd seen some AI programs before, but none of them had ever looked this realistic. The detail was exquisite. He glanced back and realized the black walls behind him were no longer visible. A small outward-facing desk rested near one wall, surrounded by modest decor that gave the office a homey feel.

"My purpose is to explain aspects of this world and the universe in general to prepare you for your journey," the AI said, causing Sam to turn his attention back to her. "These facts will likely surprise you."

Sam still found himself awed by her realism; her movements were so lifelike.

After a brief pause, she continued. "First, please tell me your full legal name."

"Sure. My name is Samuel Lance Williams."

"Are you identified by any nicknames?"

He shrugged. "Everyone I know usually calls me Sam."

She nodded. "Thank you. By undergoing this instruction," she said, her tone turning serious, "you understand that the information carries with it a significant responsibility to maintain confidentiality. If you are to return home, you will be under constant surveillance."

Sam's jaw dropped. That seemed to be a fairly extreme intrusion of privacy for protecting information.

"Do you understand these terms?" she asked. Despite the seriousness of her tone, she did not sound unkind.

"Yes," Sam replied.

"Do you accept these terms?"

Sam hesitated. If he ever went back home, these people would apparently monitor him for the rest of his life. How would they even accomplish that? Perhaps it was some kind of scare tactic. *Regardless, I've come this far. I'm not going back now. Kara certainly won't.*

"Yes," he said.

"Excellent." Alice smiled again. "Before we begin, do you have questions for me?"

Questions? He had a million questions. Everything that had happened in the past couple of hours raised countless questions. What were they again?

"I don't know. Um ... maybe continue, and I will ask as you go?" he suggested.

She smiled. "That is wise. Please stop me at any point, and I will answer your questions to the best of my ability."

The room darkened. A steel platform faded in beneath them, overlooking Earth from space, which rotated slowly below. Sam's jaw dropped as he admired the brilliant rendition of the surroundings, where billions of stars forming clouds of bright colors swirled along the axis of the Milky Way and other more distant clusters. He had occasionally savored the dazzling sky on clear nights, but the view from space was extraordinary. It made Sam feel infinitesimal—a speck among the incalculable depth of existence. His yearning to understand the fundamental workings of the universe reemerged with a vengeance.

"People of Earth have been seeking intelligent life in the universe for centuries," Alice said. "But, in fact, extraterrestrial intelligent life discovered Earth over one thousand and six hundred years ago, by Earth time scales."

The hull of a cylindrical space vessel appeared near their circular platform and descended toward the planet's surface. Sam watched it with wide eyes, the implications piling into his mind. The vessel seemed rather small—perhaps the size of a large subway car—though it was hard to judge size in space.

"This intelligent life was part of the Intergalactic Sovereignty of Rwenmar, commonly referred to as 'the Sovereignty.' You are currently inside the Sovereignty's Earthan Station, located underneath the present-day region of the Netherlands."

She paused for several seconds while Sam absorbed this absurd information. He attempted to sort through the onslaught of impacts this revelation had on his assumptions about the universe.

"So," he said, skepticism marring his tone, "a race of aliens discovered Earth over *a thousand years ago* and has been living with us in secret all this time?"

"That is technically correct. However, very few citizens of the Sovereignty have relocated to Earth since its discovery. Most citizens who live here are appointed to Earth as part of their employment."

Sam considered her response. It made sense that if a civilization with the comforts of advanced technology had discovered Earth during the Dark Ages, its people probably hadn't wanted to move there. Indoor plumbing was a nice commodity.

"Okay, so why all the secrecy? Why wouldn't the Sovereignty

share its knowledge and advanced technology?" he asked, gesturing to his surroundings.

Her expression turned sober as the stars zoomed around them, placing them in orbit around a new planet. Though its land masses differed from Earth's, it seemed to have a similar climate, with iced poles and a significant amount of water.

"The Sovereignty forbids itself from taking ownership of inhabited worlds with intelligent life," Alice explained. "The only exception is for prevention of an extinction-level event. During the period of early expansion across star systems, the Sovereignty's experience indicated that giant leaps in knowledge and technology among cultures frequently lead to devastating results."

Enormous explosions covered the land masses of the alien planet. Its atmosphere burned, and flames rippled out from the points of detonation. Heat from the planet seemed to reach Sam on their platform in the cold of space. It was a neat special effect, though physically preposterous.

"Therefore," Alice said, "it has been the Sovereignty's long-standing protocol to maintain secrecy from an inhabited world until its people achieve a certain level of technological and social advancement, preparing them for potential integration. This involves, in part, the subtle introduction of the Common language, which you now call English, and manipulations of the planet's recorded history in order to facilitate future incorporation of the planet into the Sovereignty."

Sam threw his arm up. "Whoa, wait a second. Back up. Did you just say the Sovereignty introduced English to Earth *artificially?*"

"Yes, that is correct," she responded matter-of-factly.

"That doesn't make any sense. It's been a while since my last history lesson on the subject, but from what I remember, it's very clear that English arose from other languages like Latin and French."

She smiled. "It may surprise you, but the Sovereignty's early attempts to introduce Common influenced several native Earthan languages. As mentioned before, the Sovereignty has manipulated parts of Earth's recorded history, and even some historical findings, to achieve inclusion of the language."

Sam frowned. That sounded like an impossible amount of work, even for an advanced civilization. "How is that even possible?"

The AI put on a motherly expression, mixed with a dash of concern. "I am sorry. I am not permitted to disclose any additional details of the Sovereignty's efforts to incorporate the Common language on Earth. Does this disappoint you?"

"Disappointed" wasn't quite the right word. "Skeptical" was more like it. What she said didn't feel right, and her reluctance or inability to share details made him more suspicious.

"Sorry, I'm fine," he said. "Please continue."

Alice smiled. "It is quite all right. This is understandably disconcerting information for you. Please continue to ask questions."

He acknowledged the notion with a nod.

Their surroundings faded to black, giving Sam a slight sense of vertigo. The steel platform below remained, lit by ambient light with no apparent source.

"As this incorporation of the Sovereignty's means of communication is attempted subtly to avoid detection, it is sometimes unsuccessful—or only partially successful," Alice said. "While the adoption of Common has prospered tremendously on Earth, the Sovereignty has had limited success with the adoption of our complete number system to date."

Behind her, the digits zero through nine appeared in the air. She gestured to them, keeping her gaze firmly on Sam.

"You are most likely familiar with these symbols. Is that true?" she asked.

"Yes, of course," Sam replied, walking toward them. "Those are numbers."

"The Sovereignty's number system is slightly different."

Two additional symbols appeared after the familiar ones. The first appeared to be an upside-down, flipped version of the number two, while the other looked somewhat like a backward three.

"While a ten-digit number system is most commonplace on Earth," the AI said, "the Sovereignty is accustomed to a twelve-digit number system. We refer to it as the dohnal system, though it is more commonly known on Earth as the dozenal or duodecimal number system." She walked beneath the new numbers, gesturing upwards but keeping her eyes on Sam. "While we were successful in introducing the glyphs zero through nine, the other two—called dek and el, corresponding to ten and eleven in decimal—have not yet achieved wide adoption on Earth."

Sam blinked as he stared at the two new symbols. "Am I going to need to learn this new system?" he asked, fearing the answer.

Alice nodded. "If you choose to remain in a region controlled by the Sovereignty, we recommend that you learn this new system. After your orientation is complete, Kerlo will give you a device called a Jit that will serve many functions. It will help you learn the dohnal system and perform the proper conversions to the Earthan decimal system in the meantime."

"Oh, okay. That's good, at least."

She smiled again. "Do you have any additional questions on the topic?"

Sam thought for a moment. There were question marks all over this information, but his knowledge of history, language, and the number system was not deep enough to know what else to pick at.

"Not for now," he said.

She gave him a gentle nod as the numbers faded to darkness and the view from space above Earth reappeared.

"The Sovereignty categorizes planet-wide populations on a scale of six eras or classes," Alice said. "Several factors, including technological advancement and social structures, are used to determine these classifications."

Sam stared into a cluster of clouds swirling over the Atlantic, mesmerized by the stunning visuals.

"Earth is presently categorized as a class four planet," Alice continued. "When it achieves class five status, representatives will meet with world leaders and officially offer inclusion into the Sovereignty."

Sam glanced back at the AI. Alice remained poised with her hands clasped in front of her, wearing an interested expression as she observed him. The information still felt preposterous. A spacefaring society maintaining secrecy for centuries from less advanced planets like Earth? It was ludicrous, and yet some of what the AI said seemed logical. A thought struck him.

"What do people in the Sovereignty look like?" Sam asked, stepping toward her. "I mean, I can guess that there are humans, given that I've met Kerlo and Elysia, but what are the rest of the citizens like? Is there a large mix of different species?"

Oddly shaped creatures faded in around them. One looked like an elephant without the trunk. Another resembled a cat with large bat-like wings. Sam jumped and backed away as he noticed a creature that had appeared behind him. It had four crab legs, a long rippling torso with spiky dorsal fins, two long fins for arms, and an eel head with beady black eyes. Standing upright at several feet tall, its entire body was a striking light teal color.

Alice turned to him. "The Sovereignty has encountered many unique creatures in our exploration of the universe," she said. The animals faded, and various humanlike figures replaced them. "But we have never encountered a nonhuman species with human-level intellect. Therefore, all citizens of the Sovereignty are, in fact, human."

Sam's jaw dropped. He turned about, glancing at the surrounding people, who stood motionless. They varied in shape, size, and features, but they *did* all look human in form and general appearance.

"So . . . they're all human? Not different species that just look human?" he asked.

"Correct. All of the humans the Sovereignty has encountered on other planets have manifested unique traits, but they are all genetically compatible to date. Each subspecies can procreate with any other subspecies."

The AI's answer conjured lewd images in Sam's mind. He quickly extinguished them.

"Isn't that . . . uh . . . unexpected?" he said.

"Indeed!" she replied. "When the Sovereignty first began its wide exploration of other planets, explorers expected to find varied forms of intelligent life—if such life existed at all. The discovery that all other life with human-level intellect appeared to be distinctly human astonished Sovereignty scientists and explorers immensely."

Sam imagined that scientists on Earth would find it pretty surprising as well. "But . . . why? Why only humans?"

The human figures faded, and stars zipped around them, placing them near a stunning galaxy. Billions of stars twinkled around the bright center in a magnificent swirl of brilliant purples and blues.

"An intriguing question," Alice said, "for which there is no widely accepted answer. Many have provided theories, but no proposal to date has found significant support with verifiable evidence. It is still a mystery."

Curious, Sam thought. *Still, it shows that even though the Sovereignty is highly advanced, they don't know everything.* That was something to take comfort in, he supposed.

Weariness seized Sam's mind as he stared into the spinning galaxy.

"Do you have any additional questions, Sam?" the AI asked.

"Not at the moment. Please continue."

She nodded, gesturing toward the stunning image behind her. "Though we refer to this as the Khels galaxy, you may know it as the Triangulum galaxy, which is its given name on Earth." The galaxy zoomed in around them, moving their platform near another Earthlike planet orbiting a blue-white star. Two moons surrounded it.

"This is Alvior, the planet you will travel to with your friend Kara. It is where her relative lives."

Sam could barely think anymore; exhaustion consumed him. "I assume it will take years in some spaceship for us to get there?"

The AI actually laughed at that. "Oh, no. You will rest in the Earthan station's facilities, and after you awake, you will make your way to Alvior using the acheron."

Sam blinked. "The what?"

"The acheron," she repeated. "A portal."

34

The AI actually laughed at that. "Oh, no. You will rest in the Earthan station's facilities, and after you awake, you will make your way to Alvior using the acheron."

Sam blinked. "The what?"

"The acheron," she repeated. "A portal."

Chapter 4

The Library

An arm tingled uncomfortably.

Oil. There was the scent of oil.

Rustling noises.

A man coughed.

Jeanette opened her eyes with a jolt. She had been kidnapped!

Terror gripped her as she noticed the gag in her mouth. Prickling sensations swept over her arm, which was pinned under her torso. She tried to move, but strong cords bound her hands and legs. A cold steel floor bit into her face and exposed arm.

As her vision cleared, she began to make out the small metallic interior in the dim light. Unrecognizable gadgets and tools adorned a section of the wall near her. Across the room was a door. Her eyes darted around as she searched desperately for a handle that could open it. Heart pounding in her ears, she shifted onto her chest, struggling against her bonds for a few moments before admitting they would not yield.

"Perfect timing." A low, raspy voice came from somewhere around her feet.

A strong arm hoisted her onto a leathery shoulder, forcing the wind from her lungs as the door hissed open. Powerful winds howled through the room, whipping long brown hair across her face. They emerged into the night. Large fires raged outside her view, casting a flickering image of the long circular prism of a vessel. It looked almost like a submarine. On land. With legs.

A man screamed in the distance, evoking tears of unbridled fear from Jeanette's eyes.

The steady rhythm of boot on dirt sounded against the roaring wind as the man carried her. Despite the futility, she continued to struggle against her bonds, barely able to forestall the panic from consuming her mind.

A light caught Jeanette's attention. She craned her neck up to view the large bonfire rising out of an immense square pit beneath the dirt. Fuzzy humanoid silhouettes flickered against the dirt wall on the opposite side and danced in the powerful winds. One raised its arm and stretched it forward. A loud *crack* split the night, followed immediately by cries of pain.

They walked past several more pits of torture, their inhabitants screaming. Jeanette was close enough to see a naked woman beyond the cliff, chained to the far wall. The dark skin of her upper back was raw and bloody. A whip struck out at her from outside Jeanette's view; the woman's body convulsed as she screamed in agony.

A stone archway passed overhead as Jeanette's heart raced furiously. Her neck ached from the strain of lifting it up, but she couldn't let it rest. The sudden, sharp odor of decay and excrement almost caused her to vomit. An aged stone interior surrounded her, exhibiting fine craftwork of textured columns and vaulted ceilings above bare stone walls, which displayed small bits of torn banners or plaster. The entry opened into a grand hall that stretched several stories high. The grotesque sight of blood and dead bodies decorated the stone floor, causing Jeanette to recoil reflexively.

Her captor ascended a split staircase to an upper level and then turned down a narrow hallway. Dim torches lit rough stone walls devoid of decoration, which faded into the distance as they moved onward. They passed the occasional bloody corpse—missing limbs, eyes, or both.

She squeezed her eyes shut momentarily. *This can't be real. It's a terrible nightmare.*

The sound of chatter echoed faintly from the halls alongside her captor's steps and grew louder. Soon she could make out their words.

"—s not going to happen!" a man exclaimed.

"Oh, come on, it only stings for a few minutes!" a woman's voice responded.

"Yeah, but I'd rather—Del! There you are!"

"You got the daughter?" the woman asked.

The stone surroundings whirled about as an arm flung Jeanette to the cold, hard floor. She landed firmly on her behind with a loud *thump*, her yell of pain stifled by the gag.

"Not exactly," the raspy voice said. "This is the granddaughter."

Jeanette, eyes wide with fear, glanced at the pale, thin woman before her. She wore a black top with long sleeves embroidered with swirling silver symbols, showing plenty of cleavage and a small sliver of belly. Skintight leggings with the same swirling symbols hugged her legs below a thin studded belt. Long, thick black boots rose to midthigh, ending in sharp points. She wore a full-length cloak with the hood back, exposing long black hair.

The woman frowned and placed hands on her hips. "What happened to the daughter?"

Jeanette's captor, the man called Del, pulled his hood back, revealing a pale, middle-aged face with a short, pointed beard. "She died," he said with a shrug.

They were talking about her mother. The scene flashed before her eyes—both of her parents dead on the floor of their bedroom.

"What! How did *that* happen?" the woman demanded.

"The husband fired a projectile at me, and the deflection went through her skull. Not my fault." His voice was calm. Careless.

"Well, you better hope she works." She pointed at Jeanette. "Otherwise, the Deia will not be happy when she wakes up!"

"Only one way to find out." Del grabbed Jeanette by the arm, turning to address her directly. "I'm going to release your bonds. If you try to run, you will regret it for the few remaining hours of your life."

Jeanette nodded, mind saturated with dread. He untied her bonds and released her gag. Despite her acknowledgment, she briefly considered attempting an escape out of pure desperation, but thought better of it. She was surrounded. Escape was futile at the moment. She needed to wait for a better opportunity.

Del motioned to the large wooden door at the end of the hallway. "Open that door."

Jeanette stood, trembling. She stepped cautiously toward the door, glancing at the three behind her. The large man, who had been with the pale woman before they arrived, leaned against the wall with his arms crossed, his dark eyes staring back with intensity. The woman urged Jeanette onward with a gesture, so Jeanette returned her attention forward. She found the wooden door rather plain and unremarkable. She wondered why they needed *her* to open it. Couldn't they open it themselves? Was it dangerous?

As she touched the large, brass door handle, she felt something strange: a subtle presence. It didn't feel hostile—at least, not toward her. In fact, it felt warm, comforting. She gripped the circular handle, and the presence grew stronger. As soon as she pulled the door free, however, the sensation disappeared.

The door swung open and revealed an enormous library. Shelves of books stretched three stories high around the massive open room. Small tables and wooden seating littered the interior. There were no obvious exits other than the hallway behind her, where the three others stood watching a dozen steps away.

"See," Del said, "nothing to worry about."

Jeanette turned to face him.

"Well, well, she's made herself useful," the woman said in a playful tone. "Why don't you take her to her new accommodations, Del?"

A faint smirk played across Del's bearded face.

Fear and adrenaline gripped Jeanette's body. She needed to escape—*now!*

She turned and sprinted into the library. A firm grip caught her shoulder after only a few steps. She screamed in response, swinging around to kick Del in the crotch with all of her might. His powerful arm swatted her foot away, then grabbed her throat. She brought her hands up to grasp his arm, straining to pull it away while maintaining a barrage of wild kicks toward the man.

He let go of her neck, grabbed a kicking leg with both hands, then twisted powerfully, forcing Jeanette to spin and fall on her face. In a motion far too swift to be natural, Del bound her feet together, her attempt to roll over thwarted by a stiff boot to her back. Powerful hands pulled her arms behind her and tied them together as she cried out. He lifted her and reapplied the gag around her head, stifling her screams.

"She's got some fight to her, I'll say that!" the woman said as Del swung Jeanette over his back forcefully, knocking the wind out of her once more.

Jeanette struggled and gritted her teeth at the cords that bit into her wrists. Her captor left the library to the other two, striding back through the halls of the castle with Jeanette in tow. Sore and defeated, she let her head hang low, marking their path through the castle with a steady trail of tears.

Hair whipped around Jeanette's face as they reemerged outside among the howling winds, terrible screams, and pits of fire. She craned her neck to observe the magnificent castle exterior as they departed. Its damaged walls faded upward into the darkness, above stunningly intricate carvings along the outer stone wall that danced in the flickering firelight, hinting at the massive building's former glory. She let her head hang limp again, exhausted from the strain. From her downward view, Jeanette noticed the straight edge of a pit emerge beyond her captor's legs. Her heart raced.

"Norem!" Del called out. "I've got another for you."

Jeanette's world spun, and stifled screams rattled her skull as she plunged into the hellish pit.

Chapter 5

Perspective

Kara opened her eyes—and saw almost nothing. Usually, all she could perceive was a faint sensation of ambient light.

Sam's slow and steady breathing was the only sound in the room.

The beds in the "overnight room," as Kerlo had called it, were remarkably comfortable. Her head lay on a fluffy, silky pillow. Smooth sheets and a heavy blanket kept her cozy in the cool room. Her martial arts uniform, a gi, was stiff in places from dried sweat. It was typical for her to have a hard time falling asleep in new locations and new beds, but her mental and physical exhaustion, combined with the comfortable accommodations, had miraculously allowed her to sleep. Though her body had rested, her mind was far from tranquil.

It was real.

It wasn't a nightmare. A man had killed her parents and abducted her sister. And she was in a strange facility owned by aliens calling themselves the Sovereignty.

Tears formed in Kara's eyes as anguish threatened to consume her again. She pressed the pillow up against the sides of her head, fighting to suppress it. Her parents and friends had often told her how impressed they were with her strength—both mental and physical—but she wasn't strong enough for this. Her mind had completely shut down. If Sam hadn't been there to support her, she didn't know what she would have done.

But she couldn't let despair consume her anymore. She *needed* to press forward. She had a mission now.

Jeanette.

Her fists tightened at the thought of her sister. Anger and determination smothered her sorrow. Kara hadn't been able to figure out what was happening during her sister's kidnapping, which had prevented her from taking action, but now things had changed. Her mother's cousin had information.

She was going to get her sister back.

The determination simmered in her mind for several moments before she allowed other thoughts to cool her fury.

Kara sighed, unsure how to react to everything the AI woman had told her yesterday. It appeared that her parents were from another *planet*. Before Jeanette was born, they had moved to Earth from that other planet—the name of which she couldn't remember. When she'd asked why, the AI said they had offered to support the Sovereignty's efforts and had made a specific request for the home she had grown up in. But there were no obvious reasons for their decision to relocate to Earth.

Kara was going to get some answers.

Apparently, they'd be going through some kind of magic portal to get to her relative. Sam's head must have just about exploded when the AI told him everything about the Sovereignty. He couldn't stand inconsistencies with science—seemed to take them as a personal insult, the way he reacted to nearly *every single film in existence.*

Sam's rhythmic breathing changed. He must have woken up.

"Good morning, Sam."

He yawned. "Morni—wait, how did you know I was awake?"

"Your breathing changed."

"You seriously have some superhuman hearing."

Kara turned onto her side to face him and propped her head up with an arm. "I don't think my hearing is any more sensitive than yours, just more focused."

"Okay, fair enough." His mattress rustled. "How did you sleep?"

"I slept okay, all things considered. These beds are pretty comfortable."

"Yeah, they are."

Silence settled for a few moments before Sam spoke again. "So, what did *you* think about everything they told us yesterday?"

"It's all beyond me," Kara said. "I just hope my relative can help us get to Jeanette."

"Me too," Sam said.

She reflected again on that odd conversation with the AI. "I still can't believe my parents were basically aliens."

"What?" Sam said. "The AI didn't tell *me* that! Where are they from?"

Kara sat up slowly. "I don't remember the name. Same one that my mom's cousin is on."

"Alvior?"

"Yes, that's it. She said they moved here some time before Jeanette was born."

"Why?"

Kara deliberately shook her head for emphasis. "No clue. They never said anything about the Sovereignty."

"Probably because they weren't allowed to," Sam said in a thoughtful tone. "The AI said if I returned home after orientation, they'd monitor me. Maybe they couldn't tell you because the Sovereignty would send you all away."

"Yeah, maybe."

Kara reached for the top of the nightstand next to her bed. Her fingers slid across the surface until they reached her target, a device Kerlo had given her after orientation. About the width of her thumb, it was smooth and flat, shaped like a teardrop, and bound by a small wrist strap. They called it a Jit.

The door to the room whisked open.

"Good morning," said an unfamiliar voice. "I trust you both

slept well last night? My name is Rolnauv. I relieved Kerlo a few hours ago and have clothing for each of you. I hope it is suitable until you have time to acquire new apparel. You may bathe in the restrooms down the hall if you wish."

A shower sounded wonderful, particularly since she hadn't bathed after her training—and everything that had followed.

"Thank you," Sam said on their behalf.

Footsteps, followed by the door zipping shut again, marked the man's exit. Kara rose from the bed and felt around for the extendable cane on the nightstand. Kerlo had been kind enough to obtain one for her during their orientation yesterday, since she had left hers back at the house during the turmoil.

"How can I help?" Sam asked.

She preferred to be as independent as possible, but given the fact that they were in unknown surroundings, some help would be welcome.

"You can help guide me to the restrooms."

"Of course!"

Kara put the Jit around her wrist as she took Sam's elbow. The door whisked open once more as they approached. Sam handed her the bundle of clothes that Rolnauv brought for her. They felt relatively normal and comfortable. Anything besides her dry-sweat-covered gi would be a welcome change.

When they entered the hallway, Sam paused.

"So, which way to those restrooms?" she asked. "I'm dying for a shower."

"Uh . . . I don't know."

"Aren't there signs or something?"

"Yeah, but they're not like our—Oh wait, I think that's it."

Kara followed his lead down the hall. Their steps echoed against the quiet mechanical noises of the facility. A soft buzzing rang overhead—probably from some kind of light.

"Just like the ones we used last night. There doesn't seem to be any separation between male and female restrooms," Sam said.

Doors flew open nearby as they approached.

"Looks like these are individual toilets," he said. "I don't see any showers, though."

He led her across the hall to another door, which opened for them.

"Oh, okay, I think these are the showers."

Kara snorted. "You *think*? Are you sure your eyes work?"

"Hey, this place is different! I don't know what I'm looking for."

She released Sam's arm and extended her cane. "Meet you back here after."

"Okay."

The taps of her cane echoed across the large hallway as she used the restroom, and then the shower. She spent a fair amount of time feeling out the controls and testing out how they worked, but the shower turned out to be pretty ordinary. Her fears of finding strange, exotic contraptions subsided. She also appreciated the supply of liquid body wash. Or maybe it was shampoo. She couldn't determine for sure which it was, but it seemed to do the job well—and it smelled like a mix of pleasant herbs.

After her shower, she separated the pile of clothing and ran her fingers along their smooth, soft surfaces to determine the proper orientation. She was surprised to find a bra among them. How could they know her size? Did they scan her figure or something? The thought made her uncomfortable. It appeared to be a normal T-shirt bra, though the cushy material felt unique, and it was certainly too large for her. She snapped it on anyway and marveled as the cups shrank, providing just the right amount of support. She donned the rest of the clothing, which included a simple long-sleeved, button-up blouse and elastic joggers. All of it fit rather well.

"Enjoy your shower?" Sam asked as Kara reemerged into the hallway.

"Oh yeah," she said. "Feels sooo nice after being stuck in that uniform all night." She turned around to give him a look at her outfit. "So, how do I look?"

No response.

"Please don't tell me these clothes are invisible or something."

Sam laughed. "No, no, you look great. Really!"

She felt pretty confident that her clothes were properly opaque, but her comment seemed to have caught Sam off guard. He probably enjoyed the thought of her in invisible clothing.

Kara punched in his direction, hitting his arm.

"Hey! What was that for?"

"Nothing. What color are these, anyway?" she asked.

"Your shirt is a pale green, and the pants are light gray. Like I said, I think they look nice."

"Okay," she said. Not her typical style, but they should be all right.

They wandered the halls for a bit before locating the café room they had used the night before. They entered, Sam leading them toward the side of the room.

"Kerlo said that our Jits will work on the magical food machines, right?" Kara asked. She recognized her mistake a moment too late.

"Magic is for fantasies," Sam said. "It's just technology we don't understand yet. And I plan to change that as soon as possible."

Kara sighed. "Of course you do. Let's just get some breakfast."

When Kerlo had handed them their Jits the prior evening, he'd provided Kara with her parents' dormant funds and given Sam some amount of money as well. He'd also suggested that they consider becoming citizens by entering the required educational program, since they were guests of the Sovereignty at present.

By pressing the device with their fingers for a second or two, it would beep and await a command. She found it quite similar to the way she would interact with the virtual assistant on her phone. They could issue commands to order food, and soon they found themselves enjoying a delicious meal of pancakes, eggs, fruit, and orange juice at one of the stone tables.

As Kara ate, she wondered how much of this space money Kerlo had actually given her. She'd have to budget until she found a job. She couldn't know its true value, of course, but she wanted to know the amount anyway.

She pressed the Jit firmly between her fingers, and it emitted a low but audible beep. "How much money do I have?"

"Your current balance," the device responded in a smooth, low, British-sounding voice that she liked, "is five doh four moh nine groh el doh dek Til."

Kara stilled with bewildered confusion. Unfortunately, Sam happened to be in the middle of drinking his glass of orange juice, and he coughed it up in a fit of laughter. Kara couldn't hold back her own.

"What the hell was *that*?" she said.

As soon as Sam regained marginal control over his coughing fit, he said, "I think it's"—*cough*—"that dohnal system they use. Base"—*cough*—"twelve."

"Well, I don't know what that means," Kara said. "How do I get it to talk to me in numbers I understand?"

Sam just kept up the occasional cough.

"Sam, if you're shrugging or something, please keep in mind that *I'm blind*."

"Oh! Right. Sorry. Yeah, uh . . . I don't know. Why don't you just ask it?"

Worth a shot.

She pressed the device again until it beeped. "What is my balance in . . . uh . . . what is it called?"

"Decimal," Sam said.

"Right. Decimal. What is my balance in decimal?"

"Your balance in decimal is one hun dek two thou, three dek Til," the device said.

"Ugh!" Kara said, while Sam chuckled. The sound of his laughter was contagious, and she found herself joining him.

"How am I supposed to use this stupid thing if I can't understand it?" she exclaimed.

"Maybe the way we use the decimal system is unique to Earth?" Sam said. "Try asking it for 'Earth decimal' and see what happens."

"Okay, fine, but if it talks gibberish again, I'm throwing it at your head."

Sam snickered.

Kara pressed it once more, and it beeped. "Okay, what is my balance in Earth decimal?"

"Your balance in Earthan decimal is one hundred twelve thousand and thirty Til."

"Ha, I knew it would work!" Sam said.

"Yeah, yeah. I still might chuck it at your head anyway for good measure."

They laughed again before returning to their breakfast. So, one hundred and twelve thousand. If Til were dollars, that was a lot of cash. Her gut said it was likely worth less than that.

Kara's thoughts returned to Kerlo's instruction after orientation. How difficult would the citizenship course be? Her parents had been citizens, so maybe she would take him up on his suggestion to become a citizen herself.

A voice came from the doorway. "Ah, excellent! You're already having breakfast. It is great to see you adjusting to your Jits." It was the man named Rolnauv, Kerlo's replacement. "I have some news."

Kara spun her head to face him, adrenaline spiking. "What is it?"

"We tracked your sister's kidnapper to a spacecraft which exited Earth's atmosphere just a few minutes after your encounter. Unfortunately . . ."

His change of tone made Kara's heart stop.

"It appears to have entered the target end of an acheron projection, which makes it difficult to track further."

"What is an acheron projection?" Sam asked.

"The synth told you about the acheron here during orientation, correct?"

Kara nodded. "She said it was some kind of portal."

"Yes, that's right. There are two main acheron configurations. One is linked, where two acheron gates are connected. When you enter one, you come out the other, wherever it is. The acheron in this facility is linked. The other configuration is a *projected* acheron, where one end is projected some distance out into space from the source. We use projected acherons primarily for exploration or military use, where there are no established acherons to link to.

"The attacker used one or more projection acherons to arrive at Earth, then returned through the open gate with your sister. All we know is the approximate direction of the source, based on the orientation of the gate. In other words, we have a straight line through space where that portal potentially led to—and that line stretches across *galaxies*."

Kara didn't quite follow all the technical jargon, but she got the general idea. Her sister was likely gone forever. The kidnapper was virtually untraceable. Her head and heart sank.

Rolnauv sounded apologetic. "I'm so very sorry I do not have better news. There is one sliver of hope, though."

Kara tilted her head up.

"We got a good image of the man's vessel and identified it. If it travels anywhere near a system controlled by the Sovereignty again, our detection systems will alert us."

It meant the kidnapper would have to be stupid enough—or desperate enough—to do so, but it *was* a possibility. Kara hoped her mother's cousin had more useful information.

Having finished their breakfast, they followed Rolnauv through the complex tunnels to the acheron. As they approached it, the sound of a large crowd echoed through the hallway.

"Your Jits will lead you from here," Rolnauv said. "This is where we must part ways."

"Can I ask a few questions first?" Sam asked.

By his tone, Kara knew where this was going. He'd thought through all the science conundrums over the past couple of hours, and he was going to berate the poor man with questions for the rest of eternity.

"Two," Kara said.

"Two what?" Sam asked.

"Two questions. Otherwise, we'll be here forever."

A moment of silence passed.

"But—"

"Two!"

Sam sighed. "Fine!"

Rolnauv chuckled.

Feeling pleased with herself, Kara waited. Sam took several seconds, probably sorting through his list to decide which two were the most important. Or perhaps he was trying to get the wording right.

"Okay, first: How do things like that suit Elysia wore and the pod transport ships seem to fly without any obvious means of propulsion?"

"Antigravity, of course," Rolnauv said in a smug tone.

There was a pause. Sam was going to ask a follow-up question. Kara could feel it.

"So . . . you can basically turn gravity off?" Sam asked. "And no, that's a follow-up question. It doesn't count!" he shouted toward Kara.

Kara and Rolnauv laughed in unison.

When the laughter subsided, Rolnauv replied, "No, they don't turn off gravity. The technology reverses gravity's effective direction, causes it to repel instead of attract. I believe the pod varies the amount of its hull that is in either state in order to reach the desired upward or downward acceleration. I don't know how they do the switching, though. That's beyond my knowledge."

As Sam pondered over the information or prepared for his next question, Kara considered arguing against his declaration that follow-up questions didn't count. While the dispute would be entertaining, it would probably take more time than letting it go, and she wanted to get going so she could learn more about her parents—and do whatever she could to find her sister.

"Okay, second question," Sam said. "How do you transport matter across the universe with these portals? Doesn't that break the laws of physics, like conservation of mass and energy and the speed of light?"

"I thought you might ask about that," Rolnauv replied. "I'm sorry, but I actually don't know how they work at that level. I'm not an engineer or a physicist. All I know is that more mass requires more energy from the portal."

Why does he even need to ask all this now? Kara was sure that Sam could find the information later, anyway. *The Sovereignty surely has some kind of internet, right?*

"So this portal takes us to Alvior?" Sam asked.

He broke her two-question rule. Again. She was about to scold him for it, but Rolnauv answered quickly.

"No, no," he said. "*That* is the Liris four travel hub. A space station."

Chapter 6

Alvior

Kara felt her weight decrease ever so slightly as they passed through the portal, with Sam leading her by the arm. She could tell from the acoustics that the room they'd entered was immense. Other voices with unfamiliar accents echoed all around as they followed the directions from Sam's Jit. It felt like an enormous shopping mall. The floor was a strange surface that resembled hard rubber.

If they were truly in space, there shouldn't be any gravity.

"Is this really a space station?" she asked.

"I think so," Sam said. "It's amazing!"

"How are we not floating?"

"The station is a long cylinder, and I can see stars moving in some windows, so it looks like it's using centrifugal force."

Kara wrinkled her brow. "Centri-what?"

"Don't you remember *anything* from physics class?"

"I try not to."

Sam sighed. "When you rotate things around, that rotation causes a force that pushes outward—like when you're in a car driving around a loop and you get pushed toward the side of the car. They seem to rotate this station at just the right speed to cause that force to be very close to gravity on Earth."

That sort of made sense. "What does it look like?" she asked.

"It looks like . . . a huge cylindrical room with things in it."

Kara shook her head. "You suck at descriptions. What do you see?"

"Turn right," the Jit said.

Sam led her with his arm, following the voice's instructions. "Well . . . I guess it kind of resembles an airport that curves in on itself," he said. "I can see other people walking on the ceiling from our perspective. There are also lots of trees and small plants scattered around, and thick-looking windows with a foggy view of the spinning stars outside. And there are portals everywhere, of course."

"What do those look like?"

"They're large, thick semicircles of metal. Each one seems to be, I don't know, maybe twenty feet in diameter or so?"

That was larger than she had imagined.

The Jit continued to lead them around several twists and turns. Remarkable, unfamiliar scents reached Kara's nose. She considered asking Sam if they could stop and try some of this exotic new food but decided she'd rather get to their destination as soon as possible. They walked past a couple discussing what they should have for lunch. Laughing children hurried by, followed swiftly by an unhappy father yelling at them to stop running. Despite the fact that they were walking through an alien environment, it felt familiar—quite like an airport, as Sam had mentioned.

Eventually, they crossed through the crowded portal to Alvior. Kara felt a slight but noticeable increase in weight, the only trace that they had passed through anything besides a change in acoustics. Their new surroundings were softer, less echoey.

They passed through another doorway into an outdoor urban setting. Crowds bustled about nearby as the whooshing of vehicles resounded overhead. The smooth female voice led them to a vehicle lot of some sort, where they entered something that the Jit called an ascender. It felt larger than the small podlike vehicle they had ridden in the day before, with two padded bench seats facing each other.

Kara felt the vehicle move as soon as they strapped themselves in across from each other.

"Wow," Sam said.

"What is it?"

"This thing has windows, unlike the pod we rode in yesterday. It's taking us up over the city."

"What does the city look like?"

Sam took a moment to reply. "It doesn't seem that different from a big city on Earth. The buildings look pretty similar, though some are more rounded. I guess the one big difference is all the vehicles flying around."

Others would often talk about how views from up high were a pleasurable experience—assuming, of course, they weren't *afraid* of heights. Kara had never really felt that kind of fear specifically, but there were plenty of relatively mundane things that occasionally frightened her, like crossing a busy street.

The sounds of the surrounding city faded, letting her hear the soft rumble of the ascender. It was far quieter than anything she'd ridden on Earth. In fact, it felt a bit too quiet. She longed to be outdoors again. Being cooped up in small structures and vehicles felt suffocating.

"It looks like we're heading into a storm," Sam said.

Kara's anxiety rose as she imagined flying through a thundercloud in something no larger than a car. After just a few seconds, rain tapped on the windows. Kara gasped as the flying car shifted suddenly in the wind.

"How high up are we?" she asked.

"Um . . . I don't know," Sam said, voice unmarked by any trace of concern. "Not as high as an airplane, I think. I honestly don't know how to judge."

Kara shuddered as she pictured the ascender falling helplessly out of the sky, with a sudden, violent stop at the end. She may not have a fear of heights, but she certainly *did* have a fear of being stuck in a box as it fell from the sky. After a few bumps in the wind, relief swept over her as the rain lightened and she felt sunlight warm her through the windows.

"Glad that's over," she said.

"Yeah," Sam replied absently.

A few moments of silence accompanied the gentle winds outside.

"The landscape is colorful," Sam said. "I wonder if it's fall here. Maybe trees change colors like they do on Earth. I don't recognize any of them, but they're also hard to see from this height."

He was talking about trees, but Sam's thoughts were likely elsewhere. School, maybe. Kara felt a slight twinge of guilt that he could be giving up his chance to go to college by accompanying her. Then again, he could probably learn a lot more about physics from the Sovereignty than he ever could at home.

"Do you think you'll go back home to attend school?" Kara asked.

"Probably not. It doesn't matter much now, anyway," he said.

"Sorry," she mumbled. "I know you were looking forward to that. Guess I ruined those plans."

"It's obviously not your fault, and it's fine, really. I was mainly looking forward to leaving home."

Right, Sam and his religious family didn't get along well anymore. Still, he should appreciate the time he had with them. What she wouldn't give to—

No. Can't think about that. She squeezed her eyes shut. *Jeanette. I need to focus on getting to Jeanette.*

"What about your plans to open your own dojo?" Sam asked.

Kara felt the craft descend.

"It's called an academy," she said. "And I don't know. I'd still like to do it eventually."

"You should," Sam said. "I'm sure people would love it. A blind martial arts teacher. You'd be amazing!"

She smiled.

"Looks like your mom's cousin lives in a small town," Sam said. "It's sparsely populated, and the houses look odd."

"What's strange about them?" she asked.

"They're very round, with domed roofs, and most of them are a shade of green. There are also no roads here, just small paths—though it looks like there are landing pads scattered around."

The craft settled down gracefully, with no perceptible bump to accompany their landing. The cool air rushed past them as they disembarked the ascender, and the path had a similar slightly elastic feel to that of the station. Sam's Jit led them up the path to the house. Before they reached the door, it whooshed open.

"Kara and Samuel!" an old woman's voice said. "Oh, my soul screams with excitement to see you both here safely!"

The woman spoke in a strange manner, as if she was frequently exhaling excessive amounts of air. She hugged Kara with one arm, startling her, and gave each of them a kiss on the cheek. Far too close for Kara's comfort. Being randomly touched by strangers was a rather frequent annoyance. People rarely seemed to realize how unpleasant it could be to have strangers grabbing or hugging you without warning.

The woman put her hands on Kara's shoulders. "Ah, you have your father's brown hair and your mother's—goodness child, what happened to your eyes?"

"I'm blind," Kara said.

"Oh, my poor child!"

Ugh, pity. Kara hated it. Her irritation rose as the woman embraced her tightly.

"So, I don't think we got your name," Sam interjected, probably hoping to steer the woman away from Kara's ire.

Thankfully, the woman released her and stepped back. "Oh, oh yes! Please forgive my haste. I am quite excited to have visitors, especially from a place so exotic as Earth! My name is Jesserian Kivi-Walokien. You can call me Jess."

"Pleasure to meet you, Jess," Sam said. "I guess you already know who we are."

"Yes, yes! Please, come inside." Her voice changed direction as she turned about, leading them into the house. Then she must have turned back, because her voice became direct again. "Do you need help getting around, child?"

"No, my legs work just fine," Kara said. "Sam can guide me."

"She's a little eccentric," Sam muttered softly as they followed.

"Really? I couldn't tell," Kara whispered back.

As Sam led her into the house, a strong, unfamiliar smell aroused Kara's senses. It wasn't foul, but it was rather odd—something like toasted pine with a hint of citrus and peppermint. She would need to take some time soon to explore the house and learn where everything was, but first she wanted answers.

"Are you hungry?" Jess asked. "I recently prepared some olviguck."

Whoever had named that dish didn't make it sound appealing.

"Actually, I'd like to know more about my parents," Kara said.

"Ah yes, yes. You have traveled so far. Please come and sit and I will tell you everything I know—everything I told the Sovereignty officials."

Jess led them to her living room. The seating felt like a large, fluffy pillow. Kara settled into it next to Sam.

"It seems like you knew my parents fairly well," Kara said. "Did they live near here?"

"I would not say I knew them too well. They stayed with me for a few days after returning from Tercast. I never knew why they left so suddenly, or where they were going. They were quite secretive about it."

"Where is Tercast?" Sam asked.

"Oh! It is a small religious institution in the mountains to the east. Odd place. My uncle, your grandfather Walnon, was a founder, I believe. Your parents attended and met there years ago. Some around your age go to attend for a season, like your parents did. It has become somewhat notorious across Alvior."

"We don't exactly get the galaxy's latest news on Earth," Kara said. "What's so odd about it?"

"Oh, just nonsense, child. Some call it a castle of magic."

Chapter 7

Resolve

Jeanette stifled a burning desire to scrub her skin raw. She felt disgusting.

They had violated her in ways beyond her worst nightmares. Physical pain would come and go, but memories of the acts of her oppressors refused to give her peace. Her stomach lurched with revulsion.

Tears having long since ceased their flow, she sat naked on the cold stone floor of her tiny dungeon cell, huddled with arms around her legs for warmth in the biting cold. They had moved her and the other captives from the pit into the castle after hours of torture and abuse. The stripes on her back stung fiercely. Her shoulder ached from the brief nap she had taken on the stone floor out of sheer exhaustion. Fatigue remained, however, coupled with overwhelming despair.

She shivered furiously as she stared into a corner of the cell, her back to the iron gate barring the exit several feet behind her. The square room was solid stone and stretched only about five or six feet in either direction. Its only occupants were Jeanette, a small bucket for her waste, and a trickling water spigot.

Footsteps echoed down the steps to the dungeon hall behind Jeanette and grew louder. Her heart jumped into action, and her shivering intensified. She kept her eyes fixed on the corner, too terrified to turn around. The steps continued until they reached her gate. Her heartbeat thumped in her ears. She waited, dreading the sound of the metal latch squeaking open. Instead, metal scraped against stone. The steps proceeded down the hall, followed by another scrape of metal against stone farther down.

She chanced a sideways glance toward the gate behind her and noticed a small silver bowl with green contents. Hunger gnawed at her stomach, but she remained in place, shivering in her ball.

Jeanette considered killing herself.

She could starve to death—refuse to eat until her body couldn't go on anymore. Or perhaps even drown herself in the green soup somehow. She longed for death. Her own lack of fear concerning the transition into the unknown surprised her. But people died all the time. Her parents were already dead. It wasn't anything to be frightened about. Right?

Still, that line of thinking felt horribly *wrong*.

Taking her own life clashed with something deep within her. Her parents had given her a profound sense of reverence for life. It was something to be treasured. Protected. She believed that. All life was sacred.

She couldn't let herself die if she had the power to avoid it. If her captors killed her, she would accept death. Until then, she had to keep going—even if her life was endless misery and torment. She would hold on to this ideal. Preserving life was right. Ending it was wrong. She would do it for her parents, but also for herself.

The thought gave her a grain of courage, despite her hopeless situation. She couldn't control what these people did to her, but she *could* control how she reacted and what she believed. She could control her thoughts. Her actions.

The prison guard's steps returned up the stairway. Jeanette uncurled and scooted across the floor to the small metal bowl, lamenting the loss of precious warmth as it escaped into the air. As soon as she was within reach, she huddled into her ball again.

To preserve as much heat as possible, she took the side of the bowl with one hand, keeping the other tight around her legs.

Whatever it was, the viscous substance was far from appetizing. Its primary semi-liquid was a dark green, with small brown and yellow chunks scattered throughout. She held it under her nose and sniffed, then gagged in response.

In a swift motion, while squeezing her eyes shut, she took a large gulp of the foul-smelling contents and felt the thick lukewarm fluid travel down her throat. It tasted slightly better than it smelled, resembling asparagus mixed with rotten milk and seaweed.

She finished the bowl, placed it back on the stone floor, and wrapped her free arm around her legs once more.

Shivering, Jeanette tried to focus her thoughts away from the trauma and intense cold. She thought of Kara, hoping that they hadn't captured her sister as well.

Hopefully, Sam is still with her. After learning of their parents' death, he wouldn't leave Kara's side willingly. He would be there for her. Sam clearly wanted more from their relationship, though Kara never seemed to perceive it—probably due, in part, to her blindness.

Knowing her sister, Jeanette could understand why Sam would be hesitant to express his feelings. Despite her small stature, Kara could be quite intimidating. Jeanette felt it unlikely that her sister had any romantic feelings for Sam, so if he confessed, it might just make things awkward between them. Sam must have reasoned the same.

Jeanette thought on her own past relationships, which had not ended well. Sure, her boyfriends had been charming and kind and warm—until they slept with another woman or made up some excuse to break up because they *wanted* to sleep with another woman. Kara would say that Jeanette was a pushover. Too nice. What was so wrong with her that a guy couldn't stay interested and loyal? Despair welled in her mind at the thought. She tried to think back on Sam and Kara to avoid going further down that path.

Though she was about two years their senior, Jeanette enjoyed spending time with their little trio: Sam, Kara, and Liam. They often requested rides from her into the city, since she was the only one with a vehicle. Usually, their requests weren't a problem unless she already had plans with her other friends or when work called her in for an odd shift.

The store, she realized. *They're probably wondering where I am.*

Not that it really mattered now.

Steps echoed again along the stairway leading to the dungeons, causing Jeanette's heart to race. She reflexively scooted back to her previous position near the far wall, away from the cell gate. The steps grew louder, until a despicable overweight man stepped in front of her gate: the prison guard.

He tossed two small bits of fabric toward her through the bars. "Put those on," he said in his foul mumble. "You're gonna be part o' the show."

He continued down the dungeon hall. Jeanette waited until he was out of sight before taking up the clothing. Upon inspection, they comprised some kind of sports bra and black boy shorts. She trembled to know what "the show" was, but anything to cover her nakedness was welcome.

As she put the clothing on, she heard his echoing voice give the same instructions to someone in another cell. After a few moments, he told the other prisoner to follow him. The guard reappeared in front of her cell and unlocked the latch with a squeak. Another man joined him, clasped in chains. He was tall, with curly black hair and a very thin frame.

"Come on. Let's go."

Jeanette briefly considered what might happen if she refused to leave, then determined it would probably turn out worse. They'd force her to do whatever they wanted anyway. *Better to just go with it for now.*

The guard clasped chains around her wrists as she came out of her cell. She followed him up the dungeon steps, with the other prisoner following behind. The halls of the dim, damaged castle passed by, thankfully free of corpses now, though there were still frequent patches of dried blood, and the stink of decay lingered in the air. Music played in the distance, and the pleasant aroma of spices and cooked meat pierced the stench. Pangs of hunger surfaced despite her meager meal a few minutes ago.

The prison guard opened doors to a large ballroom with intricate vaulted ceilings. Unfamiliar music poured into the hall, light and jovial. Flames danced in torches lining each of the walls, revealing brilliant paintings, and food of strange shapes and colors adorned a long table at the far end of the room. Revelers dressed in various attire ate and laughed, surrounding a large clearing in the middle. A pale, blond woman lay in a pool of blood that spilled from her split neck, her underwear pulled down around her ankles. Jeanette turned her head away instinctively at the grotesque sight.

The music stopped. A dark-skinned man at the other end of the room stood and turned to the audience. "Ah, yes! The next contestants!" His charismatic voice echoed across the hall, followed by loud cheers around the room. Red jewels lined the seams of his expensive-looking black fabric coat, and he wore a large gold necklace.

A woman dressed in a scanty maroon outfit dragged the pale woman from the clearing to the side of the room. The guard pulled Jeanette and the other prisoner into the center of the clearing, then unlocked their bonds. Jeanette turned toward the other prisoner. He wore nothing but a pair of dark briefs, displaying his slim frame. Fear stained his ashen face as he looked back at her. Her heartbeat thumped in her ears. *They're going to have us kill each other!*

"Whoever kills the other dines with us!" the man announced, confirming her fears. "Sate your lusts with the loser afterward if you'd like."

Lewd laughter rose from the audience around them.

"Begin!"

The crowd applauded. Jeanette stared at her opponent. Her fears rose as he looked her over, a primal hunger crossing his dark eyes. He stepped toward her, and she stepped back.

A man whistled and shouted from the side. "Give 'er a good poundin'!"

Cheers and laughter erupted around them, and Jeanette felt nothing but profound disgust. How could these people stoop so low—so devoid of morality that they enjoyed watching people beat each other to death?

The prisoner approached her again, and she moved to the side, lowering herself in a crouch. Flashbacks of conversations with Kara about fighting techniques flooded Jeanette's mind. What she wouldn't give to know some of her sister's moves right now. She recalled something about managing distance. Keeping him at two arm lengths, she tried to remember everything she had ever learned about self-defense. *Weak points: groin, neck, nose.*

The thin man crept toward her, fists in front of his face. As soon as he was close enough, she kicked upward as hard and fast as she could. A surprised look crossed his face as he moved to block her, but he was too slow. Her foot connected with the soft tissue under his briefs. He crumpled to the floor, howling in agony.

The crowd oohed and cheered. Some shouted at her to finish him. The man yelled and clutched at his groin, clearly in intense pain.

Jeanette hesitated as she maintained her defensive stance. She didn't want to kill him, for the same reason she didn't want to kill herself. All life was precious. She would *not* be their executioner.

Someone slid a knife toward her and urged her to kill him. A weapon was accessible now. She could try to fight her way out. There were far too many, though. It would never work.

Her fear spiked as the man arose, staring at her with intense anger. Panic clambered to take hold, but she forced it down. There had to be another way. Killing him felt wrong, but the longer this went on, the more likely his chances were of killing her—and doing whatever else he wanted with her.

He charged, running with his head forward. She kicked at him again, connecting with his forearm. He tackled her, and she landed hard against the stone floor. Her elbow connected with his face, which was against her abdomen, as he struck her side. The man lifted himself up on his knees and grabbed her throat. She punched out with a flat palm and hit the soft tissue of her target's nose. He recoiled from her blow, rolling off her and onto his back.

The audience cheered.

Jeanette coughed as she struggled to breathe. She needed to move fast. Still on her back, she turned her foot and kicked his throat. He choked, clutching his neck. She pulled herself upright and kicked his face as hard as she could. He became disoriented but continued grasping his neck and head while blood rushed from his nose. She kicked his face again, feeling pain lance across her foot as she connected.

He stopped moving. The cheering quieted. She stood over him, monitoring for signs of movement. His chest rose and fell, revealing that he was unconscious but still alive.

Someone slid the knife toward her again. "Kill him!"

Soon the room erupted in chants of "Kill him! Kill him!"

"No!" she screamed.

The room fell steadily to silence.

"You must kill him. That is the rule," the announcer said from behind her.

"No."

Murmurs broke out among the crowd.

"Last chance, girl," the announcer said, tone turning impatient. "Kill him now, or I *guarantee* you will suffer for this."

His threat caused a surge of fear within her. But she drew strength from her resolve, subduing the impulse to comply. They could control what happened to her, but she could control how she responded. She would *not* give in.

"No."

Chapter 8
Probability

Sam marveled at the stunning view from the ascender. Fluffy cumulus clouds rose in thick columns across the blue sky of the foreign planet, casting striking shadows across the multicolored, mountainous landscape below. He'd learned that it was, in fact, early fall on this part of the planet. The bright emergence of color transpired on Alvior for the same reason it did on Earth: Plant life was preparing for winter. Besides the familiar yellows, reds, oranges, and browns, a striking amount of purple littered the scenery. The plant life was exotic and unrecognizable, though he couldn't see anything too well at their current altitude.

The country of Oscertos, on the planet Alvior. He could hardly believe he was in an alien world.

The inability to share the incredible view with the girl sitting across from him made the experience bittersweet. He imagined that the ride was rather boring for her, so he tried to explain the views as best he could. Apparently, he was pretty terrible at visual descriptions. Still, she clearly preferred riding in the ascender to staying at Jess's place.

Kara had insisted that they check out Tercast to see what they could find out about this mysterious castle and her grandfather, in hopes to get a lead on locating Jeanette. Their Jit informed them that the gate town center, which provided entry, closed daily at sundown. Since it was already late afternoon in that part of the country, Sam and Kara had decided to set out the following morning.

Even Jess called the whole "magical castle" thing nonsense. She'd said that several people had spoken publicly about the magic. Most of Alvior's inhabitants considered it a ruse to attract attention—perhaps to have a larger pool of potential devotees to select from. There were some complaints of people not being allowed to leave, but the Sovereignty declared no jurisdiction over religious zones as long as citizens formally surrendered their rights when they entered.

If attention was the goal, the rumors that had been spread appeared to have the desired effect. With a planet full of people, Sam was sure they would find plenty of ignorant masses eager to see the "magic castle" for themselves, if they were anything like people on Earth.

Kara's voice interrupted his thoughts. "How much longer do we have?"

"Um . . . this thing says . . . dek. At least, I think that's a dek. It's like an upside-down two, so that means ten. I think."

"Ten what?"

"Oh, it says *M*, so I'd guess that means minutes—as opposed to months."

Kara smiled at that, which made his insides flutter.

"I'd jump out of this box before I rode in it for ten months," she said.

Sam laughed. "Easy to say when you can't see how high we are."

"I've always wanted to go skydiving."

"Yeah, but you'd also *probably* want a parachute for that."

"Why would I need a parachute?" she said with a grin. "I could just use a suit like Elysia had."

Sam chuckled. "Fair enough."

There was a brief pause as he admired the view and considered the fateful night of Jeanette's kidnapping and their flight around Earth.

"You know, the more I think about it, the less sense it makes," he said.

"Ugh," Kara said with exasperation.

"No, seriously! Gravity is tied to mass. The only way to *oppose* gravity is to have negative mass! Clearly, this thing still has mass, so it doesn't make sense."

Kara sighed. "Why does it have to make sense?"

"What kind of question is that?" Sam said. "There are fundamental laws that govern our existence. Doesn't it bother you when they don't seem to be consistent?"

"All I know is that we're in a floating car right now. And we walked through a portal that took us to a different *planet*. You can't say these things didn't really happen because they don't make sense!"

"Well, that's not—"

"You think the universe cares if you understand how it works?" Kara said.

"I'm only saying that there has to be an explanation that makes sense with our—I mean, Earth's—grasp of physics. Just because we have additional evidence doesn't mean the old results are wrong. It means our understanding is incomplete."

"Now you're just getting all philosophical about it."

"Doesn't our limited knowledge about the universe bother you too?" Sam asked. "Don't you want to know how it works? Even a little?"

She shrugged. "I take things as they come. You know that. I don't need to know how the universe works, down to the level of atoms, to enjoy life." Her blue eyes darted about as she spoke toward the window. "Analyzing all the little details about atoms and physics and particles just makes it boring."

"Well," he replied. "*I* think it's interesting."

"Doesn't mean you have to suck the fun for the rest of us."

"Ouch!"

She nodded with a playful smile. "Hard truth, Sam: You're a fun-sucker."

Sam laughed, shook his head, and let the topic drop. They'd engaged in similar discussions before. He still couldn't understand it. Physics was the most important thing there was, even if some of it was hard to comprehend. The concepts and equations of quantum mechanics were far beyond him, but he still *wanted* to understand them. How could someone not want to know how it all worked?

Sam glanced at the display. "Huh, apparently we're down to five minutes. That went by fast."

Kara raised an eyebrow. "I don't think we were talking for that long."

Sam smiled. "Questioning reality now?"

"Oh, shut up."

He laughed. "My guess is that this planet rotates faster than Earth does."

She considered his suggestion for a moment with a thoughtful expression. "That makes sense."

They passed a large, snow-capped mountain peak, bringing the castle into view. Their ascender headed toward a group of landing pads. A single path led from the pads to a large gate in the outer wall with a few small buildings around it. Small dots of people walked down the path toward the wall. Their vehicles took off behind them, leaving room for more vehicles to land.

"It really *is* some kind of castle," Sam said.

"What does it look like?" Kara asked.

Sam ran fingers through his hair. "Well, it has a giant outer wall, leaving plenty of space outside the castle. The castle itself has five towers—one of them bigger than the others. There are a few buildings near the gate at the outer wall."

"Wow, I can picture it *perfectly*."

Sam sighed. "What else do you want to know?"

She threw a hand up in exasperation. "What about landscape? Colors? Plant life?"

"Well, like I said before, the trees are mostly a mix of yellow, brown, and purple, though there aren't many trees near the castle itself." He squinted toward the area. "There are rows of crops inside the wall. Outside that, it's mostly deep-green grass, a few big trees, and lots of rocks."

"Is there anything else in the valley?" she asked.

"There's a winding river that passes by the castle wall and drops over the cliff."

"There's a cliff?"

"Yeah, the castle's right near it. It borders the ocean. Why?"

"It's something you should have mentioned!" she said, eyes darting around the vehicle.

The ascender slowed to a gentle stop on one of the concrete pads.

"Are there many people?" Kara asked.

"Sort of," Sam replied. "Looks fairly crowded up near the outer wall ahead."

"Can you lead me, then?"

Sam's heart fluttered at the thought, but he kept the elation out of his voice. "Of course."

He knew she preferred being led in sizable crowds, since she was more likely to bump into people on her own. Sam had occasionally led Kara by the arm before the event at the Joneses' house, but Jeanette typically fulfilled that role when needed. Though it was a long shot, he hoped this trip to Tercast would help them find her.

Sam guided Kara out of the ascender, off the pad, and onto the old stone path leading to the outer gate. Their ascender departed, presumably to pick up passengers somewhere else. Other vehicles landed in pads near them. People in odd clothing made their way toward the enormous wall in the distance. Some of them wore flowing robes embroidered with striking patterns, displaying elegant mixtures of color. Others wore tight, shiny jumpsuits. A man walked past wearing shorts and a simple T-shirt. The variety of styles was astounding.

The path led through the open field of tall grass and rocks. The river flowed gently to their right. As they approached the buildings outside the wall, Sam found himself marveling at the diversity of skin color. Along with the familiar shades of browns, blacks, and tans, there were some with pale blue or purple skin. Laughing, a small girl with light purple skin ran past them in a T-shirt and shorts. A stocky, pale, bearded man—no taller than four feet—talked to a woman with black skin who towered over him. Two blue-skinned, shoeless adolescents wearing brown and tan overalls crossed the path ahead of them.

Sam became self-conscious of his own outfit: the rather comfortable long-sleeved white V-neck and blue pants that Rolnauv had given him back on Earth. He wondered if others might find it strange or foreign. Given the diversity of apparel that others wore, it seemed unlikely.

Kara wore her green blouse and slim gray pants, the same outfit that had graced her figure the day before. Maybe they would have to head somewhere to get more clothing after their trip to Tercast.

The pair made their way through the sea of people, crowds thickening as they approached the outer wall. The smell of a dish from a nearby cart caught Sam's nose, reminding him of hot cinnamon buns.

"Mmm, that smells good," Kara said.

"Yeah, it does."

"How much further?"

"I think we're almost there, but there are tons of people. We might have to wait in line for a long time."

Kara frowned. Patience wasn't exactly her strong suit.

They headed toward the small cluster of stone buildings. One appeared to be a restaurant. The building next to it had a sign out front that read *Enchanted Trinkets* and appeared to be a gift shop.

Across the wide path stood a much older-looking building with two entrances. A sign labeled *Sovereignty Citizens* stood near the right entrance, while another labeled *Noncitizens* stood at the left. A massive line of people waited outside the citizens' entrance, while the other was completely devoid of any line at all.

"Hey, I think we just got lucky," Sam said. "There are two lines.

One is for noncitizens of the Sovereignty, which includes us, and it's empty."

"That's a relief. I would not be happy waiting in line all day."

They made their way through the enormous crowd, drawing eyes as they approached the building. Most of the others in line appeared to be around his and Kara's age. Jess had told them that Tercast accepted only young adults, so that made sense.

Sam pulled open the rickety wooden door for Kara, stepping in after her onto a floor of old, faded wood planks. Beige walls enclosed the small room, with an empty counter erected at the other end. Chatter about entering the castle echoed through an open door leading to the citizens' side. Sam glanced through it as they made their way to the counter, catching the eye of a female attendant in bright white-and-blue cloth. She dismissed an upset-looking pair of brothers who stormed out of the building, and she made her way across to them.

"Are you citizens?" she asked.

"We are not citizens of the Sovereignty," Sam replied.

"Let me see your Jits."

Sam and Kara both held their wrists up, and she pulled out a small device that resembled a mobile phone. She scanned each of their Jits and seemed satisfied by the result.

"Looks like you're both of the proper age," she said hastily. "Do each of you understand and accept that if you are granted entry into Tercast, you agree to abide by all laws and guidelines put forth by the Council of Grand Masters? And do you recognize their absolute authority in all matters?"

"Yes," Kara replied.

Sam turned to her. "Seriously?"

The woman sighed. "You must agree if you wish to proceed."

"Yes . . ." he said. "I guess."

She nodded. "You may not leave the castle grounds until your initial instruction is complete. Do you understand and accept?" Her voice was monotone and tired.

Sam glanced at Kara. "Jess didn't tell us *that*. You sure about this?"

Kara's face was resolute. "Yes. It's the only lead we have on my sister. We're getting inside."

"Keep in mind that you're very unlikely to be selected," the woman said.

"How unlikely?" Sam asked.

The woman shrugged. "I don't know the exact numbers, but it's pretty rare. Somewhere around one in a doh-moh, I think."

Ugh, that base twelve system again. Kerlo had said that his Jit could help with that, right? He squeezed it until he heard a beep.

"What is one doh-moh in Earth decimal?" he asked.

"One doh-moh is equal to twenty thousand seven hundred and thirty-six in Earthan decimal," it replied in its keen female voice.

One in *twenty thousand*. Their odds were pretty slim—assuming the woman was anywhere close to the mark in her estimate.

There was also another problem.

He turned to Kara. "That's terrible odds, even for *one* of us. It's nearly impossible that we will both get in."

She shrugged. "It's worth a shot."

The woman interrupted with a sigh and held out her hand before Sam could reply. "Please hand me your Jits and step through this way if you agree and wish to proceed. You may not take them into the castle. We will return them to you if you are not accepted, or when you leave Tercast at a later date."

Kara immediately handed her Jit to the woman and pulled out her folding long cane.

"Kara . . ."

"Sam, we came all this way. I'm not giving up now."

"What is that?" the woman asked, her interest suddenly piqued.

"What is what?" Sam said.

The woman pointed to Kara's cane.

"Oh, that's her cane. She's blind."

The woman blinked in apparent confusion, then gave Kara a curious look. "Please follow me."

They went around the back of the building to a row of several dome-shaped rooms attached to the massive outer wall. He guessed that the wall was at least six or seven stories high.

They approached the door of a dome, and the woman spun to face them. "Only one person per choosing room. Please wait out here, Samuel," she said.

She was going to take Kara. His heartbeat pounded in his ears. What if one of them made it and the other didn't? The odds of that happening were slim, but the thought of being separated from Kara terrified him.

"Wait!" Sam called.

They needed each other—especially right now. They shouldn't be taking this risk.

"What, Sam?" Kara said.

Studying her face, he knew that any attempt to talk her out of her decision would be futile. Emotions swirled through him. He wanted to tell her. Just in case the unlikely happened. He stared into those beautiful blue eyes as they jittered in random motions.

An urge to drop all inhibitions and go in for a kiss rose in Sam's mind. He smothered it.

I love you, he thought.

He just couldn't say it out loud.

Maybe that was for the best. It was unlikely that either of them would get in. They would probably be reunited in just a few minutes. If he confessed now, it would make things awkward between them forever. He needed to wait for the right time, if there ever was a right time, and this wasn't it.

The probabilities clearly supported this decision to remain silent. He hugged her, and she hugged him back.

"Good luck," he said.

"You too," she replied with a slight smile.

The woman opened the door. "Come inside please."

Kara turned partly around. "I know this is a nearly impossible chance. I just *have* to try it. Otherwise, I'll never forgive myself. We'll talk about what we do next afterward."

"Okay," Sam said.

He continued to suppress the irrational desire to confess his feelings for her as the door closed.

Sam exhaled some of his tension, going over the decision in his mind. He was right to stay silent. Confessing certainly would have made her feel uncomfortable. He was positive she didn't feel that way toward him. Maybe there would be a right moment one day, but this wasn't it.

The woman emerged half a minute later. "Please follow me," she said, returning to her tired attitude.

She led him to the next dome-shaped structure, and he followed her inside. It was fairly small, only ten feet or so in diameter. In the center stood an ornate pedestal, which displayed a small jewel on top. Multicolored pillows of various sizes and designs covered the well-kept wooden floor. She tapped the gem, and it glowed a brilliant pearlescent white.

"Wait here," she said. "One of us will return shortly."

"I just . . . wait here?" he asked.

"Yes. Make yourself comfortable. One of us will return shortly," she repeated.

She closed the door behind her, leaving Sam with the glowing gem. *So strange.* He inspected the gem closely, trying to determine the source of light, but it was far too bright to make out anything within. Clearly, that was part of the test, but he couldn't fathom how. He sat on a large fluffy red pillow with his legs crossed.

Several seconds passed by. How long would this take? They had hundreds of other people interested in getting into Tercast, so they probably wanted to keep the wait as short as possible.

Even though they'd only been apart for a few minutes, Sam yearned for Kara's company. She was an incredible person. He envied her strength and determination, as well as her martial arts skills. *Maybe she could teach—*

Something changed.

A new, incredible sensation slammed into his mind. The room came to life around him. He felt a bizarre connection to the surrounding pillows, reflexively distancing himself from them.

They moved.

Pillows flew into the air and crashed into the walls at an alarming velocity. Sam's eyes went wide. He moved to stand but could barely start to move before a sudden and overwhelming exhaustion consumed him.

Sam fell, his tension dissipating as the world faded.

Chapter 9

Oblivion

The Deia sat on the throne of her castle as she focused on the actions of her subjects—none of which were physically visible to her. She was most interested in the efforts of the six she had sent to the library, which had only recently become accessible. They were gathering an initial stack of potentially useful books. Many of her other subjects were asleep in the ballroom, having passed out from drunkenness or exhaustion after the crude celebration of their victory.

Her mind turned to Larv, the nearly useless subject she had tasked with handling the remaining prisoners. He was on his way down the steps to the dungeon with more gruel. The Deia closed her own eyes, observing stone walls pass by through the large man's perspective. As he reached the cell and slid the bowl under the bars, the Deia observed the defiant girl through the man's vision. The young woman huddled in a ball, facing the far corner, as was usual for her. Several red stripes lined her thin back underneath beautiful wavy brown hair. Larv had intended to chop it all off—as she had instructed—but thankfully, she had noticed the girl in time to stop him. She couldn't bear to see such gorgeous hair cut short.

Larv moved on down the row of cells, and the Deia's consciousness left his mind.

Excitement surged through her. The girl had displayed strong moral character during the festivities earlier, as reported by many of her subjects. She may have as much potential as her grandfather—whose enchantment she had unwittingly broken.

A potentially powerful disciple, indeed.

The Deia decided that after dealing with the other prisoners, and perhaps one more test of character, she would see to the girl's transformation personally. She needed more powerful top-tier devotees to carry out the next phase of her plans. No need to rush on those, of course. Everyone deserved time to celebrate and relax after the victory. But Delveton and Tess couldn't handle everything themselves.

As if on cue, Delveton Levina, the man standing next to the throne, shifted slightly at the discomfort of standing for so long. She had instructed him to wait with her. It was his triumph with the granddaughter that had granted access to the library after all. The Deia felt a spike of lust for him—a burning desire to feel his muscular body pressed against hers again.

Alas, now was not the time, and she shoved her yearning aside. Her subjects from the library were on their way to her with some wonderful finds. They brought most of the books to the desk at the side of the throne room, but she commanded a few of them to be brought to her immediately. These included volumes of *History of the Five Worlds*, which could have some interesting information; several books on biology, chemistry, and electromagnetism; and a curious, handwritten book named *On the Nature of Time, Substance, and Causality*, which had been stowed in a hidden compartment.

Her subjects piled the books next to her in silence. She wouldn't read them all now, of course, but she wanted to skim them briefly to see which volumes might be valuable. Delveton peered over as she flipped through the books on biology and electromagnetism. Through their connection, she felt his interest rise—so the books seemed to have some utility. She picked up *On the Nature of Time, Substance, and Causality* by authors Virahmgal Selevin and Elleran Laneum. The book appeared to be ancient, likely preserved supernaturally to have lasted so long. Curious, indeed.

She began reading the prelude: *Presented herein is our collective contemporary knowledge on the fundamental substratum of reality. We elucidate the structure of the macrocosm, the nature of substance, and the current understanding of the mechanisms of action, reaction, and conveyance across—*

An explosion rattled the walls.

The Deia's adrenaline spiked as she slammed the book closed in her lap and took inventory of the others within the castle. *Walnon's few remaining followers? I didn't expect them so soon. Perhaps they're attacking in desperation.* The plains of Uvlun could be brutal.

The disturbance had come from the front door. By the time she reacted, the two guards there were already dead—she could no longer sense their presence. A subject charged down the entry hall and toward the source of the explosion as the Deia entered his mind. Stone was still falling through the large hall, hurled by a massive force. Through the man's vision, she saw a hooded figure hover into the hall at a steady pace. A beam of light flashed with thunder that she could hear and feel with her own body. It vaporized the man's head, instantly cutting off her connection.

The Deia's eyes went wide.

"What is it?" Delveton asked, voice low and raspy.

"Oblivion."

Destroyer of Worlds.

Why? Why would Oblivion be here?

She stretched her mind, touching all of her subjects, commanding everyone to come to her at once and remain silent. A few more followers who happened to be in Oblivion's path faded from the Deia's perception as they began piling into the throne room. She wondered briefly if she should attempt to escape. But no, that would be futile. This being was far too powerful. There was no escaping this. Her only chance was to concentrate as many resources around herself as she could in order to meet the threat.

More forces gathered in the throne room quickly and silently, forming up by her side and filling the space. Most of them had weapons drawn. Delveton unsheathed his own sword next to her. Oblivion was getting close. She issued a silent command to Tess, who was near the door, to close it immediately. The woman slammed it shut with a telekinetic wave of her hand.

The door to the throne room burst into splinters. The Deia prepared her forces for a joint strike. It was her best chance.

"The book," a voice said, powerful, low, and booming—a sound that seemed to originate from the air itself. "Give it to me and you will live this day."

The voice echoed across the otherwise silent room.

Heart thumping in her ears, the Deia paused. That the being was speaking at all, instead of simply working destruction, was uncharacteristic of its reputation.

She looked down at the book in her lap. Perhaps Oblivion sought knowledge for the same reasons she did. But why now? Why not come and take it *before* she had gained control of the castle? Was it as incapable of breaking the enchantment on the library as she?

If Oblivion wanted it, the book must hold tremendous potential. The Deia took stock of her opponent. Its Sorcerous presence was immense. She couldn't feel anything near it, and she couldn't perceive anything past the darkness of the hood. It was clearly some kind of Sorcerer, despite what Sovereignty officials said about it. Still, her forces were formidable. Could they pose a challenge for the Destroyer of Worlds?

Best not to find out at present, she decided.

She handed the book to one of her subjects standing nearby, keeping her eyes on the cloaked figure. Was it even human? Her other subjects moved aside as the man brought the book forward amid the scattered remains of the doorway. He extended the book out toward the creature, and an invisible force pulled the book from his grip, moving it through the air toward Oblivion.

The cloak turned and floated back the way it had come, followed by the eerie, deep voice that rang through the halls. "When next we meet, you shall die."

The Deia sat in stunned silence for several minutes as she tried to make sense of the exchange. Her subjects in the room remained quiet, most of them maintaining a combat stance, following her command to exactness. She didn't understand it. To her knowledge, Oblivion had never spared a soul before. She counted herself fortunate to still have breath.

After verifying that the being's presence was, in fact, gone, the Deia released her subjects to return to their duties—or back to sleep. Some of them chatted animatedly about Oblivion as they exited the throne room.

"That is not a threat to take lightly," Delveton said.

"Indeed," she replied. "We need to accelerate our plans against Tercast."

The Deia had hoped to let the situation of the young woman's kidnapping cool before sending Delveton back to Rwenmar.

She glanced up at the man next to her, who sheathed his sword. Bitterness filled her at the thought of his departure again so soon. Her lust for him resurfaced.

Standing from her ornate throne, she looked at the entrancing man's aged face and bearded chin, which was about level with her forehead. A delicate prompting was all it took for him to pull her body forcefully against his. He engaged her in a deep, passionate kiss.

Chapter 10

Decisions

Fool.

Kara sat on Jess's guest room bed, tears streaking down her cheeks. Again. *What was I thinking?*

It had been several hours and a sleepless night since Sam disappeared, leaving her alone. The attendant had returned and taken her from that strange pillow-filled room after a few minutes and told her that Sam had been accepted.

He was gone.

They said that initiates could not leave until after "foundational instruction," which would take several *weeks*. They said it was a "tremendous honor" and that she should be happy for him.

Her parents. Jeanette. And now Sam?

Kara was alone in the universe.

Sam had been right. They shouldn't have chanced it, even if it was a nearly impossible outcome. He had a knack for being right sometimes. It was one of those things that annoyed her about him.

She'd spent the last day talking almost endlessly with her Jit, asking it everything she could think of about Tercast. Unfortunately, the place was as mysterious as Jess had suggested. They *really* liked their privacy. Almost everything she found concerned former residents who had spoken out about the castle; some called it magical and wonderful, while others commented on the terrible leadership or the controversy about students being trapped. The Sovereignty refused to do anything about it, though, since it was a religious institution.

Knocks on the bedroom door interrupted her thoughts.

"Kara, I've prepared breakfast!" Jess said through the closed door.

"No thank you."

"Please child, come eat."

Jess's tone betrayed significant concern. She was a nice enough person, but Kara couldn't stand the way she talked with too much breath, the way she was always asking if Kara needed help to get around, the way she would move things around without warning. The woman didn't understand how important consistency was to a blind person.

"Just . . ."

She was about to tell the woman to leave her alone but stopped herself. Jess *was* kind enough to let her stay, when Kara now had no one else in the world—universe, rather. It was probably prudent to be grateful and courteous, or else she might find herself homeless.

"Kara?"

Kara sighed. "Okay, I'll come out in a few minutes. I promise."

"Oh, wonderful!" Jess exclaimed. "I will have a plate ready for you!"

While the woman irritated her severely, Kara had to admit that she prepared amazing food. It was hard to tell exactly how much she had a hand in preparation, though, considering the Sovereignty's highly advanced technology. Machines like the ones on Earth might have been the real chefs. Strange noises often came from what she now knew was the kitchen, but Kara never asked about them. In fact, she still knew very little about the Sovereignty.

Perhaps her sister's kidnapper was an *enemy* of the Sovereignty?

Kara pressed her Jit. "Are there enemies of the Sovereignty?" she asked.

"There are three relatively small but significant dominions with which the Sovereignty presently contends," it responded in that confident British voice.

"Who are they?"

"They are recognized officially as the Intesu Federation, the Ingu, and the Molkinar Empire. The Molkinar Empire is the largest and most significant adversary."

"Do they ever attack planets like Earth?"

"By 'planets like Earth,' do you mean planets with a similar climate?"

Kara hesitated. *What* do *I mean by that?*

"Um ... I mean planets that are not officially part of the Sovereignty, I guess."

"Do you mean class four planets, which means the Sovereignty —"

"Ugh, fine!" Kara said. "Have those, uh, 'dominions' ever attacked Earth?"

The Jit paused for a second or two, which was unusual. "There has never been a confirmed attack on Earth from any of the three dominions mentioned previously."

"What about any *un*confirmed attacks?"

"There has been one report of a possible attack approximately four doh dek standard hours ago."

Stupid numbers. "What is that number in Earth time?"

"In Earthan time, the attack occurred approximately forty-one hours ago."

Chills descended Kara's spine. That was the attack on her house. The memory of that night threatened to unleash her grief. She tried to ignore it, focusing instead on her inquiry.

"What information is there about the attack?" Kara asked.

"The public account mentions a murder of two citizens and the kidnapping of their young adult daughter by a male with stolen exploration equipment. There is speculation that the attacker may have been from the Molkinar Empire. All other information is restricted."

Interesting. "Is the Sovereignty fighting the Molkinar Empire?"

"The two powers are not presently in good diplomatic standing. There have been recent skirmishes on Enck between the volunteer forces of the Sovereignty and the machine army of the Molkinar Empire."

So it seemed Jeanette's kidnapper *was* an enemy of the Sovereignty. Kara didn't know what to do with this information, but it could be worthwhile to look into this Molkinar Empire further.

Kara recalled her promise to join Jess for breakfast. She was likely stretching those "few minutes" far longer than she should have. Wrapping the Jit around her wrist, Kara grabbed the cane from the tabletop next to the bed and stood. She nearly stumbled as she walked toward the door. Gravity didn't quite seem to be the same here as it was on Earth.

As she emerged from the bedroom, pleasant whiffs of foreign food teased Kara's senses. She made her way to the dining room, taking in the unique aroma—meaty, with a mix of something resembling the smell of cranberries.

"Oh, wonderful! I'm so happy you came to join me! I have your plate right here." Jess grabbed Kara by the arm and led her to the chair.

Kara's ire spiked. *Why? Why do people always feel the need to yank us around like we can't do anything for ourselves?*

As soon as she sat, Jess returned to her seat across the table. Kara took the fork next to the plate and used it to get a feel for the dish: a few roundish chunks of something, some long, flexible items that reminded her of green beans, and something mushy.

She took a bite of one round chunk.

"So sorry they separated you from your friend," Jess said. "He was a nice boy. I know—"

The chunk was some kind of meat, and the seasoning was *amazing*. Kara focused on the flavors, ignoring her host. She didn't want to think about Sam again. Not now. She scooped a bit of the mush and placed it in her mouth. It was smooth and bland, with a strange fruity aftertaste. The long things tasted like an interesting mix of raspberries and squash. She continued to focus and enjoy her meal, only vaguely aware that Jess was still talking.

"—ill do next?"

Kara stopped chewing and lifted her head, reminding herself that it was polite to face someone when speaking with them. She was being asked a question.

"Sorry?" she said, her voice muffled through the food in her mouth. "What did you say?"

Jess's tone was still pleasant as ever. "What do you think you will do next, child?"

"Oh." Kara swallowed. "I guess I will enter that class to become a citizen."

"Ah, yes! Very good idea. Becoming a citizen would be wonderful for you. You will be able—"

Kara quickly tuned Jess out again and concentrated on her food. *How can anyone stand listening to that woman talk?* She needed to get out of here. She couldn't live with this every day. She'd lose her mind.

Her thoughts returned to the information she'd gotten from the Jit earlier. The Molkinar Empire, the place where Jeanette's kidnapper might be from. She wished she could do something, *anything* to help find her sister. While Sam might get useful information from Tercast, he would be trapped there for weeks. Jeanette was out there somewhere, enduring who knows what. Kara would give anything to bring the fight to her sister's kidnapper.

Realization hit like a bolt of lightning. Kara slammed her fork onto the table as she sat up straight, heart thumping. *Yes!*

"Oh my!" Jess exclaimed.

"I know what I'm going to do!" Kara said to no one in particular.

"What is that?"

The *fight*. She was a fighter. A martial artist. A warrior. All those years, the academy was where she felt at home—where she was truly herself.

Kicking ass. That's where she belonged.

"I'm going to join the army."

Chapter 11

Tercast

Sam awoke to silence.

His head felt fuzzy. As he opened his eyes, they adjusted slowly. An arched ceiling overhead filled his vision, with cool morning light trickling in through closed curtains.

"Lively morning, Samuel."

Sam flinched and sat bolt upright at the man's voice. He was older, perhaps in his sixties. A long beard fell from his face, and he wore white robes with gold embellishments. The man sat on a bed next to Sam's in a small room full of other empty beds.

"What happened? Where am I?" Sam asked hastily.

The man smiled and held his hand up slowly in a calming motion. "It's all right, calm down. You are now at Tercast. Congratulations on your acceptance!"

Sam blinked. Short gray hair contrasted the dark brown skin of the man's face, which displayed a thoughtful expression.

The unlikely had happened.

Kara. I need to get back to her. Maybe she had been admitted too, though. Improbable, but possible.

"There was a girl with me. Was she accepted as well?" Sam asked.

"Oh, I'm afraid not," the man said. "You were the only one to be accepted yesterday—the last we needed to begin the next group. Your fellow studies have already been awakened."

Sam's heart sank. "I need to leave. I need to get back to her."

The man's wrinkled eyebrows scrunched up in confusion. "I believe it was explained clearly before you entered the Room of Selection, that once you are accepted you must not leave until your instruction is complete."

Sam briefly considered lying. He could say that it was never explained to him, or that he had misunderstood. Lying about it, however, might just make things worse.

He nodded solemnly.

"Don't look so down, my young friend. You have been blessed by the Divine! You will learn incredible things during your time here."

Oh, wonderful. "The Divine"? Now I'm stuck in a society of religious fanatics?

"My name is Master Azeloram Vikacht," the man said. "It is my privilege to introduce you to Tercast castle—and provide you with these."

He presented Sam with a folded stack of white-and-silver cloth.

Sam hesitantly accepted the gift.

"You will wash and wear these robes every day during your stay. You will need to change into those prior to your group's commencement gathering. Please follow me."

The old man led Sam into a long ornate hallway lit by pentagonal windows. Elaborate wooden archways framed paths to the right and left. Colorful pieces of artwork of all shapes and sizes lined the white textured hallway, depicting scenes of angelic visitations, large feasts, and stunning landscapes. They passed a few others who seemed to be roughly Sam's age, and all of them wore similar white robes with silver linings. Each of them greeted Master Azeloram briefly as they strode past.

Master Azeloram stopped in front of a small wooden door.

"Here is the washroom. There is an instruction guide in your clothing, which explains how to put everything on." He smiled. "I will wait out here."

Sam walked in just as another robed man was leaving. Gilded sinks with flowering overhead lights lined each side of the main wash area, beyond which were individual wooden stalls. He entered one of them, staring face-to-face with his reflection. His hair was an awful mess, and he felt self-conscious of the fact that he'd been walking the halls in that state. He took off the comfortable clothes that Rolnauv had given him back on Earth and began following the hand-drawn instructions.

The shoulder piece was somewhat difficult, but once he had all the components on, Sam took a final look at his reflection. A short white cape attached by a silver ring sat on his right shoulder, atop a long-sleeved white shirt with an embroidered symbol above the left breast. The folds on the shoulder and trim of the robe were lined with silver at the edges. Curvy silver patterns ran along the forearm of the white gloves on his hands. The shirt was tucked into a pair of white cloth pants. A sash around his waist was held by a shiny clasp, and he wore thin white boots.

Sam laughed at the ridiculous look. He didn't look forward to the lengthy procedure of putting it on all the time, but at least the robes were fairly comfortable.

He made time to peruse the facilities and fix his hair at the sink before emerging to find the old man waiting patiently.

"Ah," Master Azeloram said. "Excellent job with your robes! You look grand." He slapped Sam on the shoulder. "The others are waiting. Let us make our way to the gathering hall."

"What do I do with these?" Sam asked, holding out his old clothes.

"Keep them with you for now. You will all drop them off after commencement."

The man led them back down the intricate hallways. Sam turned his head this way and that to admire the artwork and impressive architecture as they walked briskly. The hallway ended at a large, wooden double door with iron handles and intricate circular patterns. Master Azeloram pulled one door open, illuminating the hallway with sunlight. Sam squinted reflexively as they walked out onto the cool stone path leading through a courtyard. Once his eyes adjusted, he noted the impressive spires and elaborate battlements surrounding the courtyard.

As the man led him through the impressive landscaping and trees adorned with red and purple leaves, Sam's mind reeled against the jarring experiences of the past few days. He'd only just discovered a world of advanced technology—super suits, flying vehicles, and teleportation gates—and now he found himself in an almost medieval-looking castle with God-fearing cultists in robes. It was immensely disorienting.

They entered the building opposite the courtyard and strode down more extravagant hallways, arriving finally at a large door, which Master Azeloram opened for Sam. He stepped into what appeared to be a large lecture hall. A dozen or so people about Sam's age sat on padded stone benches, which curved around the front of the room. All of them wore the same robes he did. They stared at him as he entered—all except one man who sat in an old-looking wheelchair.

"Rudds. Finally!" a low, booming voice rang out. "We've been waitin' for ages!"

Sam glanced to his right toward the source of the voice, and his eyes went wide. There sat a giant of a man, easily several feet taller than Sam and three times as wide. He had an almost rectangular brown head, topped with shaggy dark red hair.

"What?" the giant said with a laugh. "Never seen a Mondrovian before?"

Master Azeloram gestured for Sam to sit, so he made his way to the third row from the front. At the other end sat a thin, black-skinned woman fiddling absently with her stark white hair, which blended into her robes.

"Here we are at last!" Master Azeloram said as he reached the front of the lecture hall. He stood behind a grand wooden podium, in front of a giant whiteboard that reached up to half the height of the room. "Congratulations to all of you for your acceptance into Tercast! The Divine smiles on you this day, the day of the commencement of your Sorcery instruction. Your group will be known as the Ulinko group, named after the majestic beast."

He motioned to the side of the room, where a purple catlike animal emerged from under a bench. It cocked its head, from which long, pointy ears stuck out. It had diamond-shaped black eyes and a white streak on its forehead. Short, thick fur covered the animal's body, which continued down its long tail and ended with a tuft of longer white fur at the tip.

"Aw, it's so cute!" a dark-haired girl near the front blurted out.

The ulinko trotted to the podium and lay down, flipping its tail quietly as the old man continued. "Now, we will go over the basics of Tercast theology."

Azeloram touched the board behind him with the tip of his finger, where black lines emerged. He traced a word—large, clear, and elaborate: *Divine.*

"First is the concept of the Divine. We use this sacred word regarding the supreme Creators and Overseers of the universe."

Sam's heart sank. He thought he'd escaped the archaic ideas of God and creationism when he'd left his parents' religion. Apparently not.

The man wrote another word underneath the first: *Source.*

"Next is the important concept of a Source. We refer to all beings that can act of their own accord as a Source—meaning a source of action. A Source's actions originate from their soul."

His finger traced a third word on the board: *Element.*

"An Element is the base entity of the universe that exists to be acted upon. If it is not a Source, it is an Element. All Elements submit to the Divine, and potentially to the will of a Source. Any direct action of a Source on an Element is called Vitalization."

Sam leaned forward and rested his chin on a palm.

"There are four primordial Elements," Azeloram continued. "They are Land, Air, Fire, and Water."

Sam fought hard to avoid rolling his eyes. *Nice. Another culture with archaic views that the universe consists of these four elements. He* was awestruck that a society within the Sovereignty—a technologically advanced civilization—could possibly believe such nonsense.

The man then wrote a fourth word: *Sorcerer.*

And here's where everything really *goes sideways,* Sam thought.

"When a Source's influence on the Elements is liberated beyond natural physical bounds, we call such individuals Sorcerers. They lie between the state of a common Source and the state of the Divine on the scale of power and influence on the Elements." He smiled as he gestured toward the class. "This now includes all of you. You are now Sorcerers. You have been blessed with the ability to manipulate the four Elements around you directly from your Source, as granted by the Divine."

Silence settled as those seated looked around at each other. Sam caught the eyes of an attractive young woman sitting in the front row of the hall. Long blond hair fell across her dark brown skin, surrounding intense bright blue eyes. The young man seated next to her had a similar appearance, though he had light stubble on his face. Sam guessed they must be brother and sister. He also noticed that their ears came to a point at the top.

Sam regarded the man in the wheelchair. He had sandy brown hair and light skin, and he hadn't moved since the lecture began. The man sitting next to him looked nearly identical. Twins?

Given the immensely low odds of Tercast acceptance, Sam found the fact that there were *two* pairs of siblings in the group to be highly suspect. Their selection process was certainly unlikely to be random. Then again, they never actually did say that it was.

"Are there questions on these basic concepts?" Azeloram asked.

Sam raised his hand, and the man gestured toward him.

"I have a lot of questions."

Their instructor nodded.

"How do you reconcile quantum mechanics with your view of the Elements?" Sam asked.

Azeloram simply blinked, clearly surprised by the question.

"You know," Sam continued, "quarks, electrons, bosons? Aren't they the fundamental building blocks of the universe, as opposed to Land, Air, Fire, and Water?"

"I do not understand your meaning, I'm afraid," the old man responded. "These terms are unfamiliar to me."

Sam sighed. Perhaps the Sovereignty used different terms for these concepts. Or, more likely, Azeloram was simply ignorant of particle physics.

"What about the periodic table? Hydrogen? Helium? Oxygen? They don't seem to fit this four-element view of reality."

Azeloram's eyes lit up. "Ah, yes," he said. "Each of those is a manifestation of one of the four base Elements. Hydrogen, helium, and oxygen are shreds of Air, for example. Iron and copper are shreds of Land, and so forth."

"That makes no sense!" Sam exclaimed. "Air is *composed* of oxygen and helium, and the same goes for Earth, which is *composed* of elements like iron and copper."

"Earth?"

"Land . . . whatever."

"I understand that the way we express these concepts may differ from explanations you are familiar with, but I believe we are in agreement."

Sam didn't feel that way, but Azeloram's tone indicated it was unwise to continue pressing the point. He couldn't help himself, though. "Also, do you really expect everyone to believe all this—" He almost said "nonsense" but thought better of it. "—*stuff* about the Divine and Sorcery and such?"

Everyone turned to Sam with expressions of pure shock.

Azeloram shook his head. "I'm surprised you desired entry to Tercast in the first place if you did not have a mind open to possibilities."

Sam scowled. *Just because I don't accept your narrow and archaic views of the universe, that doesn't make me close minded.*

"Your instruction will surely convince you of the truth," Azeloram said with a tone of finality. He turned his attention to the class. "Now, are there any more questions on these basic concepts?" he asked, gesturing toward the words on the board behind him.

Silence.

Sam wasn't surprised. Who would ask questions when the instructor was going to insult you for asking them?

"Excellent," the man said. He tapped the board, and the words disappeared. "I must now impress upon your minds one very important guideline concerning your learning at Tercast. Each of you has a book in your dormitories outlining many Tercast principles and rules, but this one is particularly important." His expression turned dark. Menacing. "You are *not* to undergo the study of Sorcery on your own under any circumstances. While you may exercise your abilities for utility on occasion, you may *not* exercise your abilities to test their limits or explore extended capabilities outside of your classroom instruction. Is that clear?"

His intent gaze settled on several students, and they nodded. His light blue eyes paused on Sam, clearly waiting for a sign of agreement. Sam's defiance wavered under the suppressive look. He nodded—more out of reflex than thoughtful compliance.

Satisfied, Azeloram's gaze turned toward the back of the room as he continued. "Anyone who fails to abide by this essential rule will be subject to harsh discipline. If you are discovered experimenting with the limits of Sorcery or with alternative forms of Sorcery, you will be severely punished. The maximum penalty for disobedience to our principles is banishment through a portal to Uvlun, a dismal underworld. We do this for your protection and the protection of all Tercast citizens."

"Is that even legal?" asked the white-haired girl across the bench.

Azeloram interlocked hands behind his back as he paced toward her position. "Absolutely. Before you could enter a Room of Selection, you agreed to accept all the conditions and laws of our society. Each of you also has a solemn responsibility to report any study who violates this essential rule." He turned and walked back to the podium, releasing his hands and holding them up. "Please understand that we do this for *your* protection, and the safety of everyone at Tercast. It is no small matter. Avoid self-study of Sorcery, and the Divine will smile upon you during your time with us."

He gripped the sides of the podium as he stood behind it. "Now, your instruction over the next doh weeks will comprise four days of Elemental instruction, one day of labors, and one day of games and evening devotion per week."

Doh weeks? Oh right, base twelve. Sam immediately regretted the loss of his Jit, which would have helped considerably with the conversions. At least he knew that doh was equal to twelve, so this meant he was stuck here for twelve weeks. Well, twelve weeks of apparently six days each, which meant seventy-two days total.

"After your base instruction, you may choose to continue your studies at Tercast or return to society on conditions of confidentiality."

So they wanted him to keep all their nonsense a secret. Fair enough. He could use the time to find out about Kara's parents and whether her grandfather was still here. When he and Kara eventually met back up, they would find out what to do from there. He had a sinking feeling that investigators from the Sovereignty would have already pursued this information, but perhaps being a part of Tercast society for a while would uncover some mysteries about the Joneses' deaths and Jeanette's kidnapping. Maybe he could learn things the Sovereignty didn't have access to. It felt like a long shot, but it seemed plausible.

"Your first lesson will be in the Land room at the ninth bell tomorrow morning. Your fellow study Tovas Qillion was the first to awaken this morning and knows where to go if you need assistance." He motioned to the man seated next to his twin in the wheelchair. "Tovas, please stand so the others can see you."

Tovas stood—thin, yet sturdily built. His short sandy hair lay straight against his head, cut a bit shorter on the sides and back. He grasped his hands behind him with his head slightly bowed in a posture of propriety, giving off an air of reverence.

"Thank you," Azeloram said. "Please ask Tovas any questions

you have. He has shown a marvelous aptitude for the Tercast ways."

In other words, he's already become one of your mindless drones.

"Now, are there any last questions for me before I let you all enjoy some lunch?" Azeloram asked.

"Yeah, I've got one." The booming voice of the giant echoed off the walls of the lecture hall. "Can you show us some magic?"

The man sighed. "It is not magic, it is *Vitalization* of the Elements by your Source. Please use the correct—"

"Yeah, yeah. Can you show us?"

Sam decided he liked the giant. He folded his arms.

"Very well."

Many of the others leaned forward in anticipation.

Azeloram raised one arm, and the glove on his hand slipped off and rose into the air, suspended by an apparently magical force. Several of the studies let out gasps of surprise. Sam had to admit that the trick looked convincing, but this could be a simple manipulation of the gravitational effects he'd seen with Elysia's suit and the flying egg vehicle—or even something much simpler.

He'd find out the truth. One way or another.

Chapter 12

Rwenmar

Kara applied foundation onto her face. At least, she *hoped* that's what it was. Jess hadn't known what she'd meant by "foundation," but after Kara described it, she had handed her a small round container. It smelled and felt about right. *Hopefully, my face won't turn out bright yellow or something.*

"What is the weather like there?"

Her Jit responded from beside her on the bed. "It is currently seventy-one degrees Fahrenheit, with partly cloudy skies in Kaalesdale, Intrenti, on the planet Rwenmar. The temperature will rise to a peak of eighty degrees Fahrenheit at doh two three doh, or fourteen thirty, local time. The temperature will then fall to a low of sixty-five degrees Fahrenheit in the evening. Skies will remain partly cloudy all day."

Kara was glad she had figured out how to change her preferences on the device. It now translated any dohnal numbers into decimal automatically and gave her the temperature in Fahrenheit rather than Kodrups—whatever those were.

She had also genuinely thanked Jess for taking her shopping the previous day, after she'd signed up for the citizenship course.

Leaving Sam behind on Alvior was regretful, but with him stuck in the secretive Tercast castle, he might as well be in another universe. She'd sent a few messages to his Jit but hadn't received a reply. Not that she was expecting to.

Kara reached out to the bed in front of her and searched for the container of facial powder. She flipped it open, swirled her brush around and began applying the powder to her face in large strokes, working to blend everything thoroughly.

"How far is it to the class again?"

"It is approximately five groh eight doh seven hexa-moh, or twenty-two sextillion, miles from Alvior to—"

"I *meant* how long will it take to get there?"

The Jit paused briefly before responding. "Travel for a direct route from your current position in Ilmar, Oscertos, on Alvior to education complex two doh el, or thirty-five, in Kaalesdale, Intrenti, on Rwenmar is estimated to take three hours and nine minutes in Alvior time with ascender transport, which will cause you to be two hours and doh four, or sixteen, minutes late if you depart immediately. Using rapid transport, travel time is estimated to be two doh two, or twenty-six, Alvior minutes, at a cost of six doh dek, or eighty-two, Til."

She filed a mental reminder to specify rapid transport later. She had intentionally avoided ascender transportation. Sitting in an enclosed box by herself for several hours would be excruciatingly *boring*.

Satisfied that she had sufficiently blended her makeup, Kara swapped out the brush for eyeliner. She closed her eyes, applying the pencil to her eyelids with delicate precision.

She was going to be a citizen—of an advanced alien race. Just as her parents had secretly been.

A smile crept onto Kara's face as she recalled the surprise in Jess's voice at her declaration to join the army. The older woman had explained that there was actually no such thing as an army in the Sovereignty. The military was all under one command called the Armed Forces, or simply "The Force."

Apparently, in order to join the Force, Kara needed to become a citizen first, which made sense. She'd asked her Jit to enroll her in the earliest citizenship course she could find, and that happened to be on the capital planet of Rwenmar. Jess had tried to talk her out of joining the military, but that was futile. It felt so *right*.

She was going to take the fight to the bastards who'd kidnapped her sister.

Completing the application of eyeliner, she placed the pencil back on the bed and felt for her mascara. Thankfully Jess had been able to locate a shorter one. Kara pulled out the wand, scraped the excess, and began brushing her eyelashes with experienced sweeps.

"How much longer until we—er—*I* need to leave, assuming I take rapid transport?" she asked.

"To arrive on time, it is recommended that you leave no later than two doh four, or twenty-eight, Alvior minutes from now," the Jit replied.

She would probably leave sooner than that, since she was just about ready to go. She was also positive that Alvior minutes were shorter than Earth ones.

Having completed her quick makeup routine, Kara picked up the cosmetics from the bed, loaded them into the makeup bag nearby, and placed the bag in the small suitcase lying next to her.

"Close my suitcase," she commanded.

A muffled mechanical noise and a few satisfying clicks indicated that her belongings were now secure. So much easier than suitcases back home.

She slid off the bed, grabbing her cane and the handle on the suitcase as she did so. The suitcase was surprisingly light, considering all the clothing she'd placed in there. She fumbled around for the touch button on top, which extended the handle. The suitcase rumbled behind her on the hard floor as she emerged from the bedroom.

"Kara!" Jess exclaimed, causing her to jump.

The woman rushed over and gave Kara an unwelcome hug.

Kara reached around with her cane-carrying hand and patted the older woman on the back.

"You are truly going through with this?" Jess asked, breaking the hug but maintaining a hold on Kara's shoulders.

"Yes. This is what I want to do."

Jess gave Kara a light pat on her shoulder. "So sad. Seems you and Sam just arrived, and now you are leaving." She sounded legitimately sorrowful. The woman was probably lonely living here on her own, even though she would spend time with neighborhood friends frequently.

Sorry, Jess, but I kind of can't stand you, even if you are nice. The woman had no apparent ambition. She didn't seem to have any solid goals in life other than enjoying her home-cooked meals, which were, admittedly, pretty amazing. Still, the woman had offered her home to them. Kara should at least show her gratitude for that.

"Thank you for letting me stay here. I really appreciate it."

That prompted another hug. "Anytime, child. If it doesn't work out on Rwenmar, please come back. My home is always open to you."

Kara almost wished she felt sad about leaving, but she wasn't. "Thank you, but I'll be fine."

"Oh, I'm sure, child. You have quite a fire about you."

She didn't know how to take that. Was it a compliment? As she considered how to respond, she remembered something.

"Oh, could you check my eyeliner?" she asked.

The woman's breathing approached as she inspected Kara's work up close. "It looks wonderful, child. No smudges."

"Thanks," Kara replied. "Well, I'd better get going—don't want to be late."

She extended her cane and walked around Jess. She'd gotten quite familiar to the layout of Jess's home. Now she would have to learn a new place. Apparently, they provided accommodations in the instruction building for prospective citizens, so she'd have a free apartment for the next few days.

"Safe travels," Jess called out from behind her.

"Thank you. Take care, Jess."

As Kara approached the front door, it opened for her and let in a cool breeze. She pressed her Jit as she stepped through, and it beeped.

"Direct me to the citizenship course with rapid transport, please."

"Providing directions to your scheduled citizenship course. Turn left on the path ahead toward the transport pad."

She followed the remaining instructions until she found herself in a small circular craft. It felt very similar to the one they'd used back on Earth to get to the Sovereignty facility. Her fingers found the straps, and she buckled herself in. Once she was secure, a low, barely audible rumble reverberated beneath her feet, and the vehicle rose with surprising gracefulness. It continued to accelerate upward as the winds outside howled against the hull.

After a few moments, Kara felt gravity pull to the side slightly just before the vehicle decelerated. Her stomach lurched when the vehicle felt as though it was in free fall. Gravity thankfully returned slowly, and the craft made a smooth stop. She unbuckled herself as the rumbling beneath the floor died down.

The door of the craft swished open as Kara approached, letting in a buzz of noises. People conversed as they moved about around her, and the rush of vehicles echoed from above. Bouncy music played in the distance. The pleasurable scent resembling cinnamon buns reached her again—identical to the scent near Tercast the other day.

Deciding she had a few minutes to spare, Kara moved toward the source of the scent, tapping her cane against a hard surface. The intoxicating scent was close, so hopefully it was a counter with an attendant nearby.

"Um, hello?" she asked.

A lid to a large container shut close to her.

"Ah! Hello, Kara," a young woman's voice answered. "Would you like a nuumyun?"

The mention of her name startled Kara. The woman must have been able to access information from her Jit somehow.

"Is that the name of this incredible thing I'm smelling?"

"Oh yes. If you haven't had one before, you absolutely must try one. Here, take a sample!"

Kara reached out with her palm facing up. A warm, soft, bread-like substance fell into her hand, about the size of a golf ball. She gave it one quick sniff up close to verify that it was her target, then tossed it into her mouth.

Pure pleasure engulfed her senses. As she chewed, the outer bread layer gave way to a dense, creamy substance. The exquisite flavor was unique and resembled a mixture of cinnamon, vanilla, and honey, though not overwhelmingly sweet. It was probably the most delicious thing she'd ever tasted.

"Oh my *God!*" she said. "I will absolutely take one of those, please."

The young woman giggled. "It'll be dek Til for a full one. Here you go!"

Kara reached out, and a much larger version of the substance was placed into her hand. "Thank you!"

"My pleasure."

Kara took another bite of the incredible snack as she turned about and made her way back to the path her Jit had directed her to, sweeping her cane before her. That Jess probably knew about this nuumyun treat and had never shared it with her was an unforgivable crime against humanity. It was surprisingly light, given the inner density. Thankfully, the food left no sticky residue on her hand.

The Jit led her into a building and teward an acheron portal, presumably the same one she and Sam came in on a few days ago. The chattering voices and steps of other travelers echoed around the large hallways. As she tossed the last of the nuumyun into her mouth, Kara's cane tapped something elastic—likely a person's shoe.

"Sorry," she said, the word muffled by the heavenly bite in her mouth.

There was no reply.

As she proceeded toward the gate, the chattering crowd around her grew denser. She soon gave up apologizing for tapping someone accidentally. She wondered how many of those around her might stare, considering her use of the cane.

Gravity became ever-so-slightly lighter again, and the air warmer. She had made it back through the gate to the space station. Thankfully, the crowd lightened as she progressed along the path according to the Jit's directions. She passed even more interesting and delightfully fresh smells from nearby food vendors.

A tightening throng of people encircled her again soon enough, telling her that she was no doubt approaching the gate to Rwenmar. The crowd dispersed once more on the other side. Curiously, she had felt no discernible change in weight. Her Jit continued to direct her across a large room, where hundreds of voices reverberated from all around. As she strode through another set of doors, the echoing sounds of the building interior gave way to the noise of vehicles overhead and city atmosphere. Warm, dry air met her skin.

Another rapid transport vehicle took her to a landing pad just outside the building where her course would be. As she stepped out onto the pad and followed her Jit's directions toward the building, she heard water falling in the distance among the sounds of flying vehicles. The air was more humid compared to the area near the portal, and still very warm. Anxiety gnawed at her as she stepped into the building.

"Excuse me, Miss Kara Jones. Please leave your bag here."

She jumped in surprise at the nearby man's voice.

"Ah, okay," she said, moving toward the source. "Um . . . where do I put this?" She lifted her suitcase, the weightlessness of which still astounded her.

"Place your bag on the pad, please."

"Sorry, I'm blind," she replied. "I don't know what pad you're talking about."

There were a few moments of silence before the man spoke again. "Place your bag on the pad, please."

"Uh, I just told you. *I. Can't. See. It.* You're going to have to give me more information."

Another pause. "Place your bag on the pad, please."

Kara let out a sigh of frustration. *Must be some asinine AI thing.* After listening for a moment, she became reasonably certain that there weren't other people around—if so, they were incredibly silent. She waved her hand around in front of her, no doubt looking immensely stupid to anyone who might walk by. Dropping to her knees, she felt around on the smooth, hard floor. *If I touch someone's spat-out piece of gum or something, I'm going to lose it.*

After a few seconds of grazing the floor with her fingers, she located a cold metallic circle, which was raised an inch or so from the rest of the hard floor. She stood and placed the bag on the section, hoping it was the correct spot. Her bag began sinking into the floor under her hand. Thankfully, the room still appeared to be absent of onlookers.

"Thank you, Miss Kara. We will take your luggage to your room. Please proceed to the lift at the end of the main hall."

"Yeah, thanks for nothing, dust-for-brains."

"I apologize for your difficulty. Your dissatisfaction has been noted and submitted to our support team," the AI said. "Enjoy your course."

Kara turned and walked down the hall, cane taps reverberating off the walls. The room smelled lightly of cleaning chemicals. She could also detect a very faint scent of mold. Her cane hit a solid barrier.

"The lift is arriving," her Jit said.

A *ding* announced its arrival soon afterward, and Kara stepped on board. The doors closed quickly with a hiss, and the platform accelerated smoothly upward. She wondered for a moment how it knew where she needed to go, then realized her Jit probably took care of that for her somehow. The little device was a godsend. She felt far more comfortable navigating the Sovereignty on her own than she ever did on Earth. People there rarely realized how difficult it was to find your way around unfamiliar territory without sight.

The lift slowed to a soft stop, and the doors opened.

"Proceed straight down the hall and enter room seven groh doh five, or one thousand and thirteen," her Jit instructed.

She walked forward and pressed her Jit, which beeped softly. "Tell me when to turn to go to the right room."

Kara didn't know if the command would work, but it was worth a shot and would save her a lot of time of awkwardly stumbling around to find the right place. Unfortunately, it didn't seem to acknowledge her command. The Jit could direct her everywhere else, so why would this be any different? Maybe the building was too old.

"Hello," a female voice called from her left.

Kara consciously turned to face the woman, hoping it wasn't another AI. "Hi. I'm trying to get to the citizenship course. Could you help me?"

"Oh, that's right in here. Didn't your Jit tell you it was in room seven groh doh five?" she asked.

"Yes, but I'm blind."

The woman paused briefly. "What did you say?"

"I said I'm blind. I can't see the room numbers."

"Oh! I'm so sorry. I was not aware. Are you sure you don't want to get that fixed before taking the course? It will be more difficult without the ability to see."

Get it fixed? They can do that?

"I'll be all right," Kara said. "I'm used to learning this way, as long as I am free to ask questions when I don't understand."

"Yes, of course you may, but . . . Don't you *want* to get your eyes fixed?"

Kara walked through the threshold of the open doorway to the classroom, tapping it lightly with her cane. "There's nothing to fix. This is just how I am. I don't consider myself broken. I just can't see like you can."

"I see. Uh, I mean . . . I understand," the woman said. "Forgive me. It's just that as far as I'm aware, everyone who is afflicted with conditions like that have it corrected as soon as possible."

"Where should I sit?" Kara asked, eager to change the subject.

"You may sit in any open seat. Would you like me to help you locate one?"

Kara could find a seat herself, but she didn't know how the room was laid out, so she'd have to wander about trying to figure out where everything was. That wouldn't do much to prove the point she just made about not being broken.

"Yes, please," she said, holding out her hand. "I would appreciate your help."

A warm hand took hers, guiding her a few steps into the room and to a desk in the front row. It reminded her of the desks at her high school, though sleeker and far more flexible and comfortable. People chatted quietly at the back of the room, and there were a few others shuffling around. She estimated about fifteen to twenty people based on what she could hear.

"Hey," said a man next to her.

Kara flinched and yelped in surprise. "My God, don't *do* that. I didn't know anyone was there."

"So you really *are* blind?" he asked. His accent was another unfamiliar one, rugged, with stiff, non-rhotic vowels.

"Obviously," she said.

"Name's Nikor."

"I'm Kara."

"There must be something wrong with my eyes too. I can't take them off you," he said.

She deliberately turned her head toward him for emphasis. "Sounds to me like your eyes work just fine. It's your brain that's the problem."

He laughed. "So where are you from?"

Kara debated whether to continue speaking with the guy but decided that as long as he didn't hit on her again, some conversation would be better than sitting around waiting.

"Earth," she said.

"Interesting. I've never heard of it. Is it part of the Federation?"

"I don't know what the Federation is. Earth is sort of part of the Sovereignty, I think."

"I meant the Intesu Federation. Anyway, if you're from the Sovereignty, then why are you here? Aren't you already a citizen?"

Kara fiddled absently with her Jit. "No. Earth doesn't know the Sovereignty exists."

"Oh, it's one of those uninitiated planets? They manipulate your history and stuff, right?" Nikor asked.

"Yeah, something like that."

"That's one thing people really don't like about the Sovereignty where I'm from."

"And where is that?"

"A planet called Enck in the Molkinar Empire."

Kara stilled. *Molkinar.* The Sovereignty suspected that her sister's kidnapper was from Molkinar.

"Isn't the Molkinar Empire at war with the Sovereignty?" she asked.

His tone became more somber. "Yeah. That's sort of why I'm here, actually. My family—"

"Good morning," the instructor called out, causing the chatter to cease abruptly. "My name is Tecsa Invilae. Welcome to your introductory course to citizenship in the Intergalactic Sovereignty of Rwenmar. This will cover the basics of Sovereignty government, economics, and citizen responsibilities, and will culminate in an examination to test your knowledge. When you pass this examination and take your oaths, you will be full citizens of the Sovereignty."

The woman's steps clacked around the front of the room. Was she displaying something to the class?

"This is our outline for the five-day course. Today we will talk briefly about Sovereignty history, our form of government, and our relationship with other notable intergalactic governments, of which some, if not all, of you are coming from."

Kara mentally prepared herself for a long, boring lecture. It didn't help that she had left Alvior in the evening. This was going to be a long day.

"Rwenmar first began discovering other inhabited worlds nearly one moh five groh standard years ago," the instructor said. "Invention of the early acheron around that time allowed transportation to distant star systems for the first time in history. The Rwenmar Republic, as it was known then, discovered nine civilized systems, openly sharing its technology and research with other worlds. This included—"

"She's showing an image of the first nine planets and where they were in the galaxy," Nikor whispered.

"You don't need to explain what she's showing, especially when it's not even that important," Kara replied under her breath.

"—and equipment, which made—"

"I just thought it looked neat, and I knew you couldn't see it," he said.

"Shh! I'm trying to listen."

"Two of the initial nine planets destroyed themselves with internal war," the instructor explained. "Three planets—Icalron, Vu, and Jakem—joined forces to overthrow the Rwenmar government, which was supported by the other three planets, Wren, Kaiwam, and Oclarion. The war lasted almost two doh standard years." The instructor paused before continuing. "In an astonishing act of treason, a team of five engineers from Rwenmar, now known as the Founders, developed a self-replicating army of drones that overpowered the armed forces on both sides of the conflict."

"Whoa, the drones remind me of Molkinar forces," Nikor whispered. "They look very similar."

"Shut up!" Kara hissed.

"—set up a new form of government on Rwenmar, which has stood ever since. The sluggishness of their republic frustrated them, particularly in military affairs. They claimed it to be the primary reason for the drawn-out war. In response, the group established a nearly autocratic government in which the supreme ruler, or Sovereign, is determined by synthetic intelligence. The Sovereign rules for an indefinite length of time that averages to about two doh standard years. The synthetic intelligence that performs the selection, known as Aldan, has selected the Sovereign ruler ever since. The factors contributing to its decisions remain incompletely known to this day."

Kara's eyes widened. Had she heard that correctly? Apparently, the Sovereignty was a dictatorship and a computer selected the ruler. She had expected a democracy, for such an advanced society.

The instructor continued. "The Founders' only official statement concerning selection criteria was the following."

A different woman's voice came from overhead. "We find the irony self-evident that those who desire power and authority are ill-suited for such power. We also have vivid evidence that public popularity and marketed political positions favor mass manipulation and are severely ineffective for determining ideal leadership. Our supreme leader, though sensitive to the popular sentiments of the public, should be of paramount moral character above all other considerations. It is far easier to teach a virtuous person to be a distinguished leader than it is to teach a natural leader to be a virtuous person."

The instructor's steps echoed around the otherwise silent room. "The Founders' enacted a universal ban on synthetically intelligent, self-replicating autonomous machines, with the notable exception of Inspec—the system which monitors citizens and provides information to Aldan. This remains a controversial decision to this day, particularly given the recent conflicts with the Molkinar Empire. The Founders destroyed their own drone army after the first Sovereign, Namon Raal, was selected by the Aldan. Our current Empress, Aiyla Covenmoor, is approaching her dekth standard year as Sovereign."

"Yeah, she's *gorgeous*," Nikor whispered.

Kara ignored him.

"We maintain a legislature and a judiciary with representatives and magistrates elected by popular vote. They perform most of the day-to-day operations of Sovereignty affairs, but the Empress maintains nearly absolute power and is supreme head of the Sovereignty's military force."

Kara could hardly fathom such power in a single person. It sounded like the system was working for the Sovereignty, though.

"The Sovereign typically meets with representatives, reviewing laws and overseeing the military, though she occasionally spends time among the people. You may have heard that Sovereign Aiyla has been overseeing the conflict with the Molkinar Empire on Enck and meeting with the refugees there."

"That's old news," Nikor said loudly.

The instructor paused for a moment before responding. "I'm sorry, what do you—"

"The conflict on Enck is over," he said, adopting a somber tone. "I just arrived from there. The planet has been destroyed."

Chapter 13

Amy

Jeanette shivered and stared into her corner as usual.

At least they had let her keep the clothing.

She'd lost track of how long it had been since hell devoured her. No visible daylight graced the dungeon, so she had no idea when days began or ended. She could tell from the dwindling noises of the jail that the number of prisoners was shrinking. They would leave with the prison guard and never come back. She assumed they had been killed—perhaps for sport, as she had almost been.

Some time had passed since the ruckus upstairs. It had sounded like an attack. Loud explosions and people running about dared to give Jeanette hope. After only a few brief minutes, however, it had become silent again, and she remained in this cold, dark pit of torment.

As the hours dragged on, Jeanette could feel her mind unraveling. Her resolve to stay in control helped to keep her sane, but only so much. She needed someone to talk to—someone who would empathize with her plight and encourage her. Imagining her parents was her first thought, but she couldn't bear visualizing their misery as they fictitiously observed her terrible situation.

Perhaps one of her friends. There was Claire, probably her closest friend, but she was a bit self-centered. Fun to hang out with when times were good, but not always the most sympathetic when times were tough. There was also Jordan. He had gone through some hard times and could be compassionate, but he didn't seem to hold up well under pressure or temptation. Probably not the best for this situation. Who else was there?

Amy.

Amy had left for college after they'd both graduated together two years ago, so they had spoken very little recently, but Amy was *perfect*. She'd endured a cruel childhood, and the experience had left her rough around the edges. They didn't always share the same worldviews, but Amy was compassionate and tough. Imaginary conversations with her might help maintain Jeanette's sanity. Just maybe.

Hi, Amy.

She imagined Amy's form seated in the corner in front of her. Wavy, dark hair stretched down to her shoulders, and she had deep-brown eyes. A dark, heart-shaped face framed her prominent cheeks and large teeth. She might wear a cute workout outfit—tight black patterned exercise leggings and a dark blue tank top over a black sports bra.

"Jeanette! I've missed you!"

I've missed you too.

"How are you and Jake?"

Oh, we broke up ages ago. Turns out he's a jerk.

Amy's imaginary form laughed. *"Sorry, but I saw that coming. You always seem to pick terrible boyfriends."*

Hey! It's not my fault, Jeanette thought in reply. *They're the ones asking me out. I'm just stupid enough to give them a shot, and they turn out to be jerks. Also, you make it sound like I've had a million boyfriends. There were only three, you know.*

"Yeah, but they were all terrible. I told you Jake didn't deserve you."

True. You did. You were right. Though, all things considered, I'd rather still be with him than where I am now . . .

Amy's expression turned sorrowful as her imaginary face scanned Jeanette's small cell. *"Yeah, this looks terrifying."*

Tears welled up in Jeanette's eyes, and she looked down at the cold stone floor. *They hurt me. They do horrible things to me . . . I don't know how much longer I can take it. I don't know if I'm strong enough.*

Jeanette imagined Amy putting her arms around her, and they cried together.

How . . . How did you put up with your father all those years? I don't think I ever quite understood how dreadful that must have been for you before now. How did you get over that?

"I never 'got over it,'" Amy replied. *"I got past it. It doesn't go away, but that doesn't mean you have to let it hold you back."*

Jeanette smiled despite her tears, still curled up in her shivering ball. She didn't truly know if Amy would have said those words, but she was glad for them anyway.

Thank you. That helps.

Amy's imagined hand lifted Jeanette's chin, and she pictured those dark eyes with stunning clarity.

"You can do this," Amy said. *"You are stronger than you know."*

Jeanette held that picture in her mind for several seconds—Amy's genuine assurance pouring into her soul.

You know, you dated a pretty big jerk yourself back in our junior year.

Amy's imaginary face laughed as she wiped tears from her eyes. *"Yeah, that's true. Iris was waaay over the top. I think she—"*

Footsteps along the stairway interrupted her fictitious conversation, sending Jeanette's heart into overdrive. Two sets of them echoed across the dungeon. By the time the steps reached the bottom of the stairwell, the thumping of her heartbeat was quick and loud in her ears. Her shivering escalated.

Please, not my cell. Please.

Her heart sank as the dreaded squeak of the metal latch echoed from behind her.

"You've got a visitor," the prison guard said in his odious mumble.

Terror gripped her chest, making it hard to breathe. She couldn't move.

"Well, look at you." It was a woman's voice. An unusual development. She sounded familiar.

Jeanette refrained from turning around. Maybe if she just acted like she'd lost her mind, they'd go away.

"Come here. I've got a gift for you." The woman's kind tone did nothing to ease Jeanette's mounting fear.

She continued to sit and shiver, heart beating furiously. She couldn't decide whether it would be worse to ignore the woman's command or to obey. Either option would lead to certain torment.

"Get up and come here. Now!" The woman's patience had faded rather quickly.

Jeanette finally decided that ignoring her would probably turn out worse, so she stood slowly and turned to face the cell opening, heart still thumping furiously. It was the dark-haired woman from the first day of her capture, the one who had chided Del for killing her mother. She wore the same outfit as she had that day. Swirling silver symbols danced along her black top, and enormous boots graced her legs, coming to points above the knees. The prison guard stood behind her with an ominous smirk on his face.

"Good girl. Now come with me," the woman said, turning on her heel.

The guard's expression turned to surprise. "You're not going to bind her?"

"That won't be necessary. She should know by now what kind of power we have and that running would be useless."

Arrogance, Jeanette thought. *Maybe I can use that to my advantage.*

Rubbing her shivering arms, she followed the woman up the spiral stairs. Her thoughts raced as she tried to recall the layout of the castle. The woman turned left in the hallway above the prison. Jeanette couldn't remember for sure, but her instincts told her that the entrance was in the opposite direction.

Without allowing herself to give it another thought, Jeanette spun and sprinted as fast as she could down the hall. She had just passed the steps to the prison when a searing pain in her thigh caused her to stumble to the stone floor with a scream.

The woman laughed. "You've got real spirit—I'll give you that."

Jeanette looked down to see a barbed dart protruding from her left thigh. Warm blood ran down her leg. She tried desperately to ignore the pain and stand, but her left leg refused to bear her weight. She continued forward, crawling as best she could, wincing at the pain.

"I can't wait till we can be friends. I like you already," the woman said as she approached from behind.

An unusually powerful arm lifted Jeanette up under her shoulder, causing a spike in pain as her leg stretched out under her. Her body reacted with an unconscious gasp of agony.

"Are you going to wise up and follow me now? Or do I need to drag you around like an animal?"

Tears fell from Jeanette's eyes. "I'll . . . I'll follow . . ."

"Good."

The woman, supporting Jeanette's weight with one arm, reached down with the other and yanked the dart from Jeanette's thigh, taking a small chunk of soft tissue with it. Jeanette screamed as blood gushed from the wound.

After placing the dart on her hip, the woman held out a small glass vial containing a few teaspoons of red liquid. She popped off the plastic lid, which swung on a hinge. "Here. Drink this."

Jeanette couldn't concentrate with the intense pain, so she took the vial without question and downed its contents. The smooth liquid evoked a pleasant taste that resembled strawberries, and as soon as it began traveling down her throat, the pain eased. After only a few seconds, the pain was nonexistent. Jeanette stared at her leg in amazement as the tissue began repairing itself rapidly. After only moments, it was back to its normal healthy state.

The woman laughed. "Your face is priceless. Come on, follow me. And don't run again, or I'm going to drag you down these halls. Neither of us wants that."

Jeanette nodded.

She walked behind the strange woman in silence through the halls of the old castle. The smell of stale meat hung in the air. Small bits of plaster and wainscoting lining a few sparse corners of the ancient hallways, along with the occasional isolated flake of paint, were all that remained of its former vivacity. All Jeanette could see now was cold gray stone. They passed only two other men, who both catcalled her. She was far too exposed.

Eventually, the woman opened a door to a small bare room, and Jeanette followed her inside. A man sat in a single wooden chair, gagged, with his hands bound behind the back of the seat. He looked up as they entered.

The woman turned to Jeanette. "All right, here's your gift," she said, gesturing to the man. "He's a murdering thief with little brains. Kill him, and we'll get you some proper clothing and a hot meal. Decline," she said, and a horrid, telling smirk crossed her face, "and I get to have my way with you."

The woman pulled a dagger from her studded belt and held the blade with the tips of her slender fingers, offering the hilt to Jeanette.

Jeanette stared numbly, her mind a blur with questions. Why? Why did they want her to be an executioner? The thought of having proper clothing was immensely enticing, and her stomach growled at the thought of a decent meal.

"Why?" Jeanette asked.

"Why does it matter? He's an evil man. He deserves to die, and we want *you* to do it."

Uneasiness gripped Jeanette. Something about this situation was terribly wrong. These people were all horrible and devoid of a conscience. They couldn't seriously be condemning this man.

A hot meal, though.

And clothing.

Jeanette couldn't deny that it was an enticing offer.

Amy's voice entered the back of her mind. *"This is wrong. Don't do it."*

"No," Jeanette said, not allowing herself another moment of consideration.

She expected the woman to get angry, but to her surprise—and dread—the woman simply smirked.

"I was hoping you'd say that. Sure you don't want to change your mind?" She waved the dagger around.

Jeanette couldn't speak. Her heart throbbed in her ears. *Amy, she's going to do something terrible to me. What can I do? I don't have a choice!*

"You always *have a choice. Stick to your principles. Don't let them win. You still have control of your actions. Don't let them take that from you."*

"Last chance," the woman said. "Will you kill him?"

Jeanette mustered her resolve. "No."

"Excellent!" The woman tossed the dagger effortlessly with the tips of her fingers. It flipped through the air and pierced the man's chest, and he let out a few muffled cries of pain before going limp in the chair.

Jeanette reflexively backed away as the woman approached her with a mischievous grin. She unfastened her cloak, letting it fall to the floor.

"Let's have some fun."

Chapter 14

Breakfast

Tovas Qillion awoke with calm excitement.

It was finally the day. The day he would begin his journey as a Sorcerer.

He pulled himself off the bed to the hard floor, then dropped to his knees. He placed his hands on top of his head, which he bowed in reverence.

Divine above, please hear my prayer. Help me be sensitive to the teachings of the Masters. Please help me learn quickly so that I may serve Thee well. I thank Thee for this incredible opportunity. For Life, Agency, and Virtue. Amen.

Tovas stood and looked around. The other studies were still asleep in their small quarters of the southwest tower. He expected the morning bell to ring soon, as they were told it would during initiation, but he should have some time to himself before then. The wooden bed frame creaked slightly as he returned to sit on the mattress. He crossed his legs, placed his hands on his knees, and closed his eyes in an attempt to clear his mind.

Sounds became more pronounced. He could hear the slow breaths of his five roommates, including his brother, Scheln. The giant Mondrovian, Vurkil, snored. Tovas focused on his own breath, slowing it deliberately.

He attempted to filter the sensation of sound from his mind, becoming more aware of the feel of the sleepwear under his hands and the bed sheets under his feet. Removing those from his conscious perception, he attempted to bring his mind and body into tranquility.

Peace absorbed his being for several minutes.

Over time, he noticed a delicate sensation. It felt similar to his experience in the Room of Selection—though far more subtle. The impression was distinct from the sensations of his usual daily meditations.

Tovas felt more aware of his own body and the surrounding room, almost as if he were external to it all. His heart pumped. Blood flowed through his vessels. Lungs rhythmically expanded and contracted. He could likewise sense the room as if he were immersed in it. Air. Sheets. Pillow. Bed frame. Stone floor. Window. Bookshelf. He felt them—not physically, but as a sequence of fleeting emotions.

The other occupied beds and the air around them felt dark. Absent. He couldn't sense them. It gave the impression of fuzzy holes in his perception of the room.

The morning bells rang, disrupting his concentration. Tovas opened his eyes as the others began stirring in their beds.

"Rudding bells," Vurkil exclaimed, pulling his enormous form into a sitting position.

The doubtful one, Samuel, sat up as well and rubbed his eyes. Fitale, the Helenestian, stirred awake but remained supine. Tall, dark, and lanky Ya'ir sat up and stretched.

Tovas rose from the bed and walked to his brother, whose eyes were open.

"Lively morning, Scheln. I hope you slept well," Tovas said, standing over his twin. "Ready for breakfast?"

Scheln blinked twice—their signal for yes.

"Breakfast sounds grand. How do we get there again?" Vurkil asked in his low, booming voice.

Tovas moved the wheelchair into position next to Scheln's bed. "I think I remember. Give me a moment to get Scheln up and we can go together."

"Any way I can help?" Ya'ir asked as he rose from his bed.

"I could use help to get him into his wheelchair," Tovas replied. "Just a moment."

Tovas pushed on the wheelchair, ensuring that the locks were engaged.

"I'm happy to help as well," Samuel said.

"Thank you, Samuel, but two sets of hands will be more than enough," Tovas said as he inspected Scheln's waste containers before attaching them to hooks on the wheelchair.

"Just 'Sam' is fine."

Tovas looked up and nodded at Sam from his crouched position. Fitale stood from his bed and left the room.

"Don't we need to get dressed?" Sam asked.

"No. They said it is customary to remain in our sleepwear for breakfast," Tovas said. "We will change afterwards."

"Oh, right," Sam said.

Ya'ir approached. "Can he . . . hear us?"

"Yes, his sense of hearing is intact. He just can't move anything except his eyes and eyelids," Tovas replied, standing up and moving around the bed. "I'll lift him out of the bed. All I need you to do is to hold his head up as I get him into the wheelchair."

Ya'ir nodded.

Tovas crouched, sliding his arms under Scheln's thin frame and lifting him up. Ya'ir placed his hands under Scheln's head and held it straight as Tovas transferred his brother slowly to the chair.

"Thanks, Ya'ir."

"Of course," he replied with a kind smile.

"Are you comfortable?" Tovas asked his brother.

Scheln blinked twice.

"Does he communicate somehow?" Sam asked.

"Yes, though not with words, of course." Tovas moved Scheln's equipment to the wheelchair and unlocked the wheels. "He uses eye movements and blinking. Two quick blinks show yes, and three show no."

"Interesting," Sam said. "Can he communicate anything other than yes and no?"

"Let's head to the lav, then we can go down to breakfast," Tovas said.

"'Bout time," Vurkil said, standing up.

Tovas wheeled his brother toward the door, the others following closely behind. As he was about to answer Sam's question, Sam himself spoke up.

"Cut him some slack, Vurkil. He was helping his brother. Didn't you get enough to eat last night?"

"Last night was a puny feast for a Mondrovian," Vurkil replied. "We will often eat whole kexlow for a meal!"

Sam shrugged. "I don't know what a kexlow is, but I'm surprised you haven't eaten all the planet's animals into extinction if your people's appetites are anything like yours."

Vurkil gave a hearty laugh as they entered the smoothly descending tower hallway. "In Mondro we are careful to protect our animals. They breed almost as much as we do!"

The hallway wrapped around the stacked rooms of the men's dormitories, declining gracefully as they walked counter-clockwise about the tower interior. Near the base of the tower sat the lavatory, which they stopped at briefly. They didn't run into Fitale, so Tovas concluded that the man must have already gone to breakfast.

As he led them down the hall toward the lunchroom, he recalled Sam's question. "Oh, Sam, about your question earlier: Yes, Scheln can communicate more than yes and no, but the other signals are subtler and more difficult to read."

Sam nodded.

They stopped briefly at the healers' room to drop Scheln off with them. They would feed him his breakfast, dress him, and bring him to the Land room before the course started. Tovas was grateful for their compassionate treatment of his brother. They didn't have all the amenities that were available in Sovereignty hospitals, but their care should be sufficient for their needs.

As they walked down the ornate hallway of the main castle structure, the sounds of chatter and clanking silverware reached them, accompanied by scents of cooked vegetables and spices. Vurkil raced ahead and disappeared into the large doors.

Ya'ir moved in front to hold the door open for Tovas and Sam.

"Thank you," Tovas said.

Ya'ir nodded at them with a slight smile.

Other studies were chatting animatedly at various tables as Tovas entered the lunchroom. To his left were long buffet tables with various food items.

They grabbed plates and filled them with dishes from the buffet. Tovas noted Vurkil and Fitale seated across from each other at one of the long wooden tables. Fitale sat next to his sister, Kulavere, with a curly brown-haired girl from their group next to her. The four other women from their group sat next to Vurkil, who was devouring his two plates of food. Everyone wore identical white sleepwear with silver embellishments.

Sam and Ya'ir settled into seats on the free side of Vurkil, while Tovas sat next to Fitale.

"So, how did you ladies sleep?" Ya'ir asked.

Talanna, the black-skinned woman with stark white hair, leaned forward in an attempt to look past Vurkil's enormous body. "I slept okay. Our room was suuuper cold last night, though."

The other women nodded.

"So cold. My hands are still like ice!" the dark-haired girl, Niu, said from her seat next to the giant.

She reached over and touched Vurkil's forearm. He flinched and recoiled immediately, dropping the pastry he was eating into his lap.

"Oy!" he exclaimed as laughter erupted around him. "Rudding woman! Don't touch me with 'em icicle fingers!"

They continued laughing as he picked up the pastry from his lap and stuffed it into his mouth.

"What does that mean, anyway?" Ya'ir asked. "I've never heard it before. 'Rudding,' I mean."

"Ah." Vurkil's low voice was muffled by his food. "'s a Mondrovian word for kexlow feces. We use it profanely." He seemed proud of the fact.

"You have a word for a specific animal's *feces*?" Talanna asked, arching an eyebrow.

Vurkil took a bite of meat and spoke with his mouth full. "'s a special animal, this kexlow. Very tasty. Raising 'em is an enormous industry in Mondro."

"Something tells me *everything* is enormous in Mondro," Talanna retorted, inciting another round of laughter at the table.

"Yes, yes!" Vurkil said through his chuckles. "Everything is large in Mondro. We are proud of our heritage!" He raised an arm into the air emphatically.

"I'm fascinated by your brawls," the girl with curly brown hair said. As everyone's eyes focused on her, she turned a bright shade of red and shrank into her seat. Tovas made a mental note to ask for her name later. He couldn't remember it.

Vurkil's voice came out muffled as he shoved another entire pastry into his mouth. "Yes! The Mondro brawls are an old tradition. Every Mondro is encouraged to compete when they come of age."

As he spoke, a fleck of pastry shot from his mouth onto Kulavere's plate across from him. She looked at it in disgust and set her fork down.

Fitale, her brother, slammed his fist onto the table. "Stop talking with your mouth full, you oaf!"

Silence ensued as Vurkil looked down at Fitale in bewilderment.

Fitale pointed emphatically at Kulavere's plate. "You spat into my sister's food!"

Vurkil's expression calmed, and he shrugged. "Oh. Was not intentional."

"Aren't you going to apologize?" Fitale's volume rose, drawing gazes from other tables in the lunchroom.

Vurkil appeared genuinely surprised at the outburst, and he swallowed his pastry. "I don't understand. Food is still good. What's wrong?"

Tovas put an arm on Fitale's shoulder. "Fitale, I don't think he —"

Fitale pushed his plate out of the way and leapt onto the table with frightening speed, sliding forward on one knee. Gasps rang out as he grabbed the large man's sleepwear shirt. "Why don't we have a brawl right here?"

Vurkil laughed. "You speak large for a small man. You cannot challenge me."

"You will withdraw, *oaf*? I thought you had more pride than that!"

Vurkil's demeanor remained calm but turned serious. "Fine, Fita. You want to spend your first day at Tercast in the medical ward? Your choice."

"Please don't—"

Tovas's words were lost as Vurkil grabbed the smaller man around the waist with a massive hand and tossed him almost effortlessly over his shoulder into the clearing between the buffet and long dining tables. Fitale rolled and righted himself dexterously. Tovas looked around, but there were no Masters in sight, just other studies staring wide-eyed at the scene.

Vurkil turned and walked toward Fitale, who ripped off his loose sleepwear shirt, revealing an impressively muscular body. A woman nearby yelped in surprise.

Ya'ir stood. "Uh, I'll go get someone." He bolted into the hallway.

Tovas and the others stood as well, moving around the tables to get a better look at the contestants, some whispering excitedly. He wanted to stop them before someone got hurt, but he was in no position of authority over these men. They had no reason to listen to him.

As the giant approached, Fitale spun into a crouch, sweeping his leg forward powerfully. It caught the larger man off guard. He stumbled to the ground, evoking a resounding *ooh* from the surrounding studies. Fitale leapt forward onto Vurkil and attempted to pin him down from a side angle. The giant grabbed the smaller man's arm and pried it off him with an annoyed look. Fitale tried desperately to loosen Vurkil's grip around his arm, but all attempts to free himself failed.

Tovas glanced over at Kulavere, who brought a hand to her forehead with a sigh, betraying little concern for her brother.

Fitale punched at the giant's torso, with no apparent effect. Vurkil lifted the smaller man over his head. An expression of frustrated determination peeked through Fitale's long golden hair as he continued to struggle. Gasps and whispers rolled from the crowd.

Vurkil knelt down, dropping Fitale to the floor and pinning his chest with a powerful arm.

"Give up yet, blondie?" his booming voice rang.

Fitale failed to gain any leverage in his efforts but maintained a remarkable degree of fierce determination.

The doors at the end of the room burst open, drawing everyone's eyes. A woman in Masters' robes stood in the doorway, an expression of surprise and indignation on her wrinkled face. Ya'ir stood behind her.

"Stop this at once!" she yelled.

Vurkil rose slowly, turned toward the old woman, and pointed at Fitale. "He started it."

Fitale stood quickly with a furrowed brow, muscles rippling across his dark chest.

"Put your shirt on!" the woman commanded. "Both of you are coming with me."

The Mondrovian shrugged, while Fitale complied with a stoic expression. They followed the woman out as everyone else returned to their breakfast, chatting eagerly about the fight.

Tovas sighed. *Those two are going to be trouble.*

Chapter 15

Vitalization

As Tovas entered the well-lit classroom, he looked around. Large brown-and-yellow-themed paintings of desert landscapes, magnificent cliff sides, stunning mountains, and deep caverns made the walls come to life. Tables with two seats each stood in two rows of three, for a total of six tables in the room. The two in the center lay parallel with the room, while the tables on either side slanted inward to face the podium at the front.

Their group mascot, the ulinko, was already curled up on the floor in the front corner. Tovas wondered where the animal slept.

One girl occupied a seat on the opposite side near the back—the girl with curly brown hair. As it was still several minutes before class began, he had expected to be the first one here. Deciding this was as good a time as ever to ask the girl's name, he approached her. She was deeply absorbed in a book, leaning back with it propped against the edge of the desk on her lap. Light freckles graced her round face. Her thin, unembellished lips were pursed in concentration.

She looked up at him with surprise, followed by fear as he approached.

"Hi," he said. "Sorry to bother you. Is it all right if I sit here?"

Her cheeks reddened, but she nodded and turned quickly back toward her book. He felt slightly guilty for disrupting her, but he hoped he could help her feel more at ease.

"I'm Tovas," he said.

"I . . . I know," she replied.

"Forgive me. I didn't catch your name yesterday. May I ask what it is?"

She blushed again, refusing to look away from her book, though clearly not reading. "It's Roseliavelirosara Zedi-Taron, but you can call me Rose." She paused before her first and last name, making the separation clear.

Yes—now he remembered. She had been on the other side of the room from him during their commencement.

He smiled. "It's wonderful to meet you, Rose."

She glanced at him briefly before returning her gaze to her book. At that moment, Tovas noticed that her deep-green eyes had intriguing flecks of purple around the iris. He decided he'd try initiating conversation once more, then leave her alone if she was still uninterested in talking.

"May I ask what you're reading?"

She closed the book over her thumb and showed him the front cover. *Hearts of Adelaide,* it read. The dark green cover depicted an outline of a man and woman hugging on the edge of a cliff. "I found it in the library last night."

The topic seemed to ease her demeanor and spark her interest, so he pursued it. "Interesting. What is it about?" he asked.

She turned toward him. "A surgeon gets pulled into a conflict between the leaders of two interstellar corporations. She falls in love with one of them. I haven't gotten very far yet, but it's okay. The author knows *nothing* about biology, though."

"What do you mean?"

"She just does things that make little sense—the surgeon, I mean. She electrocuted a patient's heart after it stopped beating!" Rose closed her fist and gritted her teeth. "Electrically stimulating an asystolic heart does almost nothing." She sighed. "Also, one character drinks a ton of sea water to survive in a desert environment. Drinking salt water just dehydrates you more, because it prevents reabsorption of water in each renal loop. The man shouldn't have survived a *day*."

Tovas stared at her, amazed at her sudden verbose outburst and apparent medical knowledge. Self-consciousness seemed to catch up to her as her cheeks flared a bright red.

"I'm not familiar with a few of those words," Tovas said with a slight laugh. "You have medical training?"

"Well . . ." She started fidgeting with her hands, clearly uncomfortable about the subject. "Yes . . . I was going to be a physician, but—"

The door to the room burst open with a loud squeak, cutting Rose off. Tovas turned around to see Talanna, Niu, and the girl with blue skin and short black hair—he couldn't remember her name. Bubbly chatter accompanied their entrance, and they selected seats at the front, pulling an extra one from a nearby table so they could sit together.

Tovas turned back to Rose, who had returned to her book. It seemed he'd inadvertently touched on a sensitive subject, so he thought it wise to leave her alone for now. He admired the quality artwork around the room instead, wondering where the locations were. Or if they even existed at all.

Sam and Ya'ir entered soon afterward wearing their robes. *Good, they remembered how to get here.* A healer wheeled Scheln into the room a minute or two later, and he had also been dressed in his robes. She parked him in the back corner near the door and then left.

"He's your brother, right?" Rose asked.

"Yes."

Her eyebrows scrunched up as she considered Scheln for a moment. Her gaze settled back on Tovas and she took a breath to speak, but seemed to think better of it, exhaling her thoughts as she focused on her novel again.

"You are interested to know what happened to him?" Tovas asked.

She nodded, turning back to him and blushing slightly.

"It's fine. I don't mind talking about it," Tovas replied, turning to look at his brother. "He was injured as we were evacuating our home a few years ago. It caused serious damage to his brain stem, resulting in what they call pseudocoma." He glanced at Rose, who looked at Scheln with a thoughtful expression. "The Masters told us that the condition should correct itself in time as his Sorcery strengthens."

Rose looked at him with wide eyes. "Really?"

He shrugged. "That's what they said."

The door squeaked open once more. Tovas glanced at Kulavere, who stood in the doorway for a split second before seating herself alone at the back table next to the one Tovas and Rose occupied.

"Why were you evacuating?" Rose asked, her gaze on Scheln.

The memory of that night caused emotion to swell within Tovas, which made it difficult to speak. He banished the painful images from his mind, attempting to consider the event more objectively.

"Oblivion attack."

She gasped and watched him with concern. "You were on Louron during the Oblivion attack?"

Tovas nodded.

"Destroyer of Worlds, they call it," Rose said. "And the Sovereignty still doesn't know who's behind the attacks, right?"

He nodded again. "Still under investigation, as far as I know."

"It's amazing you got out alive. I heard there are rarely any surv—Oh. I'm so sorry. I didn't mean to . . ."

Tovas realized that his expression must have turned sorrowful. He forced a smile. "Don't apologize. You're right. We are tremendously blessed to be alive." His smile faded. "It's just that . . . most of our family didn't make it."

She gave him a pitiful expression as chatter echoed around them. "I'm . . . so sorry."

The door opened again as their short, plump co-study Zelyra

walked in, followed almost immediately by Master Azeloram. He carried a bucket.

"Lively morning, class," the Master said as he approached the table in the back of the room near the door, where Sam and Ya'ir sat. "I trust you all slept well? You're going to become well acquainted with your beds this week."

That's a curious thing to say.

As the old man raised his hand over the bucket, a handful of sand, a single fist-sized rock, and a small glass bowl rose from the bucket and fell gently onto the table by an invisible force. Sam and Ya'ir stared at the objects—Ya'ir with delighted astonishment and Sam with scrutiny.

The Master made his way to each of the desks, moving the sand, a single rock, and a small bowl to each desk with a wave of his hand as he walked by. The three chatting girls quieted down as he finally made his way to their desk, and they gasped as the rock and sand floated onto the center of their table.

"Now, each of you will have assigned seats. Rose and Relon will be here." He gestured to the desk at the front-left side of the room, where the three women sat. "Tovas and Samuel will sit here." He pointed to the front desk in the center. "Talanna and Niu—"

The door burst open, cutting off Master Azeloram's words. Vurkil and Fitale strolled in, each of them laughing boisterously. Vurkil's low, powerful voice reverberated against the walls. They seemed to have gotten over their dislike for each other rather quickly.

"Talanna and Niu will sit here," the old man continued, nodding to the front-right table. The two seemed cheerful at the announcement. "Fitale and Ya'ir will sit in the back corner." He motioned to the table where Ya'ir sat already with Sam. "Kulavere and Zelyra will sit at the back-center table, and Vurkil and Scheln will sit at the last table at the other back corner." He waved his hand toward the area. "Please move to your assigned seats now."

Chairs scraped against the floor as most people moved about. Tovas stood and smiled at Rose. "It was a pleasure to meet you, Rose."

She gave him a slight smile back. "You too."

Tovas moved Scheln to his table at the back before making his way to his seat at the front next to Sam.

As the rest of the studies settled into their seats, Master Azeloram addressed them. "Welcome to your first instruction in Land Sorcery! As explained yesterday, we take a very hands-on approach to your Sorcery instruction. Though we will occasionally provide some historical and philosophical teachings, your classes will primarily comprise tasks for you to complete. Your first task is simple: Move the sand into the bowl without touching it."

He paused, a wide mischievous grin pressing the wrinkles up against his eyes. The silence continued to settle as he looked around at them, smiling awkwardly. Someone coughed in the back of the room.

Sam raised his hand.

"Yes, Samuel?"

"To be clear, you want us to move this with our mind?" he asked.

The old man's smile broadened. "No!" he declared, raising a finger dramatically. "I want you to move it with your *soul!*"

Tovas glanced over at Sam and nearly laughed at the look of irritation on his face.

"How do we do this?" Vurkil called from the back.

Master Azeloram raised his finger again. "Ah! An excellent question." He began pacing across the front of the room, bursting with energy. "How does a Source touch the material world? Alas, we do not fully understand this phenomenon. I'm afraid I cannot answer your question, because I do not know the answer."

"But you can do it somehow. You must know how it happens!" Talanna exclaimed.

The man turned and walked toward the other end of the room, his gaze settling on the woman. "Do *you* know precisely how you control the movement of your hands?"

Talanna inspected her right hand. She flexed her fingers for a moment before turning her head back up to address their instructor. "Well . . . I know it has something to do with nerves and muscles, but not all the details."

Tovas smiled to himself as he glanced at Rose. There was at least one person in the room who probably *did* have a pretty good understanding of the details.

Master Azeloram continued pacing past the podium at the center of the room. "It is the same with Sorcery. I can perform the act without understanding the mechanism."

"How do we learn how to do it?" Kulavere asked from behind.

"Aha!" The old man clapped his hands together. "Now *that* is the question of the day!" He pivoted on his heel and began pacing the opposite direction again. "The answer is quite simple, though difficult to master. Does anyone have a guess?"

Tovas thought back to his meditation that morning. The way he could feel the room in a strange way, as his mind was at peace.

"Serenity," Tovas said.

The Master stopped suddenly and looked down at Tovas with a curious expression. "Hmm, yes. Meditation may aid in your spiritual connection to the Elements, but there is one other principle which is even more important." He looked directly at Sam. "That principle is *faith*."

Silence settled again as Master Azeloram returned to his position behind the podium.

"You now have all the general instruction I can give for your task," he said. "Discuss the principles of faith with your fellow study at your table. When you're ready, stretch your hand toward the sand and move the Elements with your Source. With faith, you can do it, as long as it is within the will of the Divine."

Some of the other studies began conversing almost immediately. The Master walked to the table where Rose and Relon were seated and began talking to them individually about the task. Tovas turned to look at Scheln, whose head had fallen to the side. Drool dripped from his mouth. Vurkil sat next to him with his arms crossed, looking at the sand as if staring down a bitter enemy.

Tovas stood and walked to his brother. He straightened Scheln's head to ease the strain on his neck as Vurkil watched.

"Hey, Scheln. Is that better?" Tovas asked.

His brother blinked twice in reply.

"How do you think we do this, eh?" Vurkil said.

Tovas shrugged. "I don't know. I suppose we just need to get a feel for it."

The giant frowned. Tovas rotated on his heel and returned to his seat. He glanced at Sam, who looked back at him with raised eyebrows.

"This doesn't make any sense," Sam said.

"The works of the Divine are mysterious. Perhaps they're beyond our ability to comprehend," Tovas replied.

"You really believe all that nonsense? God almost definitely doesn't exist."

Tovas gave Sam a quizzical look. "What is God?"

"Oh, you don't use that word? Interesting. Just another word for the Divine, I guess."

"You don't believe in the Divine?"

"Not anymore. I grew up being taught to believe, by my parents and religious leaders. I've learned better now."

Tovas looked into Sam's dark brown eyes, gauging his conviction. It seemed firm. This man's skepticism and disbelief ran deep. Tovas felt a sense of pity for him.

"You can prove that the Divine does not exist?" Tovas asked.

Sam rolled his eyes. "It's impossible to *disprove* the existence of something supernatural like that. But just because I can't logically disprove it doesn't make it true. The burden of proof lies with the person making the claim."

Tovas considered his words for a moment and concluded that it was a legitimate argument. "Valid point. However, doesn't the nature and organization of the universe suggest that life and existence were intelligently designed?"

Sam crossed his arms, looking confident as he shook his head. "No. Not really. Even considering the fact that several planets are inhabitable, the vast majority of the universe is very ill-designed for life. This is not the universe we would expect to see if it were intelligently designed specifically for us. The idea that life arises by chance seems more consistent with nature."

His words sounded rehearsed. Tovas suspected that Sam had experience with this kind of discussion.

"What of the fact that humans are the only known intelligent form of life in the universe?" Tovas asked. "Does that not contradict your argument that life arose by chance?"

Sam appeared surprised by the question. He pondered for several seconds before responding. "Well, even though that's a surprising fact, there are other explanations. It may have been caused by another advanced alien race, for example."

Tovas smiled. "I believe you just replaced 'the Divine' with 'alien race' and made an argument for intelligent design."

Sam unfolded his arms and leaned in with a determined expression. "No, I didn't. All I said—"

"And how are things progressing here?" Master Azeloram asked as he walked up to their table.

The two looked at each other for a moment before Tovas turned his attention back to the Master. "We were discussing Tercast theology."

"Excellent!" the old man exclaimed. "Carry on." The Master moved on to the next table, where Talanna and Niu were chatting animatedly.

Sam spoke as soon as their instructor was out of earshot. "Whatever. Anyway, 'with faith, you can do anything' is a pipe dream. The universe doesn't bend to our will like that."

"Even after seeing Master Azeloram control these Elements himself—several times now—you still don't believe it's possible?"

Sam's gaze turned to the rock, bowl, and sand in front of him, and he looked thoughtful. "Well, I admit that it seemed rather convincing. I still think it's possible that it's all deception in order to get us to believe them. But even if he really moved these things telekinetically, he himself admitted that he didn't comprehend the mechanism. Why are they so quick to assume a spiritual one?"

He really has a stunningly skeptical view of the universe. He has certainly given these ideas a lot of rational thought, however. Tovas decided that he had no sufficient logical argument to Sam's statement.

"Well, I choose to have faith unless there is good reason to doubt," Tovas finally said.

A disdainful *tsh* left Sam's lips. "You're just making it easier for others to manipulate you by thinking that way. Faith makes you gullible and powerless."

"We shall see," Tovas replied.

Silence settled between them. Discussions continued to occur around the room. Tovas closed his eyes, attempting to enter a state of meditation. He wanted to prove Sam wrong, but that motivation would be misguided, driven by an inherent sense of pride. It was important that he purge the desire to make himself seem superior. He needed to do this to help Sam understand. To believe. To liberate him from the burden of skepticism and that cynical disposition.

Tovas freed his thoughts and focused his mind, filtering the sounds of chatter and movement around him. After several minutes, the odd sensations returned—the feeling of fleeting emotions associated with substances around him. His body. Air. Chair. Floor. Table. Sand. The small glass bowl.

Sam's area was a large fuzzy hole in his perceptions, where nothing seemed to exist. He opened his eyes and attempted to maintain the fleeting sensations, but they faded as he did so.

Is that Sorcery? he thought.

He glanced at Sam, who returned a smirk. Desires to prove the man wrong rose again, but Tovas forced them down. He needed to be humble. He needed to focus.

Tovas closed his eyes once more. The sensations returned somewhat more quickly this time around, as if they were at his fingertips. Emotions passed through him again. Chair. Air. Table. Sand. He tried desperately to focus on the sand, to keep the emotion from flowing away.

Something fell into place in his mind—like a leaf in the wind settling gracefully onto a lake.

He felt a connection. A single grain of sand. He sensed the pull of gravity on it, the pressure it felt against the other grains around it. Tovas opened his eyes. Focusing intently on that connection, he stretched out his hand.

Rise, he told it. The grain didn't move. *Rise.* It refused his command again, remaining stationary.

Perhaps it wasn't about thought. Master Azeloram said that it wasn't from the mind. It was from the soul. Their Source.

He imagined the grain rising. Overcoming gravity by its own force. Freeing itself from the constraints of the physical world. He imagined the feel of it passing through the air, no longer pressing against its neighbors.

Exhilaration filled him as he *felt* it rise, even before he saw it. The grain separated itself from the rest of the sand and rose into the air. He imagined and then felt it change direction and move toward the bowl. As he pictured the grain allowing itself to be constrained by gravity once more, it fell, making an almost inaudible *clink* as it struck the glass bottom. Tovas released his focus and severed the connection.

He looked over at Sam, who stared wide-eyed at the small bowl. With his jaw hanging open in astonishment, Sam turned toward him.

Tovas smiled before repeating the procedure. As the sensations returned, he attempted to grasp more of them that felt like sand. Most of them slipped through—like trying to hold water in his palm. He stretched his fingers toward the table again, imagining, and then feeling the granules rise as they defied gravity.

By his thoughts, the cluster floated toward the bowl, each grain moving at different rates. They collected into a tiny ball over the glass, and Tovas let them go. They fell, spreading across the bottom of the bowl.

Tovas unexpectedly felt tired—extremely tired.

"I don't want to believe it, but Tovas has done it!" Sam shouted.

Excited gasps and replies of "What?" and "Really?" echoed across the room as the other studies raced over and surrounded their table. Tovas looked around at them, embarrassment at the attention overshadowed by his sudden fatigue.

Master Azeloram approached as well, looking astonished. "Incredible!" he exclaimed. "I've never seen someone perform the task so quickly!"

"Show us, show us!" Talanna said.

Tovas caught Rose's gaze as she joined the group. Her green eyes stared at him with interest.

He closed his eyes once more and attempted to reenter his meditative state. It was far more difficult—despite the silence—with everyone hovering over him. Weariness threatened to overcome him. He just wanted to sleep. Eventually, he found his inner peace, the fleeting emotions of the space around him passing through his perception. This time the table was surrounded by fuzzy emptiness where the others stood.

He established a connection to just a few grains—less than his previous attempt. He opened his eyes, stretching his hand out toward the sand. Hardly a sound could be heard as everyone stared in anticipation.

As before, a few grains of sand floated into the air against the force of gravity.

Gasps arose from the crowd. Talanna covered her mouth with her hand.

Following his imagination, the sand moved to a single point over the glass again, where he released the Elements to be bound by the natural world once more. They cascaded onto the other grains present there, spreading across the bowl.

Several of the others clapped as exhaustion crashed into Tovas.

Master Azeloram looked at him with a wide smile and a twinkle in his eye.

Tovas found it immensely difficult to concentrate. With resolve, he turned to Sam, who continued to wear his look of disbelief.

"Still believe faith is powerless?" Tovas asked wearily.

Before Sam could respond, Tovas collapsed against the back of his chair, unable to keep his eyes open a moment longer.

Chapter 16

Chipper and Sunset

"Now, does anyone know any of the major trade hubs in the Sovereignty?" the instructor asked.

The class was silent for a few moments, until someone spoke up from the back of the room.

"Is . . . uh . . . Jitavan one of them?" a girl said.

"Yes, very good," Tecsa said. "Jitavan was one of the earliest trade hubs in the Sovereignty and, because of its location, has grown into the largest point of commerce in the known universe." Her footwear clapped against the hard floor of the classroom as she paced around the front. "Other notable trade hubs are Invalo, Tenrazka, and Loeh."

The woman paused for a few seconds. "Are there any last questions on Sovereignty economics?"

Finally, Kara thought. *Instruction will finally be over today.* She felt tired. Not nearly as tired as the previous day, but weary still. Keeping herself awake through the entire day of lectures on Sovereignty economics had been marginally easier than the government lecture, due to the time change coming from Alvior. *If someone asks a question, I might strangle them.*

"Excellent," Tecsa said. "I will be around for a few minutes if anyone would like to speak to me directly. Tomorrow we will discuss the rights and responsibilities of citizens. Enjoy your evening."

Kara got up from her seat as chatter built around the room.

"Hey, are you doing anything tonight?" Nikor asked from beside her.

Kara let out a sigh. "You really don't know when to give up, do you."

"Nah. Not in my blood."

She extended her cane. "Oh, so is your family just as tactless as you are, or is it only the stubbornness that's hereditary?"

He laughed. "Wow, you are brutal!"

She turned toward him. "Look, I—"

"I know, I know. I'm sorry for coming on to you like that yesterday," Nikor said. "I was just wondering if you'd like to go get something to eat, and then walk around the park and talk for a while. Unless you have other plans, of course."

Kara considered his words. He sounded genuine. What would she do otherwise? Sit around in her room? She didn't really have anything better to do, and the idea of getting some fresh air sounded amazing.

"Ok, fine," she conceded, "but this is *no* date. You put your arm around me or try to hold my hand or touch my butt or something, and I'm going to punch you in the face. Got it?"

He laughed again. "Got it."

She turned and walked toward the door. His steps came up beside her. "Nothing personal, you know," she said. "I've just been around guys who seem to think they can get away with really stupid things because I'm blind."

"That explains it."

Nikor stepped back to let Kara test the door frame with her cane before continuing, then caught up to her in the hallway. "So what do you think about the Sovereignty so far?"

Kara shrugged. "It's interesting. The government is compli-cated."

"Yeah, definitely. The three-part legislature is strange—but also elegant, I think."

She nodded as her cane bumped into the wall.

"The lift is over here," he said.

She made her way into the lift as the beep of a Jit sounded.

"Main floor," Nikor said.

The door closed with a quiet whoosh, and the elevator smoothly accelerated downward with no audible noise.

"It's interesting that the three sections of the legislature are selected in different ways," Kara said, racking her brain to recall this information, which would surely appear on the exam. "The first was the technical leaders by popular vote, the second was by random selection, and the third was . . . Shoot, what was the third one?"

"Delegation, I think," Nikor replied.

"Oh, right!" she exclaimed. "That was the one where citizens can either vote directly themselves or choose someone else to have their vote in a policy area, right?"

"Yeah, that sounds right."

The elevator slowed to a stop, and the door opened with another whoosh. "The tax system also seems to be pretty different," Kara said as they stepped through. "Way simpler than it was in my home country on Earth."

"It's different from Molkinar's as well," Nikor said. "What was it like on Earth?"

"Well, instead of an income tax where you can select the programs that get your support, our income tax was ridiculously complicated. My parents would always complain about how absurdly difficult it was to calculate how much you actually owed the government in taxes each ye—"

"Have a pleasant evening, Miss Jones and Mr. Bongar," the front desk AI said.

"Nothing would brighten my evening more than your absence, dust-for-brains," Kara said to it as they crossed the threshold to the outdoors. Warm air flowed across her skin with a gentle breeze.

Nikor laughed. "You have a problem with the attendant?"

"Stupid AI didn't help me much at all yesterday when I was trying to find the platform for my bag."

"What's an AI?"

"Artificial intelligence? Aren't there a ton of them around here?"

"Never heard them called that before. I think the usual term for them is 'synthetic personality' or a 'synth.'"

"Whatever. Same thing."

She stopped, listening to the surrounding noises. There was a whisper of vehicles overhead and of others chatting as they walked about nearby.

"So where are we going?" she asked.

"I found a park just a few minutes that way last night. It's beautiful. There's a great place to eat along the way. I was thinking we could walk around there for a while and enjoy the sunset."

"You *do* realize 'that way' tells me absolutely nothing, right?"

"Oh . . . uh . . . right. So it looks like it's west . . . mostly? Maybe a bit south?"

Those directions weren't much help either, but upon reflection, there probably wasn't a good way for him to give her a clear direction. The thought made her uncomfortable since she didn't know Nikor all that well, but having him lead her would be the most straightforward solution.

She sighed, collapsed her cane, and placed it into the pocket of her recently purchased pants. "All right, give me your elbow and you can lead me there."

"Wait, you're serious?" he asked.

"Don't get any funny ideas. This is just the most efficient way for us to get around," Kara explained, extending her hand.

Nikor placed his arm in her palm, and she lightly wrapped her hand around it. "I know what it is," he said in a playful tone. "You just couldn't resist the chance to feel my biceps."

She moved her fingers to grope his upper arm. It actually felt fairly thick and strong. She returned her hand to rest on his elbow. "Meh. Feels pretty pathetic to me."

He moved forward, taking her with him as he laughed. "You just can't stop crushing me, can you?"

"You asked for it."

"When I called you *pretty*?"

"When you said you were staring at me like a creep," she responded.

He paused. "Okay, fair enough."

Kara's thoughts turned to Jeanette as they walked in silence for a while. She wondered where her sister was. What might happen to her.

Whether she was still alive.

The thought brought latent anxiety to the surface within Kara. She needed to do something.

I am trying to do something, she reminded herself. *I'm going to join the Armed Forces and take the fight to her captors. I'll rescue her myself if I have to.*

Her parents almost certainly wouldn't have approved of this decision. They had believed in self-defense—it was why she grew up in the academy—but had never believed in aggressive violence, even against enemies. "All life is sacred," they would say. Well, Kara didn't share their idealism to that extreme, though she never confronted them openly about it. Some people were just terrible and deserved to die.

Kara longed for Sam's presence. A slight smile crossed her face as she considered what he might think of this decision to join the military. He'd probably lose it at first and then gradually come around to the idea. At least, that's what she hoped.

"So you mentioned your parents earlier when we talked about taxes. Did you leave them back on Earth?" Nikor's question broke through her thoughts.

"No. They were killed. That's why I'm here."

Nikor stopped, halting her with him. "Really? What happened?"

Kara paused as she attempted to suppress the rising grief. "I don't really know. They were killed by a man who kidnapped my sister. The Sovereignty has an open investigation but doesn't know where the killer went."

"Whoa . . ." Nikor's voice was sympathetic. "That's terrible."

A gust of wind punctuated the silence between them.

"I lost my family too," he said.

Kara's head perked up with interest. "You did?"

"Yeah. Are you familiar with the conflict on Enck?"

"No," she said.

"Well, that was my home planet. The values and intellectual liberties in the Sovereignty sounded good to me, but my family believed in Molkinar. I left them to join the rebellion on Enck. Just as the Sovereignty was gaining the upper hand, the Empire sent in an attack force. They evacuated a large portion of us refugees, but the planet was mostly destroyed." He sighed. "It's a surreal thing to see a large part of your home planet burning."

Not knowing what else to do, Kara reached forward and hugged him. Her face rested on his rather muscular chest. He smelled somewhat musky, but not foul. He embraced her in return before she finally pulled away.

"I think that's enough about our depressing situations," she said. "Let's get something to eat."

Nikor agreed and led her to a nearby place he called Yelly's. He said they had delicious chippers, which turned out to be something like a sandwich. The bread was flat and circular on top and bottom, and it had a rigid sticklike substance through the middle that held the contents together, which Nikor said was edible. The whole thing was about the size of a large burger and smelled somewhat strange, but it was not *too* unlike a sandwich.

They sat outside on a set of comfortable padded chairs, with a small glass table between them. Kara took a bite. The crust of the bready outer layers was firm, but the inside was remarkably soft and fluffy. There was a layer that tasted somewhat like beef, though less chewy. A thick, savory sauce lay between something thin and wavy and a few other soft substances. Small crunchy bits that reminded her of bacon were sprinkled throughout, and there was a very subtle taste resembling coconut.

She swallowed. "This is delicious! Kind of resembles a hamburger from my home planet, but better."

"I had my first one yesterday for lunch," Nikor said.

Kara covered her mouth while speaking through another bite of chipper. "You didn't take the meal they provided?"

"I wanted to get out and look around. This place is amazing."

Others walked about and chattered around them as Kara and Nikor finished their meal without discussion. The center piece that held the chipper together turned out to be just a larger piece of the crispy bacon-like substance. Having devoured her meal, Kara wiped her mouth with the provided napkin.

Nikor finally broke the silence. "Ready to walk around the park?"

"You're done?" she asked.

"Yeah, let's go."

Kara took Nikor's arm again as he led her further. The relative silence of such a clearly busy place amazed her. An urban location like this on Earth would be full of loud engines and people shouting over them. The ascenders were so quiet overhead. Young children ran by, taunting each other. An exasperated-sounding mother yelled after them to stop running and quiet down.

Soon Kara could hear tree leaves rustling in the wind above them as they walked. Couples were conversing nearby. It appeared they had reached the park.

This place is so different, and yet the people are so similar.

"It's so sad you can't see this," Nikor said.

"Describe it to me."

"Well, the trees overhead are a bright yellow and gold, with large spearhead leaves and thin, sleek trunks. The grass is a lush, shiny green along the sides of this white path we're on. The setting sun is a deep-red color on the horizon over the water. We have an amazing view of it here on the edge of the city."

Nikor's descriptive skills were certainly better than Sam's.

"It sounds beautiful," Kara said.

"It is."

They stopped, and there were many others chatting nearby. The residents must like to come for the vista as well.

"So what are your plans after becoming a citizen?" Nikor asked.

"I'm going to join the Armed Forces."

"*What?*" he exclaimed. "You want to enter the military?"

"Yep."

"Why in Fesda would you ever want to do *that*?"

"I'm going to do what I can to get my sister back."

"Kara, that's ridiculous!" he said. "You can't just join up and tell them 'I want to take out my sister's kidnapper'!"

"I know," she replied in a calm voice. "I may not get to choose where I serve, but they suspect it was Molkinar that took her. The Sovereignty is at war with them, so I can still do *something*."

"But . . . they're never going to let you join blind."

His words fell on her like a sledgehammer.

He was right. They might not let her join.

Panic rose in her chest. She had to know for sure.

Kara grabbed the Jit on her wrist and squeezed until it beeped. "Can blind people join the Sovereignty's Armed Forces?"

"Yes," the Jit responded, "in some roles."

"What about as a soldier?"

"No," it said. "The Armed Forces of the Sovereignty of Rwenmar do not permit individuals with significant physical limitations, including blindness, as soldiers. A level of visual capacity above a dek on the Riknalon scale is required."

Kara's heart sank. She should have known. Why hadn't she thought about this before?

"Well . . ." Nikor began, then stopped.

"Well, what?" she said.

"I know you seem to enjoy being blind for some reason, but you *could* probably get eyesight if you wanted to."

She faced downward, emotions swirling within her. She had *always* been blind, at least as far back as she could remember. Blindness was part of her. It was one of the most significant things that set her apart from most others. Memories of dear friends in the blind and low-vision community back on Earth came to her mind. She thought about Liam and how much she treasured their vision-related banter over the years. How could she give up such a key piece of her identity?

Curing the particular form of her condition was currently impossible on Earth, but she didn't doubt that the Sovereignty had some magical technology that could do it. She had the option now.

Some people on Earth would leap at the opportunity for improved vision. Liam probably would. Kara respected that, but it wasn't her. She was comfortable with her blindness. Sure, it had challenges in a world—universe—full of sighted people, but she *enjoyed* surmounting those challenges. At least, most of the time she did. That was who she was. Being able to see would change everything. How others perceived her. The way she interacted with people around her. The way she understood reality itself.

The thought of being sighted terrified her.

Then again, her life had already been upended. She was standing on an alien planet, strolling through a park with a man from another galaxy. Her life had already changed beyond recognition.

She took a deep breath, attempting to cool her racing thoughts. Regardless of how she felt, the options were clear: give up this key part of herself, or give up on her sister. When she thought of it that way, the decision was clear. She would do anything for Jeanette. Anything. She couldn't just sit by and wait for news of her sister's body to be found somewhere. She *had* to act.

"I'll do it," Kara said. "I'll get my sight."

Chapter 17

Potions

Sam scowled at the small glass vial on the table in front of him, which was filled with a red liquid. There was another next to it filled with a transparent liquid.

So far, he had failed to have any success with Sorcery. He could no longer deny that it was real. The blue-skinned girl, Relon, and the siblings Kula and Fita had managed to telekinetically move the sand after Tovas had passed out during their first day of instruction. Tovas was also the first to create a spark during their Air magic—*Air Sorcery,* he corrected himself—instruction the following day. Everyone who had success had passed out each time too. The Masters called in a team of nurses they referred to as healers, who carted the studies back to their quarters on some sort of gurney.

More than half the other studies had achieved success in creating a spark in their Air instruction—even Scheln. All of them had fallen asleep by the end of class. Less had achieved success with fire. Vurkil surprised everyone with a flaming match soon after Tovas's. Only two others had succeeded: Zelyra, the short, chubby woman, and Niu, the bubbly dark-haired woman.

So far, nearly everyone had attained some victory with Sorcery —everyone except Sam and Rose.

His table partners hadn't been much help. He'd sat with Scheln during the Air course and with Fita during Fire instruction. Scheln, of course, couldn't do anything except blink, and Fita refused to talk much at all. Sam had spent hours focusing on the tasks, which mostly comprised staring into space or at some object and willing in vain for *something* to happen.

He had little hope that today would be any different.

At least he had a more engaging table companion. Today he sat in the back-left corner of the room with Vurkil. If nothing else, the giant would at least provide him with some conversation while Sam failed to do the impossible.

Between long sessions of staring at things, Sam had read through *The Fundamentals of Tercast Theology* and spent some time in the library. Their theology was about what he would expect, with doctrine severely condemning murder, stealing, fornication, homosexuality, and, of course, experimenting with Sorcery without the oversight of a Master.

The book also contained an interesting section about those who left Tercast after their instruction. Apparently, all Adepts— graduates of the twelve-week learning period—would experience a rapid diminishing of their Sorcery if they decided to leave. The book, of course, attributed it to losing the "holiness" of Tercast. Regardless of the reason, it explained why Sovereignty society would doubt the rumors of the "castle of magic."

The castle library had little interesting material. Nearly all the books were religious texts of one kind or another, though they had some fiction as well. Rose frequently had her nose in a romance novel between classes.

"Lively morning," the woman said from behind the podium. Her light face was thin and wrinkled, with brown hair cut to only a few inches in length all around. She had completed putting two vials and a small knife in front of everyone in the room. "My name is Master Evalencia. Welcome to your first instruction in the ways of Water Sorcery."

The chatter in the room died.

"Water is the Element of life. All living things in the universe require its unique properties to surv—"

The ulinko at the front of the room yawned loudly as it stretched, cutting off the Master. Several studies laughed while Talanna and Niu uttered a simultaneous "aww." The creature trotted over to Zelyra. It seemed to have developed a particular affinity for her.

The Master smiled at it, then returned her gaze to the class. "Let's just dive in, shall we? Everyone, please take the knife in front of you."

Sam complied, curious about where this was going. Vurkil grabbed his knife as well. It looked like a tiny pocketknife in his enormous hands.

The old woman continued. "Now, please make a tiny cut in one of your fingers."

Talanna, unsurprisingly, spoke up. "You want us to *hurt* ourselves?"

"That is correct. Only a minor injury. After you have done so, please take a small sip from the vial of red liquid in front of you. Please do not drink all of it—a sip will do. Pay very close attention to your sensations as you do so."

Will it somehow heal the wound? Sam wondered with excitement.

He made a slight cut in the index finger of his left hand, ignoring the pain. After grabbing the vial, he popped open the lid, which swung on a tiny hinge attached to the glass. He sipped a small drop. It tasted pleasant, reminding him of strawberries. He swallowed and then examined his finger closely. A drop of blood oozed from the wound.

The pain in his finger quickly eased, then was no more. He stared awestruck as the cut in his skin closed, leaving the drop of blood on the healed surface. Did he just perform Sorcery?

Sam looked around to see others gaping at their hands as well.

"Rudds! It actually works!" Vurkil exclaimed.

Apparently satisfied with the studies' excited responses, the instructor continued with a smile. "As your Source gains power, your body will naturally heal more quickly. In time you will learn to heal yourself by Sorcery alone." She gestured outward toward the glass vials on the front table. "You will learn more about enchantments later on, but your task today is to copy this healing enchantment into the new vial filled with water. You must connect spiritually with the healing liquid—feel its afforded purpose, its intent, and its composition. Then connect with the water. Transmute it to match the divine purpose and composition of the other."

The Master placed her hands behind her back and stepped out from the podium. "Begin."

Sam's enthusiasm faded to irritation.

"Ugh, why can't they give useful instructions?" he mumbled. "It's all 'feel this' and 'feel that' and it will just work like magic."

Vurkil chuckled and shrugged. "Dunno, Sam. I think there isn't much else to instruct. It's spiritual, after all."

"Yeah, all that 'Spirit' junk doesn't make sense to me. How did you make the fire yesterday?"

The large man shrugged again. "Hard to describe. Just like they say: A feeling. A connection." He laughed. "Sounds strange when I say it out loud!"

Sam smiled. *At least he's self-aware enough to acknowledge how bizarre it seems.* "You don't think there could be another explanation that's not spiritual?"

Vurkil frowned for a moment. "A good question, I think. But these Masters have been studying a long time. They should know what they're talking about."

"Yeah, they should, but that doesn't mean that they actually do," Sam replied. "On my home planet, people still believe things for religious reasons that have absolutely no logical reason behind them."

A large hand reached forward and picked up the vial of red liquid. Vurkil studied it closely. "That is true in Mondro also, my friend. I think it is true everywhere." He turned to Sam. "But science is sometimes wrong too, is it not?"

"Well, depends on how you think about it," Sam said as Vurkil returned to studying the vial. Mr. Nowell's words rang in his mind. "Scientific *results* are never really wrong. They're just observations. But yes, the *interpretations* of those results can be wrong."

Vurkil turned back to him with intrigue. Being stared at by a giant who could probably tear him in half without breaking a sweat was inherently intimidating. "You are a scientist?"

"Well, not yet, but I want to be."

Vurkil let out a low chuckle. "This suits you, I think. You are a skeptic. Skeptics make good scientists."

"Well, thank—"

"But poor Sorcerers, apparently," he said, laughing as he turned back to study the vial.

So much for the compliment. Still, Sam couldn't argue with his words. He certainly seemed to be behind his peers with these bizarre supernatural powers.

Thinking about it returned Sam's agitation. He had always done well in school. Even in his worst subjects, he'd pulled off a decent grade. But if there were grades for Land, Air, and Fire Sorcery, he was positive he'd be failing right now.

At least he wasn't completely alone.

He leaned forward over the table and glanced past Vurkil toward Rose, seated at the center table next to theirs. She stared at her vial of potion with intensity. Clearly, she felt just as frustrated as he did about her own failure.

Sam leaned back in his chair. Only a few of the others remained talking, Talanna and Relon among them. Talanna was an almost nonstop chatterbox. He was surprised that she had stopped talking long enough to complete the Air task the other day. Relon, when she wasn't being caught between Talanna and Niu's conversations, was otherwise quiet and observant.

He sighed, folding his arms and letting his gaze wander about the room. Each of the four Elemental rooms was similarly laid out, but they differed drastically in color and theme to match the Element. Light blue walls and elaborate paintings of wildlife and oceans adorned the Water room. One of the larger pieces of art depicted a long, thin water creature. Sam thought it looked like a serpent with the head of a scaled fox. It emerged majestically from a crashing wave of bright blue water and stared right at the viewer.

Sam shook his head. He needed to focus on the task. *Copy a magic health potion. Right.*

He stared at the vial of red liquid, feeling stupid. Maybe he should try closing his eyes again. It seemed to work for Tovas.

He closed his eyes. Talanna was still talking animatedly with Relon. Niu was also talking with her partner, which Sam remembered was Kula. He tried to ignore them and focus on that liquid. It was on the table. Just a foot or so in front of him. He pictured it in his mind and the way it lay on its side, red liquid and air within. *Maybe—*

"Rose has done it!" Zelyra exclaimed, breaking his concentration.

Sam leaned forward to look around his enormous companion. Others turned about to do the same. The furry ulinko circled her desk, looking at Zelyra with a curious expression. Rose appeared exhausted, but she did indeed now have two vials of deep-red liquid on the table in front of her.

"Excellent!" the instructor said, making her way over to Rose and Zelyra. "That was extraordinarily quick."

Evalencia picked up the two vials and looked at them closely for a moment. "This is an excellent transmutation! You are destined for Water Sorcery."

Sam glanced at Tovas, who sat at the table in front of his own. The man had a giant stupid grin on his stupid face. For once, he wasn't the first to complete the task. Sam felt a sense of satisfaction at that.

Rose's eyes appeared dazed for a moment before her eyelids closed over them and her head slumped. She fell asleep.

"I will call in the healers for her," Evalencia said. "The rest of you, please continue working at your assignment."

Sam leaned back again, feeling even more distraught. Now he

was the only one who hadn't been able to perform any Sorcery. He let out a heavy sigh.

No, he couldn't go out like this during his first week here. He *needed* to get this.

Darkness ensued as Sam closed his eyes once more. He tried desperately to filter out the noise of chatter and the healers who had just arrived to wheel Rose out of the room. *Stop thinking,* he told himself. He needed to clear his mind.

A subtle, fleeting sensation flowed past his perception. A table. The table a few inches in front of him. *Was that Sorcery or just my mind playing around?*

"Tovas has done it!" Ya'ir yelled.

Sam opened his eyes and saw that, sure enough, there were now two vials of red liquid on the table in front of Tovas. He had a momentary urge to chuck one of his own vials at the man's head but restrained himself. Evalencia made her way over to congratulate him and give him a new task. This pattern would continue until the man passed out from exhaustion.

At that thought, Sam wondered again why there seemed to be such a strong connection between fatigue and Sorcery. If it was all "Spirit," as they claimed, and not even mental exertion, why would people get physically tired at all? It didn't make any sense.

He strained his mind to think of anything he might have read about the science of sleep and why it was needed. He remembered something about it being a mechanism to clean waste from the brain. Did Sorcery cause additional waste in the brain somehow? Perhaps the mechanism *was* mental, but they just called it spiritual because it fit their dogma better.

Whatever the mechanism, it appeared to require a meditative state—at least that was what he had observed from the others. The Masters all seemed to command the Elements easily while performing other tasks, but he suspected that was because of their experience. He needed to do it himself, if for no other reason than to find out how Sorcery worked.

He needed to know.

Sam took a deep breath and closed his eyes. Maybe he had to

try focusing on something rhythmic. He paid close attention to his breathing. In, out. In, out.

He slowed it. In. Out. In.

Several minutes of focused breathing later, he felt it again: a fleeting emotion of a desk. His mind craved to self-inspect his thoughts, but he quashed the impulse, regaining his focus on the breathing.

In.

Out.

In.

Out.

In.

Several emotions moved through him with clear localities. Chair. Table. Glass. Liquid.

As the feeling of the liquid passed by, he focused on it, and it remained with him. He felt a strange connection to it, just as Vurkil had said. Excitement surged through him as he sensed the liquid's confinement within the walls of the vial. There was something else as well. A focus on damage. Then progress. Speed. A hasty acceleration, then deceleration. Time.

A loud *thump* broke Sam's concentration—and perceived connection.

He glanced over. Vurkil had fallen out of his seat onto the floor. His partner's vial of what had once been water had now turned red.

The giant had done it.

There was no need for an announcement due to the tremendous thud. The instructor was already on her way over.

Sam sighed and turned his attention back to the glass vial of quite transparent water on the desk in front of him. None of this made any sense. But he *needed* it to make sense.

I will figure out this absurdity if it's the last thing I do.

Chapter 18

Belze

Jeanette awoke from the uncomfortable stone floor and immediately gagged from the stench. She sat up and huddled into a naked ball, staring at her corner, having fallen asleep from sheer exhaustion. The imagined form of Amy sat before her in the corner, looking somber.

So cold.

Clothing. I could have had clothing! She slammed a fist on the stone floor at the thought, then returned her arm around her legs.

Her imagination of Amy looked at her with a concerned expression. *"You know they were just trying to trick you into something. They may not have even given you those things. You have no reason to trust their word."*

I know, Jeanette thought in reply. *I just . . . I lost the little bit of clothing I had. I can't stand being so cold any longer.*

"You can. You're stronger than you think you are."

You keep saying that, but I don't know. Jeanette shuddered as she recalled the pale woman's disturbing actions. *I don't know how much longer I can stand this.*

"Don't give in. As long as you maintain self-control, there's hope."

Hope. Jeanette found it increasingly difficult to maintain any amount of hope. Her situation was dreadfully bleak. She was surrounded by abnormally strong, disgusting people with magic potions and strange weapons. There was no chance of escape. Even if she did somehow miraculously get out of the castle, she had no clue where she was. She would have nowhere to go.

Jeanette let the image of Amy fade.

Her fictitious discussions with Amy had no doubt saved her from succumbing to despair and madness, but she just wanted to be alone at the moment.

She sighed and let her thoughts dwell on the night she was brought to the castle again. They had needed her to open the library. Why? What was so important in there? Why couldn't they open it themselves? From her prior musings on the topic, she had concluded that it must have been some kind of spell preventing access. They had mentioned her being a granddaughter, and she couldn't remember for sure, but she thought they had used "he" in reference to her relative—so it could have been her grandfather.

How or why her grandfather had gotten mixed up with these people was beyond her. Her parents had refused to say much about her grandparents, only that they lived far away. She had assumed they were dead from the way they spoke about them.

Jeanette thought about it for some time in the silent dungeon, straining her mind to remember anything her parents had told her—which was depressingly little. She knew next to nothing about their family history.

Steps echoed from the stairway, causing her heart rate to spike. Breathing became difficult. *Not again. Please.*

The feet that approached the bottom of the steps had a unique signature compared to the lumbering gait of the despicable prison guard. Curiosity did not turn her gaze, however. She continued to sit and shiver, her sights fixed on the corner of her tiny cell as her heart raced furiously.

Metal crashed into metal.

Jeanette flinched and shrieked in alarm, then pivoted on her naked behind to back against the far wall. She drew her legs in close. A woman in a sleek black costume and large boots stood at the bars. Steel glinted from the buckle on a thick black belt around her waist, which holstered a dagger and three small vials of red liquid. Black leather guards wrapped around her forearms. Her face was masked and hooded, exposing only bright gray eyes and the warm brown skin surrounding them.

The woman sheathed a second dagger and pushed open the cell bars. The latch had been cut through. She then tossed a bundle of cloth at Jeanette.

"Put these on. We must be quick," the woman said as she turned to watch the stairway.

Jeanette's eyes widened in realization. She was being rescued.

"Hurry!" the woman implored.

Jeanette quickly reached out and unfurled the bundle, which turned out to be a single piece of clothing: a black, sleeveless jumpsuit with swirling gray patterns. She raced to slip it on. It was tight—but she was grateful for anything to cover her nakedness. As soon as she pulled the fabric around her shoulders, her mysterious rescuer urged her out of the cell with the wave of her hand.

"I'm Belze," the woman whispered. "I'm going to get you out. Follow me."

Jeanette followed her up the steps, unable to hold tears back at the prospect of leaving the horrible place. They stepped lightly in an attempt to remain as quiet as possible. As they reached the top of the staircase, Belze raised an arm in a stopping motion.

Jeanette froze, heart beating furiously in her ears.

After a moment, the woman motioned for her to follow again. They emerged into the hallway and turned right. The smell of seasoned meat made Jeanette's hunger flare. Belze gripped the hilt of a dagger at her waist, sliding it out as they moved quickly in silence.

They stopped at an intersection of hallways where two men stood chatting around the corner. After a moment, the men proceeded down the hallway—away from Jeanette and Belze. Once their voices faded, Belze motioned for Jeanette to continue. A few more turns later, the hallway opened into the enormous entry hall. Howling winds and rock scraping against rock echoed off the stone walls. They peeked around the corner to see a handful of individuals standing with their arms in the air. Pieces of stone were *floating* in the air toward the wall of the tower entrance, which looked as if an explosion had blown it apart.

"We cannot avoid detection here," Belze said. "Stay close. We're going to run for it."

"What?" Jeanette whispered. "That's suicide!"

Belze rounded the corner toward the staircase, and Jeanette followed, racing to keep up. Why couldn't they go back the way she had come in? They ran down the steps, apparently still undetected as they reached the bottom. As they hurried toward the gaping hole in the entrance, several heads turned toward them with expressions of surprise. *They're going to kill us,* Jeanette thought with panic.

One man pulled a bow from his shoulder, nocked an arrow, and fired at Belze with blinding speed. She brought her dagger up, deflecting the projectile off course. Some others now had swords and daggers drawn. One of them had a large mace. Jeanette's terror spiked as she panted and ran with all her might to keep up with her savior.

A concussive force rippled outward in front of Belze, sending bits of stone and all the people in front of them hurtling away.

Their path was clear.

They raced out into the windy darkness. The rugged surface dug into Jeanette's feet as they turned immediately to the right, following the castle wall. Jeanette glanced behind for pursuers but didn't see anyone. Turning her gaze ahead, she realized that her visibility was remarkably low. She followed her guide by sound, desperately hoping not to step on anything sharp. Pain gripped her chest and legs as they ran for several minutes, with powerful winds beating at them from the side.

A flash of lightning provided a split second of illumination, revealing thick, leafless, zigzagging trees scattered around them. Jeanette felt light-headed. Nausea rose in her stomach. The pain in her legs and chest became unbearable. She stopped and hunched over, placing her hands on her knees. The footsteps ahead of her paused.

"We are nearly there," Belze yelled over the gales. "We cannot stop here."

Jeanette nodded, unable to speak through her heavy breathing. They continued to run, though, thankfully, Belze had slowed their pace to more of a jog. Jeanette's eyes refused to adjust to the darkness—or perhaps there was simply no light at all. Each step shot pain through the soles of her feet.

She collided with Belze, who had stopped.

"Sorry," Jeanette said through heavy breaths.

"Come," Belze said casually, taking Jeanette's hand.

The woman wasn't even winded.

Belze led Jeanette into some kind of enclosure, which acted as a windbreak. Howling winds and the two women's steps resonated around the enclosed space. Some kind of cave?

"Stay here," Belze said. "I'll acquire some wood and get a fire going." Her steps moved into the distance.

Jeanette sat on the hard ground, still heaving. Relief washed over her throbbing feet. It amazed her that Belze could even see in the pitch darkness—and still have so much energy. That said, the woman was apparently magical, so Jeanette had no clue what her limitations might be.

Footsteps returned from the raging winds. The sound of sticks being thrown on the ground reverberated off the walls. Without so much as a spark, a large flame erupted in front of Belze and illuminated the area.

They were indeed in a cave. Belze sat down on the opposite side of the fire, leaning back on her hands. She pulled her hood down but kept the mask on her face, revealing a ponytail of dark brown hair with streaks of gold.

Jeanette scooted forward and raised her freezing hands over the glorious warmth. She had never thought she would love a warm fire as much as she did now. Days of endless chill finally melted from her fingertips with the flickering heat. Her heart rate slowed. She glanced over at Belze, who stared back with a piercing gaze.

The woman stood and walked around the fire, then sat right next to Jeanette and wrapped a warm arm around her icy back. Jeanette couldn't hold back her emotion as she reached over and grasped Belze's hand with her own.

"Th—Thank you."

Tears fell into her lap.

"What is your name?" Belze asked.

"Jeanette."

The woman's gray eyes were the only visible facial feature above the mask. They were thin, slanted upward toward the outside, giving her an almost catlike appearance. Jeanette's initial impression had been that Belze was older, but on closer inspection now, she realized that the woman may not be much older than her. There were few visible wrinkles. She wished she could see Belze's full face, but she felt it improper to ask.

"I should unseal your Sorcery before we move on," Belze said.

Jeanette raised an eyebrow. "My what?"

"Sorcery. Your dominance over the Elements. You will be able to do what I have done."

Jeanette blinked. "You mean . . . magic?"

Belze squinted. "You speak like an outsider."

"Um . . . I'm from America."

This time it was Belze's turn to give a confused look. "I have never heard of America. What planet is that on?"

Jeanette's eyes widened. "What *planet*? I'm not on Earth?"

Belze shook her head and gestured to their surroundings. "This is Uvlun."

Panic gripped Jeanette's mind. First magic, and now this? How was she supposed to get back home from a different *planet*?

She thought of Kara. Her sister was alone now, with their parents gone.

"I need to get back home," Jeanette said with urgency, moving to stand.

Belze raised a hand in a calming motion and settled her back down. "That will be difficult, since the Deia controls the only means on or off this world."

"Who is the Deia? I remember hearing about her in the castle."

"She is now the ruler of all of Uvlun, with the overthrow of King Walnon. She took Evamune Palace—the structure I rescued you from—a short time ago."

Jeanette's gaze turned distant. So this Deia controlled an entire planet using despicable magical underlings. It was a lot to take in, considering how, a minute ago, she hadn't known that other inhabited planets even *existed*.

"I should unseal your Sorcery," Belze repeated.

"What does that even mean?" Jeanette asked. "What will you do to me?"

"It is a simple process. We connect. As soon as you allow me to, I can set you free."

"Is that how you gained your abilities?"

A thoughtful expression crossed Belze's eyes. "Yes. Though I first experienced Sorcery at Tercast."

Jeanette raised an eyebrow. "What's Tercast?"

"A castle of fools. The Tercast Council of Grand Masters banished us here many years ago."

"What did you do?"

Belze gave Jeanette another piercing stare, as if second-guessing her intentions. "I experimented with Sorcery to save a man from death. His mind was failing him, and I knew I could save him." She paused briefly, looking troubled. "Personal study of Sorcery is strictly forbidden by Tercast society."

"Did you save him?"

Belze sighed. "No, they imprisoned us before I could do so. He died awaiting banishment himself."

They sat in silence for a few moments, listening to the crackling sounds of the fire and the winds howling outside the cave entrance.

"Why did you save me?" Jeanette asked.

"You have been captive there for some time. Anyone who can

withstand that lot has significant potential. I knew we could use you on our side."

Rebels.

A worthy cause, but Jeanette's thoughts returned to Kara. "I need to get back to Earth."

"The Deia controls all means of transportation on or off Uvlun. By helping us, you will also receive the means back to your home planet."

Jeanette considered Belze's words for a moment. "I'll do what I can to support you, but I won't kill for you, and I won't go back to that castle."

The woman's intense gray eyes returned another piercing stare. Jeanette turned her gaze to the fire, watching the embers float away into the darkness surrounding them.

Belze released her hand from Jeanette's shoulder. "We should proceed immediately. The sooner your Sorcery is unveiled, the sooner your skills will develop into formidable abilities."

"Okay," Jeanette said.

Belze turned directly toward Jeanette and held out her left hand. Jeanette tentatively accepted the gesture, placing her hand on Belze's. The woman brought her fingers together and gently caressed the back of Jeanette's palm. Expecting to hear some mystical incantation, Jeanette instead found the woman staring at her in silence. A subtle presence entered her perception. She had the faint impression of intrusion—of a being attempting to gain entry to a precious space.

"It's all right," Belze said. "I know it feels strange, as if I'm trying to steal something from you. You must open your Source to me. That is how it works."

Despite the words, Jeanette felt unsettled.

Amy's voice echoed in the back of her mind. *"Don't trust this woman. You don't know her."*

Uncertainty caused Jeanette's anxiety to rise, raising her heart rate with it. It was true; she didn't know this woman well, but she felt at ease around her. She sensed no ill will.

She rescued me from the most awful place in the universe, Jeanette thought. *Why shouldn't I trust her?*

"You still just met her. You don't really know what she's after," Amy said in her mind.

She just said she was part of a resistance against the Deia.

"She could be lying."

But why? Besides, if she's right about this power, I really need that. I wouldn't stand a chance against these people on my own.

"You still have your will. Don't give it up."

I'm not, Jeanette thought. She would never let others force her to kill—but this was different. This woman offered her power and asked for her trust in return. Jeanette felt she had earned it.

"You are still resisting. It is all right. You can trust me," Belze said kindly.

"This doesn't feel ri—"

Jeanette shoved Amy's voice from her mind. She knew that her imagination of Amy was just a manifestation of her own subconscious uneasiness about the situation. Right now, she needed to be rational. Realistically, she wouldn't have a chance without some kind of weapon. Abilities similar to those of her enemies were her best chance.

Jeanette took a large breath in, then let out a long exhale, attempting to ease her resistance. The presence she felt became stronger. She still had the impression of something infiltrating a precious space, but it was also an oddly pleasant sensation that resembled a dulling of pain.

"Let me free you." Belze's soft voice helped ease her fears.

Jeanette opened up.

The presence entered immediately. She had a vague, fleeting sensation of being smothered, causing her panic to rise for a moment. The presence then eased, and she felt the world come to light around her. Her eyes widened. She could feel *everything.* Air. Rock. Clothing. Muscle. Bone. She felt Belze's body in front of her own, with its own organ systems.

"What is this?" she asked in amazement.

Belze smiled fondly under her mask. "Sorcery, Jeanette."

Jeanette slipped her hand from Belze's as she drowned in new sensations she had never experienced before. Slowly, the feelings around her faded, and she felt light-headed. Belze's gray eyes seemed remarkably beautiful in the flickering light of the fire. Jeanette felt a powerful kinship with her, as if they had known each other forever.

Belze waved a hand and the fire faded, drenching them in darkness once again.

"Now light the fire," she said.

"What?"

"Light the fire. You can do it. Feel your surroundings again."

Jeanette closed her eyes—not that it really mattered in the pitch darkness—and tried to bring the feelings back. After a few moments of silence, she raised her arms up in frustration.

"I don't know what I'm doing. How do I do it?"

"Relax," Belze said. "Open your mind, and you will feel them."

Still unsure, Jeanette attempted to quiet her mind. She sat in silence for several minutes, repeatedly forcing thoughts of Kara, Sam, and her parents from her head. Remarkably, she eventually found peace.

New, fleeting emotions pressed on her perception. She felt her own heart beating in her chest, as if separated from it. Dirt. Wood. Rocks. The walls of the cave.

"Hold on to the feeling of the wood," Belze said.

Jeanette held on to the thought of the sticks, and she felt an odd connection. There was something unpleasant mixed with the beauty of the connection. A subtle feeling of suffering.

"Well done," Belze said. "Imagine the material bursting into flame. Be confident. It will follow your command."

Burn, Jeanette thought, but nothing seemed to happen.

Imagination.

She imagined the wood burning and becoming engulfed in a powerful flame, and soon she felt the stick respond. Opening her eyes, she noticed a small section of wood glowing a soft red, which then faded.

"Good," Belze said. "Your abilities will develop naturally with time and practice."

She felt Belze's presence through the wood, and the fire reignited. It grew quickly, devouring the rest of the wood. A sudden and powerful fatigue smashed into Jeanette that made her body feel three times heavier. That run must have taken a lot out of her.

Movement near the howling cave entrance caught Jeanette's attention, and her adrenaline pulled her from the sudden sleepiness.

Hooded figures in dark clothing.

Jeanette screamed as they advanced on her and Belze. A large man tackled her as she tried to run. She kicked and fought to free herself without success. Belze struggled against others nearby. Steel clanged against steel, ringing in the small cave.

Belze kicked the man atop Jeanette with her large boot, knocking him off. Jeanette immediately stood and ran out of the cave. She glanced back to see Belze clashing daggers with three other figures near the flickering flames, their shadows dancing on the cave wall behind them. A woman in a dark leather outfit lay on the ground with a large wound on her side, and her blood poured onto the rock.

Jeanette collided with something hard and stumbled over. She had run straight into a tree. A large hand gripped her arm. She turned to kick the owner but missed her mark. Cold metal clasped against her wrist. Her other arm was forced against her back and bound with it. A strong leg swept her own, dropping her painfully onto her face and chest. Large hands grabbed her feet, which became clasped by another metal device, binding her limbs completely.

She screamed. A powerful arm lifted her from the ground and wrapped a gag around her head and mouth, stifling the sound. The large man slung her over his back. As she looked around in terror, she saw an unconscious Belze draped over the shoulder of another man. He walked toward them.

Light from the fire-lit cave faded into the distance, and Jeanette was plunged helplessly back into the darkness.

Chapter 19

Two Steps Closer

"How many prime advisors does the Sovereign have?" the synth man asked.

"Two," Kara replied.

"Correct," he responded flatly.

She sat in a tiny room while the AI—or synth, as they liked to call them—drilled her about Sovereignty government, economics, and related topics. It felt very similar to the room on Earth she had sat in when first introduced to the Sovereignty, the day she'd learned that Earth wasn't alone in the universe.

The day her parents had died.

It felt like ages had passed since that fateful day, but she knew it had really only been around a week. Time was hard to track, since the length of days on Earth, Alvior, and Rwenmar were all different.

"What are the names of the two devices all citizens of the Sovereignty may use to interact with the universal network?"

"A Jit and a . . ."

Shoot. What was the other one called?

"Nit?" Kara said.

"Correct. Please briefly describe differences between the two devices."

"The Jit is a handheld thing," she said. "You press it and give it voice commands. The Nit is something like a biochip that plugs directly into the brain."

She had asked whether "Nit" was an acronym during class. It was not. Apparently, the Sovereignty government despised acronyms.

"Your answer is acceptable," he said. "Congratulations. You have completed the citizenship questionnaire with adequate answers. Are you prepared to take the oath of citizenship and become a full citizen of the Sovereignty of Rwenmar?"

"Yes."

"Please listen carefully and repeat my words if you so declare to abide by the oaths, which are presented in descending order of significance. You are also free to say no at any point, in which case you will be asked to confirm and abort the citizenship process. Is this clear?"

"Yes."

As the synth spoke the phrases, Kara repeated each one:

"I commit to honor the liberty of all beings and the experience of life."

"I commit to sustain and defend the statutes of the Sovereignty of Rwenmar."

"I commit to obey any official commands of the designated Sovereign."

"I commit to my involvement in the democratic processes of the Sovereignty of Rwenmar, in electing public officials according to my conscience."

The echoes of Kara's voice faded into silence.

"Congratulations, Kara Madelyn Jones. You are now an official citizen of the Sovereignty of Rwenmar," the synth declared. A triumphant, upbeat tune accompanied his words, which ended with a dramatic stop. "Your citizenship certificate has been attached to your profile. Have a wonderful day."

Kara thought the music was overdramatic, but she felt a sense of accomplishment nonetheless. She stood from her comfortable armchair, turned about, extended her cane, and strolled through the door at the back.

"Hey!" Nikor said as soon as she passed into the narrow hallway. "Did you pass?"

"Of course," she replied. "Did you?"

"It was a lot easier than I thought it would be, actually."

Kara nodded. "Yeah, I thought so too."

She began walking down the hall toward the elevators. His steps joined hers to the left. Their present floor smelled oddly of toothpaste.

"Let's celebrate!" Nikor exclaimed. "I've been researching some neat eateries nearby, and I think I found a really nice-looking Nevarian place."

Kara considered the offer. "Okay, but it needs to be fairly quick. I have an appointment with a surgeon."

"You do?"

Her cane hit the edge of the elevator wall. She'd forgotten to hail one, so she pressed her Jit.

"A lift to the main floor, please," she said.

"Calling a lift now. Car arriving in two doh, or twenty-four, seconds," the smooth voice responded.

Her thoughts returned to Nikor's question. "Yes, I scheduled an appointment last night after I got back from the park."

"Wow, that was fast. Sure you don't need more time to think it over? You seemed hesitant."

"No. I've made up my mind. I'm getting vision and a Nit implant."

"Nice! I'd like to do that too when I can get some Til. Having the implant would be so much more convenient than carrying this thing around all day."

Kara assumed he was showing off his Jit in some way. She'd never really had to give much thought to her Sovereignty money. She had received a fair amount of it, though she was by no means enormously wealthy. The Sovereignty provided normal transportation using ascenders and acherons as a public service, so she had mainly spent her money on food, clothing, and the rapid transports from Alvior.

"The lift is arriving," her Jit said.

The doors whisked open, and they stepped inside. Kara felt lighter as it began accelerating downward.

Nikor broke the silence. "I still don't get that number system you have your Jit set to."

Kara turned to him. "It's the number system I learned on Earth. *I* don't really get this dohnal system."

"So weird," he said, "counting by dek instead of doh."

"I always thought it seemed natural. Most people have ten fingers after all."

"Whoa, wait! You think ten fingers is normal?"

Kara found herself bewildered by his statement, and then realization hit her. "You don't have ten fingers?" she asked.

He laughed. "Nah, I'm messing with you. I have ten fingers. Everyone has ten fingers."

Kara suppressed a smile as she reached out and felt for his shoulder. When she found it, she gave it a good punch. "Jerk! I almost believed you."

Nikor laughed, but Kara pondered on the subject further.

"Well, some people are born without the usual limbs or fingers, or lose them at some point," she said. "So not everyone."

"Maybe not where you're from," Nikor replied, "but, in the Sovereignty, almost everyone uses technology to restore typical body parts and functions."

"That makes sense, but I also think that's kind of sad."

"Why?"

"Because it's *boring*. It stifles diversity. Differences in appearance and abilities are valuable. They help us get new perspectives on important things."

"Is it worth the hardship though?" Nikor asked.

"Not for everyone, but for me it is. I like experiencing life differently than most other people I meet. If I didn't need sight to be a soldier, I wouldn't be getting it."

They reached the main floor and took an ascender to the venue he had planned.

Dinner with Nikor was entertaining, and the food was wonderful. It seemed the Sovereignty in general had excellent taste in cuisine. After dinner, Nikor accompanied her to the surgeon's office.

They stood outside the entrance as Kara turned to say goodbye. Insufferable butterflies rose in her stomach. He could be insensitive and clueless, but he had a good sense of humor and she found him easy to talk to.

"Thanks for dinner, Nikor. It was fun."

"It was for me, too. You're a beautiful woman, Kara, the oasis to my desert life," he responded.

His words made the obnoxious butterflies return. *Why? That was so cheesy and stupid. And yet, oddly endearing.*

She smiled. "You say some of the cringiest things sometimes."

Her words hung in the air between them. Had she offended him?

Something soft and wet, with the scent of the fruity dessert they had eaten, collided with her face. Hands grabbed her shoulders. She recoiled, stepping back out of the grip and almost tripping over herself.

Intense frustration smothered her giddiness. "Did you just try to kiss me?"

"I, uh, well . . . I thought . . ."

"Ugh. I'm *blind,* you dolt! You can't just smash your face into me like that. I need a bit of warning!"

No response. Kara's heart thumped in her ears. As seconds passed in silence, her heart rate slowed. She wished she had some sign of what Nikor was thinking. Perhaps she had reacted a bit too harshly.

"Sorry, I didn't mean to flip out," she said, "but seriously, you can't just *do* that. I like you, Nikor. I would have been fine with a kiss. Just give me a heads-up, all right?"

"You like me?"

"Yeah, I think you're fun—when you're not being a blockhead."

No response. Kara's heart raced again in anticipation. *Please try again.*

"May I kiss you?" he said.

Kara smiled, feeling the butterflies storm again within her. "Yes, you may."

He wrapped his enormous arms around her and slid his fingers to her upper back. He pressed his warm, firm body against hers, setting her butterflies alight. She rested her chin against his chest and smelled the fruit again as his breath approached. She lifted herself on her toes and met his lips with hers. Sensations electrified her body, filling her with exhilaration. Their lips parted all too quickly as he lifted his head away. She longed for more.

"I'd better let you get to your appointment," he said. "You're already late."

She shrugged, still reeling from the experience.

His magnificent body and arms slipped away from her. "I'll come see you tomorrow morning, all right?"

She nodded. "Tomorrow."

"Oh," he said. "And good luck with your surgery!"

"Thanks," she replied, feeling elation give way to apprehension.

Nikor's footsteps fell away as she turned and walked through the door to the surgeon's office. It hissed open at her approach. The smell of something similar to peppermint and cleaning chemicals aroused her senses. Cold air gave her arms goose bumps. She wished Nikor could stay with her, but her Jit had told her that she could not have any friends or family members in the operating room, and there was no point making him wait around for her.

A warm female voice greeted her entrance. "Good evening, Kara."

"Hi," she replied. "Sorry, I'm a bit late."

"Oh, you're fine, dear. Rinzdee, the surgical technician, is ready for you now. Would you like help getting to the operating room?"

"Yes, please."

"The technician is on his way now to escort you."

She collapsed her cane and waited. Soon enough, footsteps echoing from a nearby hallway emerged and approached her. "Kara Jones?" an older man's voice said.

"That's me."

"Excellent. Please take my arm and I'll lead you to your operating room."

She reached out and found his arm. It was thick, and quite hairy. He led her forward down the hallway, passing the clacking steps of a few others on their way.

This is incredibly fast, she thought, feeling anxious. *The last time I went to a doctor, I waited for nearly an hour, and that was for a basic checkup.*

He brought her into a room that felt small and then led her to a seat. She settled into the somewhat leathery, comfortable chair and tried to relax the tension from her body. Her hands were freezing, and her mind was a blur of questions. What were they going to do? Would she be conscious? Had they done this before?

"Please try to relax," the technician said in a kind voice. "The system will take some unobtrusive measurements of your physiology while we go over your options. Nothing will touch you until we begin the procedure."

She leaned back into the chair. "Okay, I'll try. This is all very new to me."

"I see that you have scheduled vision restoration in addition to a Nit implantation. Was your blindness caused by an injury?"

"No, I was born with it," Kara replied. "Apparently, I was completely blind by the time I was five years old."

His chair squeaked. "Really? I've never been aware of such a young case that hasn't been corrected. Was there a reason you didn't have surgery earlier?"

"Well, I'm from Earth," she said. "A class . . . uh . . . four, I think, planet? We don't have the technology to restore vision yet for many conditions, including mine, and I never even knew the Sovereignty existed."

Except her parents. They *had* known. And had kept it a secret.

"Ah," he said. "Very sorry to hear that."

A machine buzzed softly near her ear.

"Don't be," Kara said. "I've actually grown very accustomed to it. In fact, the thought of being sighted is infinitely scarier to me now than being blind."

"That's understandable. This will be a big change. Do you know the cause of your blindness?"

"They said it's a rare case of Leber congenital amaurosis."

He paused for several seconds as the machine's buzzing moved around to the front of Kara's face.

"Hmm, I can't seem to pinpoint that condition," he said. "Unless a singing group from Ecantia has something to do with your blindness." He chuckled. "I suspect that our medical terminology differs somewhat from Earth's."

"Yeah, that doesn't surprise me. I'm pretty sure medical speak is its own language," she said. "I was never great with biology, so I don't know all the details. It's something about the cells in my eyes deteriorating—at least the ones that absorb light."

"Ah, yes. That is good. If the disease is in your eyes, and if the ocular nerve and visual section of your brain are still intact, we should be able to get your vision working rather quickly."

She leaned forward, recalling a question she was planning to ask. "About that. How fast is 'quickly,' exactly?"

"Please sit back," he said. "It lets the system measure you more effectively."

She complied, leaning back against the soft leathery chair.

"Timing depends somewhat on the condition and the desired solution," the man explained. "If it's the cells of your eye, as you said, the fastest method would be to replace your eyes with artificial ones. They will interface with your nervous system directly, as well as your Nit. Average recovery is . . ." He paused briefly as if looking something up. "A little over one standard week. But that's mostly with patients younger than you. Your eyes may take longer."

Couldn't their magic technology work faster? She didn't want to delay her chance to do something about her sister. Still, this was admittedly much bigger than healing a paper cut, so she decided that the timeline was good enough. It *would* give her some time to spend with Nikor. The thought reawakened the butterflies within her.

"Okay," she said. "Can they look the same as my normal eyes?"

"Yes, of course," he replied. "We can create them to look identical."

Though the idea of giving up her eyes filled her with fear, she felt some excitement at the idea of being able to see what she looked like.

"This is probably a stupid question," she said. "But, it won't be painful will it? I don't have many memories from when I still had some eyesight, but I do remember having seriously painful light sensitivity."

"Oh no, no," the man replied. "At most you may feel a dull ache just after the eyes are implanted. Nothing more, I promise."

She sighed. "That's a relief."

"Excellent," he said. "The system has your metrics and diagnostics. As soon as I configure your choices, we'll put you unconscious and the device will take care of the rest." He fidgeted with something and made a light tapping noise. "So, do you have exciting plans after you can see?"

"I'm going to join the Force," she replied.

The tapping stopped. "The *military?*"

"Yes."

Taps started up again. "I have to admit I didn't expect—Wait!"

Kara cocked her head. "Hmm?"

"If you're joining the Force," he said, "you could benefit from more advanced sensors. Ones that give you a much wider range of EM sensitivity. We could even give you finer control of visual field and magnification if you'd like. They would still work like normal eyes, of course—and that's what we would start with—but you would have *so* much more. Some people get them, but for the many who grow up with sight, the change requires a lot of time and they often cannot have complete control because their nervous system has to relearn everything. Your brain is not accustomed to those sensations, so it should adapt more effectively. These enhancements are very reasonably priced."

Interesting. I could go from being nonsighted to supersighted. I like it.

His chair creaked. "What do you think?"

"Yes," she said. "Let's do it."

Chapter 20
Elemorb

Rose awoke in her small bed under the tower window and gazed into a clear sky. Her arms ached from the physical exertion of endless scrubbing the day prior—their "service day" of the week. Apparently, that meant a significant amount of manual labor working the fields, cleaning, and cooking meals. Who needed staff when you could just make the studies do it?

There were certainly things she missed from Oscertos, her home country just outside the walls of the castle. For one, she didn't understand why these people had to live like troglodytes when technology was readily available all around them. Having even just two or three cleaning bots would be more effective than doh young adults.

Still, she couldn't go back. She couldn't be a physician. Tercast was her escape from her father's oppressive insistence. She never thought all the magical things she'd heard about the place would actually be true.

Rose turned her head, bringing her focus into the room. Most of the other women were still asleep. Zel was gone—probably hanging out with the animals or staring intently at some random wall in the hallway. Kula was also absent, likely doing her morning exercises.

Well, might as well get some breakfast.

Rose sat up, slid off the bed, and made her way across the oddly warm stone floor. She turned back briefly to grab her book, then made her way out the door as quietly as she could and progressed down the stairs. She didn't quite understand the Tercast custom of eating breakfast in sleepwear and without makeup, but she also didn't mind it much. Talanna, Niu, and Relon had been comically incredulous when Master Olana informed them of the custom on their first evening in the castle, and made clear her expectation that they follow it.

Rose had just about reached the door to the lunchroom when the morning bell sounded. As she entered the large room, she noted that it was nearly empty. One small group of four studies ate in the corner, and two others sat alone near the walls. She grabbed a plate of lillisticks and elfedder, then topped the lillisticks with a bit of yuun syrup. The food they prepared here was not nearly as good as back home, probably because it was cooked by studies on their service day. But at least it was fresh.

She settled into an empty corner and cracked open her book, *Hearts of Adelaide.* Other studies waltzed into the room as she drank her vela juice and read about the not-so-well-trained surgeon. The protagonist, Sheela, was attempting to decide whether to pursue her love in Joss or Levaan. The increasing sounds of chatter and activity faded from Rose's perception as she absorbed herself in the story. *You are hopeless, Sheela. Joss is infinitely better in every way than Levaan. Levaan just has big, stupid abs.*

"Hey."

Rose flinched and turned toward the source of the voice. It was a man from another group. She had seen him in passing once or twice. He had dark skin and hair, with forest-green eyes.

"Sorry to bother you, cutie," he said in a clearly Tolumofian accent—very nasal sounding. "I was wondering if I could sit with you."

Rose blinked as she felt her cheeks burn. *Ugh, these ridiculous cheeks. Why don't they ever stop?* She wanted to say no, but the word wouldn't come out.

The man smiled, apparently taking her shyness and lack of an answer as consent. He sat down beside her and placed his plate of food on the table.

Rose bit back a sigh. That hadn't been an invitation. The last thing she wanted was a guy to be interested in her right now. She just wanted to read.

"Name's Evan. So where are you from, girl?" he asked.

Rose's cheeks continued to burn as she tried to ignore him and go back to her book. She couldn't possibly focus on it with him there, but maybe he would go away if she didn't answer him.

He put his hand on her arm. "Come on, girl, there's no need to be so timid. I—"

"This man bothering you, Rose?" Vurkil's distinctive low voice came from overhead.

She and Evan looked up at him in unison. Relief swept over her, and she nodded more fervently than intended.

Evan flinched and released her arm. "Uh, no. No! Definitely not bothering her. I was just . . . uh . . . you know . . . making conversation!"

"You'd better move before I sit on you," Vurkil responded with a laugh. Rose smiled. He was so cheerful—even while being intimidating.

"Ah, yes. Right. I'll get going, then." Evan hastily stood and moved off, leaving his plate of uneaten food.

Vurkil sat next to Rose and set down two more plates next to the one Evan had left. He devoured all three plates of food with gusto while Rose returned to her reading. Vurkil remained by her side in silence. The only other words he uttered were "See you at the field" when she got up to return to the girls' dormitory.

"See you," she replied.

The morning bell sounded. Rose used the washroom to change into her robes. The motions came easier to her now, this being the sixth morning she'd put them on.

She read *Hearts of Adelaide* in the empty dorm room while

everyone else was at breakfast. When the next bell sounded, she made her way down the halls toward the field. On her way down the ornate hallway, past the instruction rooms, she heard familiar voices. Sam was speaking with Master Evalencia. Rose stopped outside the door and turned around, her curiosity piqued.

"—wanted to ask you if you knew of Laurel or Darren Jones," Sam said.

"I'm afraid I don't recognize those names," the Master responded.

"What about the name Walnon?"

"Hmm. Walnon . . . that sounds familiar . . ." Master Evalencia paused. "Ah yes, he was a Grand Master at the academy many years ago."

"He's not here anymore?" Sam asked.

Her tone became solemn. "I'm afraid . . . If I remember correctly, he was banished for violating the Tercast code. It was a terrible ordeal. I had only recently come to Tercast myself."

There was a brief silence. Rose glanced up and down the hallway to ensure that no one would see her eavesdropping. The hall was empty.

Sam's voice echoed from the room. "Apparently, he was the grandfather of a friend of mine who was kidnapped."

"Really?" Master Evalencia replied. "Tell me what you know so I can inform the Council. They will look into—"

Talanna, Niu, and Relon turned the corner in Rose's direction.

Rose pivoted and continued walking down the halls, wondering who Sam's kidnapped friend could be. Wasn't he from a class four planet?

After a few twists and turns, she found herself at the grand entrance. Light streamed in through the enormous front doors, illuminating the breathtaking artwork within the entrance hall. Studies and a Grand Master merged from a side hallway and made their way through the tall gatehouse at the other end. She followed them through and walked out into the bright valley surrounded by mountains.

The castle, set on a hill, overlooked the crops below and the meandering river beyond the outer wall. To the left, just outside the castle, was the playing field where today's games would take place. She made her way to one bleacher surrounding the stadium and found a seat at the farthest top corner—apart from the rest of the early observers. Their Ulinko group would only watch today, but they would need to play the following week. After their labors the previous day, Master Azeloram had urged them to pay close attention to the game.

Rose examined the field. Pairs of raised hoops stood along two lines, dividing the field into thirds. Large half-circle goals framed each side, reflecting a steel-blue color. The hoops hovering in the middle shimmered bright red and pale green in the morning light. She also noted a large scoreboard attached to the top of the stands on the opposite side of the field.

Clearly, the game was set up for scoring by moving something through the goals. Rose typically found hands-on sports like the Mondro brawls more interesting. The physiology of athletes *could* be rather fascinating, though, regardless of the sport.

Vurkil approached down the row of bleachers with a smile. She smiled back faintly, apprehension rising. Thankfully, he did not speak to her and instead plopped down without a word. He left an empty seat between them, where his right arm fell. She was surprised he could fit into the seat at all, given his size.

Rose's mind drifted into the world of *Hearts of Adelaide* as more spectators arrived. She'd gotten through over half of its pages and was still frustrated with Sheela's indecisiveness. If the woman picked Levaan, she might just toss the book and be done with it.

Sam approached them from down the row. "Hey, Vurkil. Hi, Rose."

Blood rushed to Rose's cheeks at the mention of her name. Sam sat down on the other side of Vurkil, leaving an empty seat between them for Vurkil's massive left arm.

"Lively morning, Sam," Vurkil said. "Do you know how this is played?"

Sam looked down at the field for a moment. "Uh, not really. Master Evalencia gave us a very brief description at the end of

Water class the other day, but I don't remember all of it. She said we would catch on pretty quickly by watching."

So, Rose thought, *Sam still probably hasn't had success with Sorcery if he was still conscious at the end of Water instruction.* She empathized. It had taken her several days to get a knack for Sorcery, but she was surprised how easily the potion task came to her. She'd even completed it before Tovas. Her connection with the healing potion had been an incredible experience.

Vurkil nodded.

"It sort of reminds me of a soccer field from my home planet, though the goals are smaller," Sam said.

"Soccer?" Vurkil asked.

"Yeah, it's a game where each side tries to kick a ball into a net at the opponent's end."

"Ah, sounds like rushball. It made the news recently when a player died."

"Really?" Sam responded with interest. "I'm surprised people in the Sovereignty die from anything, with all the technology."

Vurkil laughed. "Technology does not fix everything. You can't fix a broken brain."

"Why not?"

"Brains are more sensitive to changes than other organs," Rose replied, causing their heads to turn toward her. "Their function directly results from unique structure and activity. When either of those is significantly disrupted, the person is effectively dead."

Sam frowned. "Would it be possible to scan that structure somewhere and reengineer it? Or just replace it with a computer?"

Rose raised her eyebrows. "That's a dangerous idea, Sam. Past attempts to replace brains with technology haven't worked the way people hoped. It's the primary pursuit that spawned the Molkinar Empire, which the Sovereignty has been at war with for generations."

He nodded, bringing fingers to his chin in a thoughtful expression. "Interesting. So if the brain is damaged, there's no coming back from that?"

"Only biological regeneration, as long as the damage isn't too extensive," Rose answered. "Medical bots and professionals can stop bleeding and foster regrowth of brain tissue, but it isn't an exact replacement of what was there before. If those neurons powered key parts of a person's personality, that part of them is gone forever."

"Yes," Vurkil said, turning to Sam. "All other parts of the body can be replaced, but the brain cannot."

"Well, to a degree," Rose explained. "The body can deal with changes to a point, but if you change too much at once, it can't adapt well. What makes you *you* is more than your brain, you know. Every human has unique body-wide networks and signal patterns. You can't just take someone's brain out, put it into another body, and expect that person to—"

"Welcome to this week's Elemorb games!" The announcer's amplified words cut Rose short. The crowd cheered and clapped. "Our first team competing today will be the mighty Wyverns!"

Shouts rang out, primarily from a section on the other side of the field. The doh team members walked out onto the grass, wearing a lighter set of silver robes with red embellishments. The front of the robes featured a large red silhouette of the animal spreading its wings wide.

A small wyvern flew out over the team. It had scaly silver skin with red streaks along its back and long neck. Sam and Vurkil applauded with the crowd.

"They will compete against the quick and graceful Caladrials!"

More cheers, this time primarily from a section farther down on Rose's side of the bleachers. Vurkil and Sam joined again in the applause, and Rose decided she should probably clap as well. The team emerged on the other side of the field, wearing white robes with light blue edgings. Their logo featured the silhouette of a bird in flight from the side.

Their mascot, the caladrial itself, flew over the group. Morning light glinted from its bright white feathers as it soared majestically through the sky. It approached the Wyverns' mascot, and the two danced around each other in the air for a moment before settling down with their teams on the sidelines.

"Please welcome our first players of the day!"

More enthusiastic applause and cheers rose from the crowd as four members of each team strode onto the field. One stood in front of the back arch—clearly the goalkeeper—with the other three making their way to stand directly under the red and green hoops on each side. Each of the players in the center of the trio held a ball. The Wyvern player held a yellow ball, while the Caladrial player held a larger black ball.

Applause faded into anxious chatter.

"Let the game begin!"

A loud, high-pitched bell signaled the start of the match. Both players holding balls threw them into the air. The yellow ball shot forward, while the black ball soared up and remained stationary.

The Wyvern trio ran forward, yellow ball hovering over their heads. Their center player and the blond girl to his left veered toward the red hoop on one side of the field, while the third approached the green hoop on the opposite side. Caladrial defenders moved to intercept the two with the ball, the center player lifting his hands as he maintained control of the ball overhead. The blond Wyvern girl stretched her hand toward the yellow ball, and it burst into flames, then shot forward toward the hoop high above their heads. Cheers rang from the stands as the black Caladrial ball flew up further, clearly attempting to block the flaming ball from its target. It missed.

The ball of fire bounced against the rim of the red circle, evoking cries of disappointment from the crowd. It careened off toward the center of the field, and its flames dissipated.

The Caladrial player on the end sprinted toward the defending ball, which fell out of bounds near the stands. After bouncing against the grass, it moved toward the player as he stretched his hands toward it. Meanwhile, the once-flaming yellow ball moved toward the other Wyvern player on the opposite side, who stretched out his hands to receive it. A defending Caladrial girl stood only three or four feet away from him, yelling at her teammate to get their ball to her. The defending ball shot toward her position, but it was clearly too late. The attacking ball hovered over the Wyvern player's head, moving quickly and steadily against a turbulent breeze toward the pale green ring. It passed through with a sharp crack of electricity, causing Rose to flinch.

The crowd cheered as the scoreboard flipped down to a number three under the Wyverns' logo. Sam and Vurkil whooped with the rest of them. The Wyvern mascot flew over the field triumphantly.

"Whoa," Sam said. "So it seems like the red hoop requires fire and the green hoop requires electricity!"

Vurkil nodded through his applause.

Rose gave a weak clap, though she did find the game intriguing. It looked like the general strategy was to have the center players focused on *moving* the ball—a Land-associated Sorcery—while the players on either side focused more on adding the proper Fire or Air Sorcery. Where was the Water, though?

Each set of three forward players moved off the field, where three others carrying opposite-colored balls came in to replace them. The Wyverns now had the larger black ball, while the Caladrials carried yellow. The new players got into their starting positions and crouched, ready to move.

The bell sounded again, but this time the Caladrials rushed forward with the yellow ball floating forward over their heads. They split off similarly to the way the other team had, with two of them racing to the opposing green hoop. The center defending Wyvern, a purple-haired girl, moved to join her teammate in defense.

The bright yellow Caladrial ball shot forward toward the hoop, and the Wyvern ball followed a split second after. They collided, with the yellow ball ricocheting off toward the stands. The Caladrial girl sprinted after it with hands outstretched, but it bounced against the ground. A lower bell tone sounded.

Each team swapped back to the original set of players and balls, signifying the end of the short round. At the ring of the bell, the Wyverns raced forward again. Balls collided as the Caladrials successfully averted an attempt at the fire goal, but the Wyverns maintained control of it, moving it back and forth between them. The balls made their way to the defenders' green hoop, where they stood still—defending ball situated right between the smaller ball and its target. Clearly blocked, the Wyvern player moved the ball back toward the center of the field. The defending ball moved to intercept it.

The Wyverns' yellow ball abruptly changed course, firing back toward the player near the green goal. He stretched his hand up, and it arched toward the goal. The defending ball changed course to block but did so too sluggishly, clearly slowed by its larger size. The ball flew through the hoop with another crack of electricity.

The crowd cheered. Rose clapped with them, her excitement rising. The score under the Wyvern logo flipped to reveal a five.

"Oh!" Sam yelled over the applause. "Right! The goals in the center are worth less points each time you score in them, to a minimum of one. So the first goal through that hoop is worth three, the second is worth two, and every goal after that should be one point."

"What is the winning score?" Vurkil asked.

"I think they play to twelve points," Sam said.

Rose cocked her head toward Sam as Vurkil did the same.

"I mean . . . uh . . . doh points."

"What is 'twelve'?" Vurkil asked.

Sam raised a dismissive hand. "Never mind. I'll tell you later."

They returned their attention to the game, where the Caladrials failed their shot at a fire goal, missing the goal post completely. A new team of three Wyvern players entered the field, who scored a fire goal, increasing their score to eight. The game continued, with the Wyverns maintaining the upper hand. Occasionally, they would swap out a single player or two from a group once members of the team became exhausted. The defenders of the large goals at the back maintained their positions, effectively doing nothing.

After another fire goal and a third electric goal, the Wyverns were only one point away from victory. The players made their way onto the field. This time, two new Caladrial players entered with their yellow ball. They raced forward at the sound of the bell, moving toward the fire goal. The center defender raced to intercept, the black ball hovering over his head.

Cheers accompanied the Caladrial ball as it burst into flames and shot toward the goal, but it was clearly too high. The defending ball shot forward anyway to knock it further off course. The flaming ball arced over the hoop, and the defending ball also missed its target, flying off toward the edge.

Down the field, the purple-haired Caladrial sprinted past the goals toward the back arch, raising her hand as she took control of the flaming ball, which extinguished. Shouts burst from the crowd in anticipation as she approached the goalkeeper, who had barely done anything all game. Meanwhile, the Wyvern ball changed course and moved toward the other side of the field with players underneath.

The Caladrial player raced toward the opponent's large goal and stopped at a line in the grass several feet out from her target. The defender stepped sideways toward her position, placing himself closer to the straight line between her and the goal.

The Caladrial woman glanced back at the other players. After a brief pause, she stretched her arm out, almost touching the ball over her head. It shot forward toward the end of the goal, *opposite* from where she stood. The tall defender leapt to an impossible height toward its direction, stretching his hand out to intercept it. Glancing off his fingers, the ball passed just inches inside the edge of the large semicircle. The flaming Wyvern ball passed through the fire hoop, but it was a second too late.

The crowd exploded. People rose from their seats, cheering and clapping with unhindered enthusiasm. Rose applauded with them. Vurkil's low voice yelled over the crowd next to her as he stood. The majestic white Caladrial mascot soared over the field.

So that's *the Water,* she realized. *The goalkeepers must use Water Sorcery to enhance their strength and agility to defend the larger goal!*

She glanced at the scoreboard, which flipped to display a nine under the Caladrial symbol. They were now only two points down from the Wyverns, and three points away from victory. They actually had an equal chance at winning, since the fire and electric goals would still earn them three points. Each team only needed one more goal to win.

The girl who made the goal had collapsed. Her team carried her to the sidelines as a new set of players entered the field on each side. When the bell sounded, the Wyvern players raced forward toward the electric goal. The defenders followed with their own ball. As the offending ball shot toward the electric hoop, the defending ball collided with it, knocking it off course.

Rose could feel the tension in the stands as everyone watched the falling ball. It stopped just a few inches from the ground and then rose as one of the Wyvern girls dove toward it with her hands outstretched. It hovered for a moment while another Wyvern teammate approached, stretching his hand out to take control. The ball arced back toward the electric hoop, where the defending ball returned as well, blocking a clear shot. The girl who dove to the ground didn't get up, likely unconscious from exhaustion.

The yellow ball shot up—*over* the apparent target—toward the blond Wyvern girl on the other side. Players ran across the field, and the defending ball moved after the smaller target. The Wyvern girl stretched her hand up. A force sent the yellow object on a new trajectory toward the red hoop as it burst into flames.

The crowd held its breath. The ball of fire cleared its target at an incredibly narrow angle.

Noise erupted as everyone cheered. Rose stood with the rest of them, clapping with enthusiasm as the silver Wyvern flew over the field, uttering an emphatic roar. The game had been a lot more interesting than she had expected.

"What a game!" the amplified voice rang out. "The mighty Wyverns win!"

The crowd continued to clap and celebrate as the players who remained conscious made their way to the field and bowed to their opponents, then to each set of stands.

Rose's excitement gave way to apprehension as she froze mid-clap.

Their group was expected to do that in a *week*?

Chapter 21
Connections

"Before you begin your Land Sorcery task for today, we will have a brief lecture on Tercast history."

Master Azeloram addressed them from the front of the Land room, where they had been one week before. Sam sat in the same seat, with Tovas to his right—front and center in the room. A small rectangular chunk of clay lay on the desk in front of him.

"A fitting topic for Land, since an object's history can have a profound effect on its spiritual properties. We will explore this more deeply next week when we discuss enchantments."

The class sat in silence as the Master began pacing slowly, hands clasped behind his back.

"Tercast is a castle shrouded in mystery. It was discovered only about two doh and seven years ago by Grand Master Ilius Vadmon and his small group of religious followers."

Sam still couldn't think in dohnal, so he did the calculation quickly in his head. That was two doh seven, so two times twelve—twenty-four—plus seven. About thirty-one years ago.

The Master continued speaking as he paced. "They embarked on a journey into the wilderness, away from the hustle and bustle of Alvioran society, to learn the will of the Divine. They traveled for years on foot, without the distractions of technology, living off the land as they went, until"—he turned about and looked at the class with intensity—"they stumbled upon this magnificent valley and the mysterious castle along the cliff side."

Sam rolled his eyes at the man's theatrical storytelling.

"The work was of ancient architecture, and the castle was completely uninhabited. They found the Rooms of Selection near the front gate, each with a dimly lit stone within. They explored the area, noting the odd artisanship of the tools and weapons. Curiously, they found no bodies or skeletons.

"Marvelous visions passed through a few of his followers. Wind blew mysteriously. Small objects within began moving miraculously. Several of his followers fainted from sudden exhaustion."

Master Azeloram, now near the side of the room, turned on his heel and quickened his pace toward the other side. "They searched the castle and discovered a remarkable room—what we now call the Room of the Primordial. This pentagonal room contains elaborate depictions of the four primordial Elements—Land, Air, Fire, and Water—on four of its walls. The fifth wall provides a marvelous representation of darkness giving way to light."

The old man raised a finger dramatically as he returned to the podium. "It was a sign. A sign from the Divine that his quest had been fulfilled. Grand Master Ilius and his followers settled here. He discovered journals and other small writings where he found the name Tercast given, and how ancient Masters had taught Sorcery to their studies. Over time, Ilius sent missionaries to tell the nations of Alvior about the wonders of the castle. Many came to be tested, as you have, and have learned to connect with the Elements—as you are now!" He stretched his hands toward the class. "You are all now part of a glorious legacy of spiritual renewal and enlightenment!"

Sam found himself rather underwhelmed. A religious guy and his followers found a castle that granted magical powers, and he—of course—assumed it was "a sign from the Divine" because it fit his worldview. At least it explained why everyone here was so pious and quick to accept whatever these people told them. *Amaze people with "miracles" and they'll follow anyone.*

These particular miracles did have serious supernatural aspects to them, of course, but that didn't mean they came from God. That's just what Ilius and his followers wanted to believe.

"What happened to Grand Master Ilius?" Talanna asked.

Master Azeloram's expression turned sorrowful. "I'm afraid he passed away during an attack from Uvlun two doh years ago."

"An attack?" Vurkil asked.

"Yes. The underworld consumed some of Ilius's early followers. Those who explored the hellish landscape had discovered dark powers and then ambushed the gate. Grand Master Ilius and several others were killed, but the remaining Masters pushed the attackers back to Uvlun."

The room fell silent.

"Samuel," Master Azeloram said.

Sam jumped. "Yes?"

"Why do *you* think success with Sorcery has evaded you?"

The eyes of everyone in the class burned into him. He glanced to the right, expecting to see Tovas's smug face staring back at him, but his gaze was instead straight ahead, carrying an odd expression. Concern? Distaste?

Sam returned his attention to the old man, preparing for the oncoming reproach. "I . . . don't know."

"Do you still deny the existence and power of the Divine?"

Uh, yes. Yes, I do. I think it's highly unlikely. Sam felt it unwise to utter those words, however. That was sure to earn him a swift rebuke. Was there anything he could say that was true *and* wouldn't get him into trouble?

"To be honest, Master, I do not know. I'm not sure it's even possible to know."

Azeloram nodded. "Well, that is an improvement at least, but you must realize that as long as you lack faith, you will find Sorcery beyond your reach. You must humble yourself. You *must* allow yourself to believe!" He turned to address the class. "Truth is eternal. The denial of truth will only diminish your power—now and in the afterlife. Be faithful and vigilant, and you will receive joy and capabilities beyond your comprehension."

The old man turned, returning once more to his spot behind the podium and gripping it with both hands. "Now, on to today's assignment. Each of you has a bar of soft clay before you. Your primary task is to split the clay into two pieces through Sorcery. We will discuss your progress in more detail after you have attempted to complete the task for an hour. If you succeed, practice telekinetic movement of the clay in the air, or try to mold it into a particular shape. I will start at the back of the room today and make my way forward. Begin."

Master Azeloram glanced at Sam as he strode past toward the back corner where Vurkil and Scheln sat. Conversation rose around the room, the others talking about the task and their thoughts on Tercast history.

Sam looked over at Tovas, who continued to look troubled. "What's up, Tovas?"

The man flinched as if struck by something, then looked upward. "Up?"

Right, he'd forgotten that they didn't use that expression. "I mean, what's on your mind? You seem distracted."

Tovas's gaze met his, but his focus was distant. "I ... don't know. I've been getting strange feelings all morning. Like something is pressing on my mind—or on my soul."

Sam rolled his eyes. "You probably just have a headache or something."

Tovas gave no reply, furrowing his brow.

"You grew up on the Tercast religion, didn't you?" Sam said. The question came out more accusatory than he intended.

Tovas's focus returned to reality. "No. I didn't grow up on Alvior. Grand Master Ilius was, in fact, a devout follower of a branch of my faith before coming to Tercast. There are many similarities, but the doctrine has diverged in key ways, particularly regarding Elements, Sources, and Sorcerers."

"What *is* your religion, then?" Sam asked.

"Lomerianism. So named because our original sacred garden was near a river named Lomeria. We believe that our purpose in life is to learn, shed ourselves of transgressions, and become one with the Divine when we die."

"If you aren't a part of Tercast religion, why do you believe it?" Sam asked.

"Their beliefs are consistent with our doctrine. I have no reason to doubt them."

Sam narrowed his eyes. He felt a sudden urge to reach out and shake the nonsensical thinking out of Tovas. How could he possibly just accept something because it didn't seem to contradict his current worldview? That was an absolutely *terrible* way to discern truth. That was the exact kind of thinking that had resulted in the horrors of the Crusades, the Holocaust, and terrorist attacks.

"So, basically you accept Tercast theology because it seems to be compatible with your religion? What if the Masters said it was now Divine mandate to kill off a civilization with your Sorcery? Would you do it?"

"Absolutely not. That would contradict our core principles. Individual agency is fundamental to the Divine's plan for the universe. Removing a soul from mortality prematurely is morally abhorrent and is only justified in extreme need of defending the agency of another. It is a fundamental law of the universe." The abruptness and conviction of Tovas's response stunned Sam.

"I agree with you that killing is only right in extreme need for defense," Sam replied. "But the idea of morality is a social construct. It's not a 'law of the universe,' as you say." Tovas shook his head as Sam continued. "Conservation of mass-energy. Increasing entropy. Laws of motion. Those are fundamental laws of the universe. The universe itself *doesn't care* if you kill someone in cold blood—only human society."

"You're wrong," Tovas said. "The universe *does* care. Morality is just as much a law of the universe as physics is, but it operates in the spiritual plane, not the physical one."

Sam scoffed. "Oh right, of course. It's there, we just can't detect it in any way whatsoever because it's *spiritual.*" He folded his arms. "That's not a logical argument!"

Tovas sighed. "I hope you overcome your obsession with physical evidence. Spiritual things can only be discerned by spiritual means, and only individually. I cannot prove these things to you. You must experience them for yourself."

"Uh-huh," Sam said. "Sounds to me like it's all in your head. If two people can't observe the same event as independent observers, there is no logical reason to be certain in said event."

Tovas shook his head and turned to his clay. Sam did so as well, satisfied with his argument.

Now, to the impossible task at hand: slicing clay with my mind.

The clay bar was about two inches long, an inch wide, and maybe a quarter inch thick. It would fit easily into his palm. Others had mentioned that imagination worked better than thinking commands in their head, but Sam had tried everything at this point. He'd spent hours staring at sand, at nothing, at a match, at that stupid vial of water that refused to transform. He'd imagined changes in every way he could fathom. Nothing worked.

He sighed heavily, looking around the room. Rose was talking with Relon at the table next to theirs, but most of the other studies seemed to concentrate on the task, some with their eyes closed.

Sam stared intently at the clay on the desk for a moment more before also closing his eyes. He tried to relax his mind, but his thoughts drifted toward Kara. He wondered where she was and ached to be with her again. She would probably think that this was all just as ridiculous as he did . . . wouldn't she? He was unsure. She'd seemed to accept all the bizarre stuff the Sovereignty told them pretty readily. But that was different. It was advanced science and engineering, not Sorcery.

He imagined her beautiful round face. Those bright blue eyes, always moving about haphazardly. That shoulder-length brown hair, often pulled up into a tight ponytail. She usually wore a bit of light makeup, but Sam liked it on the days she didn't bother—the days he got to see her raw self.

She never gave any indication that she reciprocated Sam's

feelings, though. He had been eternally friend-zoned. Any mention of his feelings for her would almost certainly ruin their friendship. The thought filled Sam with renewed sorrow.

Faintly, Sam noticed subtle emotions about objects within him and around him. Heart. Lungs. Muscle. Chair. Table. Air. Clay.

As the emotion of clay passed through him, he tried to focus on it. He felt a strange connection to it, as he had felt with the liquid during their Water instruction. It was as if he could sense the pull of weight on it, along with the internal stress pressing up from the table beneath.

A realization pulsed through Sam like lightning. *For every action, there is an equal and opposite reaction.* Newton's third law of motion. He was feeling it in reality somehow. Gravity from Alvior pulled the clay downward, and the table pushed it upward, keeping it in place.

His heartbeat quickened with his excitement. That was one force. But what were the other forces again? Weak force, strong force, and electromagnetism. Electromagnetism—that was the one he wanted. He imagined the interactions of the molecules in the clay, pulling themselves together against the force of gravity.

What molecules made up clay? He didn't know. This was also alien clay, so who knew what was in it, but it should be held together with electromagnetic bonds regardless.

Sam felt the bonds, the material's interactions working against the forces that would otherwise pull it apart. Curious portions of darkness peppered the surface, spots where he couldn't sense anything. He wondered what they might be for a moment, before returning his focus to the substance he'd connected to. Squeezing his eyes shut, he imagined the bonds freeing themselves, letting themselves go, pushing themselves apart from each other.

The bonds broke.

Sam perceived the substance come apart, severing itself along the line of his concentration. He opened his eyes excitedly as the connection left him.

The clay was intact.

His shoulders slumped as disappointment beat down his

enthusiasm. *It was all just in my head*, he thought bitterly. *It's always just in my head.*

Something on the clay caught his eye. He leaned in closer, scrutinizing it.

There was a cut. A tiny one, but it was there—a fraction of a centimeter.

He had done it. Somehow, he had created a cut in the clay without touching it. Excitement resurfaced within him once more as he closed his eyes and leaned back. The feelings came quickly, passing through him. He moved his hand out toward the clay and felt it more powerfully. He established a connection again. Trying to focus on the entire bar, he imagined the internal bonds of the substance releasing again—the two halves pushing apart.

They complied.

Sam opened his eyes. Past his outstretched hand, two halves of the former bar of clay sat on the table in front of him, cut clean through.

"Yes!" he declared.

Tovas gasped. "You did it?"

Sam glanced over at him and grinned. "It worked!"

"Sam has done it!" Tovas exclaimed.

Fita, Vurkil, Talanna, and Niu rushed over. A few others trailed behind, including Master Azeloram.

"Ha! I knew he could do it!" Vurkil bellowed as he arrived.

As exhaustion took hold, Sam tried to let his mind go again with his eyes open, and he stretched his hand out once more. He reestablished his connection with the clay—imagined it rising, overcoming the force of gravity, releasing itself from the pressure against the table. The bar rose into the air, drawing the eyes of his spectators. Sam felt extraordinary weariness take hold. Sorcery fatigue was no joke.

"Excellent," the Master said. "You have finally accepted the importance of fa—"

"Scheln!" Tovas cried, causing everyone to jump.

The outburst broke Sam's concentration—and his connection. The clay fell to the table. Sam turned in his seat, finding Scheln as

Tovas rushed to him in the back corner. There didn't seem to be anything abnormal about him.

"What is it, Tovas?" Master Azeloram asked.

Tovas ignored him and focused on his brother as he approached his table. "Do it again!"

Silence. Everyone in the room watched with expectation, but nothing happened. The twins were just staring at each other.

Master Azeloram broke the silence. "Tovas, I don't und—"

"It's Scheln!" Tovas exclaimed. "He's speaking to me!"

Then he laughed.

"He says the left side of his butt itches terribly."

Chapter 22

Just a Scratch

Pain. Stench.

Jeanette awoke, wishing she could sleep more. The nightmares were more pleasant than her reality.

Rope bit into her wrists as she hung by them, and her body was pressed against the cold stone wall of her cell. She couldn't stop the tears, which fell down her cheeks and dripped to the stone below. The tight jumpsuit Belze had given her offered little protection from the frigid dungeon air.

She had almost been free of this hell. Almost.

A scream of frustration and despair escaped her. Her wails echoed against the walls of her tiny cell. She couldn't take it anymore; she needed to die. It was the only way she would be free of this torment.

"No, you can be strong. You can still overcome this," Amy's voice said in her mind.

"Shut up!" Jeanette screamed. "You know *nothing* about this."

"I do. You can endure." Amy's fictitious response was calm, focused.

Jeanette let out another cry of frustration. *I can't keep doing this. I can't. I can't . . .*

"You can. Have hope."

There was no hope. She was powerless.

A thought stilled her: Belze's actions in the cave, many hours ago. Jeanette had power now. Belze had given her a gift. Maybe she could use it.

Jeanette tried to calm her anxiety. Belze had told her to relax—to feel. It took several minutes to quiet her mind sufficiently, but eventually, the emotions came, passing through her. Flowing blood. Beating heart. Sore tissue. Stone. Rope.

She held on to the fleeting emotion of rope as it passed, and she perceived an odd feeling of sorrow as it connected to her. She felt its tension against the weight of her body. *Break,* she told it.

Nothing happened.

Imagination, she remembered. She imagined the rope snapping, letting her weight fall from it and releasing that tension. She felt a few strands comply with almost inaudible tiny snaps. It did little to free her, however.

Footsteps echoed from the stairway.

Her heart quickened. She dry-heaved while squeezing her eyes shut at the raging thunderstorm of emotion and dread within her.

The steps stopped. The latch to her cell squeaked as it opened. Ragged breathing filled her ears as the steps approached her. Fear smothered her thoughts.

The bond around her wrists loosed with a snap, and Jeanette fell to the cold, hard floor. She scrambled toward the corner, then turned toward her visitor.

It was the woman. The one who had asked her to kill a man several days ago and then abused her when she refused. She wore the same strange outfit as always. Spiked boots. Symbols swirling around her dark, long-sleeved top. The hood of her cloak was pulled back, revealing her long black hair and pale white face.

"Hello, Jeanette."

She knows my name. How does she know my name?

"I don't think I ever introduced myself," the woman said. "I'm Tess."

I don't care who you are, you disgusting woman.

Tess extended a hand toward Jeanette. "Come with me. I have something to show you."

This person was not trustworthy. Jeanette knew it. She was unsure which course of action led to the more terrible outcome, so she remained still, shivering in her corner and staring into the woman's dark brown eyes.

Tess laughed. "There's no need to look so terrified. I won't harm you."

Jeanette let out a skeptical "huh" before she could stop herself.

Tess put her hands on her hips. "Aww, so distrustful. Didn't we have fun last time? At any rate, the Deia just wants you to come with me for a bit, but if not, I guess I can strip you of those clothes instead."

Jeanette's eyes widened. She released herself from the corner, feeling defeated.

"Oh, don't look so glum. We're going to have some fun!" Tess exclaimed as she beckoned Jeanette to follow her out of the cell.

Jeanette still had nightmares from the last time they "had fun."

They made their way up the steps from the dungeon. As they reached the top, Jeanette reflected on the last time the woman had led her from the cell. Jeanette wasn't stupid enough to try escaping again. Perhaps if she could develop her new abilities somehow. Maybe then.

No. Even Belze wasn't strong enough to get away, and she was experienced—far more powerful than Jeanette could ever hope to be. An escape attempt was futile. Hopeless.

They made their way down the dismal, dimly lit halls. Tess led her around a corner, and Jeanette was surprised to see two women in thick robes standing near the walls with large buckets in their arms. Plaster streamed from the buckets onto the walls of its own accord, spreading quickly and evenly against the stone walls. They walked past several more buckets of plaster on the floor. Tess didn't even glance at those working.

Jeanette looked around at the freshly plastered walls. There were a few narrow windows, but no light came through them. Winds bellowed outside, and she frowned. Did the sun ever shine here?

A door opened near the end of the hallway, and a large man emerged from it. Jeanette flinched with sudden panic when she realized it was the same man who had subdued her during their attempted escape. He dragged a limp body by the arm. Long, brown hair streaked with strands of gold cascaded across the face, which contrasted with the bit of visible brown skin beneath. Black leather guards encircled her forearms, and she wore a sleek black jumpsuit with a large belt.

Belze.

The man pulled her through the doorway and away from them. A faint trail of blood painted the stone floor behind the body.

Tears welled up in Jeanette's eyes. "What did you do to her?" she asked, trembling.

Tess tilted her head to the side and giggled. "*I* did nothing." She moved forward and turned about, smiling at Jeanette as she held the door open.

Fear rose in Jeanette's gut again. She dreaded what she might find. Walking hesitantly, she entered through the doorway into a small room with bare stone walls. The sight of a man inside caused her to stop in shock.

It was *that* man. The one she had fought and spared. He leaned against the wall that separated the room from the hallway. A small table stood nearby with something steel on it. His curly black hair had grown longer since their encounter and now fell over his face. He glanced at Jeanette with widening eyes.

"I . . . What? You? This . . ." His words stumbled out but trailed off.

Tess flung the door shut behind her and raced over to him.

He backed away. "No. No, wait!"

Tess gripped the man's throat and slammed him against the wall he was backing into. He choked and grabbed her arm.

Tess, maintaining the grip on his neck, forced him to step

sideways and backwards until he fell into the steel chair at the other end of the small room. With incredible speed, she bound his wrists and ankles to the sides of the chair with cords. The man attempted to speak but was unable to get any intelligible words out, instead falling into a fit of coughing.

As the woman worked, Jeanette noticed small pools of blood on the stone floor around the chair where the man now sat, as well as the trail of blood leading to the door. She inspected the long, thin steel object on the small table across the room. It looked like a back scratcher with sharp points—more like a set of extended claws. They dripped with blood.

This man must have tortured Belze, Jeanette concluded, fury rising within her. *Why? Why would they have* him, *of all people, do it? And why would they bring me here?*

After completing the final bind on the man's left ankle, Tess stood and wrapped a gag around the man's head. "There we are. He's all yours, Jey." She moved past Jeanette, who stared blankly, and opened the door.

Jeanette's heart pounded in her ears. "Wait, what do you want *me* to do with him?"

Tess shrugged. "The Deia commanded me to leave you here with him for a while. That's all I know."

"I will not kill him."

The woman passed through the door and turned around. "No one expects you to *kill* him. Enjoy!"

The door slammed.

The man bound to the chair looked up, his expression terrified. Jeanette attempted to make sense of the situation. He had likely been driven by the Deia's forces to torture and kill Belze —the only real friend she had in this horrific place. Jeanette didn't consider that an acceptable excuse, however. He still would've had a choice. He could have said no, as she had.

He deserved to be punished.

But not by her. Who was she to execute judgment on this man?

Then again, who else was there? Everyone else was a subject of the Deia. Jeanette was the only one on Belze's side. If she did nothing about it, surely no one else would.

"*Don't do it,*" Amy said, her voice breaking into Jeanette's mind. "*They're up to something. I don't know what it is, but harming him is what they* want *you to do. Don't give in.*"

Jeanette walked toward the table and glanced at the clawlike tool. *He deserves punishment. He should have resisted as I have. I won't go too far. Just enough to let him know it was a terrible thing to do.*

"*It's not for you to decide.*" Amy's irritating voice wouldn't leave her alone. "*You don't even know exactly what happened.*"

I know enough.

Jeanette grabbed the claw by the handle and hoisted it. It was much lighter than she thought it would be.

"*It's what they want you to do!*" Amy repeated in her mind.

"I DON'T CARE ANYMORE!" Jeanette screamed.

The man stilled at her sudden outburst.

"I just want it to end," she whispered.

She strode toward the man, who strained against his bindings.

I'm not giving in, she told herself. *I won't kill him.*

Jeanette raised the claw and looked into the man's terrified eyes. *Good. He should be scared after the pain he's inflicted.* Her choice over this man's fate gave her a sensation of power she didn't realize she'd longed for. Helplessness and despair had consumed her for what seemed like weeks. Now she had agency. She couldn't choose her own fate, but she could choose this man's.

The memory of her confrontation with him during their forced combat emerged in her mind. She recalled the lust in his eyes, the way he attacked her. And now he had done something terrible to Belze.

He deserved punishment for his crimes.

She lowered the sharp claws—still colored with traces of Belze's blood—against the man's forearm. He struggled, mumbling furiously.

Jeanette swept the claw swiftly and sliced three lines against the pale skin. Blood leaked through the light scratches, and the man uttered muffled cries of pain.

She studied his face as it manifested his suffering. "That's for Belze."

She stood motionless, watching blood rise from the man's wounds.

Moments later, the door swung open.

Tess walked in, beaming at Jeanette. "Just a scratch? Why don't you give him a good slice across the face. He could use it."

Jeanette dropped the steel. It clanged against the cold stone floor. "No," she said.

Tess shrugged, still looking bizarrely cheerful. "All right then. Back to your cell. Come on."

Jeanette followed Tess out, then glanced back at the man. Streaks of blood dripped down his forearm, and his head bent forward.

They walked through the doorway and turned right, past the freshly plastered walls and the working women.

Jeanette felt a slight pang of guilt at her satisfaction. But why should she? The man was rotten. He deserved it.

Besides, it was just a scratch.

Chapter 23

To See or Not to See

The blindfold fell. Kara opened her new eyes for the first time and sensed—something?

She felt an odd mix of sensations. Things she couldn't explain. Some were familiar, some were new, but it definitely didn't feel like she was *seeing* anything.

Something caused her to jump.

"You can see that! You can see me?" Nikor asked.

"Uh, I don't know what you're talking about. I can't see anything," Kara replied.

"You flinched! I waved my hand in front of your face, and you flinched!"

Kara waved her own hand in front of her eyes, but she didn't seem to sense anything different. "I don't know. Maybe these things are broken."

"I doubt that. Besides, didn't the technician say that it would take a while for you to adjust?"

"Yeah, but it's already been several days. Shouldn't I be able to see *something* by now?"

His shoulder moved under her arm, indicating a shrug. They

were seated on the sofa in Nikor's small apartment. He had found some kind of charity community on a planet called Invar that had government-provided housing. Apparently, the community was relatively unique in that it didn't require registration; tenants could remain anonymous. Nikor said it was good for him because there was some prejudice in the Sovereignty against Molkinarans, though Kara had never witnessed it personally.

She found herself restless, eager to apply to the Armed Forces. Sight was needed before she could do so, however. The doctor had said to wait at least six days before taking off the bandages, but she couldn't stand it any longer. Besides, it was only a day early.

She had also completed some of the "acquaintance proce-dures" for her Nit, but she still had several more to go before it was "fully integrated."

"How do my eyes look?" she asked.

"They look just like they always have—without the shakiness."

"They don't have nystagmus?"

"I don't know what that is, but if it's another word for shaky eyes, then yes, it's gone."

"Huh," Kara said. "Sounds weird already."

"You miss your eyes' shakiness?" he asked.

Kara moved her arm out from under his nice, firm back and connected her hands together as she leaned forward on her knees, considering his question seriously. "I don't know. Yes? I mean, it was an aspect of my natural-born eyes, you know? They didn't work like most people's eyes, but, as I said before, that's one thing I liked about them."

He placed a hand on the back of her shirt, tracing the outline of her bra lightly with his fingertips. It sent shivers of pleasure across the skin underneath.

"Well, I'm glad you're getting sight," he said. "Then I can show you all these muscles I've been working so hard for!"

She smiled, elbowing him and looking at him with eyes that couldn't see. "Uh-huh. They're certainly dwarfed by the size of your head, though, so that must look awkward."

"Huh? My head is normal. What's wrong with my—"

Kara laughed. "It's a joke! Having a big head means you're full of yourself."

He moved his hand from her back. "Full of myself? I don't get how—"

"Ugh. You have a massive ego!" she exclaimed. "Do I have to spell it out for you?"

"Hey, it's not my fault you say weird things no one would understand."

"Well, they make sense where I'm from."

Nikor chuckled. "I'm sure they do. Anyway, I think my ego is just fine."

"Riiight. *I* think you have about as much humility as I have eyesight."

"Well, that's getting better every day."

"Or so they say," she said with a small laugh. "I still can't see your face, even though it's right in front of mine."

The sofa rustled as he shifted. "Have you read the technical manual he sent you?"

"Uh . . . no? I can't read." She pointed to her non-functional new eyes.

"I meant have your Jit read to you, you wisacre."

"Wisacre?" she asked. "Now who's saying weird things no one would understand! What the hell is a wisacre?"

"Uh . . . a wisacre. You know . . . a kind of sassy know-it-all?"

"Oh! You mean like a wiseass or a smartass?"

"What's an ass?"

They laughed together.

"You know," Kara said, "it's funny that the Sovereignty supposedly introduced this language to Earth, but they're missing out on some important terms."

"Well yeah, I'd guess they can never keep everything completely in line with current speech, right?" Nikor said. "Every place has different ways of saying things based on local culture."

"You're not even from the Sovereignty. How do you speak it so well?"

"Molkinarans speak a very close dialect. And, like I mentioned before, I joined the separatists on Enck years ago. We were a Sovereignty-supported colony—mostly plugged into Sovereignty society—but they didn't want to bring us in as citizens while we were still technically in Molkinar territory."

"I guess that makes sense."

Silence settled for a moment as Nikor placed his hand on her back and traced the outline of her bra again. "So why don't you just send me your manual? I'll look at it."

"All right," she responded.

Kara stretched her fingers down and grabbed the Jit wrapped around her wrist. She gave it a light press until the beep sounded.

"Please send the manual for my eyes to Nikor," she said.

When she had first given a similar command to contact Nikor a few days ago, she wondered if it would even work, since there must be thousands of Nikors in the Sovereignty. It always seemed to know which one she was talking about.

"All right, I've got it," he said. "Let's see . . ."

She remained leaned into her knees as he continued to run his fingers lightly across her back, supposedly reading the manual. She wondered how it displayed the information to him. Was it a projection? Some kind of three-dimensional hologram? She'd never heard Sam or Nikor talk about their Jits having screens of any kind. As far as she knew, they were the same as hers. She wanted to ask, but also didn't want to break his concentration.

"So it says here that the eyes introduce new sensory information gradually to your nervous system. It starts with an extremely dull sensation of light contrast and movement, then steadily increases the sensitivity and resolution. So, right now, you might only see very sharp changes in light, dark, and movement. It also says you're still supposed to have your blindfold on."

"Heh, I already had a sense of light and dark before," she said. "So that's nothing new."

Kara tilted her head and *did* sense something different changing, beyond her sense of balance. She couldn't understand it, though. It was like hearing a faint whisper that faded before you could listen properly.

"Can you see anything when you move your head or eyes?" Nikor asked.

She looked up, moving her head back and forth awkwardly. "Hmm. I mean . . . I can sense *something* changing, I guess, when I move my head around." She then stared straight upward. "But when I stop, I don't really sense anything."

Fleeting, fuzzy impressions danced in her mind as she alternated between staring straight ahead and moving her head around. An increasing sense of dizziness eventually stopped her.

"Well, according to the manual, it says that's normal," he said. "It will increase sensitivity to different things slowly over the next couple of days as it learns how to interpret your neural responses. You should have your sight pretty soon."

Kara sighed. "I hope so. I can't very well spend *all* my money shopping because I have nothing else to do." Well, shopping and training. She had to keep her physique up if she was going into the military.

Nikor laughed, rudely removing his fingers from her back. A light three-note jingle sounded from his position.

"What was that?" she asked.

He paused for a moment. "Oh, nothing. Just my other girl."

Kara held her mouth open in mock offense. "You jerk!" She hit him playfully, her fist landing on his large shoulder. "*Other* girl. So I'm your girl now, am I?"

He placed his magic fingers on her shoulder and stroked it. *Return to the back*, Kara thought. *They work much better there.*

"Well, I thought it was obvious, given how much time we've been spending together."

"Uh-huh," she replied. "I'll have you know that I have high standards for boyfriends, and I don't think you quite make the cut, sir."

He laughed. "Well then. Since we aren't courting, what are your plans for tonight?" he asked. "Shopping?"

She couldn't help but crack a small smile. "Oh, I don't know. Another kiss would be nice."

"Oh! So I don't make the cut to be your man, but you want me to *kiss* you?"

"Yes," Kara said matter-of-factly. "If we improve your technique enough, maybe we'll get there."

Nikor chuckled in an embarrassed tone. It was cute.

Something changed as his face came closer. Maybe she was seeing it!

It was nothing more than a subtle change as his face blocked the light. The distinctive scent of his breath approached. Her heart quickened, and the butterflies returned to her stomach. He moved his hand down to her back again, sending ripples of pleasure up her spine.

She closed the distance between them herself, connecting her lips to his. Her tongue lightly brushed against his as they kissed with passion. Light facial hair tickled her chin, and his hand traveled across her back to her other shoulder, holding her close. Fingers brushed against her thigh as he slid his left hand to a position just above her knee. She reached around with her right hand and touched his face, feeling the roughness of his cheek. His fingers tickled upward on her thigh as their lips continued to dance. His grip on her shoulder tightened. Her heartbeat thundered in her ears. The fingers on her thigh reached slowly higher.

Too high.

She grabbed his hand and broke the kiss suddenly, heart still thumping furiously. "That was a bit too far."

"What? Are you serious?" he said.

"Uh, yeah," Kara replied. "I'm not having *sex* with you."

"But you . . . you came over. We—"

She stood, her own voice rising. "All you've been thinking about is having sex with me this *whole time?*"

"Well . . . I . . . uh . . . No. Not exactly . . ."

"Ugh. You jerks are all the same!" She pulled the cane from her pocket and moved toward the door as she extended it. She didn't know the whole layout of his apartment too well, but she knew where the door was.

A hand grabbed hers. "Kara, I'm sorry. Please don't leave like this."

He sounded sincere.

She stopped and turned toward him, her thoughts and feelings churning into an indistinguishable mess within her. She sighed and then chose her words carefully and calmly. "It's okay, Nikor. I should probably go anyway. It's getting late, and I'm tired. I'll call you tomorrow, all right?"

"All right." He seemed relieved. "I'll talk to you tomorrow, then."

She gave a nod and a slight smile. He was fun to be with, but that had crossed a line. Besides, it really *was* getting late, and she really *was* feeling tired.

Her hand slid from his as she departed into the night, noting the new sensual experience as she emerged into the urban darkness.

Chapter 24

Fire

"What do you think the surprise is?" Talanna asked.

Most in the group simply shrugged, including Rose. She sat at the end of the lunchroom table, Vurkil next to her. They had been the first to arrive after the morning half of their Fire instruction. Everyone except Scheln, who was being fed by the healers. Tovas had remained with his brother for lunch today. Their psychic connection had been a surprise, but Master Azeloram told them it was actually common with Sorcerers who were identical twins.

"Maybe he will make something explode!" Vurkil said through a mouthful of chewy olgna.

A few of them chuckled.

"I seriously doubt that," Sam said through his laughter, "but who knows?"

Rose glimpsed Ya'ir at the other end of the table, who smiled fondly at Sam's words. Sam himself had gone back to eating his own plate of olgna, oblivious to the attention. Rose thought it to be a strangely affectionate gaze, lasting only a moment before Ya'ir turned away.

The group returned to their meals with occasional chatter.

Rose wasn't paying much attention. Her mind was consumed with their task for the day: transmuting air into methane and then igniting it immediately to produce a flame.

They had been given a small vial of methane gas so they could get a sense of its composition. Then they were to Vitalize some air, change it into methane, and ignite it as they had done with the match the week before. It was an exciting task, but one that proved quite difficult, even for Tovas, who seemed to be gifted with Sorcery. It built upon many of the tasks they had completed previously—transmuting water into potion the week prior and moving air the day before.

Truthfully, they had all barely focused on the task before lunch, since they wanted to make sure they remained awake for Master Farco's surprise. He had encouraged them to take it easy for that very reason.

Moving air proved tricky in and of itself, since it required quickly releasing and establishing new connections to get a constant flow in a single direction. Moving a single column of air around wasn't very useful. By the end of the class, every study had some level of success. Rose was glad that Sam had accomplished something with Sorcery after their second Land instruction. He had struggled for so long.

"What do you believe, Rose?" Talanna asked, breaking into Rose's thoughts.

"What?" she said, blushing heavily. "Sorry, I ... wasn't listening."

"You believe in the Divine, don't you?"

Oh. They're discussing religion again. I wonder who brought that topic up. She glanced at Sam. He stared back at her with an eager expression as he chewed his food.

"Yes, for the most part," she said, the weight of their attention smothering her thoughts.

"For the most part? What is that supposed to mean?" Talanna said in an accusatory tone.

Rose glanced at the faces of her fellow studies at the table, most of whose eyes were now on her. Her cheeks burned under their scrutiny, and panic rose from within.

"I do. I mean, yes! I didn't really mean anything by it."

Their eyes, thankfully, returned to their food. Rose sighed, and her nerves calmed down again.

Talanna nodded. "You see, Sam, everyone else believes. Why don't you? They've done more than enough to prove they know what they're talking about. This Sorcery is more than enough evidence."

Sam swallowed the bit of olgna he was chewing. "Well, it's not for me. I'm not buying it."

"Why are you so distrustful of religion?" she asked.

He picked at his food for a moment, looking melancholy. "It's almost always inherently hypocritical. It also causes people to discard truth when it doesn't fit their worldview."

"But it's all *about* truth!" Talanna argued. "They have *shown* us these—"

"Rudds, will you *give it up* already." Irritation laced Vurkil's low voice. "This argument is stupid."

Rose was thankful for the interjection. Talking about religion with Sam around was uncomfortable. He was frequently contentious with theological discussions. *Could it have something to do with his friend who was kidnapped?*

"We should return to class anyway," Fita said, standing up. "The bell will sound any second now."

As if on cue, the bell rang, telling the studies to return to class. Rose was impressed with the man's keen sense of time. There were no clocks in the lunchroom.

They made their way back to the Fire room. Rose settled in her seat as Zel sat in the one next to her. The ulinko showed up out of nowhere, nuzzling Zel's boot.

"Aww!" Zel scratched the creature's head fondly. "You have a pleasant lunch too? I was thinking about rainbows. Rainbows are sooo pretty. All the colors. Especially green today. I think the universe likes green today. Green is such a soothing color. Makes me think of gula slug mucus."

Zel often talked to the creature. It seemed to enjoy the attention. She also talked to inanimate objects, though, so it probably shouldn't count itself too special. That woman's thought processes were quite unconventional.

"Welcome back," Master Farco announced. His blond hair stood straight up, coming to a point over the light pink skin of his head. He had a long face with a sparse beard over his square jaw. "I hope you all had plenty to eat. We are going to take a brief break from your assignment and head to another part of the castle. Please follow me."

They rose from their seats and followed him out of the room, with Tovas pushing his brother in the wheelchair. Master Farco led them through the elaborate halls to a staircase that spiraled downward. Rose looked back at Tovas and Scheln.

Master Farco must have realized the problem as well. "Oh, Tovas, I think you're going to need to leave your brother up here. There is no other way to access this room, I'm afraid."

He turned and began his descent, the studies following his lead.

"Sorry, Scheln. I can—" Tovas paused. "Are you sure?" Scheln didn't seem to do anything, but Rose knew he was communicating telepathically to Tovas. "Okay, I'll tell you all about it from below."

She turned and descended, Tovas trailing behind. They were the last two of the group. At the bottom of the stairs was a short, plain hallway with two rooms at each end. Master Farco led them to the right and unlocked the solid steel door at the end with a key, then held it open for them to enter.

"Please do not touch anything," he instructed.

Studies ahead of her gasped as they entered, raising her own anticipation.

She crossed the threshold with wide eyes and took in the ancient weapons filling the small storage room—swords, maces, staves, spears, clubs, and all kinds of other instruments of steel, wood, and stone. They covered the walls, and three rows of shelves held even more. The studies spread out around the room, admiring the items.

Rose followed behind Fita, who looked like a child in a candy store. She smiled at his enthusiasm. It wasn't surprising, given that he was Helenestian. She didn't know their history in detail, but she knew that martial arts and ancient weapons training were an integral part of their culture.

Her curiosity got the better of her. "Did you train with these kinds of weapons, Fita?"

Fita's gaze rested on a sword with a slight curve to it that was mounted on two metal hooks. She could tell that he was itching to reach for it. "Yes," he replied. "All Helenestians train from the time we can walk. When we come of age, we choose our weapon specialty for life. It is symbolic."

It was the most she had ever heard him speak. His accent matched his sister's, heavily punctuated and proper.

"I suppose your choice was the sword?" she asked.

"The saber," he replied. "It is an elegant weapon. Quick. Versatile. There are many types."

"What about your sister?"

"Kula chose the longbow."

Their ancient weapon training was more traditional than practical, Rose knew, but she'd much rather have a firearm in any actual fight.

"Ah, I must applaud your taste in weaponry, Fita." Master Farco approached them from behind. They turned to face him as he grabbed the hilt of the sword Fita had been eyeing and moved off to the slightly more open side of the room. He called out loudly, "Everyone, please observe."

Chatter died as interested faces turned to the Master.

He gestured to the room. "These are ancient weapons, passed down through the ages and cataloged by the mysterious inhabitants of Tercast before Grand Master Ilius's discovery," he explained. "They used to be at the back of the castle in one large space, which is now our infirmary. Now they occupy two smaller rooms. The others are in a nicer display room on the west side of the castle, which you will visit during your next Land instruction."

Raising a small dagger briefly, he continued. "Each artifact is inclined to a particular Elemental effect. I wanted to bring you here because this is where we keep most of the Fire-associated items."

Master Farco pulled off the glove from his right hand, then raised the polished steel-looking sword he had taken by grasping the hilt inside the intricate, patterned guard. The blade glowed red and quickly became white. Small flames danced along its edge, growing slightly. The glow cast sharp shadows of the studies and shelves in the room as everyone shielded their eyes from the intense light.

"That is impossible!" Vurkil exclaimed from the other side of the room. "How does it not melt?"

"Excellent question," Master Farco said. "We do not know. The blade has an incredible affinity for Fire Sorcery and keeps its solidity and edge under extreme heat."

Everyone continued to watch in awed silence as the flames died and the metal cooled with abnormal speed.

The blade's affinity for heat is likely designed more for psychological rather than physical effect, Rose thought. The point of cutting was to make the target hemorrhage enough to bleed to death. That level of heat might cauterize a wound, inflicting extreme pain but ultimately reducing blood loss. The likelihood of infection from the burns could possibly cause death, but that was much slower than death from blood loss. Unless the heat was high enough to cause explosive expansion of body fluids. That would do some serious damage—and be *really* messy.

The sword returned to its silvery appearance. "Now, of course, no weapons may be carried within the halls of Tercast. They are barbaric. These weapons likely caused the original citizens' downfall. However, we can learn from their mistakes. There are some important principles that these weapons can teach us."

Master Farco walked forward and placed the sword on top of the shelf in front of him. He then picked up a thin arrow, raising it high for everyone to see. The crystal tip began glowing red, then white, just as the blade had. A small flame rose from it.

"Now, if I were to pick up a random piece of metal, do you think I could heat it to this degree?"

Everyone was silent. *How would we know?* Rose wondered.

"The answer is no," he said. "This arrow and the sword have been imbued with an affinity for Fire through their history. Master Azeloram will teach you all about enchantments in more detail, but I want you all to understand the *power* of these kinds of enchantments. I think it is easiest to visualize and appreciate with Fire."

The small arrowhead dimmed and returned to its clear crystal appearance rather quickly. He placed it back on the table.

"All right, that is all!" he said, slipping the glove back onto his hand. "Please make your way back to the classroom so you may continue working on your task."

"Can we hold some of these?" Talanna asked.

Master Farco picked up the sword and walked toward Rose and Fita. "No, no, that would be very unwise. These are really quite dangerous. You may admire them from a distance on your way out, but please do not touch." He placed the sword back in its original spot on the wall, then moved to a position where he could observe the studies.

Rose turned to walk out, leaving Fita to admire the sword a bit more. As she crossed the threshold into the hallway, a voice called behind her.

"Hey, Rose."

Her cheeks blushed at Sam's greeting. She cursed them.

"Hi, Sam," she said, stopping to let him walk up next to her.

Zelyra skipped up the stairway ahead.

"So . . . I was wondering . . ." he said as they walked together down the hallway.

Rose's stomach twisted with apprehension. This was going to be bad. She could feel it. He was going to ask to court her or something.

"Do you really believe in the Divine?" he asked. "You seemed hesitant earlier."

Her tension dispersed. "Well, I don't think I can say that I *know* the Divine exists. But I believe."

They took the first step of the spiral staircase together.

"Well, then, do you really think such a being would want us to avoid studying these gifts on our own?" Sam said.

Rose knew where he was going with this. Her apprehension rose again.

"I ... I don't know," she replied. "My family has always believed in spiritual things in a vague sense, but we feel that individual knowledge and study are important as well. I think their rule against it is strange, but he also said it was for our own safety."

She glanced over at Sam's eyes to judge his reaction. He seemed lost in thought, staring at the stairs as they climbed.

"That's why I need you," he whispered. "I trust you. I *need* to study these abilities more in-depth. You have medical training, so we can be safe doing it. There are also some experiments I can't possibly do on my own."

"Sam, that's a reckless—"

"Shh!"

She subdued her voice as she continued. "That's a reckless idea! Didn't you hear him? We could be in serious trouble!"

"I know," he said. "I don't care. This is important. I'm doing it with or without you, but I would feel a lot safer with you there."

Rose considered her options. She could inform the Masters of Sam's decision. Maybe they would prevent him from going forward with it without doing something terrible to him. It was supposedly her duty as a Tercast study to do so. But she would feel *terrible* if they *did* do something to him. What if they banished him? She couldn't possibly risk that. Another choice, of course, was to say no. He might hurt himself. Or someone else. But why was that her problem? Why should *she* risk punishment for something he shouldn't be doing in the first place?

Still, she had to admit that she was enticed by the idea of learning more about Sorcery. She knew that Sam would approach the subject scientifically rather than theologically, which was something that irked her a bit about the Masters' teaching methods. It would be interesting to see what they could discover. While she couldn't yet heal tissue with Sorcery, her medical training could definitely come in handy if something went wrong.

The duo turned to face each other as they reached the top step. Rose glanced up and down the hallway quickly to see if anyone was nearby. The only other person, Zelyra, turned the corner ahead.

She sighed, anxiety tugging at her insides. "All right, Sam. I'll do it. What's the plan?"

Chapter 25

Into Focus

Colors! My God, the colors!

Kara was outside. She *had* to go outside. Blues, greens, purples, oranges, and yellows blended across her vision as she turned her head while running around outside her temporary apartment complex they called a Swiftbode. To the others walking about, she probably looked deranged, but she didn't care. She could see colors! Things still weren't in focus, but she could see! Nikor had helped her identify some shapes and colors the day before, and she had started to understand a little bit of depth perception—but now the colors had become so much more *vibrant*. She could make out rough outlines of people, faces, tables, sofas, trees, and other large objects, though not at a distance of more than a few feet.

She'd been surprised to observe that water was, in fact, not blue but clear. Why did people always say that it was blue? It was definitely *not* blue. She could hear some of it rushing over a nearby waterfall.

Bright yellow topped the surrounding trees. Green grass tickled her bare feet. She ran toward the edge of the field. Her shoulder rammed into a tree as she passed, nearly knocking her over, but she shrugged it off and kept going. She slowed as the blurry image of the gate came into view, and she reached out until she could grab on to it. Curiously, there was nothing but blue beyond, and the sound of rushing water became stronger as she approached it. The tall gray Swiftbode structure rose to her left, and another lighter structure that was whitish or yellowish rose to her right.

Colors were amazing, but it surprised her that there were so many of them. Logically, she knew that color was a spectrum, but to her, they had always felt like discrete things. Blue was distinct from green. Yellow differed from white. But that wasn't the case at all. There were all kinds of in-between colors, ones she had no name for besides "bluish purple."

She stared out, shading her eyes from the sun as she squinted into the distance. Thankfully, sunlight didn't cause significant pain, as the technician Rinzdee had promised. Her new eyes still couldn't make anything out specifically, but there was something brown in the distance—surrounded by what Kara assumed to be a light blue sky above, and something white and moving to the left of it. A cloud? Out to the right was nothing but more blue. Maybe it was the sky reflecting on the ocean? That was a thing, right? It *would* explain why people associated water with the color blue.

Turning her body, she leaned against the railing and looked back at the blurs of yellows, browns, and greens, which she knew were the trees, their trunks, and the grass. She took a deep breath, smiling as she basked in the sensation.

She turned around again, looking out past the silvery railing at endless blue.

What time is it for Nikor?

She pressed her Jit until it beeped. "What time is it on Invar?"

"The local time on the planet Invar is currently doh three two doh two, or fifteen twenty-six," it replied.

He should be home then. Kara had relocated to a temporary apartment on Rwenmar near the primary Armed Forces recruitment facility so she could go in as soon as her sight was ready. It was somewhat expensive, so she couldn't stay long term, but she justified the cost to stay at a place that advertised incredible views.

The scene before her unexpectedly snapped into focus. She blinked rapidly, moving her head to try to make sense of the image.

The lines and ridges of a surface rose in the center of her field of view—the brown mass she had made out before—surrounded by blue. She squinted and cocked her head, trying to understand the details of what she was seeing. A cliff maybe? Wavy white blobs, what she thought might have been a cloud, moved across it. Maybe her vision *wasn't* completely in focus yet. Were the blobs moving downward? Yes, downward. It seemed to be where the waterfall sounds were coming from. So the white blobs must be water! Droplets spilled over the edge of the cliff and fell into what she assumed was the ocean, which reflected the blue sky above.

Wait. Something isn't right here.

The water contained a patch of darkness, and the waterfall seemed to fall too far beyond it. She traced the rigid lines of what she thought was the cliff side toward the ocean, but couldn't find where it met the water. She inspected features nearby to try to reason how things worked, but the images didn't make sense. The building next to her cast a large dark patch into the grass opposite from the sun. A shadow? The dark patch in the water didn't seem to connect to the cliff the same way though. It was almost as if the cliff didn't reach the water at all.

Her hand subconsciously rose to her mouth as realization sunk in.

Kara strained her head against the tall bars, looking out as far as she could to the edge of the waterfall. The brown of the cliff side came under and expanded toward her position, and none of it reached the ocean below.

She was standing on a *floating island.*

When her Jit had said it was the highlands, she'd assumed it meant *mountains.*

Turning on her heel, she ran, admiring the incredible detail of the blades of grass that cast small shadows on themselves. The trees with bare, smooth, light brown trunks rose to a peak, where large branches with four-pointed leaves spread out above. As the bark approached, her shoulder rammed into it again. She still needed to get used to depth perception, but the detail was exquisite. The black sidewalk separated the grass ahead. Next to it lay her shoes, which were deep red with black soles.

Kara reached out and felt surreal as she noticed the sight of her hand. She turned it about, admiring the lines and tiny wrinkles. With haste, she slipped on her shoes and ran toward the transports.

A sudden thought struck her, causing her entire body to tingle with anticipation: It was now possible for her to see herself. Her full self. With *all* the details.

She needed a mirror.

Kara turned and bolted in through the Swiftbode entrance, slowing at the door to avoid running into it and ignoring the greeting by the AI displayed nearby. Large columns lined the elaborate open entryway that stretched several floors up. Enormous windows allowed light to pour in. The floor was a shiny white with dark veins running through it. Up ahead was the lift. The doors were glass—transparent.

Wait. Everyone could see into those things the whole time?

She ran to the doors as they opened, purposefully forcing herself not to look at her partial reflection. The first time she saw herself had to be in a mirror. No semitransparent reflections.

"My room," she said as she entered the lift.

The glass doors hissed shut. She couldn't help but squish her forehead into the glass as the vehicle rose smoothly and quietly, giving her a view of the elaborate entrance hall shrinking into the distance below. The large windows of the room moved downward relative to the lift until it reached her floor, which was only a few levels up.

As soon as the two panes of glass opened, Kara squeezed herself between them into the hallway. The walls were a light blue, and there were portraits and various other decorations gracing them. She was tempted to stop and admire the artwork, but first things first.

Kara started walking as she reached her apartment door, which slid open for her. She stepped slowly now, heart beating furiously, due to both tremendous anxiety as well as physical exertion.

She walked onto the dark wooden floors into the small living area, air noticeably warmer than the hallway behind her. Two elaborate wooden chairs with dim green seats sat in front of a handsome dark wood coffee table. A swirly pattern of whites and grays painted the rug underneath. The small kitchen in the corner to her right had bright metallic appliances.

Walking slowly through the living area, she approached the door to the bedroom. It hissed softly as it rose, allowing her to pass through.

A simple floor-length mirror hung from the wall on the other side of her bed, which was a mess of white sheets and a comfortable, fuzzy green blanket. Kara ignored the other items in the room as she focused intently on the mirror and approached it slowly. A hand and shoulder appeared in the reflection.

Kara squeezed her eyes shut, her heart thumping uncontrollably in her chest. *This might actually be the hardest thing I've ever had to do.* She took another step to the right and a step forward, which would position her in front of the mirror. *I can't do this. Why did I think I could? I can't do this! What if I don't like myself? This could ruin me forever.*

"Here we go," Kara whispered.

She moved the hair out of her face and inhaled deeply, holding it for a moment before exhaling as she opened her eyes.

Her reflection looked back at her, light blue eyes staring into her soul. Brown hair fell down the sides and back of her head to reach her shoulders. Thin eyebrows rose slightly toward the sides of her head. Pink lips sat under a cute nose, above a rounded chin. A bright red top curved over her bust, subtle darker lines running vertically down the material. Her hips stretched outward a little beyond her torso under the relaxed top. Black, tightly fitted pants stretched around her legs, past the knees to her ankles, where a small section of skin showed above her red shoes.

An intense concoction of exhilaration and disturbance emerged as she lifted a hand to her face, and her reflection did the same. She thought she looked pretty, even though she didn't really have anyone to compare herself to. Did she even understand what "pretty" looked like? Running hands along her neck and body, she experienced the familiar tactile sensation of her form and matched them up with the lines of the image before her. Seeing herself was as unsettling as it was extraordinary.

Nikor. She needed to *see* Nikor.

Kara raced back to the elevators and pressed her forehead against the glass again as it descended. From the front entrance of the Swiftbode, she raced to the transport vehicles. She usually called ahead to let him know she was coming, but today she wanted to surprise him. On the pad were sleek metal ascenders with large open windows and a few egg-shaped vehicles, which she guessed were the fast transports.

Kara's steps slapped against the concrete before she stopped at the landing pad, panting. She felt conflicted. Fast transports were her usual form of travel, since they got her around quickly. Now she could *see*, and seeing more of the world was immensely tempting.

But she also wanted to get to Nikor as soon as possible.

She decided she could see the sights on the way back, and moved into an available fast-transport vehicle.

When the vehicle finally landed, the sights and sounds of bustling people captivated her as she walked out onto the platform. It was night on this side of the planet. The area was lit by large bright lights overhead. Vendors of various goods sold things to the people walking by. She smelled chippers and the now familiar scent of nuumyun.

She pulled the cane from her pocket and extended it. Depth perception was still difficult to her, and she wanted to avoid bumping into people. The sight of it moving across her vision as she swept it back and forth was immensely bizarre.

Passersby moved about her wearing all kinds of interesting and colorful clothing as she made her way toward the large semicircular acheron on the path ahead. Guard rails directed the flow of foot traffic through the gate. People stepped into it on the right and out from it on the left.

A pale mother with her three daughters walked past briskly, holding two of them by the hand. The youngest, following behind, was crying, complaining about something she had left at home. Her pigtails swayed as she struggled to keep pace with her mother, and she gave Kara a curious look. Her wails stopped.

"What's that?" the girl asked, pointing at Kara's cane.

Kara smiled, but before she could speak, the mother turned and shushed her daughter, looking over Kara with scrunched eyebrows. The older daughters glanced at her as well.

Kara frowned at the woman. "It's okay. It's just my cane." She turned to the girl with a soft smile. "It helps me know where I'm going."

"Come Riana," the mother said, turning and pulling the other girls with her.

"Sorry, have to go," the girl with pigtails said with a wave. She wiped her eyes and took off after her mother, calling. "Can *I* have a cool cane like that?"

Kara grinned.

A group of ten or so colorful teenagers emerged from the other side of the acheron, chatting happily as they passed her by. More stares accompanied her as she approached the gate. She did her best to ignore them.

The crowd closed in around Kara as she made her way through the portal. Her eyes widened at the sight of the cylindrical space station. Stars and a large blue planet rotated quickly in and out of view of the windows on the other side of the curved floor, which seemed like the ceiling and walls from Kara's position, just as Sam had mentioned. Trees, shops, and people walking about overhead gave her a feeling of disorientation. She followed the guidance of her Jit until she arrived at the acheron to Invar. The portal was far less crowded, with only three others passing through from the other side.

It was evening on Invar, the setting sun a deep red, bathing everything in a crimson light. Tall buildings rose all around her as she approached the vehicle pad. She took a regular transport, since Nikor's apartment wasn't too far from the gate.

She sat in a comfortable gray seat in the ascender, staring out at the passing lights, flying vehicles, rounded skyscrapers, and people down below. After only a few minutes, the vehicle landed on the pad near Nikor's complex.

Kara felt her heart quicken in anticipation as she approached the door. Nikor had given her unlimited permission to enter, so the door whisked open. She stepped into his short plain hallway, smiling at the thought of his surprise at her arrival. The edge of the wall gave way to the single room, where the light gray bed sat against the far wall.

On it was a man with black hair and white skin—kissing a blond, tanned woman. Another woman with dark black hair and skin embraced his backside.

Kara froze with wide eyes, disgust and anguish quenching the flames of excitement.

The man noticed her and stood abruptly, knocking the woman behind him backwards.

"Kara!" he exclaimed in Nikor's voice. "I . . . uh . . . didn't know you were coming!"

Her mind froze. Powerful emotions surged within her, smothering any attempt at thought. Tears started to flow from her eyes, distorting her vision before running down her cheeks.

She needed to leave.

Kara turned and rushed toward the door. Nikor's steps came after her, but she couldn't seem to tell her legs to move any faster; her body was on autopilot.

His hand grabbed hers, and she stopped.

"Hey, don't go," he said. "Why don't you join in the fun?"

It was undeniably Nikor's voice. Kara remained motionless, letting her silent tears roll down her face to the floor.

"No."

The word escaped automatically. She felt like she must be in a dream. A nightmare. Nothing felt real anymore. She stared numbly at the shiny white door at the end of the short hallway.

A large hand and muscular arm moved around her shoulder. Fingers gently slid around her left breast as the hand holding hers pulled her backwards. A warm, firm body pressed against her back.

Nikor's voice spoke from above. "I promise you'll enjoy this."

Training took over. Kara closed her eyes, stepping her right foot back behind her assailant's as she grabbed the offending arm on her right. Her body pivoted ninety degrees, and she pulled on his arm, tripping him sideways over her foot. He flipped with a yelp of surprise before landing on his back with a loud *thump*. Kara opened her eyes and looked straight into his—which were wide with fear.

"I *never* want to see you again," she said calmly, tears still dripping down her cheeks.

She released his arm and reemerged into the urban landscape bathed in scarlet.

Chapter 26

Tools

Freezing water splashed against Jeanette's face. She turned the spigot handle, stopping the trickle. The water dripped down her nose and made her feel even colder. Drops hit the floor as she shook as much off her as possible before returning to her corner of the cell. She could wipe her face with her thin sleeves, but that wouldn't do much good, and the wet fabric would just carry even more precious heat from her body.

Jeanette glanced back at the empty bowl near the bars, then sat on the cold floor. Staring at her corner, she wrapped her arms around her legs, took a deep breath, and tried to focus on anything except her endless and terrifying reality. Her thoughts settled on Kara. Where could her sister be right now? Perhaps Sam's family or Liam's family had taken her in. She certainly wouldn't have let go of the events with Jeanette and her parents easily. Perhaps by now she had given up and was pressing forward with her goal of opening her own academy. That would be nice.

There wasn't even a little chance of them finding her here—on a different *planet,* apparently. People on Earth didn't even know that other habitable planets existed. At least, not as far as Jeanette was aware. She would have known, right? It would have been on the news or something.

Jeanette hoped that Sam was still with Kara. He would keep her grounded. Sam was a realist, always thinking with his head, hiding his heart behind that shroud of logic. He would help her move on with her life after the rest of her family was gone. Maybe Kara would fall for him over time. Jeanette couldn't help but smile at the thought of them together. They complemented each other well, Kara with her fierce determination and instincts, and Sam with his cautious, analytical perspectives.

Steps echoed from the stairway.

Jeanette's heart leapt into action, thumping in her ears. Hopefully, he was just coming to pick up the empty bowl. There were two sets of feet. Her stomach churned and she squeezed her eyes shut. *Oh no. Please, no.*

The steps stopped at her gate, followed by the sound of the latch screeching loose.

Tess's cheerful voice echoed against the stone walls. "You really like that corner."

Another squeak resounded as they opened the gate to her cell.

"Well, come on. The Deia has another task for you."

Jeanette stood and turned. Tess looked different this time. Her boots were shorter, only shin height. But she still wore a nefarious grin on her pale face.

Jeanette resigned herself to her fate and followed the woman up the stairs of the dungeon once more.

"Don't look so down!" Tess said. "You get to come out of your cell."

When I can come out of my cell without being forced into something terrible, then maybe I'll enjoy it a bit more.

They reached the top of the steps. Walls now shimmered a bright teal color, and lights had been added, illuminating the hallway. The rank smell of the dungeon faded into a pleasant, flowery aroma.

Tess led her down the same path as before. As they turned a corner, the wall color transitioned to a light peach. Jeanette had to rush to keep up with the woman. The fact that she seemed excited filled Jeanette with dread.

Tess opened the door to the same room as before and beckoned her inside with a smile. Jeanette paused.

"Here you are. Go on!" the woman urged.

Jeanette tentatively stepped through the doorway and found a familiar face. It was the charismatic announcer from the night of her fight—the man who had threatened her when she'd refused to kill the other prisoner.

A bang sounded behind her as the door shut abruptly. Jeanette jostled the handle, but Tess had locked it from the outside. She turned around to face the man. Straight black hair pointed up from his dark head. Instead of the elaborate black coat he had worn the last time she'd seen him, he wore a plain gray shirt and black pants. His feet were bare. He sat bound to a chair at the other end of the small stone room.

"Ah yes, I'm looking forward to this!" he said with a laugh.

Jeanette glanced toward the small table, where there were now several instruments: a knife, a pair of pliers, some strange hooklike tool, and a rounded hammer.

"Why am I here?" Jeanette asked.

He looked over her body. "Mmm, why don't you come a little closer and sit on my lap, woman."

Anger boiled within her. She glanced over at the tools on the desk and felt an urge to put them to use.

"*Jeanette, stop. Think!*" Amy's rather annoying voice broke into her consciousness. "*This is what they want you to do! They're trying to—*"

Shut up, Amy, Jeanette thought. *I know what they're trying to do. They want me to kill him. I won't do it.*

"Come on, woman. Come, give Yester some love. It'll be well worth your while." The man raised his eyebrows suggestively. "No more sitting around in the cold dungeons. You can stay up here, with the rest of us. All it takes is a little, you know"—he raised his eyebrows again—"*personal* entertainment."

He grinned as he looked her over with lustful eyes.

Disgust gnawed at Jeanette's stomach. This was some messed-up dominatrix fantasy of his, and he somehow believed that she would play along. Clearly, he thought she might comply if he offered her freedom from that cell. She would *never* stoop so low. Not even to escape her cell. It wouldn't matter, anyway, if she couldn't leave the castle. She would be just as much a prisoner here as she was in the dungeons.

"Take off that suit so I can get a good look at that delicious body of yours."

Jeanette clenched her fist, fury pulsing through her veins. She had suffered far too much abuse to take these words from the likes of him. Emotions passed through her in an instant, surprising her. She felt the stone floor, the table, the tools, the air. The man was a fuzzy blob in her perception.

She formed a connection with the hilt of the knife by instinct. Felt its weight against the table, accompanied by anguish, as if it were suffering. She instinctively raised her left arm toward it, imagining its weight in her hands and its defiance of gravity to get there. The knife scraped against the table as it flew into the air, the hilt landing perfectly in her palm. She gripped it tightly. It was lighter than it seemed from appearance.

The man's eyes went wide. "You're a *Sorcerer?* That's . . . That's not possible!"

Though Jeanette experienced a sudden and sharp wave of fatigue, the feeling of power outweighed her weariness. She was in control. This pitiful excuse for a man was at *her* mercy now.

He struggled against the bonds. "Help! Tess, Dak, get me out of here!"

No one came.

She walked toward him, fury blazing within her. She could end him, right here and now.

"*No!*" Amy's voice rose again in the back of her mind. "*This isn't you, Jeanette!*"

Jeanette stopped and inspected the fear in the man's eyes. The words of her parents rang in her mind. *Life is precious. It is sacred.* Even the life of the disgusting man before her.

It wasn't her place. It was wrong. She couldn't kill him.

The knife slipped from her weakening grip. It fell to the stone with a loud clang, ending up just an inch or two from the man's bare right foot. He watched the knife fall, then looked back up at her with eyes still wide. His breath was rapid. She stood over him for several seconds in silence, glaring at him.

Her anger subsided and gave way to a subtle feeling of guilt. She had almost gone too far. Something was wrong with her.

No. Something isn't wrong with me. I've been locked in a dungeon and tortured for what feels like weeks! It's normal *for me to react this way.*

The man's breathing slowed. "Cuds, woman. You sure know how to get the blood pumping. If you're a Sorcerer, that opens up so many more possibilities!" He licked his lips. "Bring that luscious body over here."

Without giving herself a second to think, Jeanette turned and walked to the table. She grabbed the hammer and stomped back toward him.

"Whoa, whoa! What are you—"

She brought the head of the hammer down with all of her strength, crushing the bones in his left hand. He screamed.

"Tess!" he yelled. "Get me out! *Get me out!*"

Jeanette swung the hammer down again on the same hand and broke his knuckles. He continued to cry for help and writhe as she swung the hammer down repeatedly, until his hand was a bruised, mangled mess of flesh, blood and bone fractures.

She stopped for a moment with a sense of satisfaction as she watched him scream. She had done this to him. And he'd deserved it. The hammer fell from her grip, landing head-first with a clink, followed by the thunk of the handle.

The door opened, and Jeanette turned to see a beaming Tess walk through the door.

"Tess!" the man exclaimed through tears. "Untie me!"

The woman walked briskly toward Jeanette, who recoiled and stumbled backwards toward the wall.

Tess threw her arms around her. Jeanette waited for a stab of pain, for something to pierce her sides or her back, for some kind of torture—but it never came. Tess's head rested on Jeanette's collarbone. She was *hugging* her.

Tess released the embrace. As she moved back, Jeanette stared at her smiling face with utter confusion. The man's wails still echoed around the small room.

"Oh shut up, Yester!" Tess yelled, causing Jeanette to jump.

The cries instantly quieted.

Tess gave Jeanette a look of admiration. "We have a wonderful new guest for dinner tonight!"

Chapter 27

The Quick and Thwarted

"So, what's our strategy?" Relon asked.

"I don't know," Tovas replied as he slipped on one of his studded shoes. "What do you think?"

Master Azeloram had designated Tovas as the Ulinko team captain. He didn't feel too comfortable about the assignment but accepted the responsibility regardless. The Master had just ushered them into one of the Elemorb preparation rooms for game day. They were not prepared for this. No one had even explained the rules to them yet. Relon had surprised him by sitting next to him on the bench. Her light blue skin made for an odd mix with their robes, which had been temporarily enchanted to a new purple-and-white color scheme by Master Azeloram.

"I think we should try to get the large goal," she said, cupping her chin. "It's better defended, of course, but I don't think we have a good enough grasp on fire and electricity yet as a group to get the forward goals very well. I think we also have an inherently better defense with Vurkil."

Tovas glanced at the giant. His size likely made him a tough target to get around, so her logic made sense to him.

"Maybe you should be the captain," he said. "You seem to have more of a knack for game strategy than I do. Did you play sports before coming to Tercast?"

She brushed the hair out of her eyes and tucked it around her ear with a grin. "Yes, I did, actually. Rushball."

"That's the one where each side tries to kick a ball into a net, right?" he asked.

"Yeah," she replied.

"You played professionally?"

"No, it was a local association."

"Well, you have my attention," Tovas said. "Any other suggestions?"

She frowned in thought for a moment as she looked back at the other members of their group, who were also getting their footwear on and talking about the game.

"This one is probably obvious, but position people where they have strengths," Relon said. "Vurkil is the obvious rear goalkeeper. It's hard to tell for sure, but I think Kula, Fita, myself, and maybe Sam might be better choices for moving the ball as forward center, judging by our Land Sorcery." She rubbed her chin. "Most of us could create a spark that one day in Air, but Ya'ir and Talanna were two of the first, after you, so they would be excellent choices for the Air side. Zel and Niu have done pretty well with Fire, so they might be best for the other side. Vurkil was good with fire too, but we'll definitely want him at the rear, like I said. I'm not sure what to do with Rose. She's exceptional with Water Sorcery, but that doesn't seem to help us much here."

Tovas nodded, considering her suggestions. "What about as a backup goalkeeper? She did well with strength enhancement two days ago."

Relon shrugged. "Strength isn't everything. She's pretty small. But maybe. I'd only put her there as a last resort, though."

He nodded again, appreciative of the information since he hadn't been around to see how most of the rest of the class fared with their tasks. Being good at the tasks had its fatigue-inducing downside. "Thank you, Relon. That was extremely helpful."

"Happy to help," she said with a smile. "Of course, you're the first natural choice for the forward since you're great at everything. I assumed that would be obvious."

He smiled back at her. "I appreciate the compliment."

"Well, I'd better get my footwear on."

"Thank you again," Tovas replied as she stood.

She returned to the other side of the room with the rest of the women. Tovas noticed a strange gaze from Ya'ir, who had finished securing his shoes. The man stared briefly across the room at Sam with a fond expression before turning his gaze away. Perhaps a bit too fond. It was probably nothing. Sam and Ya'ir were just good friends.

"All right!" Master Azeloram exclaimed as he entered the room. He carried two balls—one yellow, one black. The yellow ball was about the size of his head, while the black one was perhaps two-thirds larger in diameter. "Everyone, please gather around and hold your hands out."

The Master placed the black ball near the wall and the yellow one in the center of the room as everyone stood and made their way over with their hands held out. He pulled a vial of transparent liquid from a pocket and drizzled it over their hands.

"After I put this on, please touch the yellow orb here."

Tovas, being one of the first to receive the liquid, rested his hand on the yellow ball's surface, noting the smooth, rubbery texture.

"Ah! It's cold," Talanna said.

"What does that do?" Sam asked.

"I'll explain in a moment," the old man said as he completed the circle.

Ya'ir and Sam, being the last in line, bent forward and touched the yellow ball.

Master Azeloram held up the empty vial. "This is what we call binding serum. It is enchanted to bind an object to a Source or group of Sources. It prevents the other team from Vitalizing your quickorb." He moved the yellow ball to the wall and replaced it with the larger black one. "Now we must do the same with the thwartorb."

Everyone held their hands out once more as the Master pulled another vial from his pocket and repeated the procedure for the black ball. Its surface felt similar to the quickorb.

"The rules of the game are fairly simple," Master Azeloram said. "You may be familiar with them after watching the games last week. The balls are free to go anywhere, but the quickorb must be in the air during play. Players must also stay within the white lines. The quickorb is used when your team is on assault. The thwartorb is used when your team is on guard. If the quickorb touches the ground, or an assaulting player steps out of bounds, play stops and roles switch. The group that was formerly assaulting is now on guard, and the group formerly guarding is now on assault. This continues until a team reaches a score of doh points or one team can no longer continue."

He began pacing around the room, as he frequently did during their lectures. "Each group has four players on the field at a time —one rear blocker and three forwards. You score in one of three ways." He raised a finger. "First, you may score through the Fire goal, which is coated red. The quickorb must be aflame as it passes through the hoop." He raised a second finger. "Second, you may score through the Air goal, coated green. The ball must have enough static charge to create an arc of electricity to the hoop as it passes. Each of these goals is worth three points the first time you score in them, two points the second time, and one point thereafter."

"How do we set the ball on fire?" Vurkil asked.

The Master stopped and looked up at the giant. "Excellent question," he said. "The most straightforward way is to Vitalize its surface to burn. Don't worry, it won't be destroyed. For Air, Vitalize a large electric charge on the surface."

Tovas glanced at Niu and Zel, making a mental note to place them as fire forwards, as Relon had suggested.

"Now," the Master continued, raising three fingers again. "The third goal at the rear is worth nine points if you can get the quickorb through past the blocker. However, you cannot proceed past the white restriction line in front of the goal. In addition, as soon as an assaulting player passes behind the Fire and Air targets, the defenders are free to rush forward and attempt to score with their thwartorb."

Tovas looked at the faces of his group—which were not exactly inspiring. In fact, most of them looked apprehensive. Relon, Vurkil, Kula, and Fita appeared to be the most confident among them. Perhaps he should address the group soon and try to dissolve some of their tension.

"Questions?" the Master asked.

"What if we get too tired?" Talanna asked.

"Ah yes, if you—"

"Are you all ready? This game will be over pretty quickly. It's painful to watch." Scheln's words appeared in his mind.

Not in the slightest, Tovas replied telepathically. It was an odd feeling, conversing in this manner. It required direct focus on Scheln as the target. He was out next to the stands observing, since he couldn't participate.

"Isn't Master Azeloram helping you?" Scheln asked.

Yes, but this is going to be pretty difficult. Most of the group seems apprehensive.

"Well, don't give a speech. You'll just put them less at ease."

Tovas smiled at his brother's jab. *You mean being too serious?*

"Yes. You're always too serious. Get Vurkil to talk. He knows how to lighten the mood."

I'll see what I can do. I should really start paying attention.

"Oh, all right. Tell everyone 'good luck'!" Scheln replied. *"I'll be laughing at you all from the sidelines."*

Tovas shook his head with a smile as he turned his attention back to the room.

"—ess than four are still conscious, the opposing team wins," Master Azeloram said.

The group looked just as worried as before.

"Now, take some time to discuss strategies and positions. I'll return when it is time for your match."

He turned and left, shutting the wooden door behind him.

Well, now is the time, Tovas thought.

He stood up and addressed the group. "I know this seems extremely intimidating, but don't worry. In the end, it's a game. Above all, we should focus on learning from this and having a good time."

"Getting destroyed by the opponent doesn't sound like a good time to me," Niu said.

"Who is our opponent, anyway?" Talanna asked.

"I think it's the Keglon group, the group just ahead of us," Relon answered.

"Does anyone know anything about them?" Ya'ir asked. "I mean, in terms of their strengths or weaknesses with Sorcery?"

"Great question," Tovas said.

Nods from others around the room confirmed their agreement. No one spoke up, however.

"No one knows *anyone* in the other group?" Ya'ir exclaimed.

Vurkil's booming laugh shook the air. "It's not surprising, I think. We spend all day in the instruction rooms. We only see others during meals."

The door opened, causing a few of them to flinch.

Master Azeloram peeked through the doorway. "It's time! Follow me."

That was quick.

"All right, let's go," Tovas announced. He grabbed the quickorb and handed the thwartorb to Vurkil as they started heading for the door. "Oh! And Scheln said he wishes everyone good luck."

"Ha!" Vurkil said. "Yes, we will win now for sure!"

A few of the others chuckled.

"For Scheln!" the giant shouted, raising an arm dramatically.

"Yeah!" Ya'ir shouted in response. "For Scheln!"

The rest of the team shouted "For Scheln!" in near unison. Laughter accompanied their march toward the field.

You were right, Tovas thought at Scheln. *Vurkil loosened them up by dedicating our victory to you.*

"Yes! Tell them they all better win or I'm never speaking to them."

Tovas laughed. He was glad to have his brother's humor back. It had been so long.

He gave everyone their position assignments on the way to the field. Soon enough, they arrived at the staging area outside the stadium. Overcast skies hung overhead, accompanied by chilly, moist air. The team appeared tense once more.

Here we go.

The announcer's amplified voice rang out over the field. "For our next match, we have the noble Ulinkos!"

Cheers and applause came from the crowd as the team entered. Vurkil pumped his fists in the air, reveling in the attention. The purple Ulinko dashed in from behind the team and onto the field. She was astonishingly quick. The tuft of her white tail whipped about as she raced around and then returned to the team's benches.

"They will face the magnificent Keglons!" the amplified voice announced.

Tovas squinted toward the other end of the field, where the team emerged wearing robes of dark green and silver. An animal darted out from behind them and onto the field. It had long, powerful legs and hooved feet, with a thick torso and triangle-shaped head. Its body was green and scaly, with a long mane of brilliant white hair reflecting subtle rainbows if light hit it at the right angles.

The creature made a lap and then trotted back to join its team.

"Please give them all a warm round of applause as the first players make their way onto the field."

That was his cue. Tovas, Niu, Ya'ir, and Vurkil walked onto the field, with Tovas carrying the quickorb.

Anxiety pulsed through his body as he reached the center forward position. He glanced to Niu on his left and Ya'ir on his right, who both nodded back at him.

He took a deep breath, readying himself to toss the ball upward.

The bell sounded.

He threw the ball up, opening himself up to the fleeting

emotions around him. Curiously, the grass was a layer of darkness he couldn't feel.

The ball.

He spiritually latched on to the ball, connecting with it and immediately directing it to oppose gravity. It hovered over his head as he raced forward and veered toward the green hoop ahead. The connection felt considerably weaker than in the class-rooms.

The opposing team moved to intercept—their center, a woman with dark skin and hair, moving to join her teammate, a woman with fair skin and striking blue hair. The thwartorb hovered over them.

Tovas instinctively raised his hand toward the quickorb overhead and felt his connection to it strengthen marginally. He ran straight at them with Ya'ir at his side, readying himself to change directions quickly.

The thwartorb positioned itself in front of the green hoop, effectively blocking a clear shot. That didn't matter—Tovas wasn't aiming for it.

A few feet from the goal, he switched directions abruptly, passing the opposing women and running toward the right side of the back goal. The crowd cheered around him. Fatigue was already setting in as he approached the goal. The tall blond man standing there moved to position himself about a third of the way in from the end of the large semicircle.

Tovas mentally ran through his options. He could try to shoot for the other end, or try to get it into the small corner on this side. He would need to decide quickly. The other team was surely on their way to attempt a score.

He approached the boundary line, imagining the ball passing through the goal near the edge with tremendous energy. He had to be careful not to let it touch the ground until after it was through the goal. The ball accelerated forward—but it was far too slow. The opposing blocker rushed over and swatted the ball to the ground easily, ending the round.

Tovas sighed and fought off a wave of exhaustion.

They swapped places with the main defense team, comprising Relon, Sam, and Talanna. Vurkil remained as rear guard. Relon held the center position and carried the thwartorb. The bell rang and the opposing team approached, moving toward the fire goal on Talanna's side. Relon moved to intercept, thwartorb over her head. The red-headed man in the lead pulled a similar maneuver to Tovas's, switching directions and moving to the center of the field past the forward goals. They were going for the rear goal as well!

Relon was already moving to the opposing team's side. Talanna and Sam, however, stood in place, watching the other team head toward Vurkil.

"Sam! Talanna!" Tovas shouted. "Help Relon!"

They turned with shocked expressions toward Relon, who was sprinting up the field, and then raced after her.

Relon approached the enemy's green goal as the Keglons made an attempt toward Vurkil. Their quickorb shot toward the corner, but Vurkil leapt to the side with a clear block. The ball, however, slowed to a stop before it reached him. Tovas glanced back at Relon, who was moving the thwartorb through the hoop. *She's trying to do it herself since Talanna is still too far behind!*

Tovas held his breath as her ball passed through the hoop—but there was no spark. The crowd let out an "aww" of disappointment. Tovas glanced back at Vurkil, who was on the ground. The ball floated to the other side of the semicircle goal as Vurkil raced to get back on his feet. It passed through the goal slowly, but clearly. The crowd cheered.

Tovas's heart sank as he watched the scoreboard flip to a nine under the opponent's name. This looked like it would be a pretty quick match.

He joined Niu and Ya'ir back on the field. The bell sounded, and they advanced. This time, Tovas veered to the left with Niu, her dark ponytail flowing in his peripheral vision. He raised the ball upward and attempted to beat the thwartorb to the hoop. It burst into flame as Niu stretched her arm out. Her face emitted pure astonishment and distinctive giddiness at her own achievement.

He arced the ball toward the goal, but the thwartorb nicked the bottom, sending it over the hoop. Tovas and Niu raced after it past the enemy players.

"Nooo!" Scheln's distress echoed in his mind. *"Tovas, what are you doing?"*

Tovas had taken several steps before realizing his mistake, and he stopped in his tracks and glanced back. Sure enough, the other team was rushing toward their Air goal.

By passing the front goal line, they had given the enemy leave to advance on their own goals again.

Only one thing to do.

He established a connection to the quickorb and moved it toward himself. He gritted his teeth, desperately imagining a powerful and immediate force on the rear side of the ball to fire it at the Keglons' rear goal.

A loud impact cracked overhead, which sent the ball speeding toward the enemy goal at a tremendous velocity. Fatigue crashed into Tovas. He collapsed to the ground, barely maintaining consciousness. He raised his head to see the blocker stretch for the ball. It passed his fingertips through the goal.

Cheers exploded from the crowd. Tovas smiled wearily.

"An amazing shot by Ulinko," the announcer said. "But the thwartorb shot beat it out! The Keglons triumph!"

Scheln's voice echoed in his mind, but Tovas couldn't focus enough to comprehend it. Heavy eyelids darkened his vision.

He needed to sleep.

Chapter 28

Ilkuth

"This is so much easier when I can see what I'm doing," Kara said quietly to her reflection.

She stroked the last bit of cosmetic out past the rim of her eye, creating a sharp point that matched the other side. Placing the fine brush onto the counter, she admired her handiwork. Even considering the bland, form-fitting Armed Forces uniform, she thought she looked pretty good. A thin, pale shawl covered her shoulders and upper chest, bearing the Sovereignty emblem—a droplet encircled by an octagonal, shield-like border. Beside the emblem was a single gold asterisk that denoted her rank as a Spark. The left side of the fabric came down over the upper arm, bearing the same emblem.

Underneath the shawl, she wore a skintight light gray suit that showed a bright purple depiction of the Sovereignty emblem on its chest. The purple was her choice, the only part she had any control over. Two black stripes came down on each of her upper thighs at an angle toward the inside. Subtle color variations created a heathered look throughout the uniform.

She mentally adjusted her visual spectrum range to go lower

into infrared. The sensation of her eyes cooling in her eye sockets remained a strange one. At first, she didn't understand why it would happen, but it made sense once she realized she was seeing heat. The glow of her nose clouded the inner sides of her vision somewhat, though it was clearly darker than her forehead and neck in the reflection. Her hair became nearly invisible. Her eyes appeared as eerie black orbs. She adjusted her vision back to the normal range, bringing back her white face, blue eyes, and frizzy brown hair.

The past two days had been full of physical, mental, and emotional tests to determine her eligibility for service and provide basic instruction. They'd spent an entire day on mental and emotional resiliency. She understood why it was important, but it *was* rather tedious. She passed all of their tests without issue.

She moved from the washroom into the tiny sleeping area she shared with a bunkmate named Lorelei. The sound of falling water from the shower faded slightly as Kara sat in one of the two small red chairs next to the bunk bed. She still had several minutes before her exosuit appointment.

She considered using her Nit to look up Force training information again, but she'd already spent the evening prior looking up whatever she could. Relaxing for a bit seemed like a better idea.

The ability to access the universal network directly with her mind was an amazing and bizarre experience. All she had to do was think commands toward her Nit and it would work just like her Jit—without all the talking.

Her idle mind naturally wandered toward Nikor, bringing a wave of pain with it. She wished Sam was around to talk to. He was the rational one. When one guy she'd dated in high school turned out to be a completely jealous and self-centered douche, Sam was there to supply a shoulder to cry on—after giving her the whole "I told you so" speech, of course. Liam was always good at cheering her up as well, usually by exchanging rounds of glorious insults.

God, she missed them. She wondered what Sam was up to now. Probably hating her guts for getting him stuck with a religious group. She smiled reflexively at the thought. He was going to let her have it when he finally got out.

Her thoughts turned to Jeanette, which brought her mood crashing back down.

Memories of the night of her sister's capture tormented her. Her helplessness. Her ignorance. Her inability to act. That had changed now, though. *I'm coming for you, Jeanette. Please know that I'm coming for you. I'll never give up.*

As her appointment approached, Kara left the small apartment. She was soon soaring in an ascender over the thousands of rows of military housing, flying toward the initiation field. During the short journey, dozens of soldiers in battle suits flew by. Mountains stretched into the sky to the west, and she could faintly make out the edge of a beach toward the sunrise.

When the ascender reached its destination, Kara stepped onto the landing platform. It overlooked an extensive field of grass with targets along a hill in the distance. Soldiers wearing battle suits had straight arms pointed toward the targets. She stared at one of the white targets in the distance and mentally commanded her vision to zoom in. Her eyes complied, enlarging the target to her view. It was a simple white silhouette standing at attention. A hole appeared in its chest. Her vision returned to its normal view, and she advanced to the lone building connected to the landing pad.

The door hissed open as she approached. A blond man talked to an older man behind the desk in the small plain room. As she looked at the older man's two blue circles on his shawl, her Nit reminded her of his name and rank: Commander Two Karvon Vokbon.

"—arriving today?"

"Unfortunately not, Commander," the blond man said in a rough drawl. "It seems the orbital acheron from Livneth was linked incorrectly to Ovilath, so that's where the items ended up."

The commander shook his head and sighed. "We need that shipment *today*."

"I know," the young man replied. "Several other shipments were caught in the mistake. They're sending them back through. Said they should get here by one."

The older man sighed, rubbing his forehead. "All right, Jebbs. Thank you."

Jebbs, the young Spark, bowed his head with a salute across his chest before turning and walking toward the door at the other end of the room, which opened for him. He glanced briefly at Kara before disappearing into the room beyond.

The commander stood up and moved around the desk. "Ah, Kara Jones. Lively morning, Spark."

"Lively morning, sir," she replied.

His face scrunched oddly in a way she couldn't interpret. Facial expressions were still somewhat foreign to her. "What did you call me?"

"Oh, I just said 'sir.' Should I not say that?" she asked.

He laughed. "I don't know what the hell a 'sir' is, but I'm not one of them. 'Commander Karvon' or 'Commander' would be the proper way to address me."

"Okay, sorry, Commander," Kara said. "I'm still getting used to all this."

He smiled warmly. "No harm done. Your profile says you only recently became a citizen. Is that right?"

"I want to do what I can against the bastards that kidnapped my sister."

"The Molkinarans kidnapped your sister?"

"Well . . ." She scratched her head. "That was the theory in the report I saw, but as of a few days ago, I couldn't find it anymore."

"Where are you from?"

"Earth."

He paused for a few seconds. No doubt searching for information on the network.

"Ah, Jeanette Jones. Is that right?"

Kara perked up immediately, and hope blossomed within her. "Yes! Is there any new information about her?"

The commander gave her a studying look. "I'm afraid the details of your sister's capture have been restricted. I cannot disclose them to you, Spark, but yes, additional information has come to light about her kidnapping."

Kara was both relieved and dissatisfied. So they *were* still investigating Jeanette's capture. That was a relief. Demands for more information nearly burst from her, but discipline restrained her.

"I am loyal to the Sovereignty, Commander, as my parents were. I'm ready to serve. But I would appreciate a chance to do my part in taking down her kidnappers. Whatever it takes."

The man stared into her eyes for a moment, expressionless. Finally, he nodded. "Your request is noted, but that also depends on your aptitude in combat. The better you do, the more weight your request will receive."

Kara nodded too.

Winning. She could do that.

"Please follow me," he said.

He led her into the room to the left of his desk. Inside, two dozen shiny gunmetal suits lined the long, narrow room. Other than the drastic variation in shape and size, each was identical. Sleek, thin metallic plates covered each human form, with a few spots of dark honeycomb fabric peeking up behind them around the joints and neck. A metallic version of the Sovereignty emblem was centered on the upper chest, matching the purple one on her uniform. Thicker plates cascaded over the shoulders, from which a track snaked down the arm and forearm to a point on the wrist. Each helmet bore a reflective face shield, which curved back to a crest over the ears.

The commander led her down the row of suits, stopping at the one near the end that was also clearly the smallest.

"This is yours," he said.

He gave her a moment to admire it. Her own suit of power armor. She would be a full-fledged superhero now by Earth standards. But the suit seemed too small, even for her.

"I am now transferring control to you," Commander Vokbon said.

Ilkuth armor, iteration 7.Ɛ2.4, identifier X53ƵV9S41, now in possession, the Nit communicated to her mind.

"Suit up," he said. "The system will guide you through initiation and baseline combat evaluation. Good luck, Spark. We'll talk again in a few days to discuss your assignment."

He turned and walked back down the hall of suits. Kara stared at his back, feeling stupid. No instruction at all? She didn't even know how to turn this thing on!

She looked back at the suit. It was definitely too small. This thing was going to crush her.

"Well, here goes nothing," she whispered to the empty room.

Activate armor, she commanded her Nit.

The suit came alive. It stood from its resting place against the wall and took a step toward her. She yelped and backed away reflexively, colliding with the much larger suit on the wall behind her.

Heartbeat pounding in her ears, Kara took a step toward the suit. *How do I get inside?* she asked her Nit.

Command is "open," it replied.

"Okay," she said.

Open suit.

Kara watched wide-eyed as the suit moved into a neutral pose with the arms away from the body. The front-facing metallic plates and helmet shield flung open, revealing a cushioned interior. Small grooves in the cushion contained a tiny light-emitting dot embedded within.

Kara took a deep breath. The thing was seriously going to crush her.

She turned around and stood on the open feet, laying her back against the padding. The gel-like material was rather comfortable —cool, but not cold. As soon as she got her fingers in their grooves and the back of her head into the open helmet, the suit closed with frightening speed. She let out a squeal.

Surprisingly, she didn't feel crushed. It hugged her body tightly, but not uncomfortably.

As she opened her eyes again, various widgets framed the corners of her view. The top-left corner displayed an outline of a body. A pulsing circle nestled itself into the upper right. Numbers and symbols sat in the two bottom corners, and two bar gauges framed the left and right sides of her view. The bar to the left was solid, with a lightning symbol overhead, while the one on the right was less than half full.

"Welcome to your new Ilkuth, iteration seven point el two point four," a female voice said to her through the helmet. "Please move around to acquaint yourself with the armor's motion."

Kara raised her left arm, which felt unusually light. She watched her fingers move, and they were encased perfectly by the armor. She took a step forward, amazed at the feeling of near weightlessness as she continued to move her arms around. They had an excellent range of motion. The suit was extraordinarily thin and fit snugly around her figure—like a second skin.

She sat on the hallway floor, eager to test the limits of the armor's flexibility. After extending her legs in front of her, she reached her arms out as far as they would go. Her chest, being an inch or two further out than normal and now a rigid material, lay against her metallic legs, preventing her from reaching quite as far as she normally could. Spreading her legs wide, she rolled forward into a one-eighty split. She had to plant her hands to prevent rolling to either side, but the armor was flexible enough to allow the movement.

Kara lay on her back, then planted her feet and raised herself onto her helmet, bending her back. She brought her elbows forward and stretched further, and she noted the extreme lack of resistance, until something rigid stopped her. *Not quite as flexible as I am, but pretty close,* she thought as she righted herself and stood up.

"What do I do now?" she asked.

"Please move to the nav marker," the suit said.

A small upside-down triangle appeared on her helmet's display over the door in front of her, opposite the way she entered. It whooshed open as she approached, leading her outside onto the grassy field.

"The Ilkuth Seven houses a network of doh Evelor power cells, six of which are concentrated in the ring on the upper back. Their current charge is indicated on the left side of your helmet display. There are twin Ralek projectile cannons in each shoulder, with a total of three groh doh two training rounds stored in each replaceable ammunition guard. This is indicated at the bottom of your display."

"Can I try it out?" she asked.

"Please send a target on the eastern hill to your Nit and extend your arm straight to activate the weapon."

Kara scanned the hill in the distance, finding a silhouette. When she told her Nit to target it, a reticle appeared on her helmet's augmented display. She lifted her right arm up and extended her elbow. The interlocking snakelike mechanism on the outside of her arm locked in place, keeping her upper arm, forearm, and wrist in rigid alignment.

"Whoa," she whispered.

A new reticle appeared on her display that showed where her arm was pointed. As she moved the new reticle close to her target, her shoulder locked in place.

"Press into your palm, or issue a 'fire' command to your Nit to engage the weapon."

She pressed her fingers into her right palm, and the weapon immediately responded, spraying the target with a quick stream of gunfire. Her vision zoomed in on the target and showed that she had shredded a section of it.

"Well done. Full instruction on weaponry will be provided later," the voice said. "Bending your elbow will disengage the cannon."

Kara bent her elbow, and the pieces along her arm unfastened, allowing free movement.

"That's incredible!" she said.

"The suit also features a fully integrated antigravity and aerial propulsion system."

"It can fly, right?" Kara asked, excitement pulsing through her.

"Correct," the female voice responded. "The suit's current gravity configuration is shown on the right side of your display. The gauge indicates the percentage of the suit's mass that is configured to antigravity. Gravitation state is applied uniformly to maintain proper balance and reduce mechanical stress. Please slowly increase the antigravity level of the Ilkuth through your Nit."

Kara looked around at the grassy field, the hill beyond with targets, and the mountains off in the other direction. In the upper left-hand corner, the center of her figure pulsed quickly with her heart rate. She gave her Nit a mental command to increase antigravity, slowly.

The gauge to her right steadily rose. It reached the fifty percent mark and kept rising, but Kara still felt nothing. The ground gradually left her below—which felt particularly odd since the soles of her feet maintained pressure against the suit. Her acceleration quickened. Soon she soared thousands of feet over the lone building and field below. In the distance, she could see rows of dense military housing. Snowy mountain peaks moved below her as the suit's velocity continued to rise.

Fear gripped her. If she kept going like this, she would end up in *space*. She commanded the antigravity increase to stop.

The bar stopped rising, but she was still moving upward at an alarming rate. *Stop! Stop! Keep me steady!* she thought at her Nit.

The gauge quickly slid down below to about a quarter from the bottom. Her velocity slowed suddenly, making her stomach lurch, and the gauge then rose again until she was stationary and floating above the mountains. She looked down at the landscape below. A large city bustled about in the distance—a hive of skyscrapers with tiny flying vehicles moving about. The sun reflected off the curved horizon. Clouds hung in the distance.

"Woo!" she exclaimed. "What else can this thing do?"

Chapter 29

Science

Sam lay on his bed in the dark room, staring out the window at an alien sky. An orange moon peeked in at the edge of his view. He wondered why it was orange. Perhaps it had a significant iron content like Mars. The smaller pale yellow moon was out of sight.

He sighed as his mind wandered to the game earlier that day. Tovas should have just let the ball drop when he mistakenly crossed the line into the deep zone. It would have immediately ended the round, and they might have had another shot. Instead, he had to be a show-off.

Sam turned his head and strained his eyes and ears in the darkness. Fita's breathing was slow and steady, suggesting he may finally be asleep. Sliding carefully from the bed onto his bare feet, Sam noted the warmth of the stone floor, which still bothered him. It was supposed to be cold. Hard floors were always cold. He crept over to Ya'ir's bed on the other side of the room. The man's breathing was slow and steady as well. Sam rolled his eyes before tapping his shoulder.

Ya'ir flinched, then turned his head in surprise. "Oh, sorry I—"

Sam hastily covered Ya'ir's mouth and pointed to the door. He nodded and slid out of bed. They crept into the hallway and began descending the steps of the tower.

"Are you *trying* to get us exiled?" Sam whispered across the dark hallway.

"Sorry. Wasn't thinking," Ya'ir replied.

They reached the ground-floor hallway and checked both directions. It appeared to be empty. They crept halfway down the hall and into the open courtyard. Cold air caused goose bumps to rise on Sam's arms. The magnificent sight overhead caught his gaze as they walked lightly across the courtyard. Glowing butter-flylike bugs painted streaks of purple, orange, and green in front of a breathtaking night sky. The host galaxy here was more visible than the Milky Way on Earth—or perhaps the atmosphere simply had less light pollution. The Triangulum galaxy, he remembered.

Impatience consumed him as they entered the doors on the other side of the courtyard. They descended the stairs to the hall where Master Farco had shown them the fire weapons. Sam had discovered a storage room at the other end of the hallway, which was unlocked and mostly empty.

Rose sat waiting on a crate inside. Like Sam and Ya'ir, she wore her flowing sleepwear. The single light overhead cast an eerie shadow on her freckled face.

"You brought Ya'ir too?" she said.

Ya'ir waved. "Lively evening to you too, Rose."

Sam smiled as he made his way to the corner of the dark room where the wall jutted out, creating a low ceiling. "Yes. The more people we have to test, the better our results will be."

He eyed a white stone block on the floor with a rope tied tightly around it. With both hands, he lifted it up. Seven more blocks tied to the same rope came with it, snaking down to the ground—about half a foot apart. Eight blocks were exactly one-third of the twenty-four on the rope. Sam guessed the weight was roughly forty pounds, so the entire ensemble should weigh about a hundred and twenty. Unfortunately, he didn't have access to any kind of scale, so he didn't know for sure. He'd debated trying to break into the healers' room to see if he could find one, but decided that was far too risky.

"What are you planning to do with *that*?" Rose asked.

"We're going to use it for our first experiment," Sam replied. "We know that our Sorcery gets weaker with distance. I want to measure it." He lowered the brick down to the ground again. "I found the rope and the cut stones in those crates."

Rose slipped off her crate and stood up. "Okay, so how is that going to work?"

"Simple. One of us lifts the end stone off the ground as high as we can at different distances, and I record how many stones are lifted. I can use the results to calculate the relationship between distance and Sorcery strength."

Rose nodded. "That's actually pretty smart."

"Yeah!" Ya'ir agreed.

Sam smiled. "Glad you like it."

"How are we going to measure distance?" Rose asked.

Sam walked past her to the box she had been sitting on. "Well, lacking any kind of tape measure," he said as he slid the wooden lid off and picked up another stone block, "I figured we could just use these, since they're cut pretty evenly. We can lay them out in a line and measure in brick lengths."

"Is there more rope?" Rose asked. "Why don't you just use another piece of rope and mark ticks on it with the same stone."

Sam considered her suggestion. "That's actually a fantastic idea. It will probably be more accurate that way—and easier to position. Ya'ir, the rope is in the crate next to you."

"Okay," Ya'ir replied, pulling the lid off. "What do we mark it with?"

"There's a pen and some paper on the crate in the corner. I brought them from the library. We can use that pen to make the marks."

Rose nodded and grabbed the pen while Sam and Ya'ir stretched the rope across the room. Using the stone block, Sam walked along the rope, making ticks with the pen at each block length. When he finished, he placed the block in the corner—

mindful to keep it separated from the others, since it was now their measurement standard.

"All right," he said. "Who wants to go first?"

Ya'ir and Rose looked at each other for a moment.

"I'll do it," Ya'ir said.

"Okay, stand at the end of the rope," Sam instructed.

He walked back to the connected stone blocks and, with a myriad of echoed scraping, dragged them toward Ya'ir. He stacked them at the first tick mark—only a few inches away from Ya'ir's feet—and tried to keep the stack as close to the marked line as possible. Then he walked to the corner and grabbed a sheet of paper.

"Okay," Sam said, "Go for it. Lift the top stone as high as you can."

The three of them stood in silent anticipation, staring at the pile of roped-together bricks on the floor. Slowly, the one on top rose. Tension in the rope brought three other blocks with it. As the fourth budged, the upward movement slowed, then stopped. The fourth brick teetered slightly but maintained contact with the pile beneath it.

Sam scribbled a four-column table onto the paper and placed Ya'ir's name in the second column. He marked a *1* in the first column and *4.5* in Ya'ir's column next to it. "I'll call that a four and a half," he said excitedly. "Would be nice if these blocks were smaller so we could get better precision, but we'll have to make do with what we have."

The bricks collapsed with loud chinks.

"Whoa! Gently, Ya'ir. We don't want to break them."

"Sorry!"

Sam studied the man's face. He was already showing signs of fatigue.

Tapping the end of the pen on his lips, Sam thought for a moment. "I think for now we'll just go with three trials each. Hopefully, that won't be enough to make any of us pass out, but try to gauge it if you can," he said. "If you feel you're getting too tired, just stop."

"Yeah, that's a good idea," Rose said. "We don't want to get caught sleeping down here."

Ya'ir frowned. "It's hard to tell, though. Weariness seems to be delayed. I often don't even feel it until after I *stop* using Sorcery. I don't know if your experiences have been the same, but that's how it has been for me."

Sam nodded. "I think we can still try to get by with three. What do you think?"

"Let me do another, and I'll see how I feel."

Sam moved the blocks to the fourth mark line, and they repeated the procedure, giving Ya'ir and the blocks plenty of space as Rose observed quietly from her spot on a crate near the wall. This time, the second block almost lifted from the group below it, but ultimately maintained contact with one corner. Sam marked *1.75* on the sheet next to the *4*. Ya'ir said he was still ready to go, so Sam moved the set back again to the eighth mark away.

Ya'ir lifted the block again. Sam marked an *8* in the first column and a *1* in the next as Ya'ir let the sole brick gently down to rest.

"Tired yet?" Rose asked.

Ya'ir sat on the nearest crate and lay back on it, letting his legs dangle. "Yeah. I wonder why this makes you so tired."

"Me too," Sam said as he pulled the bricks back to the first mark again. "I plan to test that another day."

"How do you know you're measuring the effects of distance and not fatigue?" Rose asked.

"I don't," Sam replied. "That's something we'll have to account for by doing the same test in reverse order another day. There are also all kinds of other potential variables—even ones we don't know about—but we need to start somewhere."

Sam volunteered for the next test. They dragged the strung bricks to the first mark and he moved into position. He took a slow breath, letting the feelings of his surroundings wash over him—amazed at how easily they came now. He connected with the top brick, imaginatively instructing it to rise against the pull of gravity and tension of the rope, and it rose slowly, lifting three other blocks with it. The fifth teetered like Ya'ir's had. Sam willed the block to rise more, but it wouldn't get any higher. He slowly eased the force and let the blocks clink softly as they rested back on the heap.

"Four point seven five," Sam said.

"I was going to say more like four point nine," Rose replied.

"No, it's only about three-quarters up."

"Exactly," she said. "That's about three point nine. Point seven five is closer to half."

"What? No, it's—" Oh. That stupid dohnal system. Eventually, he was going to have to learn how to count that way. But not today. "Never mind," Sam said. "I'm still thinking in decimal. We're probably saying the same thing."

"Decimal?" Rose asked. "Is that why you said that weird number during the game the other day?"

He stepped over and wrote a 4.75 in the second column with his name over it as Rose dragged the blocks to the fourth line. "Yes. I don't know this dohnal system very well yet, but it shouldn't really matter. We can always convert later."

Sam moved himself back into position, checking his feet to ensure he was exactly where he should be. Rose stepped back as he connected with the same block again and caused it to rise as before. Curiously, he pulled one additional block with it.

"Interesting. That's more than Ya'ir's," Rose said as she approached. The blocks dipped down, causing the second to come down and rest on the pile.

"Wait! Stop!" Sam exclaimed.

Rose froze in place. "What?"

"When you approached, my lifting power dropped a bit. Move back slowly."

He maintained his imaginative command on the block to rise as far as possible. As Rose backed away, the block rose again, coming to rest where it was before—firmly about two blocks in strength.

"Interesting," he said. "It looks like our Sorcery diminishes the closer it gets to another person as well."

Ya'ir spoke from behind. "That explains why the areas around people feel like fuzzy holes. We can't Vitalize anything around them!"

"Yes!" Sam said. "That makes sense. We'll have to look into that more too. For now, let's finish my last test."

He let the blocks fall slowly to rest. Rose and Ya'ir moved the heap back to the eighth line as Sam marked a *2.5* in the next row under his name. Returning to his position, he felt out for the block, connecting with it again as Rose stepped back and gave him plenty of room. Fatigue dragged down his mind. *Just once more,* he told himself.

As the block rose and stood steady, with the second block about halfway up, his thoughts turned to that fateful night at the Joneses' house. The bizarre image of a dresser lurching forward played vividly in his mind. Jeanette's kidnapper was definitely a Sorcerer. He'd reasoned that through many times now. Kerlo and Elysia had been wrong. Maybe if Sam had known then what he did now, he could have done more to stop the man.

The thought of Kara's immense distress and sorrow that night brought with it a surge of anger. He had to find out more about that cloaked figure. His only lead had run into a dead end when Master Evalencia told him of Walnon's fate. He suspected that Walnon's banishment and the Joneses' decision to move to Earth were connected. The Masters refused to tell him anything more about it—said they had told Sovereignty authorities everything they needed to know. Those self-righteous old Grand Masters probably had something to do with the whole thing.

"Sam!" Rose exclaimed, snapping him out of his thoughts.

The surprise also severed his connection to the block, causing three of them to fall.

"I was about to say it was surprising you could lift one and a half, but then you lifted three!" she said. "What did you do?"

Sam shook his head as he sat down on the floor, feeling the fatigue crash into him. "I . . . I don't know. I was just thinking about something that made me angry."

"Well, whatever it was, it seemed to increase your power," she said.

"Huh," he said wearily. "This is going to be harder than I thought."

Chapter 30

Books

"Wait out here, Jey," Tess said. "I'll be back soon."

The shorter woman strode into the throne room, leaving Jeanette in the bright blue hallway. Before the door closed, Jeanette caught a distant glimpse of the Deia, who was seated in her ornate throne.

Jeanette had grown appreciative of warm, comfortable clothing and a full stomach. She didn't know what the Deia was playing at. Supplying a bed, unfamiliar food, and freedom to roam about the palace would not redeem the woman in Jeanette's eyes, but she was grateful to have those privileges now.

She'd established a mental layout of the castle, though there were several areas she could not enter. The walls were still plain, but they had been plastered, painted, and lit with glowing gems that added a welcome touch of color. Winds ever howled outside the walls, and daylight never broke through the cold, endless night.

Freedom to roam about had significant downsides, since the men around the castle were despicable pigs who would pinch her or catcall as she passed. A man had nearly forced himself on her a few hours after her "freedom," and he would have succeeded if Tess hadn't shown up and shoved the guy away. Jeanette stuck around the woman after that. Tess was terrifying, but she was a known variable, unlike the palace's other inhabitants.

Though Jeanette now walked freely—so to speak—among these horrible people, she wasn't one of them. She would *never* be one of them.

"*Don't do anything they say,*" Amy's voice continually nagged at the back of her mind.

I'm not going back into that dungeon, Jeanette thought back. *I will never let them do that to me again.*

"*You'll lose yourself, associating with them.*"

I won't! I could never be one of them. I'll play their games for now to keep myself free of that hellish prison—but I won't surrender my values either.

Men came around the corner, causing Jeanette's adrenaline to spike. Pairs of them carried large bags that sank almost to the floor, suspended with two wooden poles between them, their dark robes tattered and bloody. Much of the damage looked like bullet holes.

Jeanette's nerves calmed as they paid her no attention and moved instead into the throne room. Expecting to see bloody bodies as the first bag passed, Jeanette was surprised to see an enormous pile of books instead.

What was with the Deia's obsession with books?

The last of the several passing bags did, in fact, have bloody bodies, but books and paintings filled the rest.

Jeanette leaned in toward the door, straining to hear. One man inside the room sounded like he was giving a report to the Deia.

"—took down hundreds of them. We left the few of us Del killed at the scene. He has been moving up well with—"

Footsteps approached the door. Jeanette scrambled back to her standing position as Tess emerged. She turned toward Jeanette with a friendly grin.

"The Deia has two assignments for you, Jey," Tess said.

Apprehension rippled across her skin. *This can't be good.*

Tess raised a book in her hand that read *Fundamentals of Human Physiology*. "She wants you to study."

Jeanette frowned. The Deia wanted her to study physiology?

"The second assignment," Tess said, lowering the book and smiling mischievously, "is to do combat training with me."

Chapter 31

Special Designation

"Kara, you're too far out. Bring it in."

"Yes, Chief."

Kara mentally changed her course in the air with a subtle command to her Nit, bringing her a few feet closer to the rest of the squad. She flew with eight others in what they called a column formation. The training village below appeared to be empty.

Another woman's voice came over the communication channel. "Anti-air! About three groh doh—"

A bright flash lit near the front of the group.

"Damn!" their leader, Chief Elin, exclaimed. "Spread out! C-one to the east side. C-two to the north side. Gunther, Jakele, fire on those targets!"

Several personnel indicators blinked on Kara's display to show acknowledgment of the command. A blue nav point appeared, pointing to a position north of the village. Simultaneously, a red marker emerged near a large building below. Gunfire rang out from two suits ahead. She directed her Ilkuth to change course randomly to evade fire, moving toward the blue marker with half of her team. More blinding flashes emitted nearby. One of the indicators for her team, the one corresponding with Dulvir, turned orange.

They landed at the indicated location. Dulvir's suit slowed to a stop between a group of bushes. He was in a simulated state of unconsciousness—unable to move, and his comms were temporarily shut down. Apparently, he'd been hit by one of the simulated blasts.

Kara moved into formation with the three remaining members of her cohort, forming a spaced diagonal toward the target, and lay prone against the ground with her rifle pointed toward the building. None of the doors or windows had coverings.

Members of the other cohort, which included the squad chief, landed several feet away on the east side of the village.

Chief Elin's voice came over the line again. "C-one, cover fire on that building. C-two, move to that upper deck. Eyes open."

More fire rang out from cohort one's location to the east as a green nav point appeared at an upper level of the tall building ahead.

The indicator for Kara's cohort leader, belonging to Chief Runkath, blinked on Kara's display. He spoke over the cohort channel. "Let's move. This rooftop."

A blue nav indicator appeared on top of a smaller building. Kara pulled herself up, feeling remarkably lightweight in the Ilkuth. They rushed forward in formation, several feet away from each other. As the cohort leader left the ground, Kara and Kolvan, her other cohort member, followed suit. They reached the flat rooftop and sprinted toward the other end, toward the enemy building.

A bot burst from the door on the landing ahead—thin and upright with a long gun-shaped "head" pointing in their direction. Runkath immediately opened fire, cutting the bot's thin torso in half.

"Go, go! Now!" Runkath yelled. "Kara, watch for threats below."

They lifted off from the rooftop and moved toward the open door on the landing. Kara scanned the area below, periodically zooming her sight in and out. Her teammates opened fire, but she kept her focus on the ground. It seemed to be clear.

Touching down on the landing, they ran to the side of the door, forming up in a line against the side of the building.

"C-two in position," Runkath said.

"Firmed," the squad chief said. "C-one, let's move up. C-two, push in."

"Firmed," Runkath replied. "Ready?" he asked on the cohort channel.

Kara mentally acknowledged, causing her indicator on the display to blink next to Kolvan's. A moment later, Runkath spun around and entered the doorway. Kolvan followed, flipping around and falling upward toward the ceiling. Kara entered the room after them.

Gunfire echoed across the cement walls. Runkath hovered, facing toward the enemy to their immediate left as if prone, though several feet off the ground. Kolvan stood on the ceiling overhead and sprayed the group of robots with his rifle. Kara turned to the right to cover their rear. She followed Runkath's lead, hovering in the air to present a much smaller target for enemy forces.

Three robots emerged from two hallways up ahead, with flashes of light accompanying their simulated fire. Kara raised her rifle until the red targeting dot appeared on the large lower half of the enemy closest to her. She pulled the trigger, butt of the rifle recoiling into her shoulder. The bot stopped moving, so she aimed at the next one and held the trigger until it dropped as well.

Kara's right arm went limp as her display highlighted the limb in orange. The rifle fell from her grasp, clashing against the concrete floor as she straightened her left arm and activated the cannon. Once she squeezed her fingers into her left palm, simulation rounds from the arm cannon kicked against her. Her suit moved back slightly, then quickly compensated with a forward thrust.

The room went silent as the final bot stopped. Kara kept her eyes glued on the hallways—arm cannon at the ready.

"Kolvan, with me around the corner," Runkath said. "Kara, keep covering our rear."

They rounded the corner, Kolvan still overhead, while Kara and Runkath floated stomach-down.

Something small, black, and round emerged from a hole in the wall to Kara's right. Adrenaline pulsed through her body. The object was well aimed, falling down below the group at an angle. She moved instinctively to intercept the threat. As it approached, she swung her arm to knock it away. It flashed brightly just before impact.

Her display went black, and the suit went solid. Sounds from the surrounding room disappeared, leaving her in silence.

Kara was dead.

Heavy breathing echoed against the inside of the helmet. Claustrophobia gnawed at her within the cage of her now inactive suit. *I really hope the Molkinar bots don't have anything that would disable these things. Getting stuck in here until I suffocate or starve to death would be more terrible than dying by an explosion.*

Minutes ticked by, and her battle anxiety and adrenaline faded into boredom. She hoped the rest of the team could still finish the mission, at least. The last few days had comprised training with different groups, all with varying levels of experience. This one, led by Elin, seemed to be the most experienced that she'd trained with yet. Many of her teammates had actual combat experience and were stationed at the base to await reassignment.

She needed to pee. Being dead was becoming more inconvenient by the second.

After a few more excruciating minutes, her face shield display came alive again. Green, alien foliage filled her view. She righted herself as Dulvir rose next to her.

"Hey, Kara, you got hit too?" he asked.

"Not by the anti-air. I was blown apart later by a grenade or something inside the building."

A nav marker appeared on her screen in the village.

"Yeah, they're nasty," Dulvir said as he rose into the air.

"Go on ahead," Kara said. "I'll be there in a minute."

She relieved herself in the woods, then followed the nav marker, which led them into a small one-room building near the center of the fake village. Three from the other cohort went in just before her. As she entered the room, Kara noticed that the rest of her cohort was already there.

"Kara! Good to see you, Spark," Runkath said, approaching her. He had taken his helmet off, displaying short black hair and a brown, smiling face. "We finished the mission, but that was hard seeing you go down."

She mentally commanded her own helmet to disengage, and she pulled it off as well. "Well, I was trying to knock it away."

"Wouldn't recommend batting prox bombs, Spark." Despite his grin, his tone was serious. "They detonate as soon as they get close enough."

"Why was I outside?" she asked. "If I was blown up, wouldn't I be floating around that room in pieces?"

"Nah, that kind of explosion won't do major damage to the Ilkuth." Kolvan tapped the shiny armor of his forearm with a gauntleted fist. "This stuff is nigh indestructible! But you're still vulnerable on the inside to rapid accelerations. An explosion could knock you unconscious, or even kill you if it's massive enough and close enough. With some distance, the suit can protect you from it somewhat with the plasma shield."

She nodded. "Good to know. Thanks for the tips, Chief."

"Happy to help, Spark. You're doing great. These exercises always exaggerate damage anyway. I'd be glad to have you in my cohort on the battlefield!"

She thanked him with a warm smile, and he nodded before turning to join the rest of the team.

An unarmored woman in uniform entered through the other end of the building. As she strode toward the front of the room, a glance at her insignia told Kara that she was Commander Three Yurkii Evlonin.

"Gather around, squad," she called out.

Chatter died down as everyone converged on the commander's position.

The after-action review went about as expected. She commended them on their victory but reprimanded them for their casualties. They discussed each of the stages of their assault in great detail, examining what they did well and where they needed to improve.

When the commander dismissed them, Kara's Nit reconnected to the global network. It was standard procedure to disengage all global network communications during a mission—training or not. She had a message from Commander Vokbon asking her to meet with him.

Kolvan turned about. "Hey, you two want to join us for drinks?"

"Sure!" Dulvir said.

"Can't, sorry," Kara replied. "Commander Vokbon asked to see me."

Kolvan shrugged. "Well, come join us after, then!"

She put on her helmet, watching the display come alive again as it connected to the rest of her suit. "I'll see. Thanks, guys."

Lush, hilly landscape passed below as she flew back to the commander's building. She liked the way the orange and yellow trees looked from overhead, surrounded by shades of green. It was still odd to think she was sighted now. The world felt so much larger. She was awestruck by the ability to sense things miles away. Thankfully, the suit navigated and targeted automatically from her commands, so her still-developing depth perception didn't cause her much trouble on the battlefield or while she was flying.

The suit descended and landed in front of the door, which hissed open. Inside, the commander sat behind his desk.

"Ah, yes. Kara Jones," he said, rising from his seat.

She gave him a respectful salute—thumb, index, and middle fingers extended across her chest.

He smiled. "From your scores, you seem to have some genuine talent, particularly in close-quarters hand-to-hand combat."

"I trained in martial arts back home," she replied, pulling off her helmet.

"That explains a lot. You may not be aware of this, but

experience in martial arts combat is quite rare in the Sovereignty. From the time before the Sovereignty was born, we have almost always fought at great distances, and effective policing has reduced the need for self-defense."

"Well, that makes sense, right?" she said. "It wouldn't do much good to learn how to take down enemies with your hands when they can just shoot you."

He laughed. "Indeed, indeed. And yet, here we are."

She raised an eyebrow. "I'm not following, Commander."

He straightened up. "Kara Jones," he said in a more serious tone, "I have been authorized to disclose information to you that is highly restricted. You are not permitted to repeat this information to anyone. Do you understand?"

Jeanette!

Her heart jolted into action, but she attempted to keep a calm demeanor. "Yes, I understand."

"Good," Commander Vokbon said. "I have information on your sister, Jeanette, and an opportunity to do something about it."

Finally.

"We still do not know details about her captor, but we have associated him with attacks from others with similar technology and apparel who attacked an ancient library on Tenreth a few hours ago. They do not appear to be associated with the Molkinar as originally suspected. These individuals appear to have advanced technology that deflects projectiles and other ranged attacks. Proximity combat seems to be the only effective option at present. The Sovereign has approved creation of a specially designated company in the Force for dealing with this threat."

Kara's mind was a blur. More attacks. Advanced tech—just like Elysia and Kerlo said back on Earth.

"At my recommendation, you are approved for assignment in that company. Do you accept?"

She stared into his steady brown eyes. He knew he didn't need to ask. It was a formality.

"Hell yes."

Chapter 32
Enchantments

A shoulder shoved Tovas, causing him to stumble with his tray. He caught it and prevented it from falling completely, but the movement threw his soup upward. Hot liquid and chunks of gluute splashed onto his face.

"Oh, guess I forgot to stop," Vurkil said, laughing as he continued on down the line of food.

Sam and Fita chuckled as they followed the giant. At least Ya'ir didn't join in.

Tovas wiped his face with a napkin and moved toward the other end of the room where the rest of Ulinko group sat.

I'm certainly not very popular today, Tovas thought toward Scheln.

"They're still bugging you about the game?" Scheln asked.

Tovas sat at the table next to Ya'ir, across from Zelyra. Everyone was listening to Talanna as she conveyed a story involving her family's impressive mansion. He sighed softly.

Yes, he thought toward Scheln.

"I'm sure they'll forget about it soon."

Using his spoon, Tovas picked up a few pieces of meat and

vegetables that had fallen onto his tray and shoved them into his mouth. *I should have made Relon our leader.*

"You did fine. It was our first game. Don't worry about it."

Tovas kept to himself during lunch, vaguely listening in on the group's conversation and occasionally speaking telepathically with Scheln, until the bell rang to usher the studies back to class. When they returned to the Land room, Master Azeloram announced that they would go to the Artifact Room for the rest of the afternoon.

"Yes! More weapons," Vurkil exclaimed.

"More?" the old man said. "Did Master Farco show you the weapon storage downstairs?"

"Yes, of course!" Vurkil replied. "He said we would learn more about them today."

The Master sighed. "He did this with the last group too, complaining about the Artifact Room not having enough fire enchantments."

Master Azeloram led them into the hall and opened the large doors at the intersection. The sun nearly blinded Tovas as he strode into the Tercast courtyard, pushing Scheln along in his wheelchair past the gorgeous landscaping and three giant colena trees. Cool air flowed through the light breeze, rustling their multicolored leaves and causing several to shower down on the group below. A flock of pink sky worms zoomed through the air overhead, followed by the silver wyvern, which dove through the air and snatched one with a ferocious bite. In the distance, the beautiful Ridlesh Mountains shined purple and gold—a sign of ripening fall on this side of the planet.

"This sight never gets old," Scheln said in Tovas's mind.

It is magnificent, Tovas thought back. *This has certainly been a place blessed by the Divine.*

As they reached the other side of the courtyard, Master Azeloram stopped in front of an ornate double-hung door where a woman stood. Curly gray hair fell from her head in clusters, one falling down past wrinkled features to her slightly smiling lips.

"This is Caretaker Yuulia," Master Azeloram said.

"Lively afternoon," the woman said, "and welcome to the Artifact Room. Please avoid touching anything until we tell you to."

Nodding to each other, the two Masters inserted a key into either half of the ornate door and turned synchronously. A loud clash rang from behind the door, as if something heavy had fallen out of place. They then opened each half of the door, motioning for the studies to enter.

Tovas's eyes widened as he walked through the doorway with Scheln. Glass display cases scattered across the interior, showing off amulets, shields, and all kinds of weaponry, surrounded by other artifacts covering nearly every inch of the walls. He thought it strange not to see firearms of any kind. Handguns and rifles, particularly ones powered by combustion, had been around since long before the Sovereignty.

Why do you think they don't have any guns? Tovas asked.

"*I don't know,*" Scheln replied. "*Maybe guns are evil to them or something.*"

They surely wouldn't call objects evil, would they?

"*Remember the Great Lomerian Dissent? The Scelebriars? Those people hated guns. Maybe Ilius was one of them.*"

I thought the dissenters' principal concern was condemning same gender sexuality.

"*Oh yeah, they take that one scripture literally, saying to 'spare not the rod on those which lie with like body.' Tercast's book prescribes torture to 'cure' people who are attracted to the same gender and such, so Ilius probably was one of them. It's consistent with the gun thing as well.*"

I think that's more of a scare tactic, Tovas said. *The Masters wouldn't actually torture someone.*

"*Even if that is the case, adding it to their book on fundamentals implies that harming people is the will of the Divine,*" Scheln replied. "*Harm is almost never Divine will. Tercast may have incredible abilities, but Ilius definitely took the religion in a different direction from its Lomerian roots.*"

True, Tovas admitted.

"Gather around," Master Azeloram called out near one of the display cases.

The studies returned from their awe-driven browsing to the Master's position. Tovas noted Fita's enthusiastic grin—an odd sight.

Master Yuulia walked to the glass case before them, which contained a large oval-shaped shield. "Every artifact you see here was recovered by Grand Master Ilius and his first group of followers."

She held her hands out and looked up at the walls around them. "This entire room is protected by a powerful enchantment to prevent unauthorized access and keep everyone safe. I trust that Master Azeloram has already explained to you the difference between a historical enchantment and a neo-enchantment? Can anyone elaborate for me?"

Talanna immediately spoke up. "Yes! Neo-enchantments are things like health potions. They are enchanted once for a specific purpose and lose their power over time. Historical enchantments are much more powerful, but they take a long time to do."

The woman smiled. "Yes, that is correct. Does anyone have anything else to add?"

No one replied.

"When an object is repeatedly enchanted and used in a specific way," the Master said, "it develops an affinity for that enchantment. It requires less and less spiritual energy to produce the same result."

Heads nodded around the room.

"So, what are the effects of historical enchantments on Vitalization?"

"Oh!" Talanna exclaimed. "The more an object is historically enchanted, the less other Sorcerers can Vitalize it."

"Very good," Master Yuulia replied. "The object favors its user. Everyone, take a moment to reach out with your Source."

Tovas closed his eyes and calmed his mind. Localized emotions passed through his awareness. Robes. Wood flooring. Glass. Air. The areas around his fellow studies were dark and fuzzy as usual.

Interestingly, darkness outlined each of the artifacts as well. He couldn't feel any of them.

"Interesting!" Scheln said in Tovas's mind. *"I can't feel them. That would be handy in a fight between Sorcerers. It would be over pretty quickly if one could just hurl the other's weapons away."*

"As you can see," Master Yuulia continued, "Sorcerers cannot Vitalize these relics normally, because they are bound to another soul. However, they may still be accessed with physical touch and can bind to a new soul over time with use. Follow me."

She led them to a corner of the room, where several weapons covered the wall. The most visible artifact was an enormous hammer leaning against the wall, its head against the floor. Vurkil gravitated toward it. It looked impossible to wield, even for a giant of Vurkil's size. The head was about as big around as the man's enormous thigh.

"Remove one glove and select an artifact, but please do not touch it yet," she said. "When I give you the signal, please simply touch the artifact with the tip of your finger and reach out to it with your Source. Try to feel its enchantment."

Excitement buzzed as the studies moved about to find something they liked. Vurkil remained near the hammer. Fita looked longingly at a thin sword. Kula stared at a bow. Those two likely had experience with these kinds of weapons, being Helenestian. It was part of their culture.

Fita and Kula seem to enjoy this, Tovas thought toward Scheln.

"So does Vurkil," Scheln replied.

Did you find a weapon you like? Tovas asked.

"How about that staff? It looks neat."

Tovas wheeled Scheln toward the wall where a long, straight staff hung horizontally at hip level. Solid steel formed the core, with lines of gold swirling around the circumference from one end to the other. It looked somewhat plain next to the other ornamented weapons surrounding it. A small sign hung on the wall above it, displaying the words *Staff of Dreams.*

Staff of Dreams? Tovas thought.

"Maybe it puts people to sleep?"

You first. Tovas pulled the glove off his brother's right hand. *It was your choice.*

"Yes!" Scheln replied eagerly. "Urrgh . . . Auugh . . . Euuugh . . . Okay, I might need a bit of help moving my hand. It doesn't want to listen to me."

Tovas chuckled as Scheln watched the staff with a neutral physical expression. His head leaned toward the side, drool dripping from his slightly open mouth. Grief stabbed Tovas at the sight. Despite observing the condition for many years, he disliked seeing his brother this way. Internally, Scheln was still so full of life and enthusiasm—a dramatic contrast to his externally visible body. He took his condition remarkably well, but he didn't deserve this.

"Don't look at me like that," Scheln said.

Like what?

"With that pity. Stop it."

I just hate seeing you this way. You don't deserve this.

"If I could smack you, I would," Scheln replied. "Life is what it is. Deserving has nothing to do with it."

Tovas nodded.

"Has everyone selected an artifact?" the Caretaker asked.

The studies all confirmed that they had.

"Excellent. You may proceed," she said. "Remember, use only the tip of your finger."

Tovas moved his brother's hand forward so that a finger touched the side of the metal staff. He looked back to see Scheln's closed eyes. His brother looked asleep with the drool hanging out. Returning his gaze to the staff, he noticed several tiny embellishments that were invisible from a distance. Minuscule etchings of plantlike designs covered the edges where gold transitioned to steel.

"It's incredible!" Scheln's thoughts echoed in Tovas's mind. "Feels like protection. Give it a try."

Tovas moved Scheln's hand away and placed it back in his lap. He pulled the glove from his own hand. Touching the staff with his index finger, he closed his eyes, letting serenity take him.

Unlike the weapons surrounding it, the staff almost felt like it was glowing. He could sense it, the solid steel core and swirling gold lines. He connected with the core, feeling the strain of its weight against the hooks holding it in place. Emotions of purpose flowed through him. Defense. Protection. Life. Light.

Protect my people.

The thought settled on him with extraordinary tenderness and caressed his soul. Peace radiated through his being, providing a profound feeling of warmth and illumination. Hope blossomed along with it—hope for a better existence.

He released his finger. The connection severed abruptly, but the feelings of peace and hope lingered within. He opened his eyes to find his vision clouded by tears, which he quickly wiped away.

"Tovas, I could feel that," Scheln said to his mind. *"What happened?"*

I received a revelation from the Divine.

"You did?"

Yes. A sacred duty, Tovas thought reverently.

Protect my people.

Chapter 33

Gilmar Company

Kara woke with a start, courtesy of her Nit. It was finally time to leave Rwenmar.

She sat up and stretched, though her eyes could see very little in the dim room. A subtle command caused her visible spectrum to change. The room came into view—though severely lacking in color.

The bars of the bunk ladder chilled the palms of her hands as she descended. She stared for a moment at the sleeping Lorelei. They had barely gotten to know each other during the several days they'd been together. They had both spent nearly all their time training, and command had never placed them in a squad together.

Kara felt her way into her Ilkuth, and the suit closed in around her. The brightness of the suit's night-vision display blinded her overexposed eyes, so she turned her vision back to normal. Adorning her enormous backpack, Kara walked out the swishing door and into the night.

Rows of identical military housing stretched out in each direction. To her right, past the end of the narrow street, stood the supply room and training grounds. *Well, goodbye, Garrison Keldridge. It's been fun.*

The bar at the right of her display increased, and she rose smoothly from the ground into the sky. She engaged the auto-navigator, allowing it to take control of her suit to the destination. Dimly lit mountains and the lush landscape below fell further and further until light clouds completely obscured the view. Clouds, too, fell away below, and the rushing wind gently gave way to silence.

Stars and clouds from the nearby galaxies filled Kara's view as she continued to move away from the planet. People had always told her that the night sky was beautiful. Staring at it now, Kara felt surreal. She didn't seem to feel much more weightless out in space than on the planet—probably because of the suit's tight fit.

Tiny objects came into view ahead, gradually getting larger. As Kara approached, she could make out three ring-shaped structures—acherons. Two long, cylindrical spaceships made their way through one ring as a similar vessel emerged from another.

Spaceships and teleportation portals, she thought. *Never in a million years would I have thought I'd be out in space above an alien planet.*

Her suit drifted naturally toward one portal, through which a distinct set of stars and swirly clouds of galaxies were visible. Sam was going to lose his mind when she told him about all of this.

She would be able to see him now, she realized. That would be weird.

Her suit changed direction, moving toward the Earthlike planet below named Velda. It appeared to be almost entirely water, with two large ice caps at each pole. Thick clouds swirled around its surface. The planet grew in her view as she descended toward it, and wind steadily built up around her. A glance at her antigravity bar told her that the suit was still moderating the rate of descent, so she wouldn't fall too fast.

The sky gradually gained its characteristic blueness until gray clouds abruptly surrounded her. Water droplets formed on her face shield. She emerged below the dark clouds and made out an island in the distance, heavy rain beating against the Ilkuth's surface.

Rain poured from the sky, while angry waves billowed below. She felt her descent slow as she approached a small base near the outer edge of land. An ascender took off below and made its way through the thick rain.

The suit landed gently outside the square Armed Forces building. A blue line appeared on her display that led her inside. As she walked into the building, the door shut quickly behind her, dampening the noise of the storm.

Kara stood in a small businesslike lobby. A few decorative plants hugged the walls and corners around an empty reception desk. She still felt strange entering a new building and finding herself unable to smell it. Buildings always had unique smells.

The blue line led her past the desk and into a small room filled with simple chairs facing a podium. Inside, several soldiers in Force armor talked among themselves with their helmets off. A large man with black skin and short curly hair saw her and approached with a welcoming smile. She pulled her helmet off as he greeted her with a Sovereignty salute across his chest.

"Lively day!" the man said.

She returned the salute and shrugged, then attached the helmet to its magnetic holster at her waist. "I don't know. It seems pretty rainy to me."

He raised his eyebrows before chuckling. "Rain is lively!" He held his hand out. "Commander One Olik Eniken."

She took his hand and shook it gently. Names in the Sovereignty were interesting. "Spark One Kara Jones."

"Whoa, I didn't know we were getting any brand-new recruits in this company. Welcome to the Force!"

She gave him a slight grin. "Thank you, Commander."

"Olik is just fine," he said with a warm grin. "We're not that formal out in the field." He pointed to a collection of large backpacks in the corner. "You may place your belongings with the rest of the company's things. Minister Golin will be here shortly to address us."

"Thanks," she said as she pulled the large backpack off her shoulders. She'd forgotten she was even wearing it.

Olik walked with her as she put her bag down with the group's belongings. "Where are you from?"

"Earth," she said.

"Interesting. I've never heard of it," he replied.

She moved toward a seat near the back of the room. "Yeah, no one has. It's a class four planet."

"Wow! You'll have to tell me your story sometime."

Another suit walked through the door, drawing Olik's attention.

He turned back to her. "Wonderful to meet you, Kara." He gave her another salute.

She returned it with a smile. "You too, Olik."

He moved off to greet the newcomer.

Kara assessed the others in the room as she sat near the back, marveling at the variety of appearances. Several people had skin with shades of white, brown, and black, but there were a few others with a blue or green complexion. Hair was also a variant. Most had varieties of straight black or brown hair, but a few had blond, including one of the blue-skinned girls. One woman with green skin had bright blue hair, and another girl with pale white skin had short deep-red hair. Kara wondered if the color was natural or the result of dyes. She had never had a desire to dye her hair before, but now that she was sighted, she thought about trying it out.

A blue-skinned, middle-aged man in a Sovereignty uniform entered the room, carrying a long, thin rifle. Several soldiers stood and saluted him, so Kara followed suit. As she glanced at his insignia, her Nit informed her of his name: Golin Intiliak, Minister of the Armed Forces.

He nodded in acknowledgment before walking to the front of the room. The man was the only one among them not wearing armor.

"Welin Em Onii, my friends," he said.

"Welin Em Onii," several in the room repeated.

Kara had heard the term a few times during their training.

Apparently, it was an ancient phrase from Rwenmar that translated to "for life, duty, and love." They used it as a kind of unofficial motto. Those in suits took their seats as the man addressed them.

"Thank you for accepting the invitation to serve in the Gilmar Company, a specially designated unit to combat this new and largely unknown threat."

Minister Golin held out the long black rifle he'd entered with. Kara subconsciously zoomed in with her eyes to get a better look.

"This is a Pileeken vaporizer—a plasma rifle," he explained. "I doubt many of you will be familiar with it. It is typically only used in rare industrial applications. As this new enemy appears to be highly resilient to projectile weapons, you will train to use this as your primary weapon. Our analysis of their tactics and capabilities determined it as the most effective choice. The vaporizer only has a maximum lethal damage range of about eight feet—so that means getting up close and personal. You have been selected based on recommendations from your commanding officer and your excellence in close-quarters combat."

"We are going in with deadly force?" a blue-skinned woman near the front asked. "That seems extreme."

The minister ignored her and gestured toward a man seated at the front, who stood up and made his way forward.

"Most of you are probably aware of the incident on Tenreth," Minister Golin said, "where cloaked cultists slaughtered dozens of civilians and stole priceless artifacts from the library there. We have linked them to other lesser-known attacks. They are noncitizens and extremely dangerous. Those brave few who have firsthand experience against the threat will be leading your efforts."

The other man turned about next to the minister and stood at attention. He surveyed the other suited individuals in the room. The man had pale white skin, dark hair, and a short beard, which came to a tip below his chin. His eyes rested on Kara, and they widened. A moment later, they returned to normal.

That's odd, she thought. *Has he seen me before?* Facial expressions were still difficult to read at times. It was probably nothing.

"This is your Gilmar Company leader," the minister said. "He fought personally with the cultists on Tenreth and even took a few of them down."

"Commander Three Delveton Levina."

Chapter 34

Ya'ir

Sam stared at himself in the mirror, confirming that he had put the white robes on properly. It looked like he'd lost a little weight. He hadn't made a complete habit of going to the exercise room with Vurkil and Fita in the evenings, but he would join them occasionally. Usually, he used that time to analyze the results he had, but he needed more data.

Yawning, he walked out of the changing stall and into the washroom. As he passed the ornate sinks, he thought back to his first day at Tercast—over four weeks ago, by Alvior measurements. That first week had dragged on endlessly, but after his breakthrough with Sorcery, the courses were much more engaging. The mysterious fatigue had eased, allowing them to complete several tasks each day without passing out from exhaustion. He couldn't believe it had already been over a week since their visit to the museum.

The Masters still frequently recited theological nonsense about how "Water is the Element of change" and "Earth is the Element of stability," but when Sam would ask them whether these four Elements were symbolic rather than literal, he would get nothing but scorn. "They are absolutely literal," Master Evalencia had told him. "Every speck of matter is one of the four Elements." He couldn't understand how these people could be so fervently adherent to illogical beliefs.

Their Elemorb skills had improved somewhat. They hadn't won their second game either, but they had certainly improved. At least Tovas hadn't made a fatal mistake again. He even scored once. Though Sam now enjoyed their Sorcery classes, game day was a pleasant change of pace.

He found himself in front of the Air instruction room, having walked on autopilot down the halls while absorbed in his thoughts. He entered the large door to find Vurkil and Rose seated at the front, completely silent. Niu didn't seem to mind that Vurkil was in her seat. She sat chatting happily with Talanna at another table. Zelyra sat on the floor near the front, petting the ulinko. Tovas sat at the other end of the room, staring at the exquisite green artwork.

Sam settled down in his seat near the door and looked around at the artwork himself. It was quite impressive. One image depicted a thunderstorm over a forest, with a bolt of lightning striking a tall tree. Another displayed a forest leaning from powerful winds, with leaves trailing in swirling paths.

The door opened behind him, and Sam glanced back to see Ya'ir.

"Hey, Ya'ir," Sam said with a wave.

Ya'ir plopped into the empty seat next to him. "Hi, Sam. I wonder what today's tasks will be."

Sam shrugged. "Who knows. Their curriculum doesn't seem to follow any consistent pattern—though they're getting more preachy and less hands-on."

Ya'ir nodded, his gaze settling on Rose and Vurkil. He leaned over and whispered, "Vurkil likes her, I think."

Sam chuckled. "You think?" he whispered back. "It's been obvious for weeks."

"Do you think she likes him too?"

He shrugged again. "Everyone likes Vurkil, but yeah, I don't know. Rose is pretty shy. She's been coming out of her shell a bit lately, but she's still quite timid."

"Unless you get her talking about biology or Sorcery science," Ya'ir said. "She seems fairly relaxed when discussing ideas."

"True."

Ya'ir's eyebrows scrunched up in thought. He turned to Sam with an odd look, then opened his mouth as if to speak, only to close it again.

"What is it?" Sam asked.

The man's face was troubled, perhaps betraying the result of an internal debate.

"Hey, it's all right," Sam said. "You know you can tell me anything."

"I . . ." Ya'ir trailed off, and his expression eased. "Can we speak outside for a moment?"

"Sure, of course."

They walked out the door together and Sam felt apprehensive. What could trouble him so much?

Ya'ir looked around the empty hallway before taking a deep breath. "Sam, I . . . I don't know how to say this, but I feel like I need to say it."

Worry rose within Sam. Had something happened regarding their experiments? Perhaps Ya'ir had told someone about them, like he had been suggesting recently. The thought spiked Sam's fear. If Tovas found out, they were in serious trouble.

"I like you," Ya'ir said. "A lot."

Sam's mind went blank at the unexpected statement. His initial gut reaction was to say "I like you too"—until the weight of Ya'ir's words fully sunk in.

Sam didn't know what to say. How could he tell Ya'ir that he didn't like him that way but also genuinely valued his friendship?

"I . . . hope you know what I mean by that," Ya'ir said. "More than friends, you know. I know it's strictly against Tercast code, but I was wondering . . . you know . . . whether we might get together after we graduate or something. Outside of Tercast. If . . . If you're interested, I mean."

Sam still couldn't find words. Tension rose in his chest. Why did Ya'ir have to ask this? Why couldn't they just go on being friends? Would this make their relationship all awkward now?

This was the exact problem he had been avoiding with Kara for years.

"Are . . . you going to say something?"

Sam swallowed hard. "Ya'ir," he said, scratching his head awkwardly. "You are an amazing friend. Really. I just . . . I'm actually already in love with someone."

Ya'ir's expression turned sorrowful. "Oh. Right. Of course. You . . . probably aren't even attracted to men that way anyway, are you?"

Sam's hands searched subconsciously for pockets in his robes that didn't exist. He ended up awkwardly tugging at the fabric instead. "Honestly . . . no. I'm not. I'm sorry . . ."

Brown, sorrow-filled eyes stared back at him, making Sam feel sick to his stomach. *This is exactly why I don't confess to Kara. I'd be feeling just as distraught if she told me something similar.*

Sam wanted to reach out and hug his friend, but that felt wrong. He didn't know what to do.

Ya'ir brought an agitated hand to his forehead. "I shouldn't have said anything. This was so stupid. All I wanted was for my family to accept me. All my life. They hated me for telling them. We thought maybe by coming to Tercast, something might change. We thought magic could make me 'right'—make me stop feeling this way." Tears formed in his eyes. "But it has changed nothing. I'm cursed to be like this forever!"

Stunned silence hung between them like a fog.

"Ya'ir, there's absolutely nothing wrong with—"

Ya'ir turned and ran down the hall without a word. Sam watched him, dumbfounded. The man's steps faded as he turned the corner out of sight.

Sam pivoted numbly and walked toward the Air room door, which stood open a crack. As he went for the door handle, Tovas pushed the door open and sped past him into the hall. The conversation with Ya'ir echoed through his mind on repeat as he considered what he might have done differently.

Sam knew a thing or two about parents being unhappy with their son's choices. But in Ya'ir's case, it wasn't even a choice. They should have been more accepting. More supportive. It wasn't clear whether the decision to come to Tercast was Ya'ir's or whether his family had pushed him into it, but either way, seeing magic as a "cure" for his natural desires was an extremely harmful and terrible idea.

Wait, he thought with a jolt. *That was Tovas. The door was open a crack. He heard the conversation!*

Sam spun on his heel and turned toward the direction Ya'ir had run. Tovas would certainly consider it his duty to inform the Masters of Ya'ir's "heresy." He had to stop him somehow. The last thing Ya'ir needed was a lecture about how his actions or feelings were sinful, or worse. Didn't the fundamentals book say something about beating people who confessed to "unusual" sexual attraction?

Sam ran faster at the thought, glancing through the open room doors as he passed. When he had just about reached the end of the hallway, he glimpsed two white robes through a doorway. He stopped and prepared himself to counter Tovas's inevitable condemnation with all he had.

They were hugging.

Sam stood stunned in place.

Ya'ir sobbed quietly into Tovas's shoulder as Sam watched them for several seconds, hardly believing his eyes. Tovas glanced at Sam and gave him a subtle nod.

It didn't make sense. Tovas's very existence was bent on religious devotion.

Sam turned quietly and walked back down the hall to the Air room, touched by the scene but still deeply confused. He should have been the one to comfort Ya'ir. Instead, he was the cause of his distress. Barely coherent thoughts and a sense of uneasiness accompanied him back through the Air room doors and to his table.

"What was that all about?" Vurkil asked. Next to him, Rose turned with a curious expression.

"Nothing," Sam said.

"That was no nothing! Ya'ir got upset about something out there."

Rose studied Sam's face, then turned to the giant. "Leave it be, Vurkil."

Sam expected Vurkil to continue pressing him for information, but after a moment of looking over Sam with scrutinizing eyes, he turned his gaze forward. Vurkil definitely had a thing for Rose.

The rest of the group trickled into the room over the next few minutes, including Tovas and Ya'ir. Though his eyes were red, Ya'ir was no longer sobbing. He sat in the seat next to Sam.

Vurkil turned around. "Ya'ir, what was that about?" he asked.

The infernal man just couldn't let it go.

Rose spun to face Sam with an apologetic look on Vurkil's behalf.

"It's nothing," Ya'ir replied.

"Why are you both saying this is nothing when it is clearly—" The man's face lit up in realization. "Ah! You confessed."

Tovas stood at the back of the room. "Vurkil, don't—"

"Ha! I knew it. I knew you were smitten with Sam like—"

Vurkil stopped midsentence, eyes wide.

Sam whirled his head around and stared in horror at Master Olana, whose jaw had dropped.

"Ya'ir Wenkat!" she exclaimed. "Is this true? Have you confessed a romantic attraction to Samuel?"

"Master Olana—"

"I was *not* speaking to you, Tovas!"

The room froze in tense silence before Ya'ir finally spoke. "Yes, Master."

Sam's heart sank.

"Come with me. Immediately!" she commanded.

"Yes, Master," he said, hanging his head in unmerited shame.

She held the door for him, and he walked through it into the hallway. The door slammed behind them.

Everyone in the room sat stunned for several moments. Worry flooded through Sam as he considered what these cultists might do to Ya'ir.

He took a breath and turned to Vurkil. "You dolt! Why did you —"

"He didn't intend to, Sam," Tovas said.

Sam took in Vurkil's face, which was a pitiful sight. He looked like he was about to break down, but then he turned and sat forward. Sam's anger rapidly dissolved.

A few whispered voices were all that broke the uncomfortable silence until Master Olana returned. She made her way to the front of the class as everyone migrated to their assigned seats. She looked sorrowful, causing Sam more anxiety about Ya'ir's fate.

"Master?" Talanna asked.

"Yes, Talanna."

"What will happen to Ya'ir?"

"That is up to the Grand Masters to decide," Master Olana said. "It is out of my hands now."

Unease burdened them throughout the day. The class seemed to have more difficulty focusing on their task of causing tiny pockets of air to emit light—even Tovas. Lunch and dinner breaks were abnormally quiet. Everyone had been successful with the task by the end of the day, but it did little to brighten their mood.

The empty chair at Sam's table haunted him. After Master Olana dismissed them from class, Sam walked alone toward the men's dorms. He felt exhausted—no doubt a result of his persistent anxiety about Ya'ir's fate in addition to Sorcery fatigue.

Vurkil caught up to him on the stairway to their dorms. "Hi, Sam," he said. The rampant jovial nature of his voice was absent, which struck Sam as remarkably depressing.

"Hi, Vurkil," he responded. "I'm sorry about earlier. I know you didn't mean to . . . you know . . ." He couldn't bring himself to say "ruin Ya'ir's life," since that sounded far too melodramatic—and it would just make the poor guy feel worse.

"Yeah, but you were right. I was a rudding brickhead for saying it so loudly."

Even though Sam agreed, he patted the man's enormous arm as they reached the landing to their room. He heard other steps below and the characteristic squeak of Scheln's wheelchair. The others weren't far behind.

"It's just who you are," Sam told Vurkil. "And you're awesome. Don't beat yourself up over it. It's the Grand Masters of this place and their toxic doctrine that's the problem."

"You better not let them hear you say that," Vurkil said. "Speaking evil of the Council might get you similar treatment to whatever they're doin' with Ya'ir. Or worse."

He opened the door for Sam.

"Yeah, you're probably right," Sam said as the giant followed him through, ducking under the doorway. "But this whole situation shows the issue with religious fanaticism. They're so quick to condemn people for things which are not even within their control."

Vurkil nodded as they sat on their respective beds. Fita opened the door a few moments later and held it open for Tovas and Scheln.

"Thanks, Fita," Tovas said.

Sam had been thinking about bringing more of them in on their secret experiments, as Ya'ir had suggested. He didn't fear Vurkil's contempt for their research—only his ability to keep a secret. Fita was a big mystery. Sam still didn't know him well enough to speculate about what he might do. Until today, Sam was always sure Tovas would immediately betray them to the Masters. He needed more test subjects, though. Three wasn't enough to make any significant conclusions about this whole Sorcery business. Perhaps now was the time to take the chance.

"I have something I want to ask all of you," Sam said.

All eyes turned to him. Tovas stopped his process of unlatching Scheln from his seat. Uneasiness rippled through Sam like a shockwave. This was a bad idea. It could just make everything worse. But the thought of Ya'ir gave him resolve.

He took a deep breath. "Rose, Ya'ir, and myself have been experimenting with Sorcery."

Judging from their facial reactions, he realized that this didn't have quite the impact he thought it would.

"Is that where you've been sneaking off to in the middle of the night?" Vurkil asked. "I wondered if the food was getting to you."

Sam smiled. "There's a room down near the weapon storage room Master Farco took us to a while ago. We've discovered some interesting trends, but we really need results from more people to get a better idea of the limits of these powers."

Tovas stared at him with a thoughtful expression. "This is a serious offense against Tercast rules, Sam."

Sam rolled his eyes. Of course that's all he would think about. "I know that. I just don't care. Trying to suppress knowledge is a key way to maintain power. That's all they want."

"I'm in!" Vurkil said. "I want to know more about Sorcery too."

"I will help. On one condition," Tovas said.

"What's that?" Sam replied.

"We train and explore methods for self-defense. The Divine has blessed us with these gifts, and we can use them to protect and defend the helpless."

The room fell silent for a moment. Sam could hardly believe his ears.

"Tovas, we're not superheroes," he said.

"We can make a difference for those who—"

Tovas's words cut off as the sound of the door opening made them jump. Sam stood up.

The sight before his eyes overwhelmed him.

Ya'ir stood in the doorway. Dust and flecks of red stained his white robes. His face was littered with cuts and bruises. One eye was squeezed shut from swelling. He entered and closed the door behind him. Tovas rushed forward and wrapped his arms around the man in a soft embrace.

Ya'ir wept.

Sam's vision clouded as he made his way forward and hugged them both. Vurkil's enormous arms followed soon after, encircling him and the others. A light touch on his back told him that Fita had joined in as well.

Occasional sniffling offered the only respite from the tender silence.

Chapter 35

Preparations

"Again. Maintain your stance this time."

"Don't do it. It's not you, Jeanette."

Shut up, Amy.

Jeanette held long daggers in hand—one forward, the other further back. Her opponent, Tess, raised a thin, straight sword. Gritting her teeth, Jeanette took a step and forced herself to ignore the stench. The expected thrust came toward her chest, and she jumped back. As she moved to the side, her opponent did the same.

Tess lunged. Jeanette reflexively twisted her left knife down and outward, parrying the woman's sword. She stepped forward and brought down the second blade with as much force as she could muster. It hit just below Tess's neck as she brought up her arm to block, slicing a line across her collarbone and forearm.

Tess's injured arm then flew outward, and she smashed her fist into Jeanette's face, knocking her back.

Scraping steel echoed against the stone walls as Jeanette stumbled. Immense pain accompanied a strange internal pressure in her gut, which then pulled away.

She needed to get closer.

Just as her vision was coming back into focus, Jeanette lunged forward in desperation and stabbed with her left dagger. Her opponent sidestepped. The steel blade lashed against Jeanette's outstretched arm and carved across her triceps. She tried to slash sideways toward her attacker, but her arm barely responded with a wave of agony.

A kick struck her left side, knocking her over. The dagger slipped from her fingers. The blade clanged against the floor as she landed hard on her knees and right elbow.

Pain erupted from her side with another wrong-feeling internal pressure. Jeanette screamed.

A strong blunt force hit her wounded side and turned her on her back. Nausea rose in her stomach. Her hand pressed against the hole in her side, feeling the now familiar warm wetness. Cold rippled across her skin. Her vision of the ceiling above went fuzzy as Tess hovered over her.

Red liquid fell into Jeanette's open mouth and tasted of strawberries. She swallowed automatically.

The fierce pain across her body quickly faded. Nausea subsided, and her vision cleared. She trembled as she sat up, still gripping the dagger in her right hand, disgusted by the sticky pool of blood beneath her. She glanced at Tess, who had a streak of blood running down her chest—though the gash near her neck had healed. The woman had her arms crossed, and she shook her head.

"It was a good counter, but you had too much follow-through," she said. "Left you wide open."

Jeanette remained in her sitting position on the floor, shaking furiously. She had nearly died several times during the session. Tess was merciless.

"Well, I think we are done for now," Tess said with a sigh. "That was my last potion. We'll be able to train harder once you can self-heal."

Elation filled Jeanette. Done. Finally.

"Don't let them—"

Jeanette smothered Amy's tiresome voice in her head. It was just her subconscious reminding her that something about this whole thing wasn't right. She knew that, but she would *not* go back to the prison. Never again. And if she refused the Deia's wishes, that was exactly where she would end up.

A few hours of study and rest from this torment would be hers before Tess would make her do it again. The room looked like something out of a horror film. Crusty, dried blood punctuated Jeanette's hair, her long ponytail dripping from the last encounter. Her training clothes were tattered and soaked, but thankfully, they were still somewhat modest. Red coated the stone floor and walls of the small, empty room.

"You really aren't much of a fighter," Tess said.

Jeanette agreed. Kara was the fighter. Her sister's skills on the mat, though admirable, were something Jeanette had never much envied until now. She never thought in a million years that she would be forced into such violent situations. She was the peace-maker, the helpful friend, the older sibling who drove her sister and her friends around town.

She'd never been a fighter.

Tess gathered the knife from the floor and took the one from Jeanette's hand. "Come on. Let's get you cleaned up."

"Why can't I heal myself yet?" Jeanette asked as they left the room. "Isn't that what the biology studying is for?"

"Yes, but your Sorcery is weak right now while you're in transition," Tess replied impatiently. "You won't be able to do much, if anything at all."

"Transition?"

"It'll all make sense later."

Jeanette followed Tess numbly through the halls, trying to hold the suffocating despair at bay. She had completely lost track of time. The lack of daylight didn't help. Since her release from the dungeons, she had spent hours reading the Deia's assigned books on varied topics such as psychology and astrophysics, besides the terrifying sparring matches with Tess.

There had to be a way to escape. Jeanette still couldn't figure out what the Deia planned for her, but she was sure it couldn't be good. When Tess had first told her about the combat training, Jeanette thought maybe it would provide her a chance to escape. Given her constant horrifying failures, it was becoming increasingly clear that such a feat would be impossible.

Her only hope was the rebellion.

Every day, she strained her ears for news about the rebels—Belze's people. They had to be out there somewhere. Perhaps one day they would come and free her from this misery. It was her only spark of hope left.

Tess entered the armory and stopped so suddenly that Jeanette almost ran into her. The woman stared at someone at the other end of the room, who turned to face them. Terror flooded Jeanette's mind at the sight.

Del. Her kidnapper. The man who had murdered her parents.

Instead of his black robe, he wore some kind of high-tech armor—a jarring contrast to the almost medieval-feeling castle. He was attaching a handful of small throwing knives to the back of his suit next to a sword, and he turned to face them. Weapons of all shapes and sizes littered the walls. Similar high tech suits lined the wall near him.

"What are you doing here, Del?" Tess asked. "I thought you were off training that Sorcerer-killing team of yours."

Del stared straight at Jeanette. She felt an urgent need to run, but shock froze her in place.

"Grabbing some equipment for the assault," he said in that low, raspy voice, maintaining his eerie gaze on Jeanette. "And modifying the team's armor somewhat."

Tess glanced over, then turned back to Del. "Oh, don't worry about her. She's practically one of us now."

Not a chance, Jeanette thought as she trembled at the man's stare. *I'll never be one of you.*

He finally broke his gaze from her and looked at Tess. "Are our forces ready?"

Tess shrugged. "Mostly. We found another cache of weapons in a hidden chamber down near the storage rooms. Nothing spectacular, unfortunately."

He nodded. "Hopefully, we won't need them."

"Are they actually any good?" Tess asked.

"The company? Yes, they are skilled. I'm disabling many of the suits' protective mechanisms to weaken them. It'll make it more of an even fight."

"We'll be ready regardless."

His gaze settled on Jeanette again, and he wore a disturbing smirk. "There was also a new recruit."

"They let a new recruit into the company?" Tess asked.

"Indeed."

The way Del maintained his watchful stare on Jeanette unsettled her.

"Kara Jones," he said, nodding toward her. "This one's sister."

Shock exploded in Jeanette's mind at the mention of her sister's name, followed by immense fear. She struggled to comprehend his words.

"I'll leave her protections intact," Del said. "If she survives, perhaps she will join us too."

Chapter 36

Healer

Rose threw the book onto the stone floor, drawing glances from the others in the small storage room.

"Not a good book after all?" Tovas asked from his seat on a crate across from hers.

Her cheeks still burned, but thankfully she'd been feeling more comfortable around the group. A few weeks ago, this much attention would have petrified her.

"Just a stupid ending," she said.

Most of the observers returned to their previous activities.

Tovas raised an eyebrow. "What happened?"

"Remember the surgeon I told you about several weeks ago? Sheela? Well, she had two love interests throughout the entire story and then the clearly better choice *died*, so she ended up with the other guy."

"Wow, spoiler alert," Sam remarked absently, maintaining focus on his sheets of parchment.

"None of you were planning to read it, were you?" she asked.

Tovas and Vurkil shook their heads. Silence settled as they waited for Sam to complete his work.

The entire Ulinko group had been meeting during the night in shifts now for about a week. Sam had told the men about their experiments and had asked Rose to speak to the women about it. After Ya'ir's brutal treatment at the hands of the Grand Masters and the Masters' swift rebuttal of the group's criticism, they had all agreed to join in.

They had also begun Tovas's requested training. Fita and Kula had taught them a few basic techniques and agreed to teach them with weapons—if they could get into the weapon storage room. Zelyra was working to pick the lock, with Kula standing watch.

"I think I've got it!" Sam exclaimed.

Rose stood from her crate and made her way over to him with the rest of them.

"Your 'magic-dampening equation'?" Tovas asked.

"Yes," Sam replied. "It has been really hard since it's almost impossible to correct for all the different factors that we've seen to have some kind of effect, but this equation seems to roughly explain most of the data." He held the paper up for them to read.

$$P = \frac{k}{(x+1)^{\frac{1}{k}}}$$

"Are we supposed to know what this means?" Vurkil asked.

"The x is the variable I'm most confident about," Sam explained. "It represents distance. There's a pretty clear inverse relationship between the distance of Vitalization and the maximum amount of force or change we can exert. The *plus one* is there to make zero distance correct."

Vurkil frowned. "Zero distance is what? Our center?"

"No, it appears to be our entire body. When we did the arm extension test, the strength of the Sorcery was higher when people reached out, remember?"

They nodded.

Sam then pointed to the k. "This one was tricky. The k is a very rough estimate of our knowledge on the subject, since that seems to influence distance and power. I don't know how else to explain why I can move things with more force at a greater distance than others. And Rose can do chemical transmutations more effectively, for example. It seems to have something to do with our subject knowledge of what we're manipulating."

"Why would knowledge matter, though?" Tovas said. "We don't think of specific commands about changing the Elements themselves. It's only feelings—imagination."

"Yeah, I've thought about that too," Sam replied, staring back at the paper. "Truth is, I don't know. All I know is that there seems to be this kind of correlation with our knowledge."

"Why wouldn't the Masters teach us more science, then?" Vurkil asked.

Sam shrugged. "Maybe they don't know."

"I doubt that," Tovas remarked.

Sam waved the response off. "Or they're doing it to maintain power or something. Anyway, this equation seems to capture the proper relationship for most of our tests so far. The one thing it doesn't explain is the strange jump in my results and Ya'ir's results after we brought you all in on these experiments. The jump is small but significant. I have no idea what would have caused that sudden—"

The door burst open. "Zel's done it!" Kula yelled.

The group scrambled up and raced out into the hallway—except Sam and Rose, who walked behind.

"You'd think they just found buried treasure or something," Sam said.

Rose raised her eyebrow at him. "Why would someone bury treasure?"

"I forget sometimes how much Earth culture differs from the Sovereignty in some ways."

"People on Earth bury treasure?"

"Well, not really . . . I think. We just have legends about pirates that bury treasure and such."

"Earth is weird," Rose said.

"Yeah, can't argue there."

They entered the weapon room to find the others eagerly

picking up various swords, maces, and spears. Kula had found a long bow and was drawing it back with an uncharacteristically giddy grin on her face. She must have significant strength to draw it as far as she was—or perhaps she was enhancing her muscles with Sorcery.

"Hey!" Vurkil called out, drawing their gazes. "Isn't this the sword Farco showed us?" He held the curved sword Rose had seen up close the last time she'd been in this room.

"The one that blazed hot and didn't melt?" Sam said.

"Yes!" Vurkil hefted it up. He switched it to his left hand and began slipping off his right glove.

"Fita's going to want that one," Rose told him. "He liked it even before Master Farco set it on fire."

The giant laughed. "Okay. What I really want is that hammer. Too bad it's in the display room."

"That thing was enormous," Tovas said. "It looked like it would be far too heavy to be useful, even with your size."

Vurkil shrugged. "I liked it anyway!"

"Sam!" Zel called out from the other end of the room.

"Yes?"

"I think you'll like this one." She held up a steel mace with several ornate, curved protrusions at the head.

Sam walked toward her. "Why do you say that?"

"It's all wiggly," she said. "And I feel like it likes to move things." She bent down and looked at the wall next to her. "Even says it's called the Mace of Motion."

A sudden and powerful gust of wind blew through the room, causing Rose to close and shield her eyes as several of the weapons jostled or fell with a loud clang. A large thump sounded nearby. She opened her eyes to see the others recovering from the bizarre gust.

"What was *that*?" Sam asked.

"Sorry!" Kula said. "This bow seems to create a powerful wind. I didn't know it would be—"

"Rudds, some help here would be grand," Vurkil's low voice rang.

Rose looked over to see the hilt of a dagger jutting out from his shoulder as he sat against the wall. She made her way to him and pulled off her gloves. "Vurkil, it's okay, just don't—"

He yanked the long knife from his shoulder, and blood gushed from the wound.

"—do that," Rose finished.

He looked at her with a puzzled face. "Do what?"

She sighed. "Never mind."

Rose was careful not to step on any of the weapons strewn about from the gust. She pulled the short cape of her outfit off over her head as she reached his position.

"Is it bad?" he asked. His voice betrayed no sense of pain.

"Lie flat," she commanded.

Vurkil complied, turning and laying his back against the stone floor. They needed pressure to stop the bleeding. Rose kneeled above him and pressed the bundled cape against the wound in his shoulder with both hands, causing him to inhale sharply. Judging by the copious amount of pulsating blood pouring from it, she suspected that the knife had pierced his major artery. He really should have left it in place.

"Stay calm. Don't move," she instructed.

"What can we do to help?" Tovas asked, standing above them. Kula and Sam arrived behind him.

"Sam, Tovas, lift his legs up. Kula, find something to prop them on." Rose didn't bother to check for acknowledgment, keeping her focus on applying pressure to the shoulder.

"Vurkil, have you tried to heal yourself?" Tovas asked.

Rose shook her head. "I don't think that's a good idea. We want him to stay conscious."

"He's going to be okay, right?" Sam said.

"Yes, he should be fine. We just need to keep applying pressure so he doesn't hemorrhage, until we can get our hands on one of those health potions. Is everyone else all right?"

"Yes, I don't think anyone else was injured," Tovas replied.

Zelyra arrived, looking down at Vurkil with a curious expression. "What's a hemmige?"

Rose ignored the question. She would have to try getting the cape around his shoulder so they could bind up the wound. She could ask him to turn on his side, but it would be better to lift him herself to keep him relaxed. She'd need extra strength to lift his enormous body, though.

Rose extended her Source, sensing the now familiar emotions of items around her. Vurkil was a large hole in space. Feelings associated with her own clothing and internal organs passed through her. Fabric. Heart. Blood. Stomach. Lungs. Bone. Tendon. Muscle. She latched on to the feelings of the bones, tendons, and muscles, connecting with the areas of her upper back and right biceps. She had learned that it was more effective to command the fibers as whole cells. They were Sources themselves, after all—a realization she had come to during the muscle enhancement instruction.

Vurkil's large ungloved hand touched hers affectionately. The ethereal world of emotions before her exploded with light. She could feel him. The fleeting emotions of his body and organs accompanied hers. She let go of the connection with her own muscles, instead establishing a connection to the tissue of his shoulder.

She looked up into Vurkil's eyes, which stared widely back at hers. He could sense the connection too.

The injured tissue was a mess of chaotic activity. Blood was escaping from a gash in the large artery, as she had suspected. The pressure she was applying helped, but it certainly didn't prevent all the escaping fluid. She connected with the severed ends of the large vessel, feeling the interactions of the different layers of cells, and imagined the damaged end cells being let go by the cells surrounding them. With the force of her imagination, she then brought the two ends of the vessel together, commanding junctions to re-form between each of the layers.

Blood ceased to escape from the large vessel, but the surrounding muscle, smaller vessels, capillaries, and skin were heavily damaged. She closed her eyes and worked her way from the deepest point of the puncture upward, removing damaged cells and debris and bringing together the healthy cells.

She pulled the bloodied cape away from Vurkil's arm as the last bit of his skin came together and connected at her command. The result wasn't perfect, but certainly better than a suture. His body should be able to do the rest over time. He let her arm go, but she could still feel him.

"What happened?" Tovas asked.

"Rose healed me," Vurkil said in awe.

"What?" Sam exclaimed. "That's impossible!"

"Look!" the giant said, pulling the bloodied fabric down from his neck to expose the shoulder.

"That doesn't make any sense," Sam said. "We can't Vitalize other people—or even the space around other people. We've known that for weeks!"

"It happened when we touched," Vurkil said, turning back to look at Rose. She felt his emotion—his attraction. This man had a deep affection for her. The day he guarded her from the man at lunch flashed in her mind, as well as the many instances of his quiet presence.

"That's a miracle," Tovas said. "Thank the Divine."

Sam argued the pious statement, but Rose stopped listening. She stared past the thick stubble into Vurkil's deep-brown eyes and became overwhelmed with emotion. The man was beautiful, inside and out. She leaned in slowly, feeling his heartbeat race alongside hers as she closed her eyes. Warm, full lips touched hers once she descended on him.

They kissed.

Realization electrified her, and she sat up abruptly, cheeks burning furiously. She turned around to see the others gazing down at them with wide eyes.

"Is that part of the cure too?" Zel asked.

Chapter 37

Action

Jeanette sat in her small study filled with books. The chapter titled "Weather and Atmospheric Liquid" lay unread on the desk before her. Thoughts swirled in her mind as she reeled from the memory of seeing her captor again—and hearing him utter Kara's name.

For the first time in a long while, Jeanette let herself imagine Amy's form materializing in front of the desk.

"What do I do, Amy?" she said aloud.

"Don't do anything they—"

You keep telling me what not to do. But what do I do? I can't let them take my sister too.

Amy's imagined form remained oddly silent. The beautiful dark face looked down at Jeanette with sorrow as she came around the desk and wrapped her ethereal arms around her. A tear fell from Jeanette's eye.

I don't know what to do.

"Think about what you know," Amy said.

Jeanette let the mental image of her old friend fade. What did she know? She didn't think she knew very much. Tess wouldn't provide any more details after the interaction with Del. All

Jeanette could gather was that a team of "Sorcerer killers," as Tess had put it, was coming to Uvlun. Inexplicably, Kara was with them. The other inhabitants of the castle were preparing for battle. Perhaps the Sorcerer-killer team was associated with the rebellion, and Del's involvement was a clever ruse to bring them down.

The thought of Belze and their attempted escape came to mind. That disgusting man Jeanette had spared had murdered Belze. Perhaps she shouldn't have saved him after all. If she had simply killed him during their first encounter, he wouldn't have killed Belze. The thought pained her. Her only real friend in this hellish place, tortured and murdered for trying to save her.

She would *not* let the same happen to Kara.

How her sister had gotten mixed up with the Deia's enemies was unfathomable, but if anyone was going to be caught doing impossible things like joining a rebellion against a group of Sorcerers on an alien planet, it'd be Kara. Jeanette recalled when her parents first put her into martial arts as a child. Her blindness was a severe disadvantage compared to the other students, but she took it as a personal challenge. Kara was a force of nature. She never gave up on anything.

What would her parents think of her sister now? They certainly wouldn't condone Kara's decision to join a group of mercenaries or whatever these Sorcerer killers were. "All life is sacred," they would say.

Look where that had gotten them.

It was time for Jeanette to be more like her sister—to take action. When the attack came and the castle forces were occupied with the battle, she needed to do the impossible. Or die trying.

She needed to kill the Deia.

Chapter 38

Discovery

"Okay, I'm ready," Niu said.

Rose watched as Sam raised the aptly named Mace of Motion to eye level. A small pebble rose from the ground of the storage room to his face.

"All right, here it comes," he said.

Niu nodded, closing her eyes tight.

The pebble shot toward her like a bullet and ricocheted off her skin.

Niu flinched, opened her eyes wide, and gasped. "It worked! I can finally do it too! Thank you so much."

"Ow!" Fita yelled.

Rose turned, noting the wound on the man's exposed arm. Blood poured from it. Rose reached through her connection to Fita's body—feeling its internal structures—and focused on the chaos of activity in his arm. She imagined the tissue stitching itself together, and it complied, stopping the blood flow.

The occurrence between Rose and Vurkil had taught them that it was possible to give each other control to Vitalize each other's bodies with Sorcery. The key was physical contact, coupled with a directed emotion of trust. Everyone in the group had now granted Rose the ability to affect their bodies as a precaution during their training and experiments—and were rightfully hesitant to give others that kind of intimate connection.

Interestingly, the distance rules didn't seem to apply to those connections, much to Sam's distress. Rose could heal a wound just as effectively whether she was standing right next to the patient or across the room, though she preferred to be within line of sight.

Rose stood from her crate and approached the shirtless man, inspecting her work. The path where the rock had grazed his arm was still lightly visible—an odd scar resulting from stretched tissue.

She needed to get her hands on one of those health potions. They seemed to heal tissue more naturally.

Fita nodded to her respectfully as he returned to tying his ponytail.

They had succeeded in enchanting their bodies against projectiles, as instructed during their Land course earlier in the week. Rose thought it was a clever use of neo-enchantments and an ingenious idea. Since their power was at its peak near the body, they could enchant their skin with a powerful reactionary force against fast-moving projectiles just before they made contact, delivering just enough force to send the shot away without expending enormous amounts of wakefulness.

Fatigue itself was still a strange phenomenon. The studies' capacity to enact change through Sorcery before fatigue overwhelmed them grew significantly as time went on. If they strained their abilities above baseline limits with intense emotion, their wakefulness diminished more quickly. They had spent many evenings over the past weeks aiding extremely fatigued group members back to the dorm rooms.

Rose returned to her crate in the corner next to Relon and gazed out at the storage room full of people, all present to watch Fita and Vurkil's rematch. Kula had been instructing Talanna with the bow, despite having little room for a shooting range in the small space. The two women slid a crate onto the end of the semicircle of crates—next to one where Ya'ir sat—and seated themselves on top of it. Niu situated herself between Ya'ir and Talanna. Sam sat on the other side of Ya'ir and engaged him about his plans for the next experiments. Zelyra sat alone in the corner, examining a brick with bizarre intensity.

Everyone except Tovas had arrived, which made Rose nervous. They really shouldn't all be here. Having everyone down in the storage room at once was risky.

"Ready to lose, blondie?" Vurkil taunted.

The giant pulled his own shirt off. Muscles rippled across his enormous body. Rose found herself blushing at the sight and aching to be in those arms again.

Fita's physique was quite impressive as well, and he was well-trained, but Rose thought it unlikely that he could pin Vurkil. Their size difference was simply too great.

The Helenestian smirked up at his massive opponent, then bowed. Vurkil followed suit.

He really thinks he can win, Rose thought.

Everyone went silent as the two crouched into combat stances.

The contestants pivoted clockwise—Fita with his determined, intense stare, and Vurkil with a smile of lighthearted conde-scension. Vurkil advanced, and Fita held his ground.

Vurkil laughed. "You are such a small oppon—"

Fita spun, sweeping his leg forward and tripping the giant, who fell with a loud *thump*. The smaller man fluidly crouched and sprung into a backflip from his sweep, landed on Vurkil's chest, and knocked the breath out of him.

As the crowd oohed, Rose checked on Vurkil's vitals through Sorcery. He was fine. She could feel his anger rising as Fita pinned his neck under a forearm. Vurkil attempted to roll, but Fita stretched his leg out, preventing the maneuver.

Vurkil grabbed both of the smaller man's biceps with enormous hands. Fita's proud stoicism gave way to irritation as the giant pressed him off of his body. Fita flailed his forearm, which weakly impacted the Mondrovian's annoyed face. Vurkil stood slowly, maintaining his grip on the smaller man and lifting him into the air. Fita kicked at the giant's stomach with little effect.

Vurkil bent to a knee, taking Fita helplessly with him.

Rose fought a smirk. *That was quick.*

In an act of desperation, the smaller man planted both feet on Vurkil's chest and pressed off, slipping from Vurkil's iron grip. Fita rolled and righted himself dexterously into a wide stance. He stood in front of the corner where the wall jutted to a low ceiling.

The imposing giant advanced with a menacing grin. "You fight well, Helenestian."

Fita grinned back. "You talk too much, oaf."

Vurkil laughed.

When the distance between them closed to a few feet, Fita attempted another sweep. Vurkil seemed prepared for it, though, jumping at the perfect moment. He lunged for the smaller man, who dashed to the side. Giant hands narrowly missed their target.

Vurkil righted himself in front of the low corner. Fita backstepped quickly and almost collided with Talanna, who recoiled.

As the giant stepped forward into a crouch, Fita took off in a sprint. He leapt into a flying tackle, wrapping his arms around his enormous opponent's waist as they collided. Vurkil grabbed Fita's torso and stumbled backwards. Despite his efforts to maintain balance, he fell, nearly hitting his head on the low wall in the corner.

Fita brought his legs up, planted his feet into the low ceiling, and maintained his grip on the giant's torso. Rose's eyes widened as he pressed Vurkil to the floor.

Others in the room let out breaths of astonishment.

Vurkil attempted to pry his opponent off again, without success; Fita's powerful legs were too strong. Giant hands balled into fists, and he punched at Fita's waist. Regardless of strength, his arms didn't have room for a powerful-enough swing.

Vurkil sighed. "I yield."

Applause broke out in the small room as Fita dropped to his feet. He ducked out from the corner with a broad grin on his face.

A stunned Vurkil followed him, shaking his head as he emerged from the low ceiling. The two returned to their starting positions in the center of the room and bowed to each other.

"Impressive," Vurkil said with a smile. "You fight big for a small man. Much respect from Mondro!"

Fita nodded graciously, no doubt attempting to remain stoic with a slight smile.

Vurkil turned and strode toward Rose as conversation broke out around the room. Her heart quickened, and she raised her eyebrows at him. The man shrugged before sitting next to her. She pulled herself up onto his lap, feeling his magnificent, warm arms wrap around her.

Sam gazed across the room at Rose's smiling face as she snuggled further into the giant. They were perfect for each other. Rose's quiet intelligence balanced Vurkil's enormous presence wonderfully. Sam was happy for them, though the sight caused longing to gnaw at his insides. He missed Kara dearly.

Kula helped Talanna up to continue her instruction. Fita invited Ya'ir to join him for sparring. The others in the room conversed quietly as Zelyra ran her hands along the stone walls with a curious expression. That girl was strange.

Sam found his thoughts returning to that fateful night at the Joneses' house.

The image of Jeanette's kidnapper flying gracefully out into the night played over and over in his mind. He once more considered attempting to fly using the mace but decided against it. Though it moved objects with ease, it didn't seem to enhance moving his own body. Nothing he tried seemed to work quite right. He could Vitalize his feet, causing him to rise into the air as if standing, though he found it difficult to maintain his balance. He'd also tried lifting himself by his hip bone, which worked fairly well as long as he moved slowly, but it didn't quite achieve the quick, graceful flight that the hooded Sorcerer had displayed.

Still, Scheln had been quite successful with it, eerily floating around their bedroom. He'd scared Vurkil half to death with it at first, causing the giant to think he had come face-to-face with a ghost.

A grin spread across Sam's face. Scheln had a remarkable sense of humor, given his paralysis. His powers had grown significantly in the past several weeks—likely rivaling or even surpassing his brother's—though they had only once risked taking him with them for experiments so far. Sam found it incredibly odd that Scheln could move the surrounding air more easily than his own body, adding another unknown to the endless list of mysteries surrounding Sorcery.

Rose had tried to heal Scheln on one occasion, without success. All she could say was that the disease was complex and that his brain wouldn't respond to her attempts at treatment with Sorcery.

Sam glanced at Ya'ir as the man thrust his spear toward Fita, who quickly parried it and complimented him on his form. Thankfully, Sam's friendship with Ya'ir hadn't gone sour. If anything, it had only grown stronger since the day of his confession and horrendous torture. That pivotal event had unified them as a group like never before—and had significantly reduced the others' hesitation about disobeying the Masters.

No one could believe a kind soul like Ya'ir deserved such treatment, not even Tovas. *Especially* Tovas, in fact, which was surprising. The man was still wholeheartedly devout to his own religion, but he no longer seemed to accept the Tercast Masters as religious authorities.

The door opened. Everyone turned to regard Tovas as he entered and shut the door behind him.

"Hey, Tovas," Talanna called out. "You missed it! It was amazing. Fita won!"

Tovas's eyes widened. "Really?"

"Did you get them?" Fita asked.

"Yes, I found two of them in the healers' room." Tovas raised two small vials of health potion.

Rose slid off Vurkil's lap and took one of them from Tovas's hand. "Finally," she said. "I've been wondering how these work for ages."

"Don't you already know how to heal?" Relon asked.

"Yes, but these work much faster and more effectively," Rose responded as she climbed back into Vurkil's lap. "Somehow, they speed up cellular proliferation and angiogenesis. I can only bind existing cells back together, which isn't a complete healing."

"Uh, what does that mean?" Niu said.

"It means that if you get a cut, even if it's somewhat deep, I can stitch the cells together, so to speak, to seal the wound. If something like a—I don't know—an axe tears off or damages a sizable chunk of tissue, I can't regrow it. But I think this *can*."

"It will be an essential tool when defending others or ourselves from attack," Tovas said.

Sam stood up. "Not this again. Tovas, we're not superheroes."

Tovas turned to him. "The Divine has granted us power over the four Elements," he responded calmly. "We can help others in a way few can."

"What do you expect us to do?" Sam said, throwing up his arms. "Fight crime? Stop murderers? Overthrow corrupt governments?"

"When the opportunity arises and Divine inspiration prompts us forward—yes," Tovas replied.

"You're insane."

"I received instruction from the Divine to guard Their people, and I will fulfill it. I, of course, do not expect anyone else to join me in my cause, but I welcome anyone who is willing."

"You. Are. Insane!" Sam said again, jabbing a finger in the air toward Tovas. "When you speak to a deity, that's one thing. When a deity speaks to you, that's madness. It's all in your head!"

A heavy silence filled the room. Sam glanced at the uncomfortable looks on the others' faces. He felt somewhat guilty about doing this in front of everyone, but the man really needed to gain some sense of reason.

"Sorry, Sam," Ya'ir said. "But I agree that we should use this power to help others. I'll join you, Tovas."

"I'm in!" Talanna said.

"Me too," Relon agreed.

Sam's heart sank. "Look, I'm not saying we shouldn't help people. That's not what I'm saying at all. Of course we should help people. I'm only saying that we don't need to be vigilantes. We should help when people are being attacked or oppressed. But we shouldn't go *looking* for trouble. We aren't invincible."

"Defending the weak is the highest honor," Fita said. "I agree with Tovas. We should fight evil head-on. It is our duty."

"Guys, I know your hearts are in it, but good and evil don't really exist. They're just social and psychological constructs."

"You're wrong," Tovas said.

"Yeah?" Sam said. "If that's so, and this omnipotent 'Divine' really cares so much about all of us, why is there so much 'evil' in the universe? Why is there so much agony and death? Why doesn't the almighty Divine simply destroy all evil?"

"Our purpose in life is to learn how to become good so we can become one of the Divine in the afterlife. Opposition is essential. We are only good inasmuch as we resist and conquer evil, which means evil must exist to be resisted."

Sam rolled his eyes. "How poetic. That doesn't make it true."

"Your skepticism and lack of faith are evils *you* must overcome, Sam."

Sam clenched his fist. "Your rigid belief in things that can't be objectively verified makes you a fool."

"Rudds, stop it already!" Vurkil's low voice rang out from the corner, filled with humor. "Won't you two ever stop bickering over this? Besides," he said, laughing, "I think you're both wrong."

Rose hit him playfully with a smile.

"Yeah, you two have been arguing about this since the day we met," Niu said. "Just let it rest already!"

"Haven't you ever lost someone?" Tovas asked. "Haven't you ever wished you could have saved them?"

His words struck Sam hard. The memory of Mr. and Mrs. Jones

dead on their bedroom floor flashed in his mind, and of kindhearted Jeanette going horrifyingly limp in a hooded man's arms. He remembered Kara's palpable sorrow as they held each other in that destroyed bedroom.

Tears welled up in Sam's eyes, and he found it difficult to speak. "Yes. I have."

His response, and perhaps the manner of it, quieted the group.

"What happened?" Tovas asked.

"Does this have something to do with your friend who was kidnapped?" Rose said.

Sam looked at her with wide eyes. "How do you—"

"I overheard you asking Master Evalencia about it weeks ago," she said, cheeks reddening.

Sam sighed. With everyone's rapt attention—except perhaps Zel's—he told them about Jeanette's capture and his arrival on Alvior with Kara. He told them about Jess, her mention of Jeanette's grandfather, and his banishment to Uvlun.

"That might be where Jeanette is," Sam concluded. "My theory is that their parents left because of some kind of hostility when the Grand Masters exiled Walnon to Uvlun. I think they went to Earth because they were running from someone. The Masters mentioned that those in Uvlun had discovered 'dark powers' when they attacked. I think that someone found a way out and then targeted Jeanette's parents."

Silence settled as they absorbed his tale. Niu looked horrified. Deep frowns adorned the faces of Vurkil, Ya'ir, Tovas, and Fita. Rose seemed contemplative. Kula and Talanna wore sorrowful expressions.

"This will be our first mission, then," Tovas said with resolve. "We will travel to Uvlun to help Sam's friend Jeanette."

"Tovas," Sam replied, "I truly appreciate the sentiment, but we don't even know if she's there. It's only a theory."

"Only one way to find out," Fita said, standing from his crate.

"Does anyone even know where the portal is?" Talanna asked.

"The fundamentals book mentioned that they moved it recently," Kula said. "I don't think it told us where, th—"

A rumble erupted behind Sam. He turned to find Zel, who stood in front of the stone wall—which was moving. Bricks slid around each other as the dirt behind them rose, revealing a cave. The dumbstruck look on her face told him that she was just as surprised as the rest of them. The temperature of the room quickly dropped.

"What did you do?" Talanna asked.

Zel shrugged, maintaining her expression of utter shock. "I felt that this cute little stone was different. It wanted energy, so I gave it some."

"A secret passageway!" Vurkil exclaimed.

Sam grabbed his mace. Curiosity permeated the room as they all moved tentatively forward, past the opening of stone and dirt, onto the cave floor. It stretched upward about two times Vurkil's height and had roughly equal width. Rugged rock walls led downward around the path.

"It's freezing!" Talanna said.

"I don't think this cave is natural," Sam said, ignoring her outburst. "The path here seems way too smooth."

Rumbling echoed across the cave walls. Sam glanced behind him to see the stones and dirt rearranging themselves to block their path back. Relon, who had been walking at the rear, ran toward the moving sand, but by the time she reached it, it was a solid wall of dirt.

They were trapped.

She turned to the group. "What do we do?"

Vurkil shrugged. "Only one way forward now."

"It's okay," Sam said, hefting the mace up. "If we need to break a way out, this will probably do the trick."

Ya'ir, Niu, and Talanna still appeared apprehensive, but the others seemed to accept his escape solution if needed. He hoped it would actually work.

The group made their way downward, where the path opened up to an enormous cavern with five magnificent archways. A stone wall inside each arch blocked passage through it. Above each was a different symbol: a mountain, a lightning bolt, a flame, and flowing water. The four Elements. The final archway stood at the other end of the cavern, with the weaving Tercast emblem above it.

A cluster of twelve tall crystals stuck out from the ground at the center of the cavern, surrounded by a strange black floor.

Tovas knelt and put his hands on top of his head in reverence. He was praying? Now? Really?

Sam walked around Tovas and approached a crystal, reaching out with Sorcery. Oddly, he couldn't feel anything outside his own body, except the air. As he stepped on the black floor, it sunk underneath his foot. It was a soft, viscoelastic surface. He removed a glove from his hand and touched a crystal, then connected with it, feeling its internal bonds and pressure against the floor. It ran deep.

Energy. It desperately wanted energy.

Okay, I'll bite.

He imagined power running into the material, but it resisted. Why would it feel like it wanted energy and then resist when offered?

Vurkil did the same with another crystal, sinking considerably into the black floor. In a bizarre way, Sam could feel the man's presence through the connection with his own crystal.

"Seems to want energy, but it doesn't work," Vurkil said.

"Like my brick?" Zel said, approaching a crystal herself.

"Apparently," Sam replied.

Tovas rose from the floor. "Let's give it the energy it needs."

"It doesn't work. Even if it did, we don't know what it will do."

"It's pretty clear it will power something in this cave," Tovas said. "It may be our only way out."

Sam shrugged, curiosity outweighing his unease. "Maybe."

"There are doh crystals, the same number as our group," Tovas continued. "Perhaps we all need to try together for it to work."

"Scheln's not here, though," Talanna said.

Tovas looked surprised for a moment, as if he'd only just realized his brother was missing. "Right. I will take an extra one for Scheln."

Nods and a few verbal affirmations rose from the group. Each of them stood next to a crystal, pulled off a glove, and touched it. Tovas stood between two and reached out to both.

Sam could feel the others as each connected with a crystal. Strangely, he also felt Scheln's presence. He reached out again himself, imagining energy flowing into the material as it desired.

It accepted the offering, which gave Sam a sense of being drained of something precious, and the crystal glowed a soft pearlescent white along with the others.

Vurkil fell, his large body sinking into the soft floor. Fear rippled through Sam as Tovas collapsed with him. Relon, Rose, and Ya'ir followed.

Colossal fatigue crashed into Sam, dispelling his panic as unconsciousness consumed him.

Chapter 39

The Mission

Kara stood in the shower, watching water flow over the muscles in her shoulder. She had always been relatively fit from her exercises and time at the academy, but engaging in the Force's training regimen had brought her physique to a new level. Dropping her arm back to her side, she wondered idly how long it had been since she'd left Alvior. A query to her Nit revealed it had been nearly fifty-six standard days.

By Earth standards, that was eight weeks.

She closed her eyes and thought back on that fateful day of her parents' abrupt deaths. Sorrow threatened to consume her, as it had during her first several hours in the Sovereignty facility on Earth. Paradoxically, the event felt both recent and as if it had happened a lifetime ago. She was still mentally recovering from the incident, but so much had happened since then. She'd lived in five locations on three different *planets* since their departure from Earth. That fact alone was mind-blowing.

"Questioning reality now?" Sam's words from their flight to Tercast echoed in her mind, bringing a smile to her face—followed swiftly by a twinge of longing for his presence.

A command to her Nit shut off the water. She dried and adorned her Sovereignty uniform, not bothering to do much with her face or hair, which she pulled into a ponytail. Her head would be shoved into a helmet almost all day anyway.

She walked from the bathroom into her one-room quarters, where her Ilkuth leaned against the wall in the corner. The company leader, Commander Delveton, had recently taken everyone's suits to be modified for their mission soon after their arrival. Little natural light streamed through the single window, due to the nearly endless blanket of dark clouds and heavy rain.

A plate of delicious-smelling golkin placo fell from the machine in her small kitchen, and Kara sat down at the tiny one-person table nearby to enjoy it. She didn't know what it was, but the mix of veggies and egg-like substances was the closest thing she'd found to an omelet—a meal she longed for.

As she ate, Kara closed her eyes and mentally went through the notifications from her Nit. She was assigned one-on-one training with Olik today. There was also a notification telling her that the election was ending. She'd almost forgotten about that. Thankfully, she'd done some research on the candidates previously.

There were twelve professional software engineers vying for the open position on the Sovereignty's Legislature of Technical Experts. Apparently, this was the final round of voting for that position. Unlike the constant public resolutions, however—which she had quickly deferred to delegates—this vote was one she had to cast herself. She didn't understand the Sovereignty's technology very well, though, which seemed to be the primary topic of their election campaigns.

Reviewing the candidates' names, she settled on Leeoun Ulc. The face appeared feminine to her, but Kara's research had revealed that Leeoun was regarded as vengale—the Sovereignty's catch-all term for people who didn't fit typical male or female characteristics. She hadn't personally known any non-binary people on Earth, but was certainly aware of them. Regardless, the individual appeared to be the most vocal about enhancing Armed Forces technology for increased combat safety, and fact-checking revealed them to be one of the more honest candidates, so Kara cast her main vote in Leeoun's favor. She had the option of including secondary and tertiary choices, which she cast as well.

After breakfast, she donned her Ilkuth and set down the sleek hallway to her assigned training room. Though she liked the bright overhead lighting that zigzagged along the rounded ceiling, she wished there was more to look at. The walls were plain.

She entered the room to find Olik there waiting for her. He stared forward absently with his helmet off, likely accessing something through the network.

His eyes focused on her. "Lively morning, Kara!"

"Hi, Olik."

"You mind if we just chat for a bit? I twisted my ankle like a Kamulu this morning. The suit's helping with the healing right now, but I'd like to give it a rest for a few minutes if that's okay."

"Sure, that's fine," Kara replied, stopping a few feet in front of him. There were no chairs in the plain training rooms, but standing in the suits was fairly comfortable since they bore all the weight.

"Tell me about where you're from," Olik said. "You said it was a class four, right?"

"Yep. Its name is Earth."

"So what brought you into the Sovereignty?"

She folded her arms, not knowing what else to do with them. "It's a long story. I . . . don't think I want to get into it."

He nodded and looked unsure about what to say further.

"What about you?" she asked. "Where are you from?"

"Ah, my wife an' six kids are back on Kavitar," he said, pulling a small piece of paper from the neck of his suit and handing it to her.

It was a picture. A woman with frizzy dark brown hair and light brown skin stood above five young boys and one girl, with a look of frustration on her face. The three older boys were making funny faces—one of them pressed his palm into the face of another. The girl looked like she was rolling her eyes in frustration. One of the younger boys stood up straight with a pleasant smile. The other, who looked to be the youngest, appeared to be about to eat a chunk of his sister's curly hair. Kara couldn't help but smile at the chaotic image.

"Yeah, they're wild, but I love 'em to death," he said with a wide grin. "Vellery, my wife, hates that I take this picture with me everywhere. Shows the true side of life in all its glory. I love it!" He laughed.

She turned the picture over to find words on the back.

"What does this say?" she asked.

He pointed at the words. "E vic nelen wel. Vic yalen em. Lik van desius onii."

"Uh, what?"

He smiled. "You may have never heard it, having been in the Force such a short time. It's the full expression behind the Force's informal 'Welin Em Onii' motto," he explained. "Roughly translated, it means 'Life grants potential. Duty grants purpose. Love imbues them with resplendence.'"

She nodded with a smile and turned the photo back over. Hearing Olik talk fondly of his own family brought thoughts of her parents and sister to the surface, threatening to drown her in sorrow once more. She banished them, and tried to think of another topic to steer the discussion toward so that he wouldn't ask about her family.

"So, what's the story with Commander Delveton?" she asked, handing the picture back to Olik.

Olik took the photograph from her hands. "Oh, that man's an enigma. He was a Commander One several years ago, specializing in electronics and covert operations, I think. Only rejoined the Force a few months ago, from what I heard. Rumor is that he spent the last several years at some place off the network called Tercast."

She jumped. "Tercast? He was there?"

"You know of it?"

"Apparently, my parents used to live there! A friend of mine is there now."

The memory of Sam getting taken by that stupid castle resurfaced a pang of guilt. If Delveton had been there, he might know something about her parents, or Jeanette. She made a mental note to ask him about it when she got the chance.

An urgent notification pinged her mind through the Nit.

"Speaking of, I just received a notification from the commander," Olik said. He stuffed the picture back into the neck of his suit.

"Yeah, I got it too," Kara said.

Olik stared off into the distance as Kara accepted the message. The company leader was calling everyone for an urgent meeting immediately. They had a mission.

Kara looked at Olik, who glanced back at her and nodded. They turned and strode into the hallway, where others were emerging as well.

"Do you think they found out where the wizards are?" Kara asked as they walked together down the hallway.

Olik shrugged his armored shoulders. "Possible, but not likely. The minister ordered probes sent out for electromagnetic event analysis, but I wouldn't expect that to get results so quickly."

"I remember him mentioning that," Kara said. "What is it, anyway? I meant to look it up but forgot."

"Oh, it's a method of sending out probes to different points in space so that they can analyze past events. They intercept electromagnetic radiation propagating from that event."

She turned to Olik and gave him a look she usually reserved for Sam when he was talking science babble.

Olik laughed. "You know how light takes time to travel in space?"

"Um . . . sure."

"Well, electromagnetic event analysis uses that by creating a portal in space to intercept light and other signals from an event— such as a group of homicidal cultists stealing from a library. They'll attempt to find out where the projected portal they came through was coming from, then repeat the process until they can trace the ship to its original location."

Kara nodded, still mostly lost but appreciating the man's elaboration.

"It's a long, arduous process because you have an absurdly long line through space to search for each acheron gate. It's impossible to tell exactly how far a portal was being projected—you can only accurately get its direction."

Olik's explanation concluded just as they crossed the threshold into the meeting room, the same room she had met him in several days ago.

Kara moved off and sat in one of the back seats while Olik greeted some of the other soldiers. She had mostly avoided interpersonal relationships. The last time she'd gotten close to someone, it hadn't turned out so well. The sight of Nikor schmoozing with two other women flashed in her mind, accompanied by renewed anguish at the memory. Better to just avoid most people for now.

"Welin Em Onii, my friends," Commander Delveton's raspy voice called from the front of the room.

"Welin Em Onii," a host of voices called back, including Kara's. Those still standing, which included Olik, quickly moved to seat themselves.

"We have an assignment from the minister. The following information is restriction level red: Our analysis has uncovered the location of the cultists' hideout on a planet previously thought to be uninhabited."

It appeared that the electro-whatever hadn't taken nearly as long as Olik thought. Kara turned to him, and he returned a shocked expression, followed by a shrug.

An image of a cloudy planet appeared behind the commander. "The planet was destroyed years ago by one of the earliest Oblivion attacks. Our latest probe has identified the enemy's primary location as a large castle-like structure on the surface. Surveillance shows no apparent family units or children—only members of the violent cult. We believe they may have hostages inside the structure."

Jeanette, Kara thought, anticipation rippling through her.

"We will take a Thalas-class vessel though the acheron we set up in the planet's orbit and then strike hard and fast. We don't want to give them any chance to escape. Commander Olik will lead Second Squad to set up a perimeter and keep them from escaping. Commander Rolnu will lead First Squad with myself into the building to rescue hostages."

The commander's eyes settled on Kara, causing her to wonder once more if he recognized her from somewhere.

"Make your final preparations," he concluded. "We leave in two hours."

She looked back at him and nodded with a determined expression. *We're coming for you, Jeanette. Just hold on a little longer.*

Chapter 40

Land

"Tovas. Tovas!"

Tovas opened his eyes to a large rock ceiling overhead.

"Thank the Divine you're finally awake," Scheln said into his mind.

After pulling himself into a sitting position, Tovas surveyed the cavern. Relon sat with her arms around Niu as they conversed quietly in front of the archway under the Land symbol, through which the stone wall had disappeared. Everyone else was still asleep. He nudged Ya'ir, who had fallen next to him, but the man didn't wake.

"What happened?" Scheln asked.

I don't know, Tovas replied mentally. *It seems to have drained all of us of energy. Are you all right?*

"Yes. Somehow, it affected me through you. I fell asleep as well."

Strange.

"Yeah," Scheln said. *"Make sure you all stay away from the castle for now. The whole place is talking about how you all ran away with stolen weapons. The Masters are furious. They think you sneaked*

through the front gate somehow, so they have people searching that direction for you."

I'm glad they didn't notice the wall, Tovas thought toward Scheln. *The healers are taking care of you, right? They didn't just leave you in the room, did they?*

"No. The Masters came bursting in recently looking for the group, then sent the healers up to get me." He felt an air of humor from his brother. "Master Azeloram told me to tell you, 'The Divine will burn you for your heresy!'"

Though the sense of humor was comforting, Scheln was in serious danger.

You've become much stronger with Sorcery than you let on, Scheln. Be ready to defend yourself if the need arises. They won't expect it, coming from you.

"I'll be fine," Scheln said. "You just need to find a way out of that cave."

Niu and Relon are awake. I'm going to speak with them.

"Ooh, tell Relon that I—"

No, Scheln. This isn't the time.

Tovas felt his brother's disappointment through their connection. He stood and made his way over to the two women, who watched him as he approached. He'd been telling his brother for days now that confessing Scheln's attraction to her would just put her in an awkward position. There was a time and place for everything, and this wasn't the time for awkwardness among the group.

"How long have you two been awake?" he asked.

"Not long," Relon answered. "Niu was up first."

"I tried to wake others, but no one responded! I was really scared until Relon got up."

"We looked around," Relon said. "All the other pathways are still closed off except this one." She motioned toward the open archway behind her, through which Tovas could now see another wall farther back with a faded arrow pointing downward. It had doh dark dots above it. "We thought it would be best to wait until everyone is awake before going inside."

"Good idea," Tovas replied, noting Niu's violent shivering. "Cold, Niu?"

"Yes-s-s!" she said through chattering teeth. "Why is it s-s-so cold down here!"

Tovas smiled. "It's a cave."

He stretched out his hand and connected with the air in front of it. Remembering the feeling associated with methane, he transmuted the air and set it alight with a spark. The flame burned as he continuously fed more fuel into it. He moved the fire through the air near Niu, who stretched her hands around it.

"Ah! Why didn't I think of that?" she exclaimed. "Thank you, thank you, thank you, thank you!"

Relon looked up at him with an affectionate expression as he sat down with them. The two of them joined Niu in putting their chilly hands near the fire.

"You're so good at this!" Niu said. "How are you always so good at all of this?"

Tovas shrugged. "I honestly don't know."

Relon smiled. "Your knack for Sorcery has always gotten on Sam's nerves."

"I think it's my religious devotion that he despises," Tovas said.

"Well, that too, but your abilities clash with his math."

"Yeah!" Niu said. "He's always talking about that equation, saying there's something missing. I think he needs to lighten up a bit. He reminds me of Derek."

"Ugh," Relon said, tilting her head back. "Not Derek again."

Niu blushed. "I miss him, okay!"

"Boyfriend?" Tovas asked.

Relon nodded as Niu exploded with enthusiasm. "Yes! I miss him sooo much. I never wanted to come to Tercast, you know, but my parents forced me into it. I think it's because they wanted to get me away from him."

"You're from Oscertos, right?" Tovas asked.

"Yep! Born here. I need to get out, though—see the universe. I've never even left the continent! I've always wanted—"

"What is Relon saying?" Scheln asked. *"Is she worried about me?"*

Tovas ignored the voice in his head.

Niu went on for several minutes, talking about the places she wanted to visit. Others woke during their discussion of various planets and their unique flora and fauna. Vurkil, Ya'ir, and Kula joined them, followed by Fita, Sam, and Zel. Finally, Rose came over and settled next to Vurkil. Talanna followed soon after.

"The dragons of Yolfan are a magnificent sight!" Vurkil said, his booming voice echoing in the cavern. "Like giant wyverns!"

"Those are real?" Niu exclaimed, bringing her hands to her head dramatically. "I thought they were myths!"

Vurkil laughed. "They're real! Though there are common myths about them, I think."

"Do they breathe fire?" Sam asked.

"Fire? I've never heard that one before."

"We actually have legends on my home planet about dragons breathing fire."

Vurkil chuckled heartily. "I don't know any animal that can breathe fire!"

"The fire gnocks of Ellon do," Zel said. "They blow gas from their mouth and ignite it with a spark on their tongue!"

"How do they keep from getting burned?" Talanna asked.

"I think they lick their faces a lot or something. They only breathe fire when threatened. And they eat goo flies."

"Rudds, I could go for some goo flies myself right about now," Vurkil said. "I'm starving."

Rose elbowed him with a playful grin as the group laughed. "You're always starving."

The point about food was a good one. There didn't appear to be anything edible in the cave, so they needed to find a way out—or if that failed, try to dig their way out.

"Speaking of food, we should get moving," Tovas said. "We can't go back to Tercast. The Masters know we took the weapons. They think we stole them."

"Well . . ." Sam said. "We did."

Talanna bit her lip. "What are we going to do?"

"We need to get out of this cave first," Tovas said, "then decide what to do from there."

The group nodded and stood from their huddle around Tovas's flame, which he stopped fueling. It immediately extinguished.

"I don't see any way around this second wall, though," Talanna said, walking under the arch and approaching the arrow on the wall. One dot on the inner wall glowed white.

Niu approached behind her, and another dot glowed.

"Look!" Relon said, gesturing to the dots. "It looks like it wants all of us inside before it opens."

They all stepped tentatively through the large archway into the small rock "room." As they did so, the dots continued to light up. Zel was the last to enter. They all watched as the elth dot lit up, leaving one dim. They needed one more.

"How do we get the last one?" Talanna asked.

Scheln? Tovas thought.

"Yes?" his brother replied.

The final dot glowed. With a crash, the stone wall fell from the ceiling behind them, trapping them in the rocky room. Niu screamed. The door before them with the arrow rose a moment later.

Just needed your presence to open a door, apparently.

"Oh. Strange. How does it see me?" Scheln replied.

An enchantment probably, Tovas said.

A stone path led through a seemingly bottomless pit of mists, which split into three diverging paths ahead. Rocks of various sizes floated through the air, some spinning as they moved all over the enormous cavern, which was lit by a giant glowing orb attached to the ceiling above. To the right, slightly below their elevation, were three parallel U-shaped tracks. A large swinging pendulum moved across the bottom—perpendicular to the tracks. The pendulum had a single hole in it, which swung back and forth through the tracks at their lowest point.

"Whoa," Vurkil said. "What is this place?"

Tovas shook his head. "I don't know, but whoever built it was clearly a master of Sorcery and enchantments. The crystals must have somehow used the Vitalization we provided to power all of this."

"I hope no one here is afraid of heights," Kula said as she looked over the edge into the misty darkness.

"Look," Sam said, pointing to something near the end of the tracks.

It looked like a green, glowing clock. The single arm rotated slowly around the circle, removing the glow as it swept across. A bowl of the same green color stood at the end of each track.

"It's some kind of puzzle!" Sam exclaimed. "Looks like we're supposed to put something on these tracks to reach the buckets at the end before time runs out."

"Why don't we just drop three of these floating rocks on it?" Ya'ir suggested.

"I can't Vitalize anything in here!" Relon said. "It's all dark."

Tovas found his inner serenity and reached out with Sorcery. Indeed, all he could feel was his own body. Everything else was emptiness; he couldn't even sense the air.

"What happens when all the glow of the clock is gone?" Talanna asked.

"I don't think we should find out," Relon said.

"I agree," said Tovas. "We need to explore these paths quickly. Let's split up."

The group divided into three teams. Relon, Niu, Talanna, and Zel took the left path. Vurkil, Rose, Fita, and Kula went down the center one. Tovas, Sam, and Ya'ir grouped up to take the last.

Their route narrowed slightly from the main one, surrounded on either side by bottomless pits fading into the eerie mist. Rock walls separated them from the other groups as they proceeded. The solid ceiling was convex outward toward the path center, with periodic white light sources that cast dark shadows on the crevices where the ceiling met the walls. Sam reached out and tapped a small floating rock passing nearby, sending it off in a different direction.

"Incredible," he said. "I wonder if these rocks are enchanted with antigravity the same way ascenders work. Really wish I knew the physics behind that."

Tovas led them around a bend, where the end of the path became visible in the distance. It opened up to a small cavern.

"Ya'ir, watch out!" Sam called out from behind.

Tovas turned. A large moving rock collided with Ya'ir's left side. The man's eyes went wide as he teetered on the edge, waving his arms to maintain balance. Tovas and Sam ran toward him, but they were too late. His foot slipped over the smooth edge. Ya'ir yelled, his fearful expression haunting Tovas as he fell.

"Ya'ir!" Sam shouted.

Tovas stared into the mist, mind failing to comprehend what had happened. It had occurred so fast. Ya'ir couldn't be gone. Not like this.

"Sam, Tovas!" Ya'ir's voice echoed across the walls.

"Ya'ir!" Sam called out, jumping up. "You're all right?"

"Yeah! Some kind of wind tunnel pushed me up here. I'm in a narrow hallway in the ceiling."

Tovas looked around at the ceiling but saw no sign of him. "I don't see you."

"I'm in the dark space along the edge. You may not be able to see me from there. You two should go on. We don't want to run out of time!"

The two jogged down the path in silence to the small opening where the path ended. A few feet past the end of the path was a long glass box with a smooth metal object inside. A glowing line with a wavy shape appeared on the rock wall above the box.

"Another puzzle?" Tovas asked.

"Looks like it," Sam said.

Tovas reached out with Sorcery. The metal object was the only thing outside himself that he could feel. He connected with it.

"I can Vitalize the metal thing inside," he said. "What do you think we're supposed to do with it?"

Sam frowned. "I don't know. Try moving it around inside. Maybe there's a way to get it out."

Tovas nudged the object to the left, and it slid with remarkable ease. He stopped it quickly. As it moved, one green glowing line appeared to the left of the white one. It slowly traced a path downward and upward before returning to the starting point, where it continued tracing a horizontal line rightward for a few seconds. When it finally stopped, the object returned itself to its position in the center of the box. Two green lines appeared below the first one, the final one even with the white line.

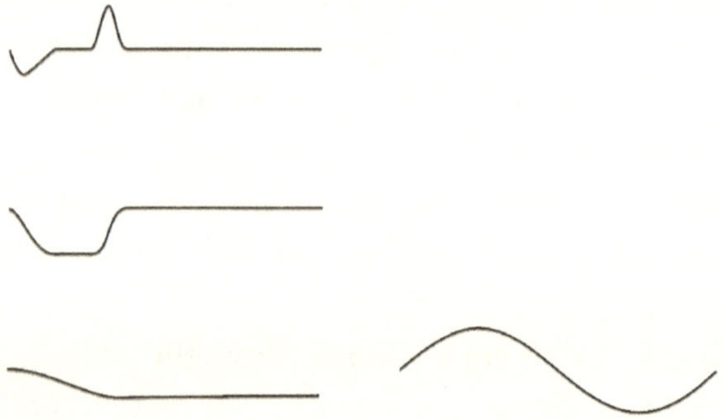

Tovas stared at the lines for a few seconds. It appeared the challenge was to trace the white line. It moved up and then down before coming back up. Up seemed to be associated with going right, so he moved the metal object in that direction. The glowing green lines disappeared, and the top one began again, moving upward slightly before returning to horizontal.

Too soon. Why had it gone back?

After a few seconds, he stopped the object. The line dipped down again before returning to its center position. Tovas scratched his head as the line stopped and the object once again returned to the center position. The two lines below it appeared again, this time tracing a plateau in the center line, followed by an upward slope in the last line, which leveled off to a horizontal.

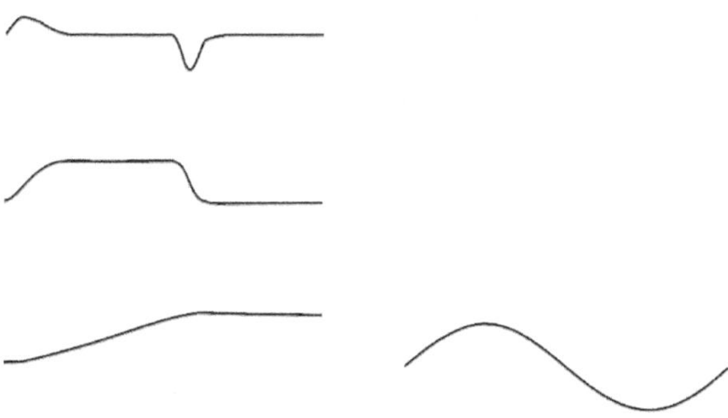

"I've got it!" Sam said. "The lines are measuring the acceleration, velocity, and position of the object. It's a puzzle about connecting the three! Here, let me move it."

Tovas released his connection as Sam took over control of the block. The green line traced Sam's movement as it drew upward, then dipped drastically down and back up before gradually leveling off. When it reached the end, the two lines below it appeared again. The middle one traced up, down, up, though not as drastically as the top one, and the final line looked quite similar to the white line next to it.

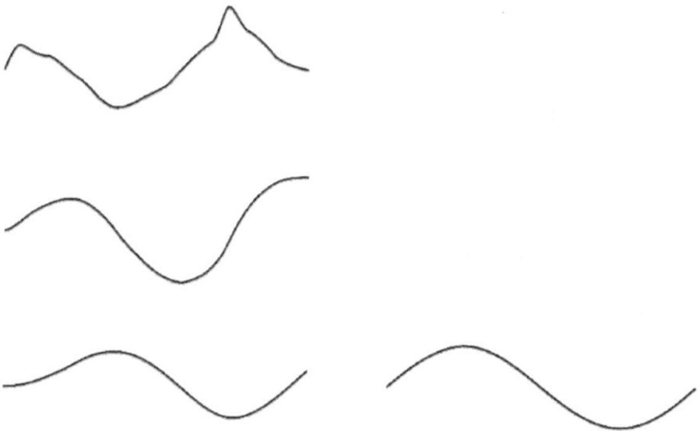

With a click, the side of the glass container opened. The shiny object slid out the side and moved through the air toward Sam, who reached out and grabbed it. It slipped from his grasp, then floated in the air next to him.

"Whoa!" he said. "This thing is extremely slippery."

"Strange," Tovas said. "But we have it now. Let's get back and regroup with the others."

Sam nodded, and they ran back down the path toward the entrance, watching for any large floating rocks. Tovas glanced at the timer as soon as it was in range. About half of the glow had disappeared, and they still needed to figure out the tracks puzzle. No one else had returned yet.

Tovas studied the track and the moving half-moon pendulum at the base.

Sam spoke first. "It looks like we have to time it right so that the objects on the tracks go through that hole in the pendulum. Otherwise, they'll just run into it. We'll also need to release them on the right track so that they all make it to the correct targets on the other side—assuming the others find similar blocks to ours."

"Will that thing slide all the way to the other side?" Tovas asked.

Sam shrugged. "Probably. The rounded shape looks like it was made to fit into the track, and it should have very little friction."

Rose, Vurkil, Fita, and Kula came running back around the bend of the second path.

"Did you find something?" Tovas called out to them.

They ran up and Rose presented a metal ball. "We found this."

"Where's Ya'ir?" Kula asked.

"He fell," Sam said.

As their expressions turned to horror, Ya'ir's voice came from overhead. "Hi! A wind tunnel pulled me up here. I'm fine! I can see you all from here."

"Well, that's good," Kula said. "At least now we know this place isn't trying to kill us."

"Rose was the genius!" Vurkil said, pointing to the ball. "There was a glass container of water with the ball inside. She figured out that we needed to get the water level down to just the right point by moving the ball out of the bowl and into the water. Then it opened up and we could get it out."

Tovas took the ball from Rose's hand and felt it with Sorcery.

"It's hollow," he said.

"Yes," Rose agreed.

Relon, Niu, Talanna, and Zel appeared from the leftward path.

"Hey!" Talanna called out as they approached. "We found something!"

Relon held out a wooden ball. "We think it goes on one of the tracks."

"Yeah, we have the other two," Sam replied.

Tovas took the ball and felt it with Sorcery as well. It was solid, weighing about the same as the metal ball.

"How do we know which one goes where?" Niu asked.

Sam reached out, and Tovas handed him the two fist-sized balls. The oddly shaped metal block still hovered beside him.

"I don't know," Tovas said, "but it's clearly another physics puzzle."

Everyone watched Sam, who looked up from his intent study of the objects. "What?"

"You're the physics expert around here," Talanna said. "So, what's the answer?"

"I'm working on it," Sam said. "Give me a minute."

Tovas turned to Relon. "What was your puzzle?" he asked.

As Relon was about to speak, Talanna interrupted her. "It was a glass box with the ball in a kind of locked trap. It had a weight on a string attached to the ceiling. Relon figured out that we could move the box by moving the ball inside it. She moved the box just right so that the weight swung up and hit the switch that opened the trap, allowing us to get the ball out."

Tovas smiled. "Smart."

"The metal ball should go faster, right?" Kula said. "So maybe that one will pass through the pendulum first."

Sam continued to ponder, betraying no sign that he was listening to them. After a few moments, he snapped his head up.

"That must be it!" he said. "It's all about moment of inertia."

"What's that?" Niu asked.

Sam moved each of the three objects through the air to the top of the distant tracks. The metal one touched down on the furthest track, which had the longest path to its green bucket. The wooden ball placed itself gently on the center track, and the solid block on the closest track, where the curved edge fit perfectly into the groove. As he placed the last piece, a green light flashed each time the pendulum reached its highest point, and the buckets at the end glowed. The three objects rested on the small lip at the top of the tracks, preventing them from falling.

"I think it's telling us to release all of them at one of the pendulum's peaks. But which one is correct?" Tovas asked.

"It's about how much energy it takes to make an object rotate," Sam explained eagerly. "The greater the moment of inertia, the more energy it takes. The metal sphere, being empty on the inside, has the highest moment of inertia because the mass is all further away from the axis of rotation." He twisted his fingers in the air. "It takes more energy to rotate. Next most is the wooden ball. It seems to have about the same total mass as the metal ball, but it's solid, so more of its weight is toward the axis of rotation. It takes a little *less* energy to rotate. Last is the slippery block. It has about the same mass as the other two, but since it will slide down the track, it loses *no* energy to rotation."

"I don't get it," Talanna said.

As the pendulum swung toward them, the light flashed green, and each of the objects simultaneously descended the track. To Tovas's surprise, the smooth block pulled out slightly ahead of the two balls and passed straight through the pendulum as it swung through the lowest point ryan the track. The other balls passed through immediately after, sliding through the moving slit. The block slowed as it ascended the other end of the track. It reached the edge with just enough momentum to pass over and fall into the green bucket at the end, which lit up brighter. The wooden sphere traveled a little further to the edge of the center track and fell neatly into the second goal, followed by the metal ball falling gracefully from the end of the longest track.

The timer overhead lit up brilliantly, showing nearly a quarter of time remaining. Stone scraped against stone as the entrance door rose, allowing them back into the main cavern.

"Um . . . okay," Niu said. "You get waaay too excited about this stuff."

The group laughed. Tovas felt inclined to agree, though Sam's knowledge was impressive.

"Interesting," Scheln's psychic voice said.

What is interesting? Tovas asked.

"The puzzle. Sam really knows physics."

You could see that? Hear that?

"Yeah, I actually just discovered it," Scheln said.

Intrusive on my privacy, don't you think?

Scheln chuckled in his mind. *"Don't worry, I'll make sure to only hack your senses at the most embarrassing times. Speaking of embarrassing times, you should really ask Relon—"*

Tovas smiled as he mentally blockaded his brother's voice.

The group reemerged into the main cavern. A stairway had opened up on the sides near the Land entrance, allowing Ya'ir to join them from the pathway above. Tovas marveled at the intricate design of the cave and the puzzles. Why had it been created? Had Grand Master Ilius or one of his successors built it as a kind of testing ground? If so, why seal it off?

Zel was the last to emerge from the large Land archway. As she did so, the stone door fell from the ceiling and closed off that room. The wall blocking the archway under the Air symbol lifted simultaneously.

Talanna sighed. "Looks like we have to do this for all four Elements."

Chapter 41

Air

"Maybe we should just dig another way out," Kula suggested.

"I actually like these puzzles," Rose said.

"I'm interested to know where this all leads," Tovas added. "It's clearly some kind of testing ground of our knowledge of the Elements."

"Yeah!" Vurkil's low voice echoed across the enormous cavern. "Let's go to the next one."

Kula and Niu seemed hesitant, but the rest of them were content to continue into the Air section. Just as before, lights glowed as they clustered into the small entry area.

Tovas reopened the connection to his brother. *Scheln?*

"There you are!" he replied. *"What was that all about?"*

As the final dot lit up, the wall blocking their exit fell with a crash.

Niu yelped. "Ugh, I hate that!"

Okay, you can listen and see as long as you're not distracting.

Scheln sighed in his mind. *"Fine."*

Tovas's eyes went wide at the sight that appeared before them. Small, pastel-colored beads of light streaked through the air in every direction at various speeds. They passed through the misty pit below and over the rocky path, which split into three, just as the Land one had. Off to the right was an identical timer to the one they had left in the Land cavern, with the hand slowly rotating over the glowing green circle.

Underneath the clock was a large metal ring with a small gap near the top. A few feet away, a Y-shaped mount held two metal rods facing each other. Cables from the rods led to a gap, followed by two metal terminals. The terminals stopped at two rectangular impressions, one lined in red, the other in blue.

"It's an electric puzzle!" Sam exclaimed.

"Didn't you say your father does electronics, Ya'ir?" Tovas asked.

Ya'ir nodded. "Yes. He taught me some about circuits, but I have never seen something like this."

"Should we split up like before?" Talanna suggested.

"I think so," Tovas replied. "We want to make sure we don't run out of time."

They split up the same way they had for the previous challenge. Tovas, Sam, and Ya'ir made their way down the path to the right.

"At least there aren't any flying rocks to knock you off this time, Ya'ir," Sam said with a chuckle.

"Hey!" Ya'ir replied. "That thing came out of nowhere. It was a lot heavier than it looked, especially since it was floating around."

One bright yellow bead moved near Tovas as he walked. He reached out for it, and a small spark leapt to his finger—bringing with it a spike of pain.

"Ow!" Tovas pulled his hand back and shook it.

The bead immediately lost its color, turning a dull white and zooming off in a new direction.

"It shocked you?" Sam asked.

"Yes. That was painful."

They made sure to avoid the glowing beads as they proceeded to the end of the path, where the wall narrowed almost to a point. Between the two sections of rock wall at the end was another glass container, this time with a gap in the middle. Two concave blocks—one red, one blue—sat at opposite ends against the rock wall.

Tovas felt out with his Sorcery. As he suspected, all he could feel from the scene were the red and blue blocks.

"Looks like we're just supposed to get the blocks out of this container through the gap," Sam said.

"Sounds too simple," Tovas replied.

He connected with the red block on the left, able to feel the familiar force of gravity pulling downward against the block, but there was another force pushing it away from the gap. As he moved the block to the right, it immediately met with increased resistance to his command. He could only move it a few inches.

"Help me move this red one out of the gap," Tovas said.

"All right," Ya'ir said.

He felt Ya'ir's and Sam's presence as they connected with it. The block moved a few more inches to the right, but still only made it about halfway to the gap. They released their connections to the object, returning it to its original position.

"It's a magnet," Sam said. "A really strong one. Can't believe I left my mace in that main cavern. It might have given me enough force to move it through."

"The blue one is a magnet too," Ya'ir said. "The sides facing each other must be the same pole, which is why they repel each other."

"Is there some way to change the magnetic field?" Tovas asked, looking toward Sam.

"I don't know," he replied. "We've never done anything like that before. I'm trying to remember how magnets work. I know it has something to do with electrons, bu—"

The red magnet began sliding slowly to the right and then exited the gap without issue. Tovas and Sam turned to Ya'ir, who grinned.

"How did you do that?" Sam asked.

"Magnetism occurs because of the alignment of magnetic fields inside it," Ya'ir replied. "All I did was change them to be more random, like most other objects. Then I could move it right out!"

The blue magnet easily slid out of its side of the container and rested in Sam's palm. He inspected it with fascination. "Nice, Ya'ir! Something about the electrons causes the magnetic fields, right? I can't remember."

"It's due to—"

"We should get back and regroup with the others," Tovas said.

Sam sighed. "Okay, okay."

They made their way back down the cavern to the electric puzzle. Rose, Vurkil, Fita, and Kula returned from their path at almost the same time. A glance at the timer showed that they had a little less than three-fourths of the total time left.

"What did you find?" Tovas asked them.

Vurkil held out a metal wire curved into a boxlike shape with a small circular base. "This."

Tovas took it and looked it over as they walked. The circular base had gaps at the halfway points between the two points connecting to the box shape.

"What do you think it's for?" Tovas asked, handing it back.

"Dunno." Vurkil chuckled. "I ripped it from a circuit leading to some kind of magnet. The shock hurt like rudding hell, but I got it out."

"I'm pretty sure that was *not* how we were supposed to get it," Rose said with her hand on her hip. "You could have stopped your heart with that much current!"

Vurkil shrugged and laughed. "Well, we got it out, so that's what matters!"

They returned to the point on the path closest to the puzzle.

"Well, clearly the magnets go in the spots designated with red and blue," Ya'ir said. "They made that easy."

Ya'ir and Sam placed their blocks in the assigned indentations. Each block slid into its groove perfectly, concave surfaces facing each other, creating a kind of open tunnel.

"Now where does this go?" Vurkil asked, holding up the box-shaped wire. "Do you think it connects that gap in the middle somehow?"

Ya'ir held out his hand, into which Vurkil dropped the wire. "I don't know. Maybe."

Talanna, Niu, Relon, and Zel rounded the corner from their path and raced back toward the entrance.

"These little light ball things *hurt*," Talanna said as she approached the group.

Tovas smiled. "Indeed. I got shocked by one myself."

"What did you find?" Sam asked.

"This thing," Niu said, holding out a black object that floated toward Sam. "It's actually two metal plates with some weird goo between them, wrapped in this black stuff."

"A capacitor?" Ya'ir asked.

Niu raised an eyebrow. "Capaci-what?"

"A device that holds an electric charge. Two conductors separated by an insulator."

"That would make sense," Relon said. "We moved it to some exposed wires, where it shocked them and opened the container it was in."

Ya'ir and Sam studied the object quietly.

"Maybe we use it to shock these wires somehow?" Relon suggested.

"Maybe," Tovas said, taking another look at the cables. He traced their path to the small gap, then to where they continued to the Y-shaped connector. The metal ring under the timer was completely separated from the rest of the circuit. "We need to figure out what's supposed to happen to that ring under the timer. I think that's our objective."

"Yeah, that makes sense," Talanna said. "But the ring doesn't even connect to the rest of the wires. There's nothing but air between that and the Y rod thing."

"Maybe somehow electricity can jump from the Y rod to the ring?" Niu suggested.

"Yes, that's it!" Ya'ir exclaimed.

Everyone watched silently as the capacitor, under Ya'ir's

command, floated to the end of the cables connected to the red and blue magnets. The metal wire moved inside the wide hole created by the two concave magnets, connecting to the metal terminals at the end of each cable.

"What does the wire do in there?" Vurkil asked.

"When I remagnetize this red block, there will be a magnetic field between it and the blue block," Ya'ir said. "If we rotate the wire, it will generate electricity, which can charge the capacitor. If we move the capacitor across the gap to the other wires, it should create the spark we need in that Y rod."

Vurkil frowned. "So how does that spark create electricity in the ring?"

"Because the spark emits radiation, including light," Ya'ir explained. "The ring can act as an antenna, absorbing the energy from the spark and creating a current in the ring."

"Riiight," Talanna said. "Those are words."

Vurkil and a few others chuckled.

Tovas glanced at the clock. They had used up a significant amount of time discussing the problem. Less than three-quarters of the glow persisted in the circle.

"We'd better solve it before time runs out," he said.

Ya'ir nodded. "Sam, can you rotate the wire? You can probably do it faster than me, which will charge the capacitor more quickly."

"Sure."

"Ya'ir really knows a lot about this," Scheln said in Tovas's mind.

Yes, Tovas replied. *His and Sam's depth of understanding is impressive. Where have you been?*

"Busy listening with my own ears. There's a lot going on here. I want to make sure I don't miss something important. Anyway, we learned some of this in our elementary studies, but these guys seem to know so much more."

Agreed, Tovas thought to him. *Perhaps we never explored the nature of Divine creation as much as we should have over the years.*

The wire spun rapidly between the magnetic blocks.

"It would be nice if we could see what was happening," Talanna said.

"You can feel it using Sorcery," Ya'ir replied. "Connect with the capacitor, and you can feel the charge difference building up."

Tovas reached out with Sorcery and linked with the two metal plates within the capacitor. He could indeed feel the difference between them, like a mounting pressure. He also felt the presence of the other group members as they connected with him.

"Okay, that's probably enough," Ya'ir said. "Here we go!"

The black capacitor moved to the wires at the other end of the gap. Just before it touched, three bright flashes accompanied large sparks between the capacitor, the Y rods, and the ring.

The timer above glowed brilliantly, and the wall blocking their exit lifted.

"That was amazing!" Vurkil exclaimed, slapping Ya'ir on the back and nearly knocking him over from the force. "So far, we're two for two!"

The entrance door rose, letting them exit to the main cavern.

Ya'ir's embarrassed smile persisted through several other congratulations from the group, and they made their way back to the main cavern. Tovas caught up to Sam as they walked.

"It's strange," Tovas said. "I would have expected more air-like challenges in there, such as air pressure or wind. Instead, it was all electricity."

Sam turned to him, his face alight with realization. "The Masters were wrong!" he cried. "I knew it."

Tovas raised an eyebrow. "What do you mean?"

"Land, Air, Fire, Water," Sam said, bursting with excitement. "They were never meant to be considered actual physical elements. They're collections of physical *concepts*! In the Land cavern, it was classical mechanics: reference frames, density, motion, inertia—things like that. Air was about electromagnetism: light, current, capacitance, radiation."

He pointed to the Fire symbol above the newly opened archway. "My guess is that Fire is all about thermodynamics—

maybe things like temperature and entropy." His finger moved toward the Water symbol. "Water is probably biology or chemistry."

Tovas's eyes widened. Sam was right. Grand Master Ilius's interpretation of the Elements had been wrong. He must have come across the four symbols at Tercast and incorrectly interpreted them.

The four Elements were *categorical*, not primordial.

Chapter 42

An Odd Conversation

Kara moved the long, thin plasma rifle to her back, where it attached magnetically with a *clink*. Anxiety gnawed at her insides.

This was it. Her relentless quest across the universe had led her to this point.

For the first time since the facility on Earth, Kara allowed herself to dwell on thoughts of her family, bringing a wave of immense sorrow with them. Her parents. Their secrets. Their deaths. She thought of her mother's gentle touch. Her father's deep chuckle. Picnics by the pond in their backyard. Their constant encouragement and support through difficulties introduced by her blindness. Tears from her eyes fell to the hard floor of her small bedroom.

She had lost them. They were gone.

But Jeanette was still out there. She had to be.

Kara rose from her cross-legged position on the floor, where she had been performing final checks on her equipment. She sniffed, wiped her eyes, and clenched her fist.

She was going to save Jeanette.

In her Ilkuth, Kara set out into the brightly lit hallway. It bustled with activity as the company prepared for departure. Most were hauling gear to the transports. The thought occurred to her that she hadn't yet had the chance to ask Commander Delveton about Tercast. There wasn't a lot of time, and he was probably busy preparing, but she headed to his room anyway to see if he had a moment.

Soldiers gave her a nod or saluted as she passed, and she returned the gestures in kind. Though she was still getting used to the Sovereignty's military culture, everyone seemed remarkably respectful—even to a lowly Spark such as herself.

As she approached the commander's room, the door slid open. She took two steps into the dark office-like room, and her eyes adjusted to the dim light. Just as she was about to call out his name, she heard his raspy voice and noticed that Minister Golin was present as well.

"—wait for the Deia's command on—"

"Yes, Spark?" the minister said.

Commander Delveton turned to her, inspecting her with that strange gaze of his again. There was something odd in it. Surprise? Suspicion? She couldn't place it. In a moment, it faded to a neutral expression.

"Oh, sorry to interrupt," she said. "I was just hoping to ask Commander Delveton a question."

"I'm afraid we do not have time for that now," Minister Golin replied. "All soldiers must report to the landing pad for departure. I'm about to send the notice now."

"Of course," Kara said, backing out through the doorway with a salute. "Sorry."

Her eyes readjusted to the bright hallway as the door slid back down smoothly.

Who's the Deia? Perhaps it's another term for the Sovereign? She probably has several titles.

A notification came to her mind that all personnel were to report to the vehicles for departure.

Her second trip down the halls was far quieter. Everyone else must have already gathered, and she quickened her pace to a jog.

When she reached the exterior door, it slid open to reveal a violent storm. Rain pelted her suit and exposed head. She donned her helmet quickly and joined the rest of the group near the sleek metallic ship parked on the pad nearby.

Commander Delveton was already among them. How had he gotten there so fast?

"Welcome to the party, Spark," his raspy voice called out over comms.

A nav marker appeared on her helmet's display, pointing to somewhere inside the vessel.

"You all have your designations," the commander said. "Get aboard."

Kara joined the rest of the company as they hovered into the end of the sleek round ship. The interior was plain but comfortable. Containers overhead held their gear. Commander Delveton was the last to land inside. The opening fell shut as soon as he passed the threshold and turned around. An old-looking sword and several small knives shimmered from the back of his suit next to his plasma rifle.

"That sword your good luck charm, Commander?" a female soldier called out. Several others chuckled.

Commander Delveton's helmet turned. "You could say that," he replied.

"We should make 'em standard issue!" a man said. "Fight like the ancients did!"

Laughter echoed across the comms channel as the vehicle rose from the ground.

"Welin Em Onii, my friends," the commander said.

The suits around the small vehicle stiffened. "Welin Em Onii," Kara said with the others.

"Let's destroy those monsters."

Chapter 43

Water

Sam glanced at the glowing timer on the rock wall, past the fiery pit.

Less than a quarter of time left.

The fire puzzle was turning out to be more difficult than the previous two. It appeared to be challenging them with thermodynamics—just as he had predicted.

An empty glass box sat underneath the timer, with a metal bar rising from the top. On the box floor lay a green glowing circle, presumably their target. A transparent, stiff tube wrapped around the outer portion of the metal bar, connecting to a mess of hoses.

The objects they had retrieved from the three branching paths included a cylindrical container with two hoses coming out, a bottle of bluish gas under pressure, and an unnaturally cold, transparent box with a thin pipe coiling through it. The cylinder contained a piston that would draw in air through the large hole and press it out through the smaller one.

The intake hose moved through the air and connected itself to one end of the hose.

"Does it fit?" Sam asked.

"Yeah, it fits," Vurkil responded.

"Do we connect the other side to the freezing box?" Relon asked.

"Looks like that's the only configuration that works," Tovas said.

Sam strained his mind to unravel the solution, but he didn't even have a clear idea of the goal. Did they need to melt the bar so that it fell into the bowl? That seemed likely, but he couldn't figure out how they would add any more heat beyond what the fire beneath was already providing. The only things they could Vitalize were the freezing box, the bottle of blue gas, and the piston cylinder, which was obviously a pump. They couldn't even Vitalize the gas itself, only the surrounding container.

The gas had to be the key. Maybe it was flammable? But how would they burn it close enough to the bar to melt it? All they had was a pump and a cold box. If the box was blazing hot, that would make more sense since they could heat the gas through it. He doubted that would be enough on its own to melt the metal bar, though. They had tried to re-enchant the freezing box to be hot, but it had refused. They could move it with Sorcery, but they couldn't change its temperature.

"The gas needs to go through the tubes," Vurkil said.

"Yeah, I figured that," Sam said, "but how do we heat it up?"

With Vurkil and Rose controlling them, the transparent hoses all came together, creating a circuit around the bar. It ran through the pump, into a narrower section inside the cold box, and back out to a wider section, which connected back to the coil encircling the bar.

"Maybe the bar wants to be cold?" Zel suggested.

"How would that help?" Sam asked. "We clearly need a liquid in there to touch the green target."

She shrugged. "Could be something else in the box."

"There's nothing else in—"

Realization flashed through his mind. Condensation. The box wasn't empty—it was full of gas!

Sam pointed a finger in the air. "Wait! You're right. This blue stuff must be some kind of coolant. We put it through the tubes and it can cool the bar so that the gas inside condenses into liquid around it!"

"Ha!" Vurkil exclaimed. "That's it!"

"Better hurry," Tovas said. "We're running low on time."

Sam glanced at the timer, which displayed a small slice of time left, perhaps only three to four minutes. He connected with the bottle and moved it to the larger side of the pump.

"Disconnect that side from the tube so we can suck the gas out with the pump," he said.

At Vurkil's command, the rubbery transparent tube pulled out from the one connected to the bar. Sam caused the bottle's tight rubbery opening to slip over the tube, submersing the tube in the bluish gas within.

"I'll pump it," Relon said to Vurkil.

"All yours," the giant replied.

The piston pulled away inside the pump, and blue gas immediately flowed through the transparent tube into the chamber. Relon compressed the piston back toward the end, and the colored gas shot through the other tube into the much narrower coil inside the freezing box. As she continued to pump the piston, blue gas passed through to the larger section, then twisted around the bar, where it turned purple. It then came back around until it started spilling out from the open end.

"Neat!" Zel said. "It turns more red with heat!"

Sam now desperately hoped the gas *wasn't* flammable. If any of those flames from below ignited it, a bomb would explode in their faces.

"Okay, let's seal that back up after the next pump," he instructed.

Relon let the piston suck in from the bottle one final time, then Sam pulled it off the tube. He moved it back toward him and let it rest on the rock pathway. The open end of the tube from the cylinder reconnected to the sturdy one with purplish gas leaking out.

Thankfully, no explosions took place. Everyone watched in

silence as Relon continued to pump the substance through the system.

"You okay, Relon?" Tovas asked.

"Yeah, it's actually very easy to move," she replied. "Probably enchanted for it."

Sam glanced at the clock. It only had a small sliver of glow left. The gas quickly turned from a purplish color into a bright red in the section immediately following the piston, then faded to a cool blue as it passed through the cold box. It turned a deeper blue at the point where the pipe widened.

Talanna pointed at those sections. "Why does it get a lot hotter here and colder there?"

Sam opened his mouth to speak, but Zel beat him to it.

"Pressure," she said. "Pressure increases, temperature increases. Pressure drops, temperature drops."

Talanna nodded.

"On my home planet, we call it the ideal gas law," Sam explained. "Because of conservation of energy, pressure multiplied by volume is roughly proportional to mass multiplied by temperature. Mass of the gas is constant in this case—so when the pressure or volume changes, the temperature changes, just like Zel said."

Talanna looked at Niu. "Did you understand a word of that?"

Niu smiled and shook her head. Sam rolled his eyes.

"Look!" Relon said. "It's working!"

Glowing green liquid condensed around the metal bar inside the container. A drop fell onto the green target below.

Niu screamed as the eerie fire rising from the pit below turned bright green, then faded out. The remaining time—a dangerously small slice—glowed powerfully, and the stone wall lifted, letting them all back into the main cavern once more.

They walked through the open archway with idle chatter among the group.

"That was close," Ya'ir said. "I was terrified we wouldn't get it in time."

"Yeah," Sam replied. "But we're fine. The last one should be a breeze with Rose—assuming it actually is biology like I think it is."

"Didn't you say it could also be chemistry?"

"Yeah, that's true. If I have to do stoichiometry, we might be screwed."

Ya'ir's brows furrowed. "What's stoichi—"

"Are we going straight to the next one?" Relon asked. "I really need to . . . uh . . . you know . . . relieve myself."

Sam became uncomfortably aware of the pressure from his own bladder. The puzzles had provided plenty of distraction from that and his hunger up to this point, but they really needed a bathroom break.

"Divine, yes!" Talanna exclaimed. "I've been needing a lavatory since we woke up!"

"I think we've just kind of been ignoring it up to this point," Ya'ir said with a chuckle. "But where exactly do we go?"

A stream of liquid hitting rock echoed from behind. Sam turned to find Vurkil facing the wall, urine flowing along the floor between the wide gap in his legs. Sam turned with a laugh as several others averted their gaze as well.

Talanna gasped. "Vurkil!"

"Rudds, I'm glad someone said it," he said. "I can't hold this no longer."

"Disgraceful," Fita said, shaking his head.

Niu covered her eyes. "That's *disgusting*!"

Rose shrugged with a laugh. "Everyone needs to do it. I'm going to go find more privacy, though."

The men remained in the cavern while the women headed back up the path toward the castle. Fita took a bit of convincing but eventually gave in to the fact that they probably wouldn't see a toilet for a while. The men spread out across the room to relieve themselves, then reflected on the challenges together while waiting for the women. Several minutes later, they returned.

"Ready for the Water puzzle?" Sam asked.

Though Ya'ir, Relon, and Rose seemed to share at least a

fraction of his enthusiasm, Fita, Kula, and Niu looked weary. The others appeared relatively indifferent.

"I'm just ready for some food," Vurkil said.

"Well," Sam replied, "hopefully when we finish this last cavern, it'll open a path out of here."

"What about this one?" Talanna said, pointing to the archway on the other side of the cavern with the Tercast symbol above it.

Sam shrugged. "Maybe that's the way out?"

"Or it might be another challenge," Tovas said.

"Let's do it," Rose said. "I'm curious to know what's at the end of all this."

The group entered the now open archway under the Water symbol. As before, all twelve lights over the arrow lit up—Scheln somehow activating his light through his connection to Tovas. The stone wall behind them dropped as the one with the arrow rose, revealing a significantly smaller cavern. Unlike the other challenges, no path branched off into three sections above a misty —or burning—pit. The enclosure had a smooth rock floor. Searching the jagged cave walls, Sam couldn't find a timer, or any sign of a puzzle. The cavern room was empty.

Niu hugged herself. "Why do these caves have to be so cold? Except the last one. That fire was nice."

"This one is different," Talanna said. "There aren't any paths."

"There isn't a timer either," Tovas said.

They stood looking around the empty cavern. It appeared they were trapped.

Vurkil threw his arms up. "What kind of rudding challenge—"

Water poured in from all around, cutting him off with a loud rush. Screams and yells reverberated through the small cavern as they huddled toward the center. Lukewarm water lapped at their feet and lower legs.

"What do we do?" Talanna shouted.

Sam reached out with Sorcery. Fabric. Bone. Muscle. Heart. He could feel nothing beyond his clothing and his own body.

"I can't Vitalize the water!" he yelled.

It was rising with tremendous velocity, already up to their

knees. Tovas placed hands atop his head and closed his eyes in prayer.

"We need to find something!" Vurkil said.

"Can everyone swim?" Relon called out.

Thankfully, everyone indicated they could.

Sam looked around desperately, failing to find anything but rising water and their rocky prison. The water had already reached most of their chests. Rose was nearly up to her shoulders, her pale freckled face wide-eyed with terror.

Tovas snapped out of his prayer and said something into Rose's ear before Vurkil lifted her onto his shoulders. A current beneath pushed them around, separating them from each other. The water's surface rose rapidly. Soon everyone treaded water except the giant.

This doesn't make any sense, Sam thought, panic rising. *Why would this place suddenly want to kill us?*

Maybe this was the puzzle: stop the water. But how could they do that when they couldn't control anything except their own bodies?

Their bodies.

That was it. It had to be. They had to do something to their own biology—but what? Turn their arm into some kind of drill to bore through the rock? That didn't seem possible, even with Rose's expertise.

Sam looked around frantically for any sign of an exit, or anything out of the ordinary. Vurkil was swimming now, Rose off his shoulders and swimming herself. They had only a few feet of air left. Panicked voices echoed against the rock walls as the others talked over each other. Sam ignored them. He had to think.

Where was the air going? If water was coming in, the air had to leave somewhere. He looked closely at the ceiling and saw tiny crevices next to the points of light. That's how the air was escaping. How could he use that?

He glanced at the others. Many of them watched him in desperation. They expected him to solve this. Talanna looked to him for hope through her brilliantly white, wet hair. Relon's face reflected mild panic. Even Fita's typically stoic eyes looked fearful.

He had failed them. All of them. He didn't have the answers. It didn't make any sense.

Tears from his eyes mixed with the rushing water as their heads neared the cavern ceiling.

"I'm sorry," he said. "I'm so sorry."

With the few inches of air left, he took a deep breath. The water quickly filled the gap, leaving them trapped underwater. The group became nothing but fuzzy images to his view. He could tell Vurkil's large shape from the others only by its size.

Heart thumping, Sam swam to the bottom and back toward the entrance, feeling around the seams of the door for any sign of give. It was shut tight. His lungs strained for oxygen. He desperately wanted to breathe, but knew that any attempt to do so would only be his demise. His diaphragm convulsed. He let a little air out of his lungs, causing him to sink a bit more.

There were too many unsolved mysteries. They had never found out who built this place, or who had kidnapped Jeanette and why. He still had so much more to learn about the universe, and Sorcery. He'd never get those answers now.

Anguish swept over Sam as he thought of Kara. He'd never get to see those incredible, unsteady blue eyes of hers again. He'd missed his chance to confess his love for her. Now he would never get another shot. He was going to die.

Something changed.

Sam couldn't tell what it was exactly, but he suddenly felt relieved. Activating his Sorcery, he sensed Rose's presence. She was doing something to him.

His lungs.

The air inside them was changing. He wasn't familiar with the feelings of the chemicals, so he couldn't tell exactly, but she must be magically creating oxygen—allowing his lungs to breathe without actually taking a breath.

He swam toward the others. Many of their fuzzy outlines were holding hands. They still needed to determine a way out. Rose's amazing skills were keeping them alive, but she couldn't keep it up forever. Eventually, they'd need to breathe on their own. He felt around the rock ceiling, looking for any sign of an exit.

Abruptly, water currents flowed, which pushed Sam away from the group. He looked up to see the water's surface drop away from the rock. Arms and legs straining against the water, he broke through the surface with a massive breath. The sounds of others doing the same resonated across the cavern.

"Rose, was that you?" Ya'ir asked.

Sam wiped his eyes and glanced up to see Rose's wet face nodding in the distance.

The water level quickly fell. Coughs echoed against the cavern walls. Eventually, their feet rested against the smooth cavern floor once more. Niu and Talanna shivered, water dripping from their pitiful faces. Kula wiped droplets from her eyes and flipped her blond hair back. Zel and Ya'ir wrung water from their robes.

"How did you do that?" Fita asked Rose.

She sniffed, then wiped her nose with her sleeve, trembling slightly. "Oxygen. I just changed the carbon dioxide in everyone's lungs into oxygen."

"You saved us," Ya'ir said. "You saved all of us."

She smiled. "I can't take all the credit. Tovas had the idea. I was too panicked to think straight."

The door opened and revealed the way back into the main chamber.

"Let's never do that again," Talanna breathed through chattering teeth, wringing water from her stark white hair.

Niu nodded. "Never again."

They shuffled their way back toward the archway while dripping water along the way. Sam passed through the opening first. The water wetting his hair, skin, and robes fell abnormally to the floor, lifting a significant weight from him.

"Whoa!" he said, "the entrance dries you off!"

Talanna ran through the archway, drying immediately as she did so. Niu and the others followed closely behind, and soon everyone was dry again, though their hair was no longer quite as neat and orderly as it was before the challenge. No one seemed to mind much, having narrowly escaped death.

Sam glanced at the final archway under the Tercast symbol. It was open.

Inside he found a small enclosure with a horizontal line running across the center, hovering in the air. The line faded from a solid dull gray at one end to a transparent center, which then transitioned to bright, vibrant color at the other end.

He walked tentatively inside and glanced around at the rocky, irregular walls and ceiling. The smaller cavern contained nothing but the strange line. A gray outline of a figure emerged from the center in the shape of a man. Another one formed up next to it, creating a faceless woman. The figures stood motionless for several seconds as Tovas and the others arrived, all of them transfixed by the curious sight.

The two gray images faded into smoke. A new character emerged slightly to the right, appearing a sapphire blue. It was a woman planting a seed. Two more arose from further down the line, depicting a brown man with a shield defending a violet woman from a dull gray sword. The scenes progressed at a glacial pace, their motion barely detectable.

The bright images faded, and more figures appeared from the line slightly left from the midpoint. Two semitransparent gray women pointed mockingly at another woman. A gray man beyond them laughed as he lit a small green animal on fire. Further down, two more opaque, gray, humanoid figures emerged, one mercilessly beating the other with its fists.

"It's a lesson about morality," Tovas said.

The original outlines of a man and woman surfaced from the center of the line once more. They raised their hands as if holding something up. Their standing figures strode to the right, and color emerged within them, blending across the spectrum. A point of pearlescent light appeared above their hands. As they moved further, their color-shifting bodies became more vibrant, and the light above their hands increased.

They stopped, then quickly walked toward the other end of the spectrum. Their colors faded. The light above their hands dimmed to nothing as they passed back through the center and became a point of eerie darkness above their hands as they moved further down, their figures turning a dull gray.

"Sorcery," Tovas remarked. "It depends on our moral standing. Where we stand between good and evil determines its strength. Moral ambiguity suppresses its power."

Sam considered Tovas's interpretation. That did appear to be what the line was showing.

The two figures faded, and the line expanded into a plane, maintaining the gradient between dull, opaque gray, transparency, and vibrant color. Several additional smoky characters rose across the spectrum—the colorful ones engaging in uplifting or protective actions, and the ones on the gray end depicting increasingly despicable actions. Each was more transparent toward the center, and had a point of light or darkness above its head, which increased in intensity toward the ends.

Sam and the others treaded slowly around the room and inspected the magical imagery, which disappeared as they passed through it.

One vibrant image caught Sam's eye. A group of multicolored men and women encircled a distraught figure in a warm embrace, bringing a similar scene to mind of the men huddling around a brutalized Ya'ir.

Realization settled on Sam like a warm blanket. His eyes widened.

This was the unexpected jump in his power. The missing piece of his equation. That night, his and Ya'ir's Sorcery had increased because of their actions somehow. Tovas had been right. Morality seemed to have some kind of effect.

A solid, dim gray figure appeared at the end of the spectrum. It threw out clattering chains which latched on to all other figures near it, pulling them further leftward as they struggled against each other. Another figure appeared at the far end of the right side of the spectrum, glowing a brilliant range of colors. It opened its arms, and the figures on the light side turned and began walking toward it, shining more vibrantly as they moved further from the transparent center.

The plane morphed, forming magnificent swirling galaxies of various color around the room and the figures within. Sam marveled at the stunning depiction of the universe. Some of the colorful figures flew across the room and clashed with the dull gray ones, vigorously striking their chains.

A single bright female figure hovered to the center, her pearlescent color shifting wildly. Light exploded from her, illuminating the room. The galaxies and smoky inhabitants stopped moving—frozen in place—as colors and lights swirled around the woman at the center. She raised a hand, and the galaxies and figures surrounding her spun rapidly in reverse, eventually collapsing in on each other. The smoky images then imploded into a single point, which faded.

The group was left in darkness.

A point of light appeared overhead, illuminating the cavern and an opening on the other side.

Sam turned to Tovas, who had his eyes closed. He appeared to be praying again.

"That was amazing!" Talanna exclaimed.

"Finally," Vurkil said, striding toward the opening. "Let's find something to eat!"

The cave shook with a dull boom.

"Rudds. What was that?"

"Quakes?" Relon asked.

More low blasts shook the caves from above.

"What's going on?" Niu asked.

Tovas jolted as though he'd been struck by lightning. He turned and looked at Sam with wide eyes.

"Scheln!" he yelled. "Tercast is being attacked!"

Chapter 44

Cyborgs and Sorcerers

Kara crouched on a wall set with battlements, her arm cannons lowered at the evening-lit courtyard as she scanned for enemies. Commander Delveton descended with First Squad onto the neat grass below. The squad split into two groups, which stacked up and entered the north and south ends of the castle simultaneously. Gunfire ensued.

Kara's squad had set the welcome mat—blowing the courtyard entrances wide open with explosives. She kept her position on the west-side battlements with Tilna to provide cover and keep the enemy from escaping. Two other members of her squad, Bavan and Rico, crouched on the east side to do the same. Commander Olik and two others covered the front entrance, while the last two covered the rear of the building.

She glanced up at the clear night sky. "I expected rain, given the cloudy planet in the briefing."

"Me too," Tilna said next to her, looking up.

"Stay focused," Commander Olik said over the channel. "You can chat about the weather later."

Kara returned her attention to the courtyard, wishing she could be part of the squad storming the halls to find her sister.

"Contact at the front!" Olik called out. Gunfire rang out from the front side of the building to her right.

"What are these people?" Penali asked over the squad channel.

"Hell if I know," Olik replied. "But they're not getting past us."

A dark-skinned woman in white robes emerged into the courtyard from the south opening. Kara opened fire. Projectiles tore up the door near the target, deflected somehow from the woman's skin or robes, and she retreated inside. The distinct electric sound of plasma fire rang out from the opening—followed by an explosion that shook the walls. Strange that they would wear white. All the cultists in previous attacks wore black.

The situation felt off, but perhaps that was their intention.

She opened the company channel. "Contact in the courtyard. Target retreated into the south building."

"Contacts!" Jin called out. The sound of plasma blasts rang out from the north side of the building to Kara's left. "They're coming out from a rear entrance. Tons of—"

A low blast echoed from that direction. Both Jin's and Ernilow's indicators turned red.

"Tilna, Rico, get around to that rear side *now*," Olik instructed.

Two acknowledgments from each squad member pulsed on Kara's display, and the suit next to her flew off to her left.

"Kara, Bavan, maintain your positions."

She fired off her own acknowledgment, heart thumping.

Red. That meant they were in critical condition. What did these people possess that could damage the impenetrable Ilkuth?

Gunfire rang out to Kara's left, followed by more plasma blasts.

"Engaging!" Tilna's high-pitched voice called out fearfully over the channel.

Olik's reply was stern and full of urgency. "Do not let any of them escape, Chief Tilna."

The woman's acknowledgment blinked as additional plasma and arm cannon fire ensued around the building.

The indicator for Mul, one of the squad members with Olik, turned red.

"Mul is down!" Olik called out over the company-wide channel. "They didn't even hit him hard. Somehow, they've disabled the armor's defenses!"

"Steady on," Delveton replied calmly. "Keep them from escaping."

Something white hot and flaming collided into Kara with a loud bang. She felt the temperature rise slightly before the suit compensated with cooling. Adrenaline pulsed through her as she spun on her heel and unloaded several arm cannon rounds through the door at the end of the battlement. It was the black-skinned woman wearing white robes. She held some kind of medieval-looking spiked mace.

"Contact on the west battlements!" Kara called out over the squad channel.

The rounds seemed to have no effect as the woman quickly approached. Kara pulled the plasma rifle from her back. A powerful gust of wind came out of nowhere as the woman stretched her arms out, causing the electric blast from Kara's rifle to miss its target. The gale made Kara lose her footing as it pushed her back. The Ilkuth compensated with antigravity and propulsion. Kara hovered as the winds subsided. Her enemy approached with a yell, readying the mace for a blow.

It abruptly burst into fiery white flame. Kara's eyes went wide.

The woman brought the mace down as Kara raised her forearm as a shield. She felt the temperature quickly rise again before the suit adjusted itself a split second later. Kara spun, sweeping the woman's legs out from under her, causing her to fall.

Others in white robes started to move out the battlement door. Kara fired her arm cannon at the area above the opening. They retreated inside as debris fell and blocked their exit.

The woman beneath her rose up, swinging the flaming mace at Kara's head. It glanced off with little effect. A kick at the woman's hand caused her to cry out in pain as the mace flew off the battlement into the dimly lit crops beyond. The woman reached out her uninjured hand, and a bright shock arced to Kara's helmet before dissipating across her armor.

"You devils cannot take this holy place!" the woman yelled as she pulled a dagger from her hip.

Kara leveled the plasma rifle at the woman and pulled the trigger. The brilliant light and distinct sound left a massive hole in her chest. The plasma shot hadn't yet fully charged, but Kara was close enough that it didn't matter.

That's for Jeanette, she thought. The woman's wide eyes faded as Kara continued checking the battlement door and courtyard for other targets. Soon enough, the woman's twitching stopped.

"West battlements secure," Kara said.

Olik's acknowledgment light blinked.

"Another target in the courtyard," Bavan called out.

Something floated out of the south doors of the courtyard below. Kara's eyes went wide. It looked like a sleeping young man in white robes, floating in the air. His head and limbs hung limp. Bavan opened fire at the ghostlike figure from the battlements across. As Kara leveled her arm cannon to shoot as well, a powerful whirlwind pushed her backward, centering on the man.

Dirt and debris rose from the ground and pelted Kara's suit. The Ilkuth strained to keep her arm cannon level at the target amid the tumultuous wind. How was this possible?

A large rock smashed into Bavan's helmet at a tremendous velocity, knocking him from the wall and out of Kara's line of sight. His indicator turned red. Kara's suit went abnormally rigid, and something smashed into her side—an enormous slab of stone. Her suit rolled with the blow automatically, righting her. She dodged another rock and strained to get a clear shot, but the wind and debris prevented her arms from remaining steady.

Many of the squad's indicators turned orange or red as the sounds of battle raged all around.

"Kara!" Olik instructed over the squad channel. "Help from the other squad is on its way."

She gave her acknowledgment as arm cannon fire erupted

from the north doorway of the courtyard. Two suits emerged from the doors, hovering in the air as they pressed against the maelstrom. They moved toward the center of the storm, continuously firing their arm cannons to no apparent effect. Through the gap in the battlements, Kara watched the eerily limp, hovering man at the center of it all.

Slowly, the raging winds subsided, giving room for the sound of arm cannon fire. The limp figure gradually fell to the ground and lay in an awkward position as the suits continued to fire at him ceaselessly. A few bullets seemed to break through the invisible protection, marring the robes with holes and flecks of blood.

A blond man in a white cloak emerged behind the two soldiers with a flying kick. He sent one of them sailing headfirst into the wall across the courtyard. The other soldier reached for his vaporizer, but the robed man was too quick. He jumped onto the shoulders of the Ilkuth. Kara reached over the battlements and fired, but the shots ricocheted off the man's body. He pulled the helmet from the suit with a loud crack, destroying the fastening mechanism and exposing Chief Eranim's feminine blue face and blond ponytail.

Kara ceased firing. Eranim was exposed. Quent, the other soldier, ran toward the pair.

Eranim grabbed the enemy's ankle and threw him to the ground, then reached for her weapon again. The robed man kicked dirt from the ground into the woman's face, causing her to recoil in pain. He pulled the sword from his side and sliced upward in a swift motion.

Blood spilled from her head, and she fell with a thump. Her indicator turned bright red on Kara's display.

An electric blast rang as Quent moved into range. It caught the blond man in the head, illuminating the courtyard. A kick to the enemy's chest sent him flying back several feet, robes tainted with dirt and blood. Without pause, Quent ran back through the open door, where more gunfire ensued in the hallway. The blond man remained motionless.

"Kara," Commander Olik called out, "Tilna needs your help at the rear. Go—"

"No," Commander Delveton said calmly over the squad comms. "I will help Tilna. Maintain your position, Kara. If you see anything else, inform us but do not engage."

Why was he taking her out of the fight? What had she done?

Now isn't the time to be questioning authority, she thought before firing off her acknowledgment. Disorientation clouded her mind as her heart beat furiously. Nearly everyone in the company was down. This was supposed to be an easy win.

Something about the whole situation was terribly *wrong*.

Chapter 45
Choosing a Side

It made no sense. Two men outside Jeanette's door spoke about the battle—but as if it were happening somewhere else. Jeanette had expected to hear explosions and gunfire as soldiers stormed the castle. Instead, there was nothing but tense silence.

Now was the time. She knew that the Dcia was still directing her subjects' actions from the throne room due to the hallway chatter. Kara was in danger. Jeanette needed to make her move. *Now.*

"I'm going to kill that woman," she said to the small, empty study. "Or die trying."

She rose and strode into the hall, carrying long daggers on her hip, which she had kept from her last practice session. Unbridled rage flowed through her, giving her confidence. This was it. The Deia's life or her own. That was the only way this would end. Jeanette was ready to die. She'd been ready since the day they'd brought her to this hellish place.

The ornate hallway was unusually empty. Swirling patterns of black lines danced along the colorful paint. Gorgeous images of fantastical landscapes embellished the walls, making them come alive. Jeanette marched past one that depicted a snow-capped mountain beyond rolling hills of orange vegetation.

Jeanette rounded the corner toward the throne room and stopped in her tracks at an impossible sight.

Him. Again.

She faced the man she'd fought and spared. The one she'd let off with only a scratch for Belze's murder. He stood in front of the doors to the throne room, looking anxious. He'd lost even more weight since their last encounter.

His dark eyes widened as he saw her, and he raised his hands. "Don't come!" he yelled.

Jeanette's fury surged within her. This man would not stop her. She marched toward him and unsheathed the daggers from her waist.

"No!" he exclaimed, glancing back at the doors. "You . . . You must not come through here. Turn back. Please!"

The man was paler than usual under his curly black hair. Though he looked terrified, he balled his hands into fists and took a fighting stance.

He had no weapons. This would be easy.

Jeanette jabbed forward with her dagger as soon as the man was within range. He stepped to the side, avoiding the thrust, and threw a wild punch at her. She brought up the other dagger and sliced his hand as he did.

He recoiled with a yell and held the wrist of his bloodied hand with the free one. She advanced on him, and his thin frame shrunk back, falling into the wall behind him. Bony arms lifted above his head.

"Don't!" he cried. "Please . . . Please don't! She . . . She told me to stop anyone from coming through, or else they would torture me again. Please . . ."

"*This isn't you.*" Amy's quiet voice pierced Jeanette's mind— barely more than a whisper now. "*Leave him be.*"

Jeanette stared at the pitiful man, feeling powerful. *He killed Belze. This man doesn't deserve to live any longer.*

"*Jeanette, whose side are you on?*"

She was done being pushed around—being forced into submission. She would not do what anyone else wanted. Ever again. Not her parents. Not Amy's stupid imagined voice. Not Tess. Not the Deia. Not anyone. She was through submitting to the will of others.

"I'm on my *own* side!" she shouted, slashing down at the man's arms with her dagger.

Fury took over her body as she sliced over and over. The man screamed below her as blood dripped from the cuts in his arms. Jeanette screamed with him, tears running down her cheeks. She thrust a final blow downward and caught the man in the chest below his arms.

She stepped back, anger fading into shock. The dagger remained. Bloody, pale arms fell from where they had shielded the man's head, and they dropped limply to the side. He looked at Jeanette with wide, dark brown eyes as blood spilled from the hole in his chest.

A change occurred within her. A subtle shift. Something ethereal.

Numbness consumed her mind as she stood in the hallway and watched the man die.

Chapter 46

Lightning

Rose checked everyone's vitals as she stood with them at a fork in the dark, narrow caves. They were anxious or frightened but otherwise healthy.

Kula returned from the rightward path. "This leads to the forest outside the wall."

"Finally! Let's go," Talanna said.

Sam held his mace out, stopping her. "Let's wait for—"

Fita came running from the leftward path. "This leads to a hidden storage area behind the Artifact Room. The room appears to be empty at the moment, but there's a battle raging up there."

Sam nodded. "The other path leads outside the wall, so we can get out that way."

"Wait!" Relon said. "Where's Tovas?"

"Over there." Vurkil pointed back the way they had come.

Ya'ir adjusted his light onto the path, revealing Tovas as he knelt in prayer against the cave floor, hands atop his head.

Relon walked to him, and Rose followed with the others. Points of light hovered in the air with them and illuminated the cavern.

"Hey, Tovas," Relon said as she approached him. "We found—"

She stopped and bent down to put a hand on his shoulder. Rose walked to them, Vurkil and Sam trailing behind her.

Streaks of tears reflected light down Tovas's cheeks. He opened his eyes and slowly dropped his hands to his sides.

He looked at Relon with eyes full of anguish. "Scheln is gone."

Relon's blue face crumpled. She lurched forward and embraced Tovas.

Rose felt numb as she approached the two and dropped to her knees, putting her arms around them as well. She reached out with Sorcery and was unable to establish a connection to Scheln. Tears fell from her eyes as a stab of sorrow pierced her. They'd never really gotten to know him well. Tovas would only occasionally tell them what he was thinking.

"What happened?" Fita asked from somewhere Rose couldn't see.

The embrace broke.

"It's Scheln," Vurkil replied sorrowfully. "He's—"

"I need to go," Tovas interrupted. "Scheln said he was going to do what he could to help others escape. I must help as well. I need to save whoever I can."

"We're incredibly lucky we happened to be in this cave when it happened," Sam said. "I'm sorry about Scheln, but getting ourselves killed isn't going to make his sacrifice more meaningful."

"Those who have the power and disposition to do good have a responsibility to act," Tovas said. His voice was calm, steadfast.

Fita nodded. "Yes."

Sam opened his mouth to protest, then closed it. To Rose's amazement, he nodded as well.

"Escape if you want, but I'm going back," Tovas said, striding toward the fork in the cavern ahead.

Fita followed. "As will I."

Vurkil reached a hand to Rose, and she took it, looking up into his hazel eyes. She nodded, and they followed Tovas hand-in-hand. They weren't going into battle without a healer.

Sam, Ya'ir, Relon, and Kula followed behind. Activating

Sorcery, she felt their anxiety through her special connection to each of them. Talanna and Niu hesitated at the fork, and Rose thought they might escape to the forest for a moment, but they followed the group down the path toward the castle.

The cavern led to a small storage room with a few ruined weapons strewn about. The wall separating it from the Artifact Room lay in ruins. Sounds of gunfire and explosions rang out nearby.

"Enchant yourself against projectiles," Tovas said as he entered.

Rose followed him cautiously with the others, enchanting her skin to deflect high-speed objects. In the dim light, she searched through the wreckage of the Artifact Room for anything useful.

"Vurkil," Sam called out.

"Over here."

"I found your hammer."

"Yes!" Vurkil said, turning and making his way toward Sam, who indeed held the giant hammer aloft in one hand. It looked like an impossible feat, given the weapon's enormous size, but he appeared to be holding it effortlessly.

"It's a lot lighter than it looks," Sam said, handing it to the giant with a strained movement.

Vurkil took it as Rose approached beside him. "It's actually called the Maul of Ruin."

Sam pointed at the oversized weapon. "I'd bet it's enchanted with antigravity to make it lighter."

Rose looked for a shield while the others sifted through rubble and weapons around her.

"Everyone, over here," Tovas called, bringing the group together.

They took inventory of their findings. Relon had found a pair of daggers. She stood next to Niu, who hefted something resembling a halberd. Tovas held a long silver-and-gold staff, while Talanna knelt next to him and picked up a double-bladed sword. Zelyra strode up next to her with a handful of throwing spades. Kula had found arrows among the rubble, and a quiver to put them in—ammunition for the bow she had brought into the cavern. Ya'ir held a short spear. Fita still carried his heat sword, and Sam wielded the Mace of Motion.

Rose had found nothing for herself, but hopefully she wouldn't need it. Her focus would be on making sure everyone else stayed alive.

"Rose," Tovas said. "Is everyone safe from gunfire?"

"Yes," she replied. "Everyone has an active deflection enchantment."

"We need a strategy. Fita, what are your thoughts?"

Rose turned to regard him. Fita glanced at the rest of them, no doubt taking inventory of their weapons and abilities himself.

"It is hard to say. We don't know what we're up against," Fita replied. "My first thoughts are to strike hard and fast. Hesitation could mean death. We must protect Rose so she can heal any injuries."

"Agreed," Tovas said.

"Let's move with Tovas and Kula in the lead. I'll bring up the rear with Zel and Sam. The rest of you should stay alongside Rose."

Tovas nodded. "Let's go."

They emerged past the rubble into the foul-smelling hallway. Rose gasped.

Corpses.

Blood and bodies lined the corridors. Niu and Talanna froze, wide-eyed and trembling. Tovas led them through slowly as they stepped over the remains. Rose saw one face she recognized—the man who had approached her one morning in the lunchroom. His face hung to the side, and he had a fist-sized hole in his chest. Something had burned straight through his body.

"Tovas," Talanna said in a quivering voice, "we should leave. We're too late."

He turned around, face grim but determined. "Please go if you want. I'm going to do what I can. The rest of you don't need to come."

"No chance," Vurkil said. "These people need to be stopped."

"These are Armed Forces suits!" Kula said, pointing to a fallen power suit. Though the suit itself appeared intact, black residue indicated some kind of explosion, which may have shaken the occupant's body violently enough to kill.

"Wh-Why would the military attack Tercast?" Talanna asked.

"I don't know," Tovas said, continuing down the narrow hall.

"It looks like it was hurt by an explosion," Rose said. "That armor is probably impossible to pierce. Blunt force may be the best way to attack."

Vurkil hefted his hammer. "Got us covered there."

Whether out of a sense of personal duty or fear of leaving the group, they all pressed onward. As Rose rounded the corner, an electric blast flashed through the hallway.

Vurkil yelled out next to her, while Fita lurched forward with a glowing white sword, melting the forward grip of the emitting weapon clean off. The suit threw down the pieces of its rifle and straightened its arms, spraying the group with gunfire which ricocheted off their skin. Fita swung again and the cyborg raised an arm up, deflecting the blow. An immensely powerful gust of wind struck the hallway as an arrow smashed into the suit helmet with a loud clang, shattering into splinters as it did so. The powerful blow caused the suit to flip backwards and fall to the ground. It remained motionless.

"Rose!" Vurkil yelled.

Her heart pounded in her ears as she turned to him.

Eyes wide, Rose fought down the rising panic. He had a giant hole in his abdomen.

She took a deep breath, forcing herself to remain calm. Whatever that weapon was, it had vaporized the tissue straight through Vurkil's massive body underneath his rib cage. She connected with him, feeling blood drain from his face and pool around the cauterized tissue as he sat down against the wall. She knelt next to him, and the others gathered around.

Rose put her hand into the sash of her robes and pulled out the small vial of potion Tovas had given her earlier. She flicked open the cap and held it up to Vurkil, who drank eagerly. Heart racing, she closed her eyes, focusing on the sensations through her connection to his body.

Blood. Tissue. Skin. Causality.

His neural activity calmed somewhat. The enchantment cleaned the charred and dead cells from his body, holding his fluids in place. Cells of his skin, intestines, and vessels began proliferating with incredible speed.

Time, she realized. The enchantment involved manipulation of time by increasing the rate of causality. She struggled to trace the details—everything was happening too quickly. She guessed that waste products were being transmuted into nutrients and perhaps even oxygen around the rapidly proliferating cells, giving them the means to press forward without a constant supply of blood. Within a few seconds, the tissues of his intestines, mesentery, vessels, and skin had completely healed beneath the hole in his dirty white robes.

Vurkil pulled himself from the wall and embraced her with his enormous, warm body. "Rudds, you saved me again."

She wrapped her arms around his giant frame, thanking the Divine for the miraculous potion.

"—can't just leave him." Fita said. "He may awaken and attack us from behind."

Rose let go of Vurkil and glanced over to see Sam, Fita, and Tovas talking over the fallen enemy. Fita still held a flaming white sword. *He should put that thing out before he accidentally burns someone. Or himself.*

"I will not let you kill him," Tovas said calmly, raising his staff in a defensive stance.

"He nearly killed Vurkil!" Fita yelled.

Sam nodded.

Rose stood, and Vurkil did the same next to her. She wiped a tear from her cheek, striding toward the fools on the brink of fighting each other.

"I've got it," Ya'ir said as he kneeled next to the body.

"Ya'ir, I won't—"

"I won't harm him," he said, cutting Tovas's protest short.

He turned the suit over and touched several spots across the back of it in silence. A tap to the neck resulted in the helmet popping free, and Ya'ir lifted his hand. "Done. Power is cut off from everything, so even if he wakes up, he'll be immobile."

"Nice thinking," Tovas said. He pulled off the soldier's helmet, which revealed a middle-aged man with dark skin and short curly hair. "Let's keep moving. Vurkil, will you please take this man? I don't want to leave him here."

Fita stepped forward. "I'll do it." He bent down and grabbed an arm of the armored figure. He dragged it across the floor without too much difficulty, showing that the suit likely had antigravity in effect to make it lighter. The sword in Fita's hand had cooled back to its shiny steel color.

As they progressed, it became more and more dismally apparent that Talanna had been right. They were too late to help Tercast. A few fallen power suits accompanied the many bodies of studies and Masters. Rose attempted to avoid glancing at the faces as she passed by. When they reached the doors leading into the courtyard, Vurkil and Ya'ir pulled them open as Kula and Tovas led the way cautiously. Kula nocked an arrow.

The courtyard appeared as though a tornado had hit it. Debris and downed trees littered the area. A dark night sky hung overhead. The two moons provided eerie illumination of the dismal scene. As the group cautiously walked through the doorway, Tovas rushed forward toward the corner of the courtyard to their right and kneeled next to a body.

Scheln.

"Kula, Ya'ir, and Zel, stay and watch the hallway behind us," Fita instructed. "Sam, Vurkil, Rose"—he pointed to the battlements overhead—"keep a close eye on the top of these walls and yell if you see anything. Talanna, Niu, Relon, come with me to cover the east door."

Niu and Talanna trembled with fear. Tears fell from their eyes. Zel appeared distant as usual—though her typical cheery attitude was absent. Rose was surprised they all had enough grit and determination to keep moving through the gruesome scene.

Dragging the power suit behind him, Fita accompanied Niu, Talanna, and Relon to the east door, which had been thoroughly destroyed. Rose, Sam, and Vurkil moved to Tovas, each of them scanning the battlements for any sign of movement.

"Rose, is he gone?" Tovas asked, perhaps too afraid to check himself.

She turned and knelt next to him. Scheln's abnormally thin body had several bullet wounds. Touching a hand to his head, she reached out with Sorcery and inspected Scheln's organs. His heart beat weakly.

"I think he's alive!" she said. "But he's lost a lot of blood. I'll patch him."

Tovas threw out his hand and stopped her. "No. Save your strength. I'll do it."

He dropped and touched his brother's arm, and his eyes went misty. In almost an instant, the holes in Scheln's body began closing, and blood multiplied in his veins. His heart thumped with renewed vigor, and his lungs moved. Thankfully, the damage wasn't too extensive. Saving her wakefulness and their last potion was a wise call.

Tovas lifted his head. "Will he be okay?"

She nodded, smiling. "I think so."

"Why couldn't I connect with him after he fell unconscious?"

Rose shrugged. "I don't know."

Talanna screamed.

A loud electric blast rang out from the direction of Fita's group. Talanna's tall figure fell to the ground—her stark white hair tainted with red. Niu's cry cut off instantly as a flaming knife pierced her eye. Rose reached out with Sorcery, no longer feeling her connection to them. She intimately felt Relon's pain as a long dagger pierced her forehead with a loud crack of electricity. Her body went dark to Rose's perception.

Fita stepped forward with a yell, bringing down the flaming sword. The armored target moved with extraordinary speed and deflected the sword with a forearm. It punched Fita in the gut with enough force to send him flying backward. Through her connection to Fita's body, Rose felt his destroyed sternum and traumatized internal organs. She quickly relieved some of the pressure—but he needed more healing than she could provide alone.

An arrow rode powerful winds toward the enemy. The suit dodged, narrowly escaping the impact. Two more dark knives flew out from the armored figure, stabbing Kula in the shoulder and Ya'ir in the leg. More knives raced through the air toward Rose and Vurkil. Tovas appeared in front of them with blurring speed, deflecting the knives into the ground with a twirling staff.

The enemy pointed the long rifle in its hands down at its fellow soldier's exposed head and pulled the trigger. A bright white light accompanied an electric blast, which echoed against the castle walls.

Heartbeats thumped in her ears.

Rose could hardly process what was happening. It had occurred in a matter of seconds. They needed to get Fita to safety. Talanna, Niu, and Relon were gone. The enemy was gathering knives from their bodies, rifle at the ready in its other hand. Kula and Zel supported Ya'ir as they rushed toward the rest of the group's position in the corner. Rose felt at their wounds. They would be okay—for now. Fita's vitals, however, were dire. She couldn't save him with her power alone. He needed the potion.

"Fita," she said, trembling. "He's still alive."

Vurkil emitted an earsplitting roar, saturated with anguish.

He leapt to an impossible height, lifting the giant maul high over his head. His target rose from a crouch and raised its forearms as the hammer fell with tremendous force. The impact sent sparks flying with the sound of thunder, driving the suit into solid ground up to its waist. The rifle flew across the courtyard, propelled by the immense collision. Vurkil immediately ran to Fita and flung him into the air toward the group. Tovas caught Fita's body as the giant engaged the enemy again, which had pulled itself out of the ground.

Rose clenched her fists as she watched. *Destroy him!*

Vurkil approached his enemy and swung the maul, which the suit deftly evaded. She needed more time to help him.

Simultaneously connecting with her own body, she gave an imaginative command of an increased rate of causality, and the world slowed around her. Vurkil spun in slow motion, his body stronger and heavier than usual—an effect from the maul. The powerful sideways blow missed its target as the suit cartwheeled with blurring speed. It kicked the maul from Vurkil's grip.

Rose's breath caught, heart thumping. Vurkil was already propelling a punch toward the enemy with his other hand, shouting with unbridled fury.

She connected with the skin, bones, and muscles of his body, willing the bonds between cells to strengthen—to become unyielding. She gave his muscles almost all she could bear, strengthening them to her limit. As the suit righted, Vurkil's punch landed on the helmet with incredible force, knocking the suit back with a visible shockwave. Vurkil didn't let up as he repeated blow after blow. The suit appeared dazed, stumbling under the onslaught of superhuman punches from the giant above. A blow smashed the face shield of the helmet and sent large cracks across its surface. Exhaustion poured over Rose as she tried to maintain the enchantments that were likely keeping Vurkil alive.

The suit stepped back and pulled something from its back: A sword.

As Vurkil threw another punch forward, the suit brought the weapon to an angle toward the giant's head. A powerful flash of lightning blinded her vision.

Rose's connection to Vurkil ruptured—his presence and body gone to her perception.

She let the Vitalization of her own body fall. The world returned to its normal speed, and she fell to her knees, tears streaming from her eyes.

Agony and exhaustion devoured her.

She wanted to scream, but sudden insurmountable fatigue made the feat impossible.

Sam took a deep breath nearby before Rose's consciousness faded to the abyss.

Chapter 47
Deceived

"Vurkil!"

Kara flinched.

That voice was familiar—but impossible.

She pulled off her helmet in haste. Her eyes zoomed in between the battlements, on the man who had yelled. His face was a subtle brown, with monolid eyes. She'd never seen that face before, but what she saw was consistent with her knowledge.

It was *impossible*.

Questions assaulted her mind. Why had Commander Delveton killed Commander Olik? Where was Jeanette? Why had that sword emitted a blast of lightning?

Why was Sam *here*?

They were here to destroy a band of evil wizard cultists with strange technology. But Sam was at Tercast.

Unless this *was* Tercast.

She glanced at Delveton as he recovered from the fight with the giant. The enormous man lay sprawled on the ground nearby—missing half of his head. The commander had deceived them. They weren't attacking evil wizards at all. They were attacking

Tercast. Having control of the company and their ship, he must have changed the destination to Alvior and led them to attack Tercast instead of their original target. But *why*?

Delveton and Kara were now the only two of the company still alive.

His raspy voice came through her helmet over the company channel. "Olik was compromised. Help me destroy them, and we will go to your sister."

Chills ran across her skin as she studied the damaged face shield. It was *him*. It had to be. Delveton had kidnapped Jeanette! She threw her helmet back on, burning with colossal fury.

"Where is she?" she yelled.

"Help me take them down, and I will take you to Jeanette," he replied calmly. "She's one of us now."

Us? Who the hell is "us"?

"Where is she!" Kara repeated, nearly screaming.

The man pulled his cracked helmet off, brandishing the electric sword as he faced the opposition across the damaged courtyard. They clustered into the corner, wielding medieval-looking weapons. Somehow, Sam was among them, gripping some kind of mace.

Delveton was possibly her only chance of getting to Jeanette.

But why was *Sam* here?

I'm the reason he's here, she realized. *I led him into this mess by pushing him into Tercast.* Tears fell into Kara's helmet as she glanced over at the black-skinned woman's dead body next to her. A terrible pang of guilt gripped her. The woman was probably innocent. *All* the people here were probably innocent. They were just protecting their home in some stupid battle for nothing because of the manipulations of this despicable man.

She stood on the wall, resolve piercing through her misery. The image before her remained blurry through tears she couldn't wipe away.

Chapter 48

Convergence

Sam watched in horror as another suit flew to its ally from the battlements across the courtyard.

"A-Another one?" Ya'ir said from the ground, voice shaking.

Kula and Zel sat next to him and attempted to wrap his leg with the shawl taken from his shoulders. Kula struggled with her own bandaged shoulder.

"We should run," Zel said through tears.

Tovas shook his head. "We can't. We *must* stop him."

Despite Tovas's ridiculous sense of hope, Sam admired his courage. He stared at the suited man who had killed so many of his friends, sensing a bizarre familiarity. That beard. He had seen it before. And the sword.

"I know this man," Sam said, goose bumps rising across his skin. "I don't know why he's here, but he's the one who kidnapped Jeanette."

Tovas turned to him. "You're sure?"

"Yes. He has the same sword. Same face. It's him."

The two suits began walking toward them.

"Sam, Zel, get ready to hit them as hard as you can," Tovas said, moving out in front of the group and brandishing his staff.

Sam lifted his mace and Vitalized a bowling-ball-sized piece of rubble nearby up to eye level. He aimed at the man wielding the sword. They would not go down without a fight. For Jeanette. For Scheln. For Talanna, Niu, and Relon.

For Vurkil.

The smaller, more feminine suit to the left pulled a rifle from its back by the grip. It aimed at the group, then spun.

Boom!

An electric blast and a stream of bright light illuminated the courtyard.

Everyone watched in stunned astonishment as the suited man fell with a thud.

His supposed ally raised a hand and put the smoking rifle down in an act of submission. Tovas looked at Sam with wide eyes, and Sam shrugged.

The suit pulled off its helmet.

Sam froze, his mind reeling at the impossible sight.

He dropped the mace, and the hovering piece of debris fell with it. Rubbing his eyes, he stared again.

It looked like Kara.

But it couldn't possibly be her. She stared straight back at him. Kara couldn't do that. It wasn't her. Kara was *blind*.

Tears fell from the non-Kara's eyes.

Numbly, Sam ran forward, ignoring Tovas's protest. His heart beat furiously with the vortex of emotions within him. As he approached, he took in her round, slim, familiar face and short figure. It looked so much like her, but it was *impossible*. Kara was *blind*. There was no reason why she would be here—wearing a power suit, of all things—but he had to know for certain.

"Kara?"

He could barely get her name out through the knot in his chest.

"Sam?" she replied.

It was her.

Pure joy pierced through the whirlwind of feelings within him.

He rushed forward and embraced her. Tears streamed from his face as words failed him. He had innumerable questions. Nothing made any sense—but Kara was *here.*

She had saved them.

He pulled back and looked into her blue eyes, which stared oddly straight back into his.

"I love you," he breathed.

The words escaped before his mind had a chance to reconsider. He decided he didn't care. He would not let it go a second more unsaid.

Kara gazed into Sam's kind eyes for the first time in her life. This was her best friend. A boy she had known for most of her life. The way he looked at her now set the butterflies in her stomach aflame. This wasn't an expression of friendly affection.

Sam was in love with her.

Her mind raced through their years together, and it all started to come together. The way he always seemed unusually bitter toward her boyfriends. His protectiveness. His willingness to give up everything to be with her when her world ended. This was no spur-of-the-moment development. He had loved her for years.

As the thought hit her, she felt her own feelings for him blossom throughout her being. Although she had never thought of him in a romantic way before, seeing him for the first time in her life brought new life to her feelings toward him.

She kissed him. A brief moment of peaceful bliss among the tempest of destruction and death. It ended quickly, and she looked into his light brown eyes once more, which were wide with surprise.

"I love you too," she found herself saying.

"What are you doing?" a taller sandy-haired man said. He approached on Sam's left and brandished a staff.

Sam waved him down. "This is Kara, Tovas."

"We were supposed to be saving Jeanette," Kara said, gesturing at the bastard lying next to her with a gaping hole through his temples. "I only just found out that he was behind it all and deceived us into coming here instead."

"What happened to your eyes?" Sam asked.

"I got new ones. Long story."

The man named Tovas lowered his weapon. "I don't think we should stay here."

"Let's take the ship," Kara said, pointing to the vehicle hovering above. "As the only one left in the company, I have control of it."

"You can fly that thing?" Sam asked.

"I don't need to," she replied, tapping the back of her neck where the Nit had been implanted.

Sam raised his eyebrow.

"If you trust her, Sam, then I trust her," Tovas said. "We need to get everyone on board, and all the weapons we can carry too." He pointed at the fallen murderer. "We don't want people like him getting hold of them."

"Where will we go?" a slender dark-skinned man asked as he approached. "We'll need supplies."

Another woman with a bow came up behind him, glaring at Kara with suspicion. "There are supplies here we could take."

"Not easily," Tovas replied. "The storeroom is rubble. And more enemies may arrive. We need to leave as soon as possible."

Kara nodded, thinking back on the exchange between Delveton and Golin. "I agree. I'm pretty sure there are more from his cult in the Armed Forces. High up in the command chain too. More could show up at any moment. That also means we shouldn't go anywhere the Sovereignty can track us."

"Where can we go for supplies, then?" the slender man asked. "Doesn't the Sovereignty track people everywhere?"

"Not quite," Kara said. "I know a place."

Sam raised an eyebrow at her again. She returned a soft smile, issuing a mental command to the ship above to land in the courtyard nearby.

"Okay, we need to move," Tovas said as the vehicle began to

descend gracefully into the courtyard. "Let's get everyone onto that ship." He put a soft hand on Kara's shoulder. "Thank you."

She gave him a quick nod of acknowledgment.

Sam accompanied Kara toward the bodies near the courtyard door. He knelt down, tears shimmering on his face as he checked the three fallen women there.

Kara knelt next to Olik and tried to ignore the disturbing hole through his forehead. The rest of his face had severe burns from the blast. A small slice of white in the hexagonal under-fabric of his neck caught her eye. She pulled it out, finding the picture of his family: frustrated mother, rambunctious sons, and exasperated daughter.

Tears blurred the family's faces. Kara blinked, causing them to fall to the suit with a light *clink*.

"Welin Em Onii," she said softly.

Chapter 49

The Deia

Jeanette stared down at the man she had murdered, his guttural sounds having ceased minutes ago. His mouth and eyes hung open.

The faint sound of a door opening down the hall broke her trance. She shook her head. There was no time to linger.

She had one more person to kill tonight.

Jeanette turned to the double throne room doors and pushed one forward slowly, hoping the commotion hadn't roused suspicion. She peeked her head through, finding the throne empty. Purple carpet with gold, swirling embellishments traced the floor to it. Elaborate, bright gold decorations streamed across the ceiling. In the room's corner, the Deia sat at her desk—reading.

A fitting demise for this book-loving tyrant.

She squeezed through the crack in the door, then closed it softly behind her. Creeping forward, she slowly drew the dagger from its sheath, holding it palm-down. The Deia's brown hair, which was streaked with strands of gold, fell over her shoulders as she leaned over the book before her. She wore a mauve dress with intricate gold ornaments. Through the woman's hair, Jeanette could see a sliver of the dark brown skin beneath. That was her target.

She raised the knife high, eyes fixed on that sliver of brown. Gritting her teeth, Jeanette squeezed the dagger and brought it down toward the woman's flesh.

A powerful emotion of cessation slammed into her.

Jeanette's muscles immediately responded, halting the dagger inches from the woman's neck. Her eyes widened as the Deia turned, gray eyes looking calmly back into her own.

Emotion swirled in her gut as her mind struggled to comprehend the sight. She knew those eyes—that hair.

Impossible. It can't be. She's dead.

Belze.

Tears fell from the Deia's eyes.

Jeanette remained stationary, her arm stopped mid-swing.

"He's gone," she said softly, voice full of anguish.

Jeanette's arm fell. She had too many questions, so she asked them all at once. "Why?"

Belze—the Deia—sighed heavily, wiping her eyes as she spoke. "I've been expecting this moment, but I was not sure if you would yet make the leap."

"What moment?" Jeanette asked.

"Your transition," she replied calmly. "You are truly one of mine now."

Realization crashed into Jeanette. Belze's rescue. Their escape into the woods. The "unsealing of her Sorcery." The woman had done something to her. Changed her. Gotten into her head somehow.

"Why me?" she asked.

Belze smiled. "You had strong moral convictions. You refused to kill. That gave you great potential. The deception was necessary to unlock that potential as a Sorcerer under my care."

"I don't know what you're talking about," Jeanette said.

She felt an unnatural draw to the woman. Something subtle— an invisible force.

"When you killed the man out there," Belze said, nodding at the throne room door, "you freed yourself from your moral bounds, releasing your Source to me."

"My Source?" Jeanette said.

Belze nodded.

Jeanette felt the woman's presence in her mind. "What did you do to me?"

"I made you powerful," she replied, pushing the hardwood chair back and standing. She stood about as tall as Jeanette.

No time to lose. It was now or never. Jeanette moved the dagger upward to stab the woman.

An unnatural feeling of cessation again compelled her arm to stop despite her own will. Fear tightened in her chest.

Jeanette lowered the dagger and turned about—unable to resist the powerful prompting to do so. Belze made her way to her throne. An impression came into Jeanette's mind, pressing her to follow.

"What about Kara?"

Belze looked back, and her eyes betrayed a look of sorrow once more. "I was hoping your sister would join us, but Delveton died before he could locate the portal. I fear she is lost to me now."

Relief swept over Jeanette. At least her sister was safe from this tyrant—for the moment.

"Why are you doing this?"

Belze sat and looked down at Jeanette from her high throne with a piercing glare. "After freeing ourselves from your grandfather's despicable rule, we were ready to take our revenge on Tercast. Those old fools never should have banished us here. Unfortunately, we have a significant danger to prepare for. Oblivion will come for me sooner or later—I am certain of it."

Belze was cold, analytical. She played games of strategy with people's lives. Jeanette couldn't let herself be used. She wouldn't. This was going to end.

She spun the dagger in her palm and shoved it toward her own stomach. Her arm abruptly stopped with the tip of the blade inches from her gut—again she was bound by a sudden impression to stop.

"Now, now," Belze said. "No sense unnecessarily damaging that gorgeous body of yours. Tess would be quite upset. She's grown rather fond of you." She sighed heavily, looking weary. "We have much to do now that Delveton is gone. I have sent Tess's group to Tercast to recover the artifacts there and to take care of any stragglers before Sovereignty forces arrive. Backlash from the slaughter of the castle will facilitate the next stage of our efforts. I need your power at its peak."

The piercing gray eyes settled on Jeanette. "Return to your studies."

Questions in Jeanette's mind faded to grief as an unseen force compelled her to turn abruptly and walk out of the throne room. Tears streamed down her face.

As she moved through the doors, she glanced down at the pale, curly-haired man. The man she had murdered. The hilt of the dagger still protruded from his chest.

Sorrow and regret drowned out all other emotion.

I'm sorry, Amy. You were right. You were right all along.

Amy's voice didn't respond.

Jeanette walked numbly around the corner and stopped as she nearly ran into someone coming the other direction.

The prison guard.

"'Ey, girl!" he said with a disgusting smile. "Lookin' fine in—"

Pure fury exploded within her. The unseen force within her caused Jeanette to reach out reflexively and grab the man by the throat. She activated her Sorcery out of pure instinct. Skin. Muscle. Bone. She connected to all of it, and imagined a raging blaze of incineration.

The man struggled to scream as he raised his arms against hers. His body suddenly burst into flame. The rank odor of burning flesh nearly made her gag, and the fire scorched her hand and forearm, sending searing pain up her arm. She didn't care. Pain was nothing now.

Jeanette released her grip, and he fell to the ground.

She stepped over the smoldering ruin of flesh, feeling the weight of immense and sudden exhaustion accompany her profound despair.

Chapter 50
Reconciliation

Sam stared sorrowfully at the mounds of red dirt among yellow and green vegetation. Tovas, Fita, Kula, Ya'ir, and Zel stood around nearby. *We should wear black for this sort of thing*, Sam thought. All they had were their dirty white robes, except Kara, who wore a form-fitting Sovereignty uniform as she sat in the grass away from them. She stared past the trees into the rolling hills below.

The sky above was a dismal gray, sprinkling sparse droplets onto their heads and reflecting the dreary mood. Sam noticed that no drops reached the ground nearby, where their invisible, cloaked ship stood, undetectable. He wondered how that worked.

Shaking his head, he returned his attention to the graves. Not the time for that.

Someone should say something. Other than the distant cry of alien bugs and rustling trees, the air was far too quiet.

"They were heroes," Sam said. "All of them."

"They still are," Tovas added.

The afterlife. Sam wished he could believe in such a thing right now, but it felt like false hope. *Even if there is some kind of soul, who we are—our memories, our experiences—is tied to our physical bodies. When those have dissolved away, what's left?*

Ya'ir sobbed. Tovas turned to wrap his arms around him. Sam walked over and joined them, along with Zel, Fita, and Kula.

They had all lost dear friends. Rose had lost more than that.

Slowly, the sorrowful embrace subsided.

They removed their outer robes and gloves, stripping down to their plain white shirts and pants. Kara joined them on their hike to the charity complex at the edge of the city a few miles away. Zel remained behind to watch over Rose and Scheln, who were still unconscious, as well as the mascot creatures she had rescued from Tercast. The group made little idle chatter as they walked through the alien forest, across an ascender landing pad, and through a well-manicured yellow park to the tall urban landscape beyond. The charity complex was only a few blocks down from the park.

The complex officials provided them with plenty of food and supplies, and never asked for any identification, as Kara had said. Carrying a box containing some kind of nutrition bars, Sam walked into the nearby community park, their designated meeting place. A few well-groomed green trees stood amid a rolling field of yellow grass. It was warmer at this location on Invar than Tercast was on Alvior—he guessed late summer or early fall, though he had no idea of their latitude.

The cloudy sky above cast a grayish orange on the evening scene. Fita, Kula, and Ya'ir were already at the park conversing, their supplies stacked on the grass nearby. Tovas prayed on his knees under a tree. Kara sat on the peak of the park hill, looking out at the landscape beyond. The location overlooked the ascender landing pad and the untamed hills to the west—where their ship remained hidden.

He quietly ascended the hill and sat next to Kara in the soft yellow grass.

"Jeanette's still out there, Sam," she said. "I failed."

He put an arm around her shoulder. "No. You did everything you could. You saved our lives."

Her worried eyes looked up at him. "Del said she had joined them. Why would he lie about that?"

"I don't know," Sam admitted. "Jeanette's the kindest person in the universe. She'd never join a group of murderers willingly."

"We need to find her," Kara said, returning her gaze to the hills beyond.

Sam gave her shoulder a soft squeeze of reassurance. "We will."

"How?"

He considered the question for a few moments. "For now, we need to stay hidden. If, as you said, this Minister Golin is with them, we can't trust anyone in the Sovereignty military. We'll lie low for a while, find out what we can, and make our move from there."

Kara nodded.

The sun peeked out underneath the overcast sky, casting the scene in a deep crimson.

"I've thought about it," Kara said, "and I'm going to turn these eyes off, at least for a while."

Sam turned to her. "Really? Why?"

She shrugged. "They're overstimulating. And ever since I gained sight, I've been seeing things I wish I hadn't. I don't think sightedness suits me."

He stared into her bright blue eyes, which stared oddly back into his. Every logical bone in his body took issue with her statement. Sight was useful. Removing a nearly ubiquitous human sense because it didn't suit her felt logically absurd. However, for reasons he couldn't explain, it also felt . . . right. It was who she was. Sightedness really *didn't* seem to suit her.

"I understand," he said with a mischievous grin. "You just don't want to see my face anymore. I get it."

She smiled at the self-deprecation before punching his shoulder playfully. "Jerk. You have a beautiful face."

Her unexpected comment made his insides flutter.

Kara rested her head on his shoulder. They watched the red sun slowly descend toward the hills in silence for several minutes. People in strange clothing passed by on the path below. They were all so diverse. Sam could still hardly fathom the fact that human beings lived across the universe—unknown to those back on Earth.

A well-built man with dark hair and light skin made his way up the path from the landing pad below, his arm around a chubby blond girl. As he glanced up at Sam and Kara, his eyes went wide. He quickened his pace considerably up the path and dragged the annoyed girl with him.

"What was that all about?" Sam asked. "Do you know him?"

"Long story," Kara replied with a smirk. "You don't want to know."

Sam decided he'd ask about it later. The man's physique reminded him of another question.

"Are you actually going to spar with Fita?" Sam asked.

"Yeah," she said. "We could all use something to loosen us up after that nightmare."

Sam nodded.

"I'm surprised you're friends with Tovas," she said. "He seems pretty religious. I thought you hated that stuff."

A gentle gust blew a few strands of Kara's light brown hair into Sam's face. He removed them with his free hand. "It's true that religion can cause all kinds of problems, but somehow I think Tovas does it right. It suits him. Kind of like your blindness suits you."

"I know you didn't mean for that to sound condescending, but you probably shouldn't phrase it that way. You *should* tell him, though."

"Why?"

"Because it would mean a lot coming from you," she said.

She was right. He had argued with Tovas countless times over his beliefs, and even called him a mindless drone on more than one occasion. The thought caused him a pang of guilt.

He turned his head to find Tovas sitting under the tree, apparently having finished his prayer.

"I'll go talk to him now, before I think better of it."

Kara lifted her weight from him, and he stood up and brushed the grass from his robes. He walked over to Tovas, who glanced at him briefly before dropping his gaze back to the manicured yellow grass beneath him.

"Hi, Tovas."

"Lively evening, Sam."

Sam struggled to find the right words as he settled down next to him.

"I must apologize to you," Tovas said.

"For what?" Sam asked.

"When I first observed your skepticism and lack of faith, I saw it as a flaw in your character. Now I thoroughly believe it to be one of your greatest strengths. Forgive me for not seeing it sooner."

Sam glanced over in disbelief. That was the last thing he'd expected to hear.

Tovas's eyes turned misty. "I failed. I failed to protect them. You were right."

Sam put a hand on his shoulder. "No. We had nowhere else to go. They would have found and killed us all if you hadn't led us back when you did. I'm sure of it. And they may have taken Kara, just like Jeanette. Everyone made their own choice to follow you." He sighed. "Though I can't accept it myself, I've come to respect your unrelenting faith. It's one of *your* greatest strengths."

Tovas turned, his misty eyes wide at Sam's words. Sam could hardly believe he was saying them himself. He released his tender grip on the man's shoulder.

"Come to think of it," Sam continued, gazing out over the field, "any philosophy has its blind spots."

Words from a physics lecture echoed in his mind.

"Perception is not reality."

Tovas nodded with a slight smile, returning to stare outward as well. "I think you are right."

They watched in silence as Kara descended the hill to the others, where Fita—shirt removed—began stretching his muscular arms.

Tovas rose, and Sam stood with him. They walked toward the rest of the group.

"You think she can actually win?" Tovas asked. "Fita can best a man three times his size."

Sam gazed at the woman he loved with a knowing smile.

Kara trod across the field of springy yellow grass toward her opponent, a relatively tall, dark-skinned man with blond hair and pointy ears. Fita, was it?

"Ready to lose, Frito?" she said.

He scowled, giving her a sense of satisfaction.

Kara turned about and glanced at the others, who had gathered to watch their match. Sam approached behind her with a grin on his face. He knew who was going to win. Kara felt confidence blossom within her as butterflies tickled her stomach.

She still found it surprising that Sam, of all people, would be giving her butterflies.

If he had confessed his love to her before this ordeal, she didn't know what she would've said. It would have been too weird.

Somehow, things were different now. It felt right.

Sam was apparently magical too—a "Sorcerer," like the others at Tercast. It was quite a mind-boggling development, given his profound skepticism.

His face faded away as a command to her Nit switched off her eyes and returned the familiar lack of visual sensation. Her other senses took over, giving her a perception of her surroundings that she had missed—one where visuals didn't overwhelm her mind. Cool air caressed her skin with the passing breeze. Soft grass tickled her bare feet.

Isolating the sound of her opponent's feet against the smooth grass, she entered a wide stance. Fita's quiet breath disturbed the air nearby. She took in a deep breath herself, letting her training consume her mind.

Breathe.

Focus.

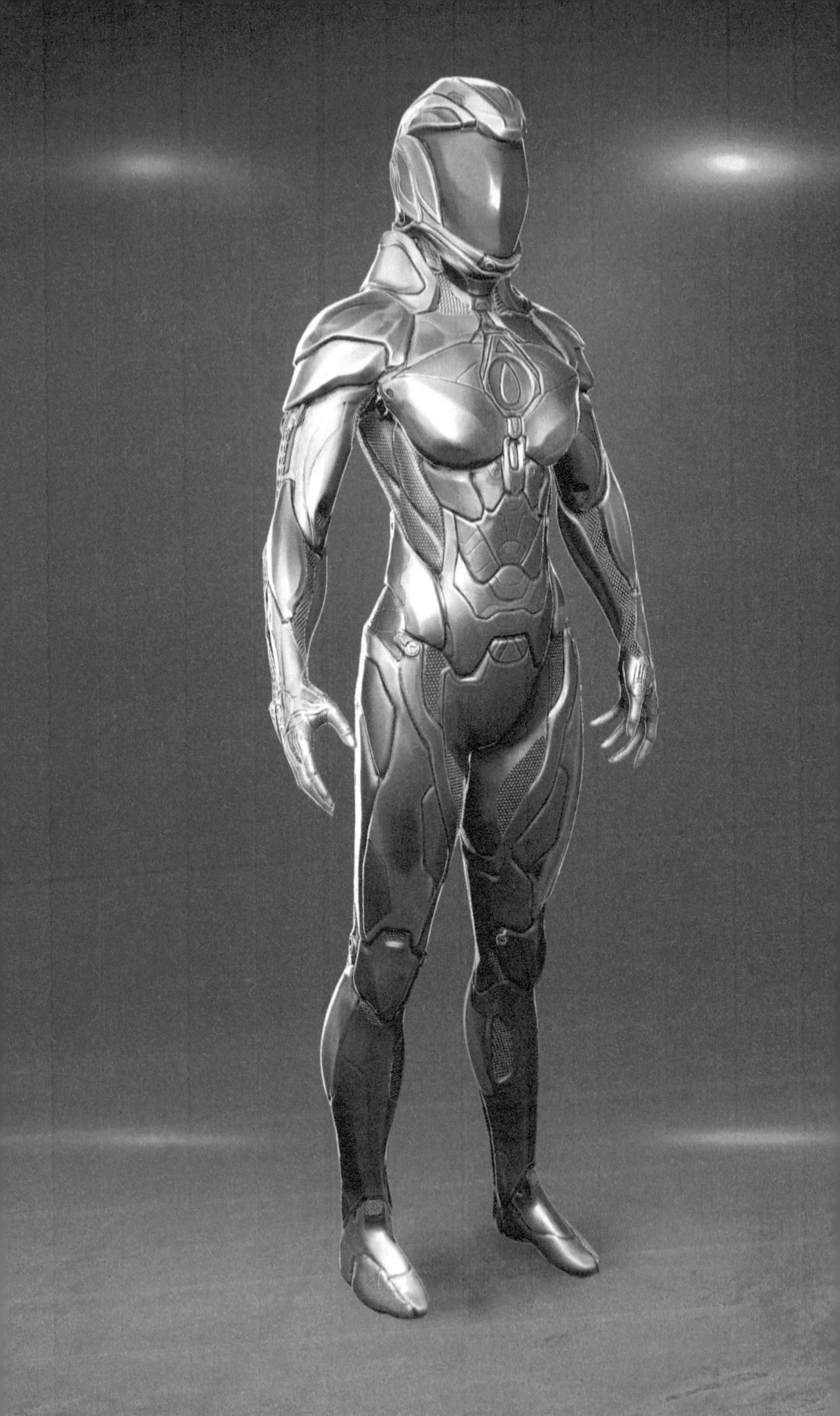

Ryan Sivek has been developing aspects of this particular story since he was in his early teenage years. He loves spending time with his wife and kids and enjoys his day job as a software engineer. He currently resides in the eastern United States.

www.ryansivek.com